SHARING THE WEALTH

The Zany Adventure of a First-Year Counselor

By Jack Dempsey

RPSS Publishing - Buffalo, New York

Book design by Mark D. Donnelly, Ph.D.

www.rpsspublishing.com

publisher@rockpapersafetyscissors.com

ISBN:978-1-956688-05-4
Printed in the United States of America
Second Edition

11 10 9 8 7 6 5 4 3 2

This book is dedicated to my four children, Kyle, Ian, Jude and Eamon.

They are without question my greatest joy in life.

CONTENTS

INTRODUCTION

This is a story about a young man named Jack O'Leary. Mr. O'Leary has just recently earned a master's degree in the field of Vocational Rehabilitation Counseling, and he is now eager to set his sights on seeking employment so that he can make his way in the world.

As the reader will discover, Jack O'Leary is an extremely focused young man, however, he does have a tendency to let his imagination run rampant from time to time, and he has been known to have some very spirited and uncensored conversations with himself.

Yes…, life according to Jack O'Leary is not always what it seems, and people sometimes say and do the strangest things.

Although O'Leary would have preferred a different career path in life, he puts his hopes and dreams aside and ultimately decides to pursue a career in the field of counseling instead.

Despite the fact that counseling wasn't exactly O'Leary's first choice of careers, he puts his nose to the grindstone and intends to make the best of it. O'Leary has invested a great deal of time and money in achieving his educational degree, and so he decides to take a job with an agency that specializes in hiring the handicap

CHAPTER ONE

Well, here it is…, graduation day and I still haven't found a job. It's supposed to be an up-and-coming field, jobs galore. Well…, that's what the career counselor told me at the College Job Fair anyway.

So guess who has a master's degree in hand and no job prospects?

Yeah, you guessed it…, me!

I've got a few irons in the fire and one or two return phone calls to make, so it's not as though things are totally hopeless. Apparently my classmates all seem to have jobs waiting for them, that is…, after they take their customary two weeks off down in the Caribbean, but me, well…, I'm still scratching my head and making up excuses.

In any event, I'm hoping that my employment prospects will change after this graduation weekend is over, but for now I think I'm just gonna kick back, crack open a beer or two with Dad, and try to simply enjoy the moment.

So after all the hoopla of graduation weekend, I decided to follow up on some of the job leads that I had sizzling in the fire, or should I say "smoldering." I'm optimistic, but not totally confident that the employment embers that I'm stoking have any flicker.

One of the places that I contacted, called WEALTH Industries, was planning on calling me in a few days because a counselor position at their agency had just become available.

WEALTH Industries is a nationally recognized employer for the handicapped, and an agency that I became quite familiar with through my graduate studies over at the university.

The name WEALTH is an acronym that stands for Workers Earning and Learning Through Help. I thought it was a pretty catchy name for an agency because it provided the perfect vehicle for public relation campaigns and self-promotion.

Anyway, the recruitment specialist that I spoke with on the phone was very personable and seemingly quite eager for me to set up a time and a date to visit the agency and discuss the position. I was happy to see that all of the hard work of preparing my resume had paid off.

Naturally, I would've liked to have gotten right down to the nitty-gritty by asking the recruitment specialist such questions as salary, benefits, and time off.

Yeah, time off…, getting paid for lounging around in my easy chair at home and doing nothing. I was hoping there'd be plenty of time off at this job!

Then again…, I knew that this was not the time or the place to be asking such bold inquiries. I mean, after all…, didn't I learn any counseling skills in graduate school?

As I hung up the phone, I began dreaming of my first real paycheck. Now I will admit that my thoughts were a bit premature. After all, I hadn't even seen the place yet or spoken to the person in charge to see if I was even remotely interested in the position.

I guess you could say that I was putting the proverbial cart ahead of the horse.

At that point, all I saw were dollar signs. Like that brand new car I wanted to buy, and what about that stereo I was longing for, not to mention a whole new wardrobe.

Yeah, I couldn't wait to start earning some real money, instead of the fast food restaurant pay that I had grown accustomed to making. When it came right down to it, I was thinking more about financial security than job satisfaction.

Quite honestly, I think I justified job satisfaction by convincing myself that I was willing to do virtually anything as long as I was being compensated for it with a paycheck.

Well, as time was drawing nearer for my job interview I could sense an extreme state of nervousness coming over my Dad, and he seemed to be a lot more anxious about the impending job interview than I was.

Dad works as a truck driver for one of the local freight companies in town, and from what Mom tells me, he has been bragging nonstop to all of his friends and coworkers down at the terminal that his son "Jackie boy" was getting ready to interview for a big job and that I was well on my way to becoming a successful and high-powered psychiatrist.

Now I did try telling Dad on more than one occasion that I was not a psychiatrist, but a vocational rehabilitation counselor, however Dad couldn't quite make the distinction.

Dad would simply say to me, "You deal with people's problems, right? So you're a psychiatrist."

Of course, it eventually got to the point where I was just too tired of arguing with him anymore, so I just decided to acquiesce to his convictions.

I'm scheduled for a job interview at three o'clock today over at WEALTH

Industries, and I'll be meeting with a Mr. Robert Watson, who is the Executive Director of the agency.

So I guess that means I'll be forced to break out the old graduation suit again, and try to put my best foot forward so that I can impress Mr. Watson.

Mom went to the trouble of having my suit dry cleaned, and Dad…, not to be outdone, shined my shoes and went out and bought me a brand new necktie.

So before heading downstairs I took one last look at myself in the mirror, and I actually thought that I didn't look half bad. As I stood there admiring myself in the mirror, I was beginning to have some mixed feelings about my interview today.

I guess professionals in the field would characterize this as having ambivalence.

Anyway, I then decided that I needed to start thinking in more clinical terms. So at that point I began to rehearse some questions and answers in my mind, so that I would appear to be somewhat prepared for any hypothetical situations that might arise in today's interview.

I then gave myself a little pep talk, and focused all of my energy into convincing myself that I had nothing to worry about this afternoon.

After all, I have a professional degree in the field and I'm trained to do the job.

Well…, at least on paper anyway!

As I grabbed the car keys off the kitchen counter, Mom and Dad wished me good luck. I then walked out of the house, started up the car, and before I could even shift the car into reverse, I saw Dad frantically running out of the house toward me.

For a fleeting moment there I thought that Dad was coming to tell me that Mr. Watson just called, and after careful scrutiny of my resume he has decided to cancel my interview.

Obviously, these negative thoughts that I'm having don't bode well for my confidence level in this afternoon's upcoming job interview.

Anyway, as Dad approached the side of my car, panting and completely out of breath, I rolled down the window and calmly asked, "Yeah Dad…, what is it?"

His dark brown eyes were wide, and with this startling look on his face, he boldly said, "Jackie boy, whatever you do…, don't take their first offer. Play hard to get!"

I looked at Dad a little bewildered, and all I could say was, "Okay Dad…, thanks for the advice. I'll keep it in mind."

As I was backing the car out of the driveway, I happen to glance over at Dad who was waving "good-bye" to me, as if I was all packed up and leaving for summer camp.

So as I headed cross-town, my mind kept ruminating over Dad's eleventh hour advice.

Dad wants me to play hard to get? Is he for real? He actually wants me to reject their first offer? Has Dad completely lost all of his faculties? I'll be lucky if they even make me an offer!

Well…, either Dad has a lot more confidence in me than I have in myself, or else he has less of a handle on reality than I thought.

The directions that the agency provided me were pretty good, and surprisingly I only made one wrong turn. I should've made a right hand turn onto Harris Road, but I missed my turn and had to double-back, and then I wound up asking a pedestrian where Harris Road was.

So before we precede any further, I probably should tell you that my eyesight really isn't all that good. In fact, I guess I'm pretty lucky to have a driver's license in the first place.

But with the help of some eye drop medication, a sturdy pair of coke bottle glasses, and my solemn vow to the ophthalmologist that I'll be dutiful in obeying all of the posted traffic laws and voila…! I now find myself firmly planted behind the wheel.

When I drive a vehicle I like to navigate via landmarks, as opposed to the more conventional methods of reading street signs or observing route numbers.

For instance…, when I drive I like for people to tell me to turn right after the Economy gas station and then go down to the second traffic light and make a left hand turn at the pizzeria.

That's basically how I get around. I like to refer to it as the "landmark theory," and although it might sound a little unorthodox, it really seems to work for me.

In fact, I may get lost a few times in a strange new place, but once I get to my destination I have this uncanny ability to remember future trips to the same location, even after being away from that location for very long periods of time.

I guess you could equate my memory for landmarks as being similar to an idiot-savant skill, although my close friends will adamantly tell you that I'm more idiot than I am savant.

Anyway, my vision impairment is a congenital eye defect, and was essentially the main reason for my getting into the field of counseling in the first place.

Originally, I had intended to go into the field of broadcasting. I envisioned myself sitting behind a microphone and broadcasting sporting events heard all over the world. I wanted to be a household name, like some of the famous broadcasters that we've all come to know and admire.

Yeah, broadcasting was my dream job, but due to my physical limitations I knew that dream would never be realized so I had to settle for something else.

It killed Dad the day he talked me out of pursuing broadcasting as a career. Dad knew that I loved sports, but he also knew that I didn't have the visual acuity needed to proficiently do the job so that I could become a top notch broadcaster someday.

Dad knew that I spent every waking moment brushing up on all the team rosters and player statistics. I was like a sponge, soaking up every piece of sports trivia that I possibly could, and then spewing it out to whoever would listen.

Yeah, what a waste…, especially since I was so articulate, witty, and funny.

Well…, perhaps now I'm getting a little too carried away with myself!

In most ophthalmologic circles I was considered to be legally blind, and I will admit that there were times when I felt quite sorry for myself. I knew that there were much worse afflictions to have in life than mine, but growing up with congenital cataracts was not an easy cross to bear.

Often times, I felt very self-conscious, especially out in public. It seemed like I was constantly being scrutinized by adults and ridiculed by kids. Not only was the lens of my eye severely compromised, but my cataract condition caused my eyes to be extremely sensitive to light as well. I had to resort to wearing dark sunglasses all the time, but even then I was still forced to always squint and shield my eyes from incoming light the best way that I could.

This constant squinting caused me to have tremendous eye strain all the time, and as a result I suffered with severe migraine headaches, which often restricted me to indoor activities.

It got to the point where I actually welcomed cloudy days, so that I didn't have to strain so hard to see.

As a young boy I was very passionate about sports, and I can vividly remember playing sandlot football and wearing dark sunglasses under my football helmet so that I could compete and try to keep up with the other kids.

Of course, modern medicine has made some tremendous strides in the field of ophthalmology, and nowadays cataract surgery is quite routine and performed on an outpatient basis. This however was not the case when I was a young boy growing up, and ultimately I had to forego my career in broadcasting.

Yeah…, I guess you could say that I was disappointed, but I believe that things happen for a reason, even if we don't know exactly why.

The simple reality was that I was born in the wrong era, and the broadcasters that I grew up listening to as a kid did not have the luxury of using computers or state of the art equipment as a visual aide. They relied solely on their wits and an old pair of binoculars.

That is…, if the technician remembered to pack the binoculars into the equipment bag!

Broadcasting was a pretty antiquated profession when I was growing up. There were no directors, producers, or statisticians spoon-feeding broadcaster's information, or a teleprompter to tell you what to say and when to say it like the modern day broadcasters have it now.

Gee…, if only I had been a child of the twenty-first century!

Well, since broadcasting wasn't in the cards, I really didn't have a clue as to what it was that I should do with my life. Dad thought it might be a good idea for me to work with people who had disabilities. He thought that since I had a disability that perhaps I may have an affinity to relate to other disabled people.

When I was a youth, I had a lot of professional assistance from voluntary agencies. One such agency, the Industrial Home for the Blind, assisted me to better cope with my disability in terms of providing me with support, tutoring, and various educational aids, such as audio and large print books. This was a very positive experience for me, and Dad ultimately convinced me that I might thrive in the field of human services.

Uh…, I don't know if this is too early in the story to get into this or not, but I also believe in life after death, you know…, reincarnation. And as bizarre as it may sound, but I even think that I was a woman in a past life.

Hey, - how do you think I've been able to develop my sensitive side as a counselor?

Anyway, I think it's quite apparent the volume of wild and crazy thoughts that I have floating through my head as I proceed to take the short ride over to my job interview today. I'm sure that all of these extraneous thoughts I'm having are all attributed to some sort of nervous energy about this afternoon's job interview, and hoping that I can land the job.

As I continued to proceed down Harris Road, I saw a sign that read WEALTH Industries, so I pulled into the parking lot. I shut off the car, took a deep breath, and then said a little prayer that I could nail this job interview today, so that I could make Dad proud of his "Jackie boy."

I cautiously got out of my car and then sized up the building. At first glance, the building was not very appealing to the eye, and it looked rather austere.

Then again…, maybe dumpy would be a better description!

The outside of the building looked like it hadn't been painted in years. I guess I had envisioned a more state of the art looking building. The main entrance had a half-painted plywood sign hanging onto an awning, and it was barely hanging on at that. The sign on the outside of the building plainly read WEALTH Industries, so I knew I was in the right place.

Suddenly, I experienced a sinking feeling in the pit of my stomach. It may have been anxiety or perhaps disappointment at the sight of the building.

Then again…, it could have simply been indigestion from the corn beef sandwich that Mom made me for lunch earlier.

As I approached the front entrance, I happened upon two Down-syndrome men who were exiting the building. These two young men were both quite engaging, as they pleasantly said, "hello sir," and then proceeded to hold the door open for me.

At that point, I seemed to forget all about the shanty facade of the building, and thought what a nice place this is and that perhaps these two demure and congenial young men will be on my caseload when I get the job.

See that…, I was already viewing things in a positive light!

Then again…, if I do get the job then I'll be low man on the totem pole, and I'll be getting all of the "square pegs" so to speak. The good clients are probably already taken by the most senior counselors, you know…, - "To the victor go the spoils!"

Then again…, maybe the senior counselors are assigned to work with the more difficult clients because they're senior counselors, and they have more work experience.

I don't know…, it's just too much for me to process right now. I haven't even stepped through the front door of the agency yet, and I was whipping up one scenario after another.

When I entered the building, I once again noticed how stark the inside décor was. There was some pine trim molding around the front door jam, but other than that the place looked rather dingy, like an old warehouse.

This to me was not really a deterrent, because I felt like I was in dire straits for attaining a job…, any job!

As I made my way down the hallway, I saw a plaque on the wall that read, "Main Office This Way," with an arrow pointing in that direction so I headed that way.

When I entered the Main Office, I saw a young woman sitting behind a desk. She was absolutely gorgeous, and I couldn't stop taking my eyes off of her.

Frankly, I thought she might be the reason why people came into work every day, well…, at least the male staff anyway. It certainly wasn't because the place felt homey.

I approached the young lady's desk and introduced myself, and then proceeded to tell her that I had a three o'clock appointment with Mr. Watson. She quietly smiled, and then glanced down at her appointment book and confirmed my statement.

The young lady then cordially asked me to wait for Mr. Watson in the outer room. The outer room consisted of nothing more than a small table with a few metal chairs, and a variety of vending machines that were filled with an assortment of snacks and drinks. So at that point I quietly sat down in one of the squeaky metal chairs and then waited for further instruction.

So as I sat there in my spiffy graduation suit, I felt a little bit self-conscious. People were parading back and forth in front of me making all sorts of purchases out of the vending machines and then stopping to stare in my direction, as they whispered, "Hey, who's that guy?"

As you can only imagine I had a sea of thoughts floating through my head, which ordinarily would be quite funny, well…, at least to my way of thinking anyway, but given my current situation I thought I would just tuck them all away for future reference.

So as I anxiously sat there the constant noise and chaos of my surroundings was making it quite difficult for me to concentrate on my thoughts. I was trying very hard to focus all of my energy on some witty snippets of information that might help me to impress Mr. Watson today.

I was trying to rack my brains in remembering the exact initials of some of the more prominent professional journals in the field, as well as jogging my memory with some of the more notable articles that were required reading in my graduate coursework. I really thought that if I could pull this off then I might have a fighting chance at landing this job today.

Obviously, I'm not a subscriber to the aforementioned journals, and my feeble attempts to look good in front of Mr. Watson today was seemingly nothing more than smoke and mirrors.

It was my sole intent in this interview today to only scrape the surface of the subject matter, and not delve too deeply into anything too specific. I was actually trying to convince myself that this could work, as long as I didn't mix up any of the initials of the journals, or screw up the correct names and order of the various professional organizations in the field.

Suddenly the area that I was waiting in was now becoming noisier and noisier, and I found myself engulfed in a sea of frenzy and commotion all around me.

Apparently the employee time clock was situated in the general vicinity of where I was sitting, so people were lining up to punch their time cards because it was now quitting time.

At that point, hordes of people were buying soda and treats out of the vending machines for their ride home, and excitedly saying their never-ending good-byes to their coworker friends.

By now, the outer room was so congested that people were accidentally stepping on my feet and bumping into me. Although the atmosphere was affable, it was quite unnerving and very chaotic as well, and I was praying that no one would spill anything on my spiffy graduation suit.

I then thought to myself, "Why the hell didn't Mr. Watson schedule me to come at a less conspicuous time of day, without all of this hubbub surrounding me?"

Just then a tall slender middle-aged man approached me. He then extended his hand and casually said, "Excuse me, but you must be Jack O'Leary?"

I stood up and respectfully replied, "Yes sir…, I am."

We shook hands, and then this tall slender man countered my reply by saying, "Well, it's very nice to make your acquaintance Jack. I'm Robert Watson, Executive Director of WEALTH Industries. Why don't we step into my office and chat a bit."

Mr. Watson and I then proceeded down a small hallway away from the commotion of the vending machines and the time clocks, and entered a rather large and luxurious looking office.

As I panned the room wide-eyed, Mr. Watson humorously remarked, "This might be your office someday Jack."

I innocently said, "Well, you haven't offered me the job yet, sir."

Mr. Watson chuckled at my naïve response, and then replied, "That's pretty funny, Jack."

As I continued to pan Mr. Watson's office, it was truly a sight to behold. It was adorned with all sorts of memorabilia, including pictures of him with famous people…, and I mean some really prominent people. The walls were dotted with awards, plaques, photographs, and he even had several autographed baseballs on display from some famous big league ballplayers.

Now that in itself was worth the trip over here today!

Mr. Watson noticed that I kept staring at his collection of autographed baseballs, and then he casually asked me if I liked sports, to which I replied, "yeah."

The word "yeah" no sooner came out of my mouth, when I immediately thought to myself that I must've sounded like I was five years old.

For crissakes…, what the hell am I thinking? I'm in the middle of a job interview trying to make a good impression on this guy, and the best response that I can come up with is "yeah."

Well, I better come up with a better response than "yeah," if I expect to land this job!

Now if saying the word "yeah" wasn't bad enough, I couldn't believe what came out of my mouth next, as I inadvertently said, "Well, I initially wanted to go into the field of sports broadcasting, but my Dad talked me out of it, so I wound up going into human services instead."

Suddenly, it occurred to me that I might have made a serious tactical blunder. The fact that counseling was not my first choice of careers might be viewed as a red flag.

Mr. Watson just smiled, and quietly said, "Really…?"

There was a moment of uncomfortable silence, and then Mr. Watson interjected, "Jack, do you think human services was my first choice of careers? Well…, it wasn't. I have worked in many capacities over the years, such as sales, the insurance business, and public relations, just to name a few. I even tried my hand at writing the "great American novel," which…, I'll have you know, I still may do someday." Watson then lightly chuckled to himself.

"I see…," I quietly said.

Watson continued by saying, "I appreciate your candor, Jack. Actually, it's been my experience that sometimes people will fabricate information in a job interview so that they can look good in front of the interviewer."

Suddenly, I felt quite guilty because my initial strategy in this job interview today was to do exactly what Mr. Watson had just alluded to. I thought if I could dazzle him with enough bull shit then I might be able to fool him into thinking that I was worth taking a chance on.

Gee, maybe I didn't have to resort to bamboozling him after all!

Watson could see that I had something on my mind, so he ended the brief silence by saying, "Jack, the fact that you went to college and earned a professional counseling degree tells me an awful lot about the kind of person you really are."

I thought to myself, "Boy that really sounded good, I only wish I had said it!"

"Thank you, sir." I replied.

Watson then asked, "So do you like the name WEALTH Industries, Jack?"

"Yes sir, it's a great acronym to describe what you're all about."

"My sentiments exactly, Jack. I'm glad you concur." Mr. Watson remarked.

There was another brief moment of silence, and then Mr. Watson asked, "So I'm assuming you know what the acronym stands for, right Jack?"

"Yes sir, I do." I adamantly said, while thinking to myself, "Yeah! I know one of the answers on the test."

I then proudly stated, "WEALTH stands for Workers, Earning, and Learning Through Help."

Mr. Watson replied, "That's correct, Jack! Ya know…, you'd be amazed at how many applicants that I've interviewed over the years that have no idea what the word WEALTH even stands for. I'm sure you heard a lot about us in your graduate studies over at the university, but let me refresh your memory as to who we really are."

Watson then proceeded to tell me a brief history about WEALTH, and also provided me with some background information on the demographics of individuals working at the agency.

He then finished up his little canned spiel by telling me what the mission statement of the agency was. I asked a few benign questions to make it look good, and to give him the appearance that I was trying to be remotely interested in what he was saying.

So after about twenty minutes of getting to know each other, we left Mr. Watson's office and then took a leisurely tour of the building. The tour was rather perfunctory and only amounted to about ten minutes because all of the clients and staff had already left for the day.

We took a quick sweep of the offices, and then walked out back where the clients work to see nothing more than empty chairs, workbenches, and boxes and boxes of material to be worked on for the next day.

So once the tour was over, we headed back to Mr. Watson's office and made ourselves comfortable. He then asked me if I had any questions or comments, to which I attentively replied, "No sir…, but I was quite impressed with what I saw."

Mr. Watson then strapped on his game face and became a little more serious as he said, "Okay, well…, if you don't have any questions then let's get right down to business, shall we? Jack, I think you'd fit in quite nicely here at WEALTH Industries, so I'm prepared to offer you the vocational counselor position, level one. So whatta ya say Jack, would you like the job?"

I quickly replied, "Yes sir…, I'm very interested in taking the job, however I'm not quite sure what a level one position is."

Watson then casually said, "Well Jack, a level one position simply refers to the salary level, and frankly all of our new counselors start at level one, which is our base salary. Once you gain experience in the position, it will enable you to achieve higher salary levels down the line."

So after dispensing with his explanation about the salary, Mr. Watson then outlined the benefits package and the educational and training incentives that were "on the table."

Watson explained everything to me in great detail. The look in his eye and the ease in his voice indicated to me that he has reeled off this patented little spiel of his many times over the years. He had a real good poker face, and he was pretty crafty at not tipping his hand.

Quite frankly, I couldn't tell if Mr. Watson was holding a full-house or a pair of deuces!

As Watson continued to onslaught me with information, he surmised that I was a bit overwhelmed, and I think he felt quite confident that he had me right where he wanted me.

Once again, Watson uttered the magic words, "So, would you like the job Jack?"

Well, as crazy as it may sound, but suddenly I had thoughts of Dad running through my head, and all I could think about at that moment was Dad's eleventh hour advice as I was backing out of the driveway.

And if that still wasn't crazy enough to admit, I actually listened to the little voice inside my head that prompted me to take Dad's shaky advice to heart, as I squeamishly uttered the word "no" to Mr. Watson's enticing job offer.

Upon hearing my reply, Mr. Watson looked rather stunned. He then said in astonishment, "Really…, so what's the problem Jack?"

I then bravely said, "Well Mr. Watson, I would prefer to start at a level two salary instead of a level one because I did complete a one-year internship, which you yourself said was "quite impressive." This should warrant whatever experience is needed to command a level two salary."

As I waited for Mr. Watson to respond, I was nervously thinking to myself, "Please hire me, please…, please…, hire me!"

Even I have to admit that I sounded very convincing, and gutsy…, in the way that I negotiated with Mr. Watson. It was something that I didn't know I was capable of doing, especially since I've always considered myself to be a very timid and complacent kinda guy.

Quite honestly, elevating me to a level two position would only mean an annual increase of about five hundred dollars to my base salary. Now I know that isn't a lot of money, but at that point it really wasn't about money, it was more about making a statement to your boss that you know you are of value, and that it would be in his best interest in obtaining your services.

And as far as the extra money goes…, it would be nothing more than a secondary gain.

So as Mr. Watson continued to mull over my reasons for wanting more money, he then decisively said, "Okay Jack, you have a deal. As long as it's only five hundred dollars a year more and nothing else."

"No sir, that's all I want…, over and above what you have already outlined."

We shook hands, and then Mr. Watson boldly said, "Welcome aboard!"

At that point, I couldn't wait to get home and tell Mom and Dad the good news. I knew that Dad would be proud of his "Jackie boy," and that he'd want to hear all of the details.

As I pulled into the driveway, I could see Dad sitting at the kitchen table. Apparently, Dad had been sitting at the kitchen table the whole time that I was gone because he didn't want to miss the expression on my face when I got home.

Dad liked sitting at the kitchen table for a number of reasons, but mainly because he felt like he was the "Neighborhood Watch Commander," which I'm sure was due to some residual fallout from his days in the Army. When Dad was sitting at the kitchen table he was "on duty," and in his mind I'm sure he felt that the neighborhood was a much safer place to live.

Yeah, Dad enjoys spending countless hours sitting at the kitchen table, staring out the window, drinking his coffee, and listening to his favorite music on the radio station, such as the sounds of the big bands, "Tommy Dorsey," "Count Basie," or any type of swing music that the radio station would play. Dad enjoys the solitude of sitting at the kitchen table, but today Mom decided to join Dad at the kitchen table and keep him company.

As Mom sat at the table with Dad, she clutched her rosary beads, and quietly prayed to all the angels and saints that everything would turn out well for her "baby" boy.

Mom is very religious, and during "crunch time" she likes to pray the rosary. Crunch time is any time that divine intervention is needed to help sway an important situation.

I guess I'll never really know what the determining factor was in landing my first real professional job. Was it my incredible wit, or Dad's eleventh hour advice, or Mom's vigilance at praying the rosary?

Then again…, maybe it was a combination of all three!

As I approached the house, Dad stood holding the front door wide open for me with a look of nervous anticipation on his face. He wasn't exactly sure if he should be excited or consoling.

Dad then eagerly said, "So Jackie boy…, do you have any good news for us?"

I then proudly said, "Yeah Dad, I got the job!"

Dad then gave me a big bear hug, and excitedly said, "Well, get the heck in here boy and tell us all about it! Mom made her world famous potato salad while you were gone. C'mon into the kitchen and grab a plate. That is, after you go upstairs and change out of that fancy new suit of yours, so that you don't spill anything on it. And when you come back downstairs, I'll have a big plate of potato salad and an ice cold drink waiting for ya. Goddam, this is a great day!"

Mom then sternly said, "Jack Sr., watch your language!"

I chuckled at Dad's exuberance, and quietly replied, "Okay Dad, I'll be right down."

Yeah, I'll admit it…, Dad was treating me like I was ten years old again. But you know what, I wouldn't have wanted it any other way. Because I was his "Jackie boy" and this was his way, and it made us both feel special.

So after changing out of my suit, I sat down to a huge plate of Mom's homemade potato salad. I took a healthy mouthful, and then excitedly said, "Boy, that sure tastes good Mom!"

Mom's potato salad was the best damn potato salad in the whole wide world, and maybe even in the whole galaxy. Any time we were at a social function and it was the duty of everyone to bring a covered dish, well…, everyone would ask Mom to bring her homemade potato salad.

Hey, it must be her Irish heritage. You know how the Irish feel about their potatoes, and beer, well…, that was Dad's department.

As I sat there enjoying my potato salad, I began filling my parents in on what transpired in my job interview. Dad listened intently, while Mom was busy cooking up a pork shoulder to go with the potato salad.

Mom would occasionally interject, "That's nice, dear." Mom only said it to be kind, because she knew that Dad would rehash all of it with her again later that night.

Wow! I have a job, and Mom and Dad are proud of their "Jackie boy."

Life is good!

CHAPTER TWO

"Why the hell is that alarm clock going off," I muttered to myself.

As I lay in bed, it suddenly occurred to me that it was Monday morning, and I'm scheduled to report for my first day of work today. I really didn't feel like dragging myself out of bed, but I knew I had to.

When I glanced at the clock it read six-thirty.

Man…, I haven't been up this early since high school!

Although I didn't have to report to work until eight o'clock, Dad thought it might be a good idea for me to get into work a little early this morning, so that I could make a good impression on the boss.

As I shuffled toward the bathroom, I could tell that Dad was already up and that he was downstairs making breakfast, because I could smell the intoxicating aroma of bacon that was permeating throughout the house. Dad always believes in starting the day off right with a big breakfast. You could always tell when Dad was cooking breakfast, as opposed to Mom. When Dad cooked breakfast the bacon sizzled different. I don't know why…, maybe he threw some extra shortening into the pan. Mom's a great cook, but Dad is the breakfast king.

So after my shower I felt totally revitalized. Upon re-entering my room, I saw that my bed was made and that Mom had laid out some brand new clothes for me to wear.

Mom had done some serious clothes shopping during the week, so that her "baby" boy would look good going off to work on his first day.

Apparently Mom caught a half-price sale down at the local department store, and a store that our family has been shopping at for years. The store is also on Dad's truck route, so the department store staff sees Dad several times a week when he's in there making his deliveries.

The day that Mom was down there buying out the store, she proudly announced to all of the store clerks that I landed a new job. The store clerks have known me ever since I was a little boy, and frankly they were more like extended family than department store workers.

When Mom made the big announcement all of the store clerks were tickled pink, and excitedly said, "Tell Jackie congratulations…, and good luck!"

Mom wound up buying me four shirts, two pairs of trousers, socks, and of course brand new "clean" underwear. For some reason, Mom likes to refer to new underwear as "clean."

Every once in a while, I would point out to Mom that if the underwear is new then it must be clean, but Mom never found my whimsical remark to be all that funny.

And Lord knows that I've been sent to my room a few times without dessert to prove it!

Anyway…, during my week off I basically lounged around the house and Mom treated me like a king. I found myself indulging in a little too much of the good life, and when Mom asked me to try on my new trousers, I found them to be a little bit too snug in the waistline.

At that point, Mom suggested that I eat light over the weekend, so that I didn't look like a stuffed sausage for my first day at work on Monday.

So after getting dressed, I came downstairs to a mighty breakfast. Dad told me that he couldn't sleep last night, and wound up tossing and turning all night and woke up at the crack of dawn. Since Dad couldn't sleep he decided to drive over to the bakery, and actually got there before the bakery opened up, so he wound up waiting outside the bakery for over fifteen minutes.

Mr. Migliori, the owner of the bakery, was wondering who was waiting outside his shop that early in the morning.

Upon opening his shop for business, Mr. Migliori saw that it was Dad and warmly said, in his beautiful Italian accent, "Hi-a-Jack! I-didn't-a-know-it-was-a-you-waiting-outside-in-a-da-car. Why-didn't-a-you-knock-on-a-da-door? I would-a-had-a-you-in-for-some-fresh-a-coffee. I was-a-beginning-to-think-that-a-someone-was-a-casing-da-joint…, capisce!"

Dad just laughed and told Mr. Migliori that he couldn't sleep, and so he thought he would swing by the bakery to pick up some rolls and assorted pastries. I've known Mr. Migliori ever since I can remember. Our family has been buying baked goods from him for years.

Mr. Migliori was born in Italy, and then he came over to this country when he was a young man. As a matter of fact, Mom not only bought my graduation cake from his bakery, but every birthday and special occasion cake that we have ever had too.

Dad not only knows Mr. Migliori from buying baked goods for our family, but you guessed it…, the bakery shop is also on Dad's truck route as well.

Any time Dad stepped into the bakery, Mr. Migliori would always give him a large container of coffee just the way he likes it and a big jelly bun, which is Dad's favorite donut.

Mr. Migliori did this because Dad was always doing him favors. Dad always picks up and delivers parcels for Mr. Migliori free of charge, and in return Mr. Migliori would not only treat Dad when he walked into the bakery, but he would usually leave several bundled boxes of baked goods on the back step with a note attached saying, "Jack, thanks for the freebies! Now here are some freebies for and your family…, grazie!"

In fact, when Mr. Migliori heard that the rolls and pastry were in honor of my first day at my new job, he threw in an extra dozen hard rolls, "on the house!"

So while Dad and I chitchatted over breakfast, Mom was at the kitchen counter making me a delicious "five-star" lunch and admiring me in my new clothes.

When I was done eating breakfast Mom handed me my lunch, which I promptly secured into my backpack. I then gave each of my parents a big hug and thanked them for their efforts.

Yeah, I know what you're probably thinking…, this morning sounds like a 1950's television show, but that's how it was in our household and I wouldn't want it any other way.

I grabbed the car keys off the counter, and as I was walking out the door, Mom encouragingly said, "Try to remember everything you learned in graduate school, dear."

My initial thought to Mom's gratuitous remark was, "Uh…, you're probably not referring to my drinking or carousing," so I just blurted out, "Okay Mom…, I will."

I jumped into the car and then headed over to WEALTH Industries. I had the directions already resigned to memory, the "landmark theory" remember…, - turn right at the big yellow building that says Carpet Warehouse, - this was Harris Road, and one-half mile down on the left was WEALTH Industries.

When I arrived at work, I saw that one vehicle was already parked in the parking lot. Of course, with it being my first day I had no idea who this particular car belonged to, but whoever owned it sure had great taste in cars. It was a luxurious Lincoln Town Car, and it was to die for.

As soon as I walked through the front door, I could hear some noises coming from the back portion of the building, as if someone was moving chairs or equipment.

At that point, I wasn't too eager to go exploring, so I decided to sit down in one of the squeaky metal chairs where all of the vending machines were situated and wait for Mr. Watson to come strolling through the front door. I then glanced at my watch and saw that it was 7:45, so I knew that I still had enough time to make a good impression on Mr. Watson.

As I continued to sit there, time was beginning to tick away. People were slowly filing into the building, however there was still no sign of Mr. Watson.

Suddenly I could feel my autonomic nervous system in rapid fire, as the clock kept creeping toward eight o'clock. I couldn't figure out if all of my anxiousness this morning was due to being scared about starting my new job, or because my efforts of coming in early this morning and impressing Mr. Watson were going for naught.

Just then the secretary arrived and walked over to her desk. Finally..., a familiar face!

The secretary's name was Dolly, and she was probably expecting me. I approached her as she was removing her jacket, and then proceeded to introduce myself.

At first, she looked a bit puzzled, but after glancing down at her day planner she saw my name and that I was scheduled to start today. To tell you the truth, I was a little surprised that she didn't immediately recognize my face and give me a rousing, "Welcome aboard!"

Anyway, I then proceeded to ask her when Mr. Watson would be arriving. As I waited for her to reply, I was thinking in the back of my mind that my efforts for coming in fifteen minutes early this morning were completely wasted.

Although as the Nuns would often say back in parochial school, "People should perform acts of kindness out of the goodness of their hearts, and not expect anything in return."

"Yeah, sure Sister..., a lot of good that will do me." I thought to myself.

Actually, it wasn't until years later that I would fully appreciate the genius of those words, and the life lessons that the Nuns were trying to bestow upon us young whipper-snappers.

Dolly then broke my train of thought about the Nuns, and politely said, "Gee, I saw Mr. Watson's car out in the parking lot. I'm surprised you haven't already seen him yet."

Just then I felt a hand on my shoulder, which prompted me to flinch. I then turned and saw that it was Mr. Watson, who amusingly replied, "Whoa..., steady Jack, you seem a little jumpy. I'm glad you decided to join us today. Did you just arrive?"

I promptly replied, "No sir, I've been here since a quarter of eight..., maybe sooner."

I then thought to myself, "Good, I got it out there, so now he knows I was here early this morning." I actually felt pretty good at that point, as if I had just won some type of moral victory.

Watson then cagily said, "Really? Huh…, I've been here since six o'clock straightening up the back room. Funny, I didn't think I heard anyone arrive. So were you looking for me?"

I then started to backpedal, as I defensively said, "Well…, uh…, no sir, I did hear some noises coming from the back area of the building, but I didn't want to overstep my bounds."

"I see. Well…, don't worry Jack, the place won't bite ya, we're not haunted. You should have walked out back so that we could have had a chance to chat." Watson casually said.

At that point, I felt pretty stupid. Here I am bragging that I was fifteen minutes early this morning, meanwhile Mr. Watson has already been here for two hours. Boy, they must be playing by a whole different set of rules than the ones that I'm accustomed to playing by.

I then quickly replied, "Um, well…, I'll make a point of doing that next time, sir."

"Okay, well…, your actions today were understandable. I just want you to feel as comfortable as you possibly can here Jack." Watson said, reassuringly.

So after our brief social exchange, Mr. Watson showed me to my office, which was no bigger than a storage closet. He quickly pointed out the filing cabinet that had all of the files of the people who were currently on my caseload.

Mr. Watson then informed me that there would be a staff meeting at 8:30, and that the meeting would last about an hour. Upon conclusion of the staff meeting, I could then start reviewing all the files of the people that I would be responsible for.

Watson then suggested that I grab some coffee out of the break room and get situated at my desk, and that Dolly will buzz me on the intercom when the staff meeting is ready to begin.

Mr. Watson then shook my hand and gratuitously said, "Welcome aboard," and then he exited the room, to which I attentively stated, "Yes sir, thank you, sir!"

I looked down at my desk, only to look right back up again, as I heard Mr. Watson's voice say, "Oh Jack, by the way."

"Yes sir…, what is it, sir?" I dutifully replied.

"Jack, you keep calling me, sir. Do me a favor, will ya…, don't call me sir all the time. It makes me sound, well…, old." He said, jokingly.

I then smiled, nodded my head, and almost blurted out "yes sir" again, but managed to catch myself in time.

So as soon as Mr. Watson left my office, I unpacked a few personal items that I had brought from home, and then arranged them to my liking on top of my desk.

Gee…, that took all of about two minutes to do.

Suddenly I noticed that the noise level in the hallway was starting to build, due to the fact that the clients were now beginning to arrive.

As I peeked out into the hallway, I observed a plethora of activity going on. Over and above the laughter I could see people punching their time clock cards, buying soda and treats out of the vending machines, and casting one last smile to their friends before making it off to their work assignments. Meanwhile, others were trying to get in one last puff of a cigarette before it was time to punch their time card, and stay on the good side of their line supervisor.

When the hallway finally cleared out, I could see Dolly in the reception area. She was trying to pour herself a cup of coffee, and at the same time she was answering the telephone and attending to the needs of the male clients who surrounded her desk.

As I watched the clients jockeying for her attention, it brought a smile to my face. It was quite obvious that they were all infatuated with her. They all seemed to have a crush on her, and who could blame them! She was an absolute knockout, and apparently kind-hearted as well.

Just past Dolly's desk I could see two professionally dressed men. Maybe they were two of my peers, - my colleagues, yeah…, that's got a nice sound to it I thought. They were milling around the front office, sifting through their mail and working off their first cup of coffee.

Unfortunately, I just couldn't seem to muster up enough nerve to go over and introduce myself to them. For now I just wanted to be a spectator, and see first-hand what I've gotten myself into here at WEALTH Industries.

As I turned to return to my desk, I heard Dolly's voice call out, "Mr. O'Leary…!"

For a fleeting moment there, I thought that maybe Dad had dropped by to pay me a quick visit in-between deliveries, but then realized that Dolly was addressing me. I wasn't accustomed to people calling me mister, just plain old Jack, and occasionally answering to "numb nuts."

I looked back at Dolly, who was pointing in the direction of the conference room, as she said, "The staff meeting is ready to begin. They'll be convening in the main conference room, which is the room right next to Mr. Watson's office."

"Thanks Dolly, I'll be right there."

At that point, I grabbed a pen and a pad of paper off of my desk and then made a bee-line down to the conference room. I must admit that I was pretty nervous, so I took a couple of slow deep breaths before entering the meeting room.

The conference room was quite nice. It reminded me a lot of Mr. Watson's office. In the center of the room there was a massive mahogany table with ten matching mahogany chairs.

As I quietly sat there, I was thinking that the furniture was probably donated by some wealthy benefactor or philanthropist, as a show of appreciation that the agency may have demonstrated toward a family member. I would later discovered that my hunch was correct.

Once again…, I'm attuned to my psychic energy. I just wish that I could harness these mystical powers of mine, so that I could devise a way to win the mega-million lottery.

As I awkwardly sat there, I sensed that everyone in the room knew that I was the "new guy," but strangely enough no one extended a welcoming hello or even a hearty handshake.

Undaunted, I just sat there in complete silence, as I listened to the various conversations that unfolded around me. I heard one guy talking about his weekend, another was complaining about how much work he was behind on, and still another who was saying that he couldn't wait for work to be over today because he had front row tickets to the biggest rock concert of the year.

Although I was quite intrigued with the stories that were being bantered about, I must confess that these were not the types of conversation that I was expecting to hear on my first day. I had envisioned conversations with more professional substance and far less personal content.

Just then Mr. Watson walked into the room, with Dolly one step behind him.

Upon seeing Mr. Watson, everyone in the room abruptly quieted down and gave him their undivided attention. Dolly sat down in a corner chair and began flipping through her steno pad, so that she could begin recording the minutes of the meeting.

As Mr. Watson stood at the head of the table, he struck me as someone who demanded a high level of documentation for accountability purposes, that way his staff couldn't finagle their way out of assignments by saying that they weren't present or didn't get the correct information.

At least that was my "dime store" impression anyway.

There I go again…, overanalyzing situations and making snap judgments.

Gee, I wonder if there's some kind of fancy pink pill on the market that might help me to control these types of erratic thought patterns that I'm prone to having all the time!

Anyway, so after commanding everyone's undivided attention, Mr. Watson then sat down at the head of the table with all eyes riveted on him.

I must say that I was quite impressed with the respect that the staff gave him. My eyes then shifted over to Dolly for a brief moment, and I was wondering if her shorthand was as good as the legs that were coming out of that skirt of hers.

Mr. Watson then cleared his voice, and said in grand style, "Good morning, everyone! So before we begin, would you please join me in welcoming the newest member of our counseling staff, Mr. Jack O'Leary."

At that point, I decided to stand up. I don't know why, but I did. I stood for a second or two, and then thanked Mr. Watson for his gracious introduction. The counseling staff responded by giving me a small round of applause.

For a fleeting moment there, I thought that the group may have been thinking, "Misery loves company."

Mr. Watson then went on to say that I would be managing Allan Farnsworth's caseload. I'm sure that this was already common knowledge to everyone sitting in the room, but for documentation purposes, Mr. Watson needed to state the obvious for the minutes of the meeting.

As I took my seat, Watson thanked the group for their enthusiastic show of support, and then remarked that I would be a tremendous asset to the agency.

Perhaps it was my imagination, but as soon as Mr. Watson made his rather grandiose comment, I thought I heard a few moans and groans from around the table. I really didn't know what to make of it, so I thought I would just file it away for future reference.

Mr. Watson then decided to put me right on the spot by asking, "So Jack, do you have anything that you'd like to share with the group at this time?"

I quickly responded, "Um, no…, Mr. Watson. Only that I'm pleased to be here today, and I hope to get to know each and every one of you a little bit better as time goes by. Thank you."

Mr. Watson replied, "Thank you, Jack. I'm sure you will."

Watson then said, "Well, on that note…, can we please go around the table and introduce ourselves to Jack, that way he can put a face with a name. Barry we'll start with you."

At that point, everyone around the table proceeded to introduce themselves to me. Although I found it to be an extremely nice gesture, it proved to be nothing more than an exercise in futility, because I'll be darned if I could remember even one person's name.

So once the housekeeping chore of introducing me was completed, Mr. Watson then pulled out his agenda for the meeting and proceeded to get right down to business.

Mr. Watson then systematically covered everything from referrals, budgets, expenditures, and even scolding some of the counselors for spending more time in the break room than with their clients down on the contract floor. He made it quite clear to everyone in the room that they needed to be spending considerably more time evaluating the clients' progress, so that they didn't appear to look like total idiots at the determination meetings.

As I glanced around the table people were rolling their eyes and looking at their watches, and feeling like a "pork roast" at a barbecue. It was my definite impression that they couldn't wait for the meeting to be over, and I wondered if this tongue lashing tactic on the part of Mr. Watson was a common practice of his, or did he simply wake up on the wrong side of the bed.

The meeting lasted an hour, just like Mr. Watson predicted. I was coming away with the notion that Mr. Watson was a stickler for being right all of the time, and a perfectionist to a fault.

Thus far, it's my distinct impression that this agency was not a democracy, and if people wanted to continue to work here then it was either going to be Mr. Watson's way or the highway.

All in all, I found my first professional staff meeting to be quite illuminating, even though much of the content that was discussed was Greek to me.

At one point in the meeting I did feel rather uncomfortable, when Mr. Watson began criticizing one staff person in particular, Mister, "I-can't-wait-for-work-to-be-over-today-so-that-I-can-go-to-my-rock concert-tonight."

For some reason, I'm sensing that Mr. Watson roasts this guy quite often!

So after the meeting concluded, I decided to grab a quick cup of coffee out of the break room, and then get right down to business in familiarizing myself with some of the files on my caseload, which consisted of a total of seventy people.

Geez…, does that mean that seventy people are actually depending on me to navigate their lives and help realize their dreams?

Boy, if that's the case…, then these people are certainly in for a rude awakening!

What do I know about shaping people's lives? Staying on top of seventy lives will certainly be a daunting challenge.

I then had a passing thought regarding my predecessor Allan Farnworth, and wondered if he was rose to the challenge of staying on top of seventy lives. I also wondered why he left.

Did he crack under the pressure, or did he leave because he got a better job offer?

So as I entered the break room, I had my favorite coffee mug in hand. This was the same coffee mug that got me through a lot of all-nighters in graduate school. I thought having my favorite coffee mug at work might bring me some good luck in my new job.

As I reached for the coffeepot, I discovered that all of the coffee was gone and that no one had bothered to make a fresh pot.

Shit! I was hoping to be in and out with my coffee, but I can see that's not gonna happen.

As I stood there holding the empty coffee urn, I didn't know what to do. I didn't have a clue as to where any of the fixings were to even attempt making a fresh pot.

Just as I was ready to high-tail it out of there, I heard a gravelly voice from behind me sternly say, "Hey kid, did you drink the last cup of coffee? I mean, uh…, I know it's your first day and all, but rules are rules, and whoever drinks the last cup of coffee makes a fresh pot!"

I immediately went on the defensive, and replied, "Well…, that sounds like a really good rule, but apparently someone is not playing by them. When I walked into the break room, I discovered that the coffeepot was as dry as a bone. I was actually toying with the idea of scouring the room to find all of the fixings, so that I could make a fresh pot of coffee."

"Well…, that's very noble of you kid, seeing how no one even told you about the "golden rule" of the break room." The older gentleman said, with a happy-go-lucky smile.

The gentleman that I was speaking with looked to be the most senior counselor on Mr. Watson's staff. He looked to be in his late fifties and seemed a little eccentric, (probably as a result of working with these clients for so long).

As I watched him rustling up the coffee, I was wondering just how much money Watson was paying this guy. I also wondered what kind of credentials he had.

This guy struck me as someone who was probably "grand-fathered" into the position, and given a title that he is most likely not qualified for.

Although grand-fathering is quite common in human services, personally I'm not a big proponent of the concept, because in my opinion it tends to water down the profession.

I guess it's the old supply and demand theory. Agency Directors like Watson are sometimes between a rock and a hard place, and are subsequently forced to hire people who are simply not qualified to do the job, but learn the job as they go. I felt a little uneasy knowing that this guy held the same type of position that I did.

I then thought to myself, "Could I possibly turn out to be like this guy someday? Gee…, I hope not!"

The older gentleman then asked, "So you haven't had any coffee yet, Mr. O'Leary?"

I calmly replied, "No, like I said, the pot was drained dry when I walked in."

"Okay, well…, let's see if we can do something about that, shall we?"

"Oh, by the way, do you think you could call me Jack and not Mr. O'Leary. Well…, that's if you don't mind?"

He casually replied, "Sure, Jack it is," as he rifled through the various cupboards, so that he could whip up a fresh pot of coffee.

Although I initially drew some negative conclusions about this guy, I decided to cut him a little slack, and try to make a concerted effort to extend myself to him.

Once again, the old Irish Catholic guilt coming to the forefront, as it usually tends to do.

I then said, "Sorry, but I've forgotten your name. I know I saw you in the staff meeting earlier, but remembering people's names in large groups, well…, it's a little overwhelming."

The older gentleman replied, "Hey, no problem, I totally understand. My name is Charlie Dowell, but everyone around here calls me C.D., so put it there kid!"

We shook hands, and as fickle as it may sound, but I made a complete one hundred and eighty degree turn on how I felt about this guy. Perhaps I may have slightly misjudged him.

Usually my initial first impressions about people are pretty good, but not today.

In a way, C.D. kinda reminded me of Dad, and I think in time C.D. and I could really hit it off and become pretty good friends.

So while the coffee was brewing, C.D. showed me where everything in the break room was kept, such as, the filters, the coffee grounds, the silverware drawer, and even the refrigerator of all things. C.D. was explaining everything to me in great detail, much like Dad would do.

Once again, I felt like I was ten years old, but it was okay…, because it was a familiar role for me to play.

Obviously, C.D. took his coffee seriously. It was becoming quite apparent to me that coffee was a very big priority in his life, and perhaps even the focal point of his day.

When the coffee finished brewing, C.D. poured me a cup. After taking a sip, I gotta say that it was the best damn cup of coffee that I've ever had in my entire life. There's no doubt in my mind that C.D. has had many years of practice in honing his coffee making skills.

C.D. and I chitchatted a little while longer. He told me a little bit about himself and the caseload that I inherited, and what he told me was a real eye-opener.

As I listened to C.D., he struck me as someone who didn't sugarcoat anything. For one thing, he didn't seem to have a lot of good things to say about my predecessor Allan Farnsworth.

To be perfectly honest, the more I heard the more I was beginning to develop a whole new mindset as to what I was getting myself into here at WEALTH Industries.

C.D. poured himself another cup of coffee, and then he came back to the break room table and began talking some more. C.D. was definitely someone who shot from the hip, and from what I could gather he didn't seem like the sensitive type. I was beginning to wonder how he even got into the field of counseling in the first place.

Hey, maybe there were no openings at the local mini-mart!

Anyway, he began telling me things that Mr. Watson had failed to mention in my job interview, - that's for sure! It's sometimes the information that you hear from your coworkers that serves as the true barometer of a situation. Supervisors often omit some of the more sordid details, and I was beginning to wonder if Mr. Watson was that kind of supervisor.

Additionally…, your coworkers usually tell you things that you don't generally find in the case files either. I was certainly getting a quick overview of the agency from C.D., or should I say, the "unedited" version.

As I sipped my coffee and listened intently to what C.D. was telling me, I was starting to wonder if I was in way over my head.

Then again, like my Dad often says…, "You gotta consider the source."

Maybe C.D. is nothing but a big blowhard, who likes to stir the pot and make up stories. I guess I'll need more time to draw my own conclusions.

But hey, - it's my first day…, and I wasn't going to rush to any hasty decisions just yet!

In wrapping up my conversation with C.D., I told him that it was nice chatting with him, and I reassured him that I would uphold the "golden rule" of the break room, - so help me God!

So after my strange but interesting encounter with C.D., I went back to my office and began sifting through the case files. I was actually quite content, as I sipped on my coffee and familiarized myself with the stories that were beginning to unfold.

Although, I will admit…, that some of the information I was digesting from the case files was comparable to that of a scary science fiction novel.

It then suddenly occurred to me that the people I was reading about were actually going to be on my caseload, and that I'll be interacting with them at some point in the very near future.

When I glanced at the clock on the wall, I saw that it was well past four-thirty, which was thirty minutes past quitting time. I must say that my first day of work went by rather quickly.

As I slung my backpack over my shoulder, I noticed that the building resembled a ghost town. Apparently, I was so engrossed in reading the case files that I was totally unaware of the mass exodus surrounding me, as everyone cleared out as soon as four o'clock rolled around.

It then occurred to me that I didn't even stop to eat the delicious five-star lunch that Mom had made for me.

Now that in itself is highly unusual!

As I was leaving the building and walking towards my car, I saw that Mr. Watson's car was still parked in the parking lot. You know the one…, that gorgeous Lincoln Town Car that I couldn't stop taking my eyes off of this morning.

Mr. Watson really impressed me today. He wasn't all show. The man led by example. He doesn't even designate a parking space for himself. Then again…, why should he? He gets here so damn early every morning that he has the pick of the litter to park his car wherever he wants.

As I unlocked my car door, I noticed that Mr. Watson's office window looks directly out onto the parking lot. I began to quietly chuckle to myself because I was thinking that Mr. Watson probably instructed the architect to design the building that way. I'm sure that Watson wants to have a "bird's eye view" of all the comings and goings of his staff, and based on a few of the staff that I observed today I can certainly understand why.

Well, the thought no sooner left my mind, when all of a sudden I heard Mr. Watson call out to me from his office window, "Jack, I see you survived your first day!"

I quickly said, "Yes sir…, I sure did. It was a good day, and I'll be back tomorrow!"

Watson replied, "Great, that's the spirit! And uh…, Jack, remember, try not to call me sir." He then lightly chuckled to himself, as he shut his office window.

Well, my first week of work was progressing nicely. I was taking copious notes, and trying to make sense out of all the volumes of paper that were stored in each of the case files. I was becoming more and more adept with the terminology and the flow of the reporting process.

Periodically, Mr. Watson would check in with me and ask me how things were going. He said that once I was finished reviewing the files, then I should start to initiate contact with the clients on my caseload, such as making phone calls and scheduling interviews.

Mr. Watson pointed out to me that there was a transition period that needed to be made, and tried to impress upon me that the rehabilitation counselor was the lifeline to the outside world for the clients that I worked with.

In fact, on several occasions he adamantly stated, "Other than family, the rehabilitation counselor may be the most integral person in the client's life."

Watson may have been slightly overstating the point, but in theory I had no problem with his expectations. I was quite eager to begin rolling up my sleeves and facing the challenges that lay ahead. I wanted people to stand up and take notice of Jack O'Leary, and say great things about me behind my back. I still had no idea of the cast of characters that I would grow to know on this caseload. Even after a thorough and careful examination of the case files, it is still quite difficult to ascertain the full gravity and scope of the situation.

In other words, familiarizing yourself with the case is one thing, but living the case and having reality stare right back at you from across your desk is clearly another.

Well…, I survived my first full week!

Yeah, I would say it was a good week, a successful week, and I got a lot accomplished. I was beginning to get my feet wet so to speak, and I was getting to know the staff that I work with a little better. I was now on a first name basis with most of the people here, and I was trying to give everyone the distinct impression that I was a regular guy and not at all pretentious.

Sure, there's a number of people here that still don't know my name and simply refer to me as the new guy, but maybe in time they'll really get to know me, and see that I'm trying to survive in this job just like they are.

Well, week two began in much the same fashion as week one did. Dad had the breakfast going full-bore every morning, and Mom was making me a delicious five-star lunch every day.

I was still making the effort of getting into work fifteen minutes early each morning, but my reasons for doing so have shifted. Last week I was attempting to falsely impress Mr. Watson, but this week I was coming into work early because I really wanted to.

As I pulled into the WEALTH parking lot, I saw that Mr. Watson's Lincoln Town Car was already parked in its usual spot. His car was pristine and glimmering, - inside and out.

Where does the man find the time? Mr. Watson gets here two hours before everybody else each morning, and only God knows what time he leaves in the afternoon.

As I was walking toward the front door, I began to ask myself, "What motivates Watson to be the first person into work every morning and the last one to leave?"

Quite honestly, I couldn't determine if it was love, duty, or compulsion which drove him. The man has over thirty years of experience, yet he's hungrier than a greenhorn.

Whatever the reason, Watson was making a bold statement to his subordinates. I'm not really sure if Watson was making an impression on the rest of the staff around here, but he was certainly impressing the hell out of me, and he was definitely the right man to be at the helm of the USS WEATH.

Watson reminded me of a Field General, who not only knew battlefield tactics, but he didn't mind looking the enemy square in the eye and doing some hand-to-hand combat as well.

Mr. Watson struck me as someone who did whatever had to be done, and he would never ask you to do something that he wouldn't do himself. I was very fortunate to start my career with a boss like Mr. Watson. He wasn't the milquetoast type, or some burn-out of a human service's supervisor, who was merely putting his time in and collecting a lousy paycheck.

Agency Directors like Watson really need to be on the cutting edge, if they want their agency to remain solvent. They need to be creative, innovative, and crafty enough to follow the all-important money train, so that the agency not only stays on track, but also stays in the black.

As I entered the building, I could distinctly hear noises coming from the back room. It was like déjà-vu all over again from the previous week. Watson was probably rearranging the back room. This must be a standing routine that he does every Monday.

I then surmised that it was not something that he merely did last week to impress me. Once again, the man did whatever had to be done and he was very unassuming about it.

At that point, I began following the sounds of tables and chairs clanging in the back area of the building. The area that all of the noise was emanating from was known as the contract floor, and this area was where the bulk of the clients spent the majority of their day.

These client workers were involved in all sorts of assembly and packaging jobs that were subcontracted to our agency from local and interstate businesses. These businesses found it to be fiscally advantageous to farm out the work to us, instead of processing the work themselves.

Frankly, these subcontracted jobs that the clients worked on were very menial in scope, and to tell you the truth, businesses probably couldn't get anyone in the general population to perform this type of drudgery work anyway.

However, be assured that this was not busy work, but work that was invaluable to the overall solvency of the businesses that subcontracted with us. The clients had an affinity for this type of work, and Watson did everything in his power to take full advantage of the situation.

As I walked onto the contract floor, I looked around the room and saw all types of industrial machinery, workbenches, and all sorts of supplies and paraphernalia that were neatly labeled and organized in big metal bins. The area was absolutely immaculate, and void of any sign of disarray or clutter.

From what I understand, the companies that we subcontracted with not only provided WEALTH with the material needed to do the work, but they also purchased the industrial machinery as well. This was actually great for us because the expenditures for the machinery didn't have to come out of our overhead budget. And to take it one step further, if the machinery were to breakdown then the companies would either fix it or replace it for us free of charge.

Yeah, Mr. Watson was certainly happy about that, and I was beginning to realize that he knew how to play all of the angles and maximize all of his resources.

So after a brief inspection of this part of the room, I walked around the corner where I spotted Mr. Watson straightening out the long line of workbenches and chairs.

Watson was still unaware of my presence, due to the scraping sounds that the furniture made, and also because he had his back to me.

As I observed Watson, he reminded me of someone who was "old school," and someone who relied strictly on his own initiative. He did whatever had to be done without being told what to do. He probably wishes that he had a few more "old school" subordinates on his staff, so that they could help take some of the burden off of his shoulders.

I then thought to myself, "I need to step up and be one of those subordinates that he sorely needs, so that I might lessen his load."

So not wanting to startle Mr. Watson, I slowly crept into his peripheral line of sight before uttering a word. I know how startled I would be if someone unexpectedly snuck up on me.

Mr. Watson then saw me out of the corner of his eye and turned his full-attentions toward me, as he pleasantly said, "Good morning, Jack. So I see you decided to take me up on my suggestion from last week and go exploring…, eh."

I attentively said, "Yes sir…, because I knew you were back here and you gave me permission."

"Permission…," he said, in a rather surprised tone of voice.

Watson continued by saying, "Jack, I don't want you to feel inhibited here. I want you to feel completely comfortable in your surroundings."

I simply nodded my head, and then proceeded to help him move the last few remaining chairs into place. I then glanced at my watch and saw that it was still before eight o'clock.

A week ago, I would've been jumping for joy in knowing that I was making a good impression on Mr. Watson, but today it really didn't matter. Today I was here early solely because I wanted to be.

"So Mr. Watson…, would you like me to move the tables and chairs into place for you on Monday mornings? That way it would free you up to do other things." I quietly asked.

Watson smiled, and then graciously said, "Well…, thanks for the offer Jack. That tells me a lot about you. It tells me that you don't view yourself as being above any one duty that we have around here. In my day, we use to refer to someone like that as being a "company man." I don't know…, maybe you're too young to be familiar with that expression."

"Actually Mr. Watson, I'm very familiar with the term because my dad has taken great pride in being a company man his whole career." I replied, proudly.

Watson smiled, nodded his head, and then said, "Well, I grew up in a blue-collar family too, and I'm sure that you and I have a lot more in common than you realize."

"No doubt…," I quietly answered.

Watson and I finished straightening up the back room. He never gave me a definitive answer as to whether he wanted me to rearrange the back room on Mondays or not. I wasn't going to press the issue. I offered to do it, and now it would be up to him to decide.

After all…, he's the boss!

We left the back room and then headed toward the offices. Watson casually asked me how I was coming along with the case files, and I told him that I should be finished with the balance of the case files sometime today.

Mr. Watson patted me on the back, and then said in a gregarious tone, "That-a-boy, Jack! I knew you were a real go-getter!"

Watson then continued by saying, "Now Jack, once you finish reviewing all of the files then let Dolly know. Once Dolly is notified then she will send out a form letter to each of the clients on your caseload. The letter will basically say that Allan Farnsworth will no longer be handling their case, but that you…, Jack O'Leary, will be the new counselor of record."

"Okay Mr. Watson, I understand."

Watson continued by saying, "I'd like to see the letters go out today. Dolly will need you to sign each letter, and then she can take them over to the post office in bulk mail. It will then be up to you to schedule some preliminary interviews, so that you can get better acquainted with the clients. It will also be up to you to field any phone calls that the clients may have as well, and to deal with whatever life disasters that may come up. Well…, within reason of course."

I paused a moment, and then inquisitively asked, "Um…, what constitutes within reason, Mr. Watson?"

Watson looked me dead in the eye and said, "Believe me, you'll know, and if you still don't know…, then come see me."

"Okay Mr. Watson, sounds like a plan."

As Watson turned to walk away, I could hear him quietly chuckling under his breath. Then he must've thought of something really funny, because I could see the back of his shoulder blades bobbing up and down with laughter.

Obviously, Mr. Watson didn't want to share his humorous thoughts with me. He was probably thinking to himself, "This kid has no idea what he's getting himself into."

I'm sure Watson didn't want to say too much, but at the same time he couldn't seem to restrain himself from laughing in my presence. For crissakes…, he could have at least waited until he left my office before he started doubling over in laughter.

For the rest of the day, I made a concerted effort to finish up reviewing all of the case files so that Dolly could mail out the form letters.

At about three o'clock, I walked over to Dolly's desk and told her that she could begin preparing the form letters. She indicated to me that she would make the copies and then place the letters on my desk for signature.

Dolly knew the drill, and I'm sure she has done this little administrative exercise for Mr. Watson a million times.

At that point, I was feeling pretty good about myself, especially since the letters couldn't get mailed out until they had my signature on them. I was officially representing the agency.

It took about a day or two before I started fielding any phone calls. I have to say that it was a bit of an adrenaline rush when Dolly buzzed my office and told me that I had a client on the line that wished to speak to me. I would then proudly pick up the phone and blurt out my name and then think to myself what a wonderful thing this was. I was in a position of authority.

I really enjoyed setting up appointments to meet with people, and to discuss whatever needed to be discussed. I would take out my day planner and schedule times that were more to their liking than mine. I'm sure I was in a bit of a honeymoon period, but it really didn't matter.

In a way, I felt as though I was saving the world. I would lay in bed at night and think of vivid metaphors in which I was "tilling" the human services field, and hoping that some of the human services program "seeds" would somehow "germinate."

Essentially, I envisioned myself as a gardener. My job was to systematically turn over the soil in the human services field, level the soil to a workable grade, plant the seed, water occasionally, and then pull up any weeds that might be encroaching on the plant.

The "plant" of course was my client.

Well…, I hope it all sounds this easy when the clients are sitting across from me and we start delving into our counseling sessions.

Let's hope it's not going to be "ashes to ashes," or dust to dust!"

As I glanced at my day planner, I saw that it was beginning to fill up nicely. I enjoyed filling in all of the available slots and having as few empty spaces on my day planner as possible.

Yes indeed…, things were certainly moving along quite smartly, until the next moment when I heard the intercom buzz, and Dolly nervously say.…

CHAPTER THREE

"Excuse me, Mr. O'Leary."

"Yes, what is it Dolly?"

"You have a phone call on line one, it's Mr. Sampson. He said it's extremely urgent, and he really needs to talk to you right away."

"Mr. Sampson, huh…, that name sounds familiar." I thought to myself.

"Okay, Dolly. Thanks, I'll take the call." I pleasantly replied.

I walked over to my desk, sat down, and picked up the phone and then cheerfully said, "Hello, Mr. Sampson. This is Jack O'Leary…, how can I help you?"

An extremely deep and intimidating voice came over the line and grunted, "Yes, you can help me, Mr. O'Leary. My wife and I will be right over to your office, so that you can fix the problem that we're having with our money from Social Security."

"Gee, I'm sorry Mr. Sampson, but I can't see you on such short notice. I was told that you simply wanted to speak with me on the phone, not come over and see me."

"No…, we want to come over right now!" Sampson said, with a raised voice.

"Well Mr. Sampson, I'm looking at my day planner, and I see that I have an appointment with you and your wife Charmayne for next Wednesday afternoon. Perhaps the matter can keep till then." I stated reassuringly.

Sampson interrupted violently and shouted, "No…, I don't care about that! I need to see you right away! You're my counselor, and you need to fix my problem!"

"Mr. Sampson, wait a minute…," I said, wincing from the sound of his voice.

Sampson then bellowed, "I just received a letter from the Social Security Office! They said that I'm gonna get less money in my paycheck because of my job at the restaurant! Mrs. Sampson's money is gonna be cut too! We wanna see you right away and find out what you're gonna do about it! I'm coming down to see you on the next city bus!"

"But Mr. Sampson…," I pleaded.

"No buts…, we'll see you in fifteen minutes!" He yelled, and then the phone line went dead.

There was apparently no getting through to Mr. Sampson. The counselor that was previously in charge of Mr. Sampson's case, Mr. Allan Farnsworth, left WEALTH to take a job with the State Office, and from the looks of it that's where I'd like to be right now too.

Why you may ask?

Well, not only does the State Office pay their counselors almost double the paltry salary that I'm earning here at WEALTH, but I'm sure that none of the counselors down at the State Office has to put up with the likes of Mr. and Mrs. Sampson.

With each passing day, it was becoming more and more apparent to me that every counselor working here at WEALTH was quite disenchanted with their job, and that they were all simply biding their time until they could get hired by the State Office.

I've worked here for three weeks now, and even I find myself making some subtle inquiries to a few of the counselors on staff regarding State employment, but nobody's talking.

It seems to be the best kept secret in town, and almost bordering on "national security!"

Now I will admit…, but it certainly doesn't bode well that three weeks into the job and the new kid on staff is already asking questions regarding alternate employment.

Apparently Mr. Watson frowns on this type of chatter around the water cooler, and rumor has it that he once fired someone right on the spot for engaging in such idle repartee.

So after hanging up the phone with Mr. Sampson, I began reminiscing about the dreams I had as a child. Like any other kid, I wanted to be a great athlete or even a famous rock star.

As I've mentioned before, my true ambition in life was going into sports broadcasting, and delivering some of the great play-by-play sports moments of all time to millions of people all over the world. I certainly never imagined myself sitting behind a desk trying to sort out the lives of people who were mentally and physically challenged.

These people were actually counting on me for answers. They were expecting me to set them free from their personal prisons, but then…, who would set me free of mine?

Suddenly, I was jarred out of my daydreaming state by a loud knock at my office door. I looked up and saw this immense black man standing directly in front of me, and he was being shadowed by someone who was standing closely behind him.

It was the Sampson's!

I had momentarily forgotten that the Sampson's were stopping by to see me. I guess Mr. Sampson wasn't kidding when he said that he would be right over on the next available city bus.

The Sampson's got over here so fast that they must've flagged one of the city buses down in the middle of the street. I thought perhaps his ranting was nothing more than an idle threat.

Mr. Sampson looked extremely agitated, and I could plainly see the steam rising off the top of his head. He was clutching onto something. No doubt…, it was some sort of bureaucratic form letter that he had made reference to in our previous telephone conversation.

I had heard from some of the counselors on staff that this husband and wife tag team was big and loud, and they were notorious for using intimidation tactics to get their own way.

Well, despite the staff's well-intentioned heads up, their forewarnings paled in comparison to what was now standing directly in front of me. These two hulking individuals wanted immediate action to their problem, or else they were prepared to kick some butt, specifically mine…, if they didn't hear or get the results that they wanted.

Anyway, I simply can't express in words how vertically challenged I felt in the presence of these two immense individuals. They were certainly two of the biggest people that I had ever seen before in my entire life. Their reputation preceded them, and they were now firmly planted two feet in front of me in my tiny little office.

Just to give you some idea of what I was experiencing. Mr. Sampson was approximately six-foot eight…, maybe bigger, and he was easily four hundred pounds. Everything about him was big…, his hands, his head, and his huge bulging eyes.

His counterpart, Mrs. Sampson, was approximately six-foot two, and she probably weighed in at a svelte three hundred and fifty pounds.

It was certainly a sight to behold when they both simultaneously crossed over the threshold of my office doorway.

For a minute there I thought they were going to unhinge the brackets that were affixed onto the door jam. Then they sat down and totally engulfed the two poor defenseless chairs that were sitting directly across from my desk. I was utterly speechless.

To say that I was nervous, well…, that would be an understatement!

Anyway, I wanted to get off on the right foot with the Sampson's, so I stood up and extended my hand to greet them once they were "officially" in my office.

Mr. Sampson had no time for formalities. He then slapped the crumpled Social Security determination letter that he was holding in his sweaty palm into my already outstretched hand.

Apparently the Sampson's were quite content in receiving full benefits from the Social Security Administration along with the pittance that they were earning from their menial dishwasher jobs at the restaurant. They were completely in the dark on just how convoluted the Social Security system was.

Their previous counselor, Allan Farnsworth, informed the Sampson's that they needed to be involved in some level of employment, or else they might be in jeopardy of losing their Social Security benefits. I'm sure Farnsworth never informed them that from here on out they would be subjected to a volley of bureaucratic form letters from the Social Security Administration.

Farnsworth didn't care because he was on the short road to the State Office, and he probably figured that the next counselor, or should I say the next "schmuck," - that would be me…., would be forced to clean up his mess and futilely attempt to explain all of the gory details of the flawed system to the Sampson's.

The Sampson's had no idea what they were getting themselves into regarding the never-ending saga of threatening correspondence that the Social Security Administration is notorious for. Due to their limited intelligence, the Sampson's could not fully appreciate the gravity or the logistical quagmire that they were now immersed in.

I was really hoping that my initial encounter with the Sampson's, which was scheduled for next Wednesday afternoon, would have been more hospitable and homeostatic.

Instead I find myself in an adversarial situation, and the consternation of getting off on the wrong foot is not the way I had intended to start our new relationship.

Well, after some long-winded explanations, and perhaps one or two empty promises that I made to the Sampson's, I finally convinced them that everything was going to work out fine.

I basically told the Sampson's that I would personally look into the matter for them, and that I would hash out all the particulars with the Social Security Office.

Upon hearing my reassurances, Mr. Sampson seemed pleased. As he was walking out of my office he said, in his rather intimidating voice, "So you'll take care of it, right Mr. O'Leary?"

I just smiled, and replied in a deflated tone, "Yes… yes…, I'll take care of it Mr. Sampson, good-bye."

Just then Dolly buzzed me over the intercom, "Mr. O'Leary, you have a phone call on line one, it's Mr. Burroughs of OVR."

Dolly saw that the Sampson's had just left my office, so she knew that I was available to take the call.

"Thanks Dolly, you can patch the call through." I said, wearily.

Yes, our secretary was really named Dolly. She is a beautiful woman, but in addition to her beauty she is also helpful, kind, courteous, and very efficient.

The men in the office always seem to find time to check their mailboxes every chance they can, and yes…, you guessed it, - the mailboxes are all in close proximity to Dolly's desk.

It was also quite customary to see the male counselors making a concerted effort at hand delivering their reports up to Dolly's desk, instead of having one of the office couriers doing it.

I guess for them it was just another excuse to sneak a peek, or better yet…, catch a whiff of her intoxicating perfume. They would then look for reasons to just hang around her desk and act like awkward school boys, as they did everything in their power to impress her.

Actually, it was rather amusing for me to watch, and I must say that I found it to be a welcomed distraction, especially on the days when my caseload was stressing me out.

So the phone call that Dolly was transferring over to my office was from a gentleman named Mr. Burroughs, who works as a vocational counselor for a State agency called OVR.

OVR stands for the Office of Vocational Rehabilitation, and this agency sponsors many of our clients here at WEALTH Industries for vocational evaluation and training. And from what I understand, these sponsorships generate a lot of revenue for our agency.

In fact, this particular State agency is home to many of the counselors who started their fledgling careers right here at WEALTH Industries.

OVR is certainly a State agency that I would entertain working for someday, well…, if the opportunity ever presented itself anyway. I'm ashamed to admit it, but I find myself doting on these OVR counselors hand and foot in meetings, such as shagging them coffee and danish out of the break room, so that they might go back and tell their bosses about a certain young counselor over at WEALTH Industries who is a real go-getter.

Watson has certainly taken note of my exemplary actions in pampering the OVR counselors, and he wholeheartedly applauds my efforts.

In fact, on more than one occasion, he has mentioned my zealous deeds at the Monday morning staff meeting, and has emphatically stated to the other counselors on staff, "I want you all to follow Jack's lead in dealing with OVR."

Hey, Watson knows where his bread is buttered, and that OVR pays a lot of the bills around here.

I don't think Watson is aware of my true motives in sucking up to the OVR counselors, but I think all of the WEALTH counselors are. Watson has made it abundantly clear to all of the counselors on staff, "That whatever OVR wants...., then OVR gets!"

Dolly, after transferring the call, then pleasantly said, "Go ahead Jack, Mr. Burroughs is on line one."

As I reached for the telephone, I attempted to collect my thoughts..., especially after the mentally fatiguing session that I just endured with the Sampson's.

Suddenly, my mind went blank, and I completely forgot my reasons for taking this phone call in the first place. I remember talking with Mr. Burroughs the other day, but the substance of our conversation seems to have flown right out the window.

At that point, I thought I would buy a little time by exchanging a few light pleasantries with Mr. Burroughs, whose first name actually escapes me at the moment.

Just as I remembered my reasons for wanting to talk with Mr. Burroughs, out of nowhere one of the clients came barging into my office, and then proceeded to pick up one of my office chairs and fling it against the wall causing the plaster to buckle. He then lunged across my desk in a fitful rage, with the explicit intent of inflicting me with bodily harm.

This extremely agitated young man's name was Michael Wallace. Michael was a young deaf man on my caseload, and he was currently undergoing an evaluation here at WEALTH.

For some reason Michael was quite angry, and he was targeting his anger toward me. Michael had a hold of my shirt with one hand, and with the other hand he was lining me up to punch me in the face.

Just before Michael could throw the deciding blow, two rather large men who work on the contract floor intervened, and managed to subdue Michael and wrestle him down to the floor.

Apparently, these two men had been in hot pursuit of Michael because he had just trashed the back room of the contract floor, and then made a quick getaway toward the front offices.

Fortunately, these two rather large men were able to chase Michael down and intercept him in my office before he was able to unleash anymore additional harm or chaos.

In the midst of being wrestled to the floor, Michael managed to reach across my desk and grab my eyeglasses, which were sitting on top of a pile of papers. As he clutched the glasses and crushed them with his vise-like grip, a satisfying smile seemed to sweep across his face.

It was a rather surreal moment, and all I could do at that point was just watch in utter disbelief, as he went plummeting to the floor with these two large men firmly in control of him.

As Michael lay on the floor, he had a rather bizarre look of contentment on his face, and then like magic..., an eerie calm seem to sweep across his entire body.

The two men then helped Michael up to his feet, and as Michael was exiting my office, he smiled at me and gave me a slight wave good-bye, as if nothing had ever happened.

Although I found Michael's actions to be utterly astounding, I have to say that deep down inside I really felt bad for him. These outbursts that Michael was prone to having are no doubt a direct result of his being misunderstood by the speaking world.

So after Michael was safely escorted out of my office, I took a couple of deep breaths so that I could try to compose myself. I then bent down and picked up the stack of papers that had fallen to the floor during the melee, and when I reached under my desk to retrieve my eyeglasses, I saw that they now resembled a twisted pretzel. I then glanced down at my brand new shirt, and I noticed that it was badly ripped and that several buttons were missing.

Suddenly, I heard a faint voice calling out to me on the telephone, "Mr. O'Leary, hello..., Mr. O'Leary!"

It then occurred to me that the voice was that of Mr. Burroughs, who had been hanging on the telephone line during the entire fracas. Oh, my God..., what must he be thinking?

Wait, Richard..., that's Burroughs' first name.

Anyway, I had a call into Richard Burroughs the other day because I wanted to speak to him about Michael Wallace, and discuss how Michael was progressing thus far on his vocational evaluation. And to be perfectly honest, the update that I was about to give him was far from rosy.

Michael was currently being sponsored by OVR, and Burroughs was the OVR counselor assigned to young Michael's case. Burroughs has been advocating strongly for Michael since coming to us three weeks ago.

Boy, talk about coincidences!

I've called Richard Burroughs several times now to discuss Michael's erratic behavior, and frankly we are at wit's end as to what we should do with Michael. Based on everything that we've seen so far, Michael's chances of remaining at WEALTH were pretty slim.

Quite honestly, Michael's evaluation is really not working out very well, and at this point in my career I didn't feel competently equipped in guiding this young man in the right direction.

I'm ashamed to admit it, but I guess I wanted to bail out on Michael just like everyone else has in his life, except for Burroughs, who seems to be in young Michael's corner.

Although Burroughs knew that Michael was exhibiting some major compliance issues here at WEALTH, I couldn't bring myself to tell him about the harrowing incident in my office, and that in all likelihood Michael was destined to be an unsuitable candidate for our program.

Was it the old Irish Catholic guilt that prevented me from rubber stamping his rejection slip?

No..., the Nuns can't take credit for this one, because this one belonged to Watson.

As a rule, Watson frowns on having the counselors reject anyone from the program. So that being said, I guess it was nothing more than pure unadulterated fear that prevented me from telling Richard Burroughs the naked truth regarding young Michael's poor performance thus far.

Frankly, Michael would have to be the "anti-Christ" for a decision of termination to be made, and even then Watson would scrutinize the decision and explore any and all avenues so that Michael could remain in the program.

Man, two weeks into the job and all I could think about was that two of my cases were seemingly in the toilet, and I had a caseload of seventy people assigned to me.

Geez..., what must the other sixty "odd" clients, (pardon the pun,) be like?

I fumbled for the receiver, and then hurriedly said, "Hi Richard, sorry about that..., but one of the clients just came by my office for an unscheduled counseling session."

As I continued to converse with Burroughs, I could hear Watson's voice in the back of my mind saying repeatedly at our Monday morning staff meetings, "Counselors should not make any hasty decisions regarding denying enrollment into our program."

I then asked myself, "If someone wanted to tear your head off, such as young Michael Wallace wanted to do to me this morning, would this then constitute being a hasty decision?"

Quite honestly, I was beginning to wonder where the line was to be drawn. After all, Watson's motto was, "We want these client's to succeed at all costs!"

The counseling staff all felt that Watson purposely used the word "cost" because we were operating under a tight budget, and every client that was denied access into the program meant less revenue being generated.

So the motto, "at all costs," reminded us that it costs a lot of money to operate WEALTH, and keep its doors open for business.

Watson would often say, "Revenue people…, that's what pays your salary. So let's take a real hard look at all referrals, shall we?"

So while I have Richard Burroughs on the line should I tell him the unadulterated truth about Michael Wallace, or should I simply turn a blind eye, and say that any discussion on the matter is a little too premature and nothing more than pure conjecture.

At that moment, I felt as if I was between a rock and a hard place because I really liked Burroughs, and I didn't have the heart to break the discouraging news to him regarding young Michael's horrendous performance thus far.

Burroughs then chimed in and said, "Jack, I know Michael can be a real handful at times, but please give him every consideration."

I quickly replied, "Richard, we give everyone here strong consideration, and Michael is certainly no exception. I hope you realize that."

Burroughs countered, "I know that Jack, but he's had a lot of bumps in the road over the last couple of years. He comes from a really nice family, and they would love nothing more than to see him land a spot at a really top notch program like WEALTH."

"Well Richard…, you know we make every effort to be very objective, but there is also a certain level of subjectivity that comes into play as well. Let's just see how the rest of the evaluation plays out, okay." I said, diplomatically.

Quite honestly, I couldn't believe all the poppycock that I was spewing out to Burroughs with regards to objective and subjective criteria. It's nothing but a bunch of bull shit that I'm rambling on about. Burroughs must know how Watson and this agency operates. He's gotta know that we rarely deny anyone access here, especially if Watson has anything to say about it.

It would take an "Act of Congress" for Michael Wallace to be denied services!

In all likelihood, we're going to take Michael Wallace into the program. Watson makes sure that he circles his calendar when it comes to attending all of the determination meetings, and he usually has the final say on the matter anyway. The WEALTH counselors are simply viewed as figure heads in the whole process, with Watson doing all of the real wheeling and dealing with the OVR counselors, and insuring that all of the necessary paperwork is signed in triplicate.

Actually, I was just thinking the other day that Watson should erect a replica of the Statue of Liberty and place it near the front entrance of WEALTH, with an inscription on the plaque that says, "Give us your square pegs and your underachievers!"

As my subconscious mind continued to wander haphazardly, I was hurled back into reality when Burroughs said, "Jack, there must be something down there that he is good at. He has a lot of energy and he is very strong. I think he has a real fighting chance to make something of himself, if given the right opportunity."

"Wow!" I thought to myself. Is Burroughs psychic…, because that was an unusual choice of words that he just used?

Burroughs is right, Michael is a formidable fighter, however he's not exactly the kind of fighter that we're looking for here at WEALTH.

"Well Richard…, time will tell. We still have a couple of weeks left in his evaluation. In my opinion, Michael has a lot of anger management issues, and I think it is directly related to his communication deficits. I think his chances for success could increase dramatically, if OVR contracted the services for a speech therapist. A therapist might be able to unlock the door of what's really troubling him."

"That's a great idea, Jack! I know our agency uses the speech services of a Jill Woodson. I'll contact her today, and see if she's available. Thanks for the tip!" Burroughs replied.

"Hey, don't mention it Richard, I'm glad we had a chance to talk. I'll be in touch, and I'll keep you up to speed on how well Michael is fighting, uh…, I mean…, doing." I said, as I inadvertently blurted out a Freudian slip.

Burroughs then said, "good-bye," and although I sensed some hesitation in his voice, I think he thought better of not asking me to further explain my accidental slip of the tongue.

Well, it's been about a week now since I had my little "tête-à-tête" with

Michael Wallace. I probably should head down to the contract floor and inquire on how young Michael is doing, along with the rest of the clients on my caseload who work down there, but I seem to be psychologically paralyzed in doing so.

It then occurred to me that I haven't set foot onto the contract floor since taking over my caseload. I have no idea as to who works down there, or what they do or how they do it.

Although I know that I should get down there and make some observations, I'm afraid of what I might find if I do.

Every day when making out my "to do" list, or better said…, my "wish" list, I always jot down visiting the contract floor as a high priority. I really need to familiarize myself with the work that is being done down there, and to get to know the people performing the work as well.

Frankly, I don't want to be viewed as a counselor who just sits in his office all day, and is oblivious to the day-to-day dynamics happening around him. I need to see my caseload in action, so that I can make some cohesive and well-thought out vocational treatment plans.

Several of the OVR counselors have been calling to ask me how their referrals are doing. I'd really like to provide them with some definitive answers, and not be compelled to go running down the hallway making some half-baked inquiries or persistent phone calls to line supervisors because that just wasn't my style. I want to be respected by the line supervisors, and not be looked upon as an incompetent, or heaven forbid…, be seen in the same light as that C.D. fellow.

Well, call it what you want, but every day I was a "no show" down on the contract floor. I opted to remain in the friendly confines of my office, but then realizing that my office wasn't all that friendly, seeing how I'd already been attacked there once before by Michael Wallace.

So maybe it's time for me to roll the dice and head down to the contract floor and take my chances.

For two weeks now, I've been telling myself that this is the day that I throw caution to the wind and visit with my clients down on the contract floor, especially since there were a lot of clients on my caseload that I haven't even met yet.

I kept asking myself, "Why am I so afraid to make the leap? Am I afraid I'll find more people like young Michael Wallace and the notorious Sampson's down there?"

Excuses, excuses, and more excuses kept popping up throughout the course of my day as to why I didn't go down to the contract floor. Classic excuses like, it's Friday…, and it's the end of the workweek, so I'll do it Monday. Then Monday rolls around and I'll say that I'm tired from the weekend, so I'll do it tomorrow, especially when most people are usually cranky on Monday mornings anyway. I just kept putting obstacles in my way every single day, which prevented me from going down to the contract floor.

It was kinda like exercise…, you know you should do it, but you find all sorts of reasons not to. Once again, another week would slide by and still no visits to the contract floor.

It's another Monday morning, and once again I'm trying to convince myself that today is the day that I'm finally going to visit the contract floor.

So after slugging down my last cup of coffee, I shuffled a few papers on my desk, and then attempted to find the courage to get up from my chair and head down to the contract floor.

Suddenly, I could feel the adrenaline pumping through my veins, as if it were the big game, and the head coach just gave me the nod to go warm up.

Yeah, I know what you're probably thinking, and you're absolutely right…, my thought processes sound somewhat delusional, but please hear me out.

As I reluctantly got up from my desk, I made sure that all of the piles of papers on top of my desk were in order. It's, well…, an obsessive-compulsive tendency of mine.

Apparently, I just can't seem to leave my office without straightening up the top of my desk. I'm sure that this neurotic behavior of mine can all be traced back to the Nuns, and my parochial school education, which I seem to attribute all of my weird and quirky tendencies on.

Anyway, so after straightening up all of the papers on my desk, I took a deep breath and then slowly walked toward the door. I decided to take a pad of paper and a pen with me, so that I could jot down a few notes on the people that I was about to meet.

I cautiously opened my office door, and as I was locking the door behind me, I was continuing to tell myself, "This is it…, it's really gonna happen today!"

So with my paper and pen in hand, I wield around and make my way down the dark and dingy hallway that leads to the contract floor. After making it halfway down the hall, whom do I see walking up the hallway towards me, but none other than Mr. Watson.

Watson looked me straight in the eye, and then decisively said, "Good morning, Jack. I'm sorry for the short notice, but we have an emergency staff meeting in five minutes. I need you down in the conference room, ASAP. I hope it won't be an inconvenience for you."

"No sir, Mr. Watson! No problem…, at all! I'll be right there!"

A reprieve…, hallelujah, and "saints b' praised!"

No contract floor visits today!

Hey, at least this time I made the effort. I was halfway down the hall before I was intercepted by the boss. I would say that's pretty good progress, but today's contract floor visit just wasn't in the cards.

Gee, maybe if things really work out for me, I won't have to go down to the contract floor at all this week. It was kinda like going on a diet, tomorrow, and tomorrow, and tomorrow.

Well, needless to say…, but I didn't make it down to the contract floor that week. I have totally convinced myself that the honest to God reason for my shying away from visiting the contract floor was fear. I kept ruminating over Michael Wallace, the notorious Sampson's, and the "Pandora's box" of problematic clients that I might encounter down there. The unadulterated fear of getting to know more people on my caseload, and the onslaught of potential disasters that might occur were just too much for me to think about.

The following Monday rolled around, and once again the thoughts of making it down to the contract floor were swimming through my head. I checked my voice mail and saw that I had three new messages from OVR. I always made sure that I responded to these messages "ASAP," as Watson would say, and since OVR was our primary sponsoring agency and paid most of the bills around here then my immediate response to them was imperative.

Anyway, the three messages that I received involved three clients who were all slated for determination meetings this week.

I'm embarrassed to admit it, but I was totally unfamiliar with two of the three clients in question, and I was scratching my head as to how I was going to remedy the situation.

So after thinking about it for a few minutes, I then concluded that my only recourse was to go down onto the contract floor and see what I could find out about these three clients.

Quite honestly, I needed to come up with some fast answers to some pretty technical questions that the OVR counselors were posing to me, such as, production rates, earnings, and work capabilities. This was all information that I needed to secure from the line supervisors, and I really didn't want to extract this information from them over the phone.

In theory, the determination meetings should really be an integral part of the process, but with Mr. Watson chairing the meeting, it always seemed more like a formality than a necessity.

To be honest with you, the determination meetings always reminded me of an auction house atmosphere, because both the WEALTH counselor and the OVR counselor would jockey for position in deciding on what they felt was in the best interest for the client.

Watson of course played the role of the auctioneer, and he would carefully present each and every item that was up for bid, while both counselor combatants waged a bidding war.

The first usual item up for bid was Supportive Employment. The client who was lucky enough to be recommended for supportive employment would receive On the Job Training or any other training that he or she may need to help solidify a work placement in the community.

Supportive employment was the number one option that OVR wanted for each and every one of the clients they sponsored. Not only was supportive employment dynamic for the client, but it also provided OVR the opportunity to recoup a sizeable amount of money from the federal government, especially if the client they sponsored was able to secure competitive employment.

The next item up for bid was the SEP option, which was a less desired option, and stood for the "Sheltered Employment Program." The SEP did not allow for OVR to recoup any of its money, and actually OVR was charged a nominal fee for the client to continue on at WEALTH in that capacity.

Of course, there was a third item up for bid, which was termination from the program. But suffice to say, Watson usually kept that item safely under wraps and rarely up for bid.

Sometimes the determination meetings became rather heated, and depending on how the wind was blowing, Watson would have to decide on whether he would allow the bidding wars to continue or else be forced to play the role of the moderator.

In fact, there were times when the discussions became so heated that it looked as though Watson was "refereeing a heavyweight boxing match."

Generally speaking, but the WEALTH counselors always felt like they were at an unfair disadvantage in the determination meetings because their arguments had to be pretty compelling in order for them to convince Watson to rule in their favor. For obvious reasons, Watson usually sided with the OVR counselors, and merely used the WEALTH counselors as pawns.

Now oddly enough, but there were limits to what Watson could do in terms of giving the OVR counselors everything they wanted at these determination meetings. Watson realized that he couldn't give the OVR counselors the Supportive Employment option all the time.

Typically, the OVR counselors would usually play along with Watson's little charade, but the minute they heard the dreaded recommendation for SEP, then all hell would break loose!

At that point, the OVR counselors would then moan and groan and feverishly attempt to have Watson overturn his decision.

After all..., the OVR counselors had bosses too!

And none of them wanted to go back to the office and tell their supervisors that all the money they just spent on a sponsorship for the last four months went for a SEP placement.

Actually there were times when I felt bad for making a SEP recommendation, but I also knew that I had to use the best judgment possible in placing people in the right situations.

From what I was told, the SEP was essentially a holding tank for clients until something better came along. The SEP is where we did most of our subcontract work, and from what I hear the people that worked in the SEP were really quite capable, as well as extremely productive too.

Unfortunately, the cruel reality was that virtually everyone that was referred to us for vocational evaluation was ultimately headed for the SEP when their evaluation was completed.

So that being said, I convinced myself that I needed to get down to the contract floor so that I could be adequately prepared for my upcoming determination meetings this week.

Well, just in case you were wondering..., I knew where the contract floor was located. I didn't need to consult a floor plan.

As I left my office and proceeded down the dark and dingy hallway that led to the contract floor, I could tell that I was headed in the right direction because the noise level in the building was getting louder and louder.

It kinda reminded me of the Coliseum in ancient Rome!

Suddenly, I envisioned myself as some sort of revered gladiator, who was walking into the heralded arena for the first time, and being awestruck by the crescendo of the crowd.

Well..., maybe my visualizations are a bit dramatic!

Anyway, at the end of this dark and dingy hallway was a set of swinging wooden doors, with a twelve-by-twelve inch plexi-glass window centered right in the middle of each door.

So before setting foot onto the contract floor, I decided to take a quick peek at the room through the window. To my surprise, I observed a plethora of activity unfolding before my eyes.

It kinda reminded me of Santa's workshop!

I kept cocking my head in all sorts of positions, so that I could see all of the different angles of the room. It actually caught my interest more than I was expecting it to.

Although I was rather intrigued by the amount of activity that was happening before me, I was still pretty hesitant to push through the door. I felt as though my feet were glued to the floor.

Just then one of the double doors swung open, and a young Down-syndrome man bolted through it. He had a big smile etched on his face, as he said in a very businesslike fashion, "Hello, sir. I'm sorry if I startled you, but I forgot my lunch box up front."

I calmly replied, "Hey, that's okay buddy..., no problem."

The young man was certainly quite exuberant and seemingly harmless. I was wondering if maybe he was one of the clients on my caseload. Boy, I could sure use a couple of cupcake clients like him to help balance out the likes of Michael Wallace and the notorious Sampson's.

Well, from what I could see the coast was clear, so I decided to slither my way through the two double doors and take a closer look at the contract floor.

So here I am, finally on the contract floor!

This is the place that I have been dreading to set foot on for over a month now.

"One month...," I thought to myself.

Gee, I was wondering if I had just set an agency record for a counselor not getting down to the contract floor sooner than this.

Well, maybe not..., I'm sure that C.D. is probably the all-time reigning champion for that dubious distinction.

Suddenly, I realized that I had forgotten my client roster list. I was meaning to take the list with me so that I could use it as a reference, but in my haste to get down here this morning I just plain forgot it. I had intended to put a face with a name.

Well..., so much for that theory!

To tell you the truth, I guess this could have been the ideal moment for me to make an about-face and beat it back to my office, but I didn't..., and so I decided to forge ahead.

Undaunted by my blunder, I found myself being more and more intrigued with my surroundings. I watched people doing all sorts of assembly work and packaging jobs, which frankly were several notches above my meager mechanical ability, or lack thereof.

From what I could observe the clients on the contract floor were visibly happy and quite productive. The line supervisors certainly had good control of the situation, and the whole operation seemed to run as smooth as a Swiss timepiece.

Walking up and down the rows of workbenches, I observed nothing but productive men and women. They truly had a zeal for the work they were doing. I didn't see one malcontented person nor did I see any lollygagging or horseplay of any kind. I only wish that the WEALTH counseling staff had as much enthusiasm for their jobs, as these clients seemingly had for theirs.

These first-hand experiences of the SEP were quite illuminating, and it wasn't at all what I had envisioned it to be. The clients looked a helluva lot happier in their job than I was in mine.

I then amusingly thought to myself, "Well, that's probably because they didn't have to deal with the likes of young Michael Wallace or the notorious Sampson's."

When I arrived to work the next day, I was very eager to visit the contract floor and try to replicate some of the same positive feelings that I had experienced from the day before.

So after rifling through my mail, and then returning all of the phone calls that I needed to return, I made my way down the dark and dingy hallway that led to the contract floor.

Upon entering the contract floor, I quickly spotted the same Down-syndrome man that almost bowled me over from the day before.

As I watched the young man find his spot on the line, I marveled at all of his little quirks and mannerisms, especially the meticulous way that he arranged and organized his work station.

I then nonchalantly strolled over to one of the line supervisors, and quietly asked who the young Down-syndrome man's counselor was. I was really hoping that the line supervisor would say Allan Farnsworth, because then I would know that the young man was assigned to me.

But to my chagrin, the line supervisor said, "Oh, you mean Kevin, he's on C.D.'s caseload."

I then thought to myself, "Boy, no wonder why C.D. gets to spend so much time drinking coffee in the break room, he's got nothing but cupcakes on his caseload."

Anyway, the day proved to be very productive. Not only did I get the opportunity of meeting many of the people on my caseload, but surprisingly none of the people I met even remotely resembled young Michael Wallace or the notorious Sampson's. So I guess you could say that all of my fears and apprehensions regarding the contract floor were for nothing.

Actually, I discovered that I had quite a few "blue chip" clients assigned to me, and I was beginning to realize that maybe things weren't as bleak as I had envisioned them to be.

The next few months went by like the blink of an eye. I'm happy to say that I generally have a good rapport with most of the people on my caseload, and I've managed to balance my time evenly between my office responsibilities and the contract floor.

Watson of late has been almost a total recluse in his office, and rumor has it that he's been busy developing several new work initiatives for the agency.

One of the initiatives that Mr. Watson is working on is to expand our janitorial services program. Watson is planning on having our job placement specialist, Mr. Joe Atkins, head up the new program. Joe was selected because of his vast experience in grass root development for the agency, and also because of his extensive contacts in the business community.

Joe is someone who is always looking to promote new and exciting employment opportunities for our agency, so that the agency can maintain a more competitive edge in our local job market.

Sadly, Watson's new work initiative may need to be put on hold because Joe was recently stricken with a severe heart attack, and he's currently out of work and convalescing at home.

Last week at the Monday morning staff meeting, Watson announced that he would be putting the new janitorial program on hold until Joe returns to work, and in the interim Watson has decided to evenly distribute Joe's job placement responsibilities amongst the counselors.

Needless to say, but this announcement made for a few moans and groans from around the table because the counselors were already overwhelmed and clearly behind in their work.

Suffice to say, but none of the other counselors relished the fact of having any more work thrust upon them. Nevertheless, Joe is extremely optimistic that he will be returning to his full-time duties after he recovers from his illness, and we are all certainly cheering him on.

So let me tell you a little something about Joe. In my opinion, Joe was just about as good a job placement specialist that you could ever hope to have working for your agency. For a guy who has never had any formal education, Joe was a real "pro."

Joe was a natural born salesman, and before taking the job at WEALTH he worked twenty years selling farm equipment for a local distributor.

By all accounts, Joe was a little rough around the edges, and he wasn't your typical smooth-talking salesman. Joe possessed a certain je ne sais quoi, although if the truth be known, not everyone on the counseling staff thought he was as charming to be around as I did.

To put it mildly, I guess you could say that Joe wasn't exactly schooled in the fine art of diplomacy.

So if I had to describe Joe, I guess the word abrasive might come to mind. But if I was being totally honest, then I would have to classify Joe as being a royal "pain in the ass."

Joe's life consisted of loving God, his family, and getting the word out to the local business community about hiring the handicapped.

Say what you want about Joe, but the bottom line was that Joe could get the job done. And when it came to placing clients into the job market, Joe knew how to "close the deal."

Essentially, Joe had a real knack at talking anyone into anything. Joe loved what he did, and he especially took a lot of pride in placing clients into employment opportunities that no one ever dreamed possible.

Whether Joe was kibitzing in a coffee shop or simply standing in line at the grocery store, he viewed every waking moment as a potential job lead for our clients.

Every morning, Joe had a routine. Well, actually…, it was more like a ritual.

Joe would sit at his desk with a piping hot cup of coffee and carefully examine his job bank, which was nothing more than a dinky little metal box filled with scratched-out index cards that he kept safely tucked away in a locked bottom drawer of his desk. Joe would meticulously study the contents of the job bank each day, and then plan out his day accordingly.

The information that Joe had stored in the job bank was called his "contacts." Joe felt that his contacts needed to be reviewed on a daily basis, or else his contacts would get ice cold.

Prior to Joe taking the job here at WEALTH, we had a guy named Stanley doing job placement. From what I understand, Stanley was not a very good job placement specialist, and to put it bluntly, Stanley was basically incompetent and seldom took any initiative in developing any new job leads for the agency. Stanley rarely left the building, and he would usually confine himself to the existing leads that we already had on file. The skimpy leads that Stanley did come by were shaky at best, and often times they were given to him by someone else.

Joe on the other hand was constantly beating the bushes, so that he could take advantage of seizing every opportunity that he could. Stanley would rather spend his time hanging around Dolly's desk, then developing any new job leads out in the field where he was supposed to be.

Lately, the counselors seem to be reminiscing more about the comical exploits of Stanley. I'm surmising that this recent trip down memory lane is because job placement has now become such an integral part of our overall job responsibilities. The stories regarding Stanley are pretty funny, and rehashing them has been a much needed source of comic relief for the counselors.

On the flip side, the counselors have been doing a lot of mumbling and grumbling behind Mr. Watson's back with regards to job placement, and when hearing their constant gripes and bellyaches it often makes me feel very uncomfortable.

Personally, I really didn't mind doing the job placement component, but I was afraid that if I expressed my true sentiments on the subject then I would be ostracized by the group.

Actually, we haven't heard much from Joe or his family in over two weeks. When Joe was first out of work, he would check in with us every day, but lately communication has been sparse…, not only on Joe's end, but on our end as well.

The last time we spoke to Joe, he indicated that the cardiologist was recommending that he undergo quadruple bypass surgery when he got a little stronger.

But then knowing Joe…, he's probably more concerned about the contacts in his job bank getting cold then he is on any upcoming or impending surgery that he might require.

When it was my turn in the rotation to do job placement, my mind was usually consumed with thoughts of Joe.

"Hitting the streets" is what we generally say when we go out into the field to do job placement, and one of the things we dabble in when we hit the streets is "head hunting."

"Head hunting" is when we canvass area businesses that really don't know much about us. It gives us an opportunity to educate them, hand out a few pamphlets, and if we're lucky, maybe even solicit services from them.

"Hitting the streets" and "head hunting" were just two of the many pet phrases that Joe coined in describing what he did. I think it's safe to say that I was the only counselor on staff that not only appreciated his witty euphemisms, but thoroughly enjoyed listening to his little pearls of wisdom as well. The other counselors on staff couldn't be bothered with any of Joe's anecdotal tales or descriptive metaphors, and thought that Joe was simply blowing smoke up their ass.

Joe took his job very seriously, and I can only imagine what he must be thinking when he's lying in bed at home recuperating. He's probably rolling his eyes or shaking his head when he thinks about me and the other counselor's doing his job, or should I say, "screwing it up."

Yeah, I can hear Joe now, "Kid, you mean well…, but you're doing it all wrong!"

Joe was all business, unlike his predecessor Stanley who was all "monkey business."

There were no subtle differences between the two men whatsoever. Their approaches to the job were like night and day. Joe took his job personally, whereas Stanley was solely in it for the money. Joe was strictly into quality and Stanley was into quantity. Joe wouldn't place anyone in a job unless the person had an eighty-percent chance of succeeding in that job.

Whereas, Stanley's idea of orchestrating a successful placement was getting the client there safely, packing them a measly lunch, and then crossing his fingers and hoping for the best.

Stanley took the attitude that if the placement didn't work out according to plan, then it wasn't his fault, but the counselor's fault for not making the necessary adjustments.

Yeah, a real stand-up guy that Stanley…, wouldn't you agree?

Stanley had no substance or integrity. He was strictly all for show. He was solely into the numbers game, and the only thing that Stanley really cared about was placing as many clients into jobs that he possibly could regardless of whether they were suited for the placement or not.

If the truth be known, the only thing that Stanley was concerned about was trying to impress Watson at the Monday morning staff meeting. He loved giving his report and spouting off inflated placement numbers, or outlining upcoming planning sessions or appointments with area businesses that he had no intention of keeping. Stanley would pompously gloat during his presentation, and then sit back and sneer when listening to the others give their reports.

It shouldn't come as any big surprise, but Stanley was not that well-liked by any of his coworkers. Even the clients thought he was an idiot, and told him so every chance they could.

Joe on the other hand had a proven track record, and the people he placed in jobs actually remained in those jobs for years and years. Stanley only concerned himself with the short term windfalls of job placement, whereas Joe was in it for the long haul.

To tell you the truth, Joe was so damn good at matching the right client to the right job that he actually had area businesses begging him to place clients at their companies. They all knew that if a problem arose then Joe would be right there to fix it. Joe did it the way I was taught in graduate school, and he could have easily written the textbook on job placement.

Every so often, I would jokingly call Joe, Dr. Joe Atkins…, Professor of Job Placement.

Joe would laugh when hearing me reference him like that, and then boldly say, "Gee, it's too bad you didn't have me teaching you job placement in that fancy-schmancy school of yours kid, you might have learned something!"

Now theoretically, Joe's placement responsibilities ended after he placed the client into a work location. It then became the counselor's responsibility to provide follow-up services for the client, and to deal with whatever problems occurred so that the placement could be maintained.

However, and if the truth be known…, this was rarely the case. Joe simply couldn't determine the line where his responsibilities stopped and the counselor's responsibilities began, even though Watson has made this point abundantly clear to him time and time again.

Over the years, Watson has had to consistently counsel Joe on what his exact job duties were. And these closed door sessions between them were often quite spirited to say the least.

Like clockwork, Joe would be summoned into Watson's office several times a week for his routine tongue lashing, but then Joe would continue to do job placement the way he saw fit.

Time and time again, Watson would have to remind Joe that the counselor was solely responsible for all aspects of follow-up services after the placement was made. And although Joe was fully aware of what the repercussions would be if Watson found out, he would continue to demonstrate interest in the placement, and invariably "poke his nose" where it did not belong.

Often times, Joe would freelance by making unannounced visits to the worksite, so that he could inquire as to how the client was doing, and he couldn't be bothered with protocol or getting prior approval from the counselor of record. If a problem developed then Joe would handle it, and he was subsequently dubbed by the counseling staff as the "lone wolf."

Joe would often say, "I'm not gonna let some incompetent counselor foul up my placement, because I've got too much at stake!"

Actually, there were a number of times when several of the counselors took exception to Joe's bold characterizations regarding the way in which they did their jobs. But I on the other hand tried to keep a more level head, and chose not to take Joe's colorful remarks to heart.

Joe was a very demanding man, and often times he had a tendency to fly off the handle when things didn't go according to plan.

Let's just say that Joe wasn't out to win any popularity contests!

I'd never admit this to Watson, but as far as I was concerned follow-up services was basically passing everything by Joe, and then getting his opinion on the situation.

To my way of thinking that was the best way I knew in stabilizing the placement. Joe would wind up giving me tips, and better yet…, show me ways in which I could manufacture a more successful placement for the client, so that I didn't have Watson breathing down my neck.

Of course, at the sake of repeating myself, but what I was doing wasn't exactly standard operating procedure, and if Watson found out then surely there would be hell to pay.

I actually enjoyed doing follow-up services, and I would have to say that I was probably the only counselor on staff that seemed to get any real pleasure out of the whole experience.

Quite honestly, it was fun being out of the building. I got the chance to go around town and visit the various job sites and talk with the client and the employer.

At times, problems occurred and adjustments needed to be made, but I always felt good in knowing that I had Joe in my corner to back me up. Joe was essentially my safety net.

Everyone on the counseling staff, including myself, felt that we were often between a rock and a hard place when it came to follow-up services because Watson wanted results, and he didn't want to hear any long-winded excuses or explanations as to why a particular job placement wasn't panning out. So in order to keep Watson happy and safely off our backs, we were forced to either lie or get Joe involved in the case.

Usually, when the counselors were stymied in salvaging a placement, they would ask Joe what he had in his "bag of tricks." Joe's "bag of tricks" was simply a euphemism to describe the economic incentive package that Joe used at his discretion in appeasing disgruntled employers.

Hey, Joe was no fool…, and he knew full-well that the business community listened more intently when it came to saving money.

So that being said, these economic incentives that Joe had up his sleeve was an effective way to help stem the tide in persuading the employer to reconsider a shaky placement.

Quite honestly, the counselors all felt that these economic incentives that Joe was peddling were nothing more than smoke and mirrors. But the minute one of their placements was in jeopardy, it was amazing how fast they got on the horn to Joe so that they could ask his advice about the incentive program. Joe would then visit the placement, do his magic, and then low and behold, the employer would begin to look at the client in a more favorable light.

Our agency has had an amazing track record for maintaining work placements, and having these placements remain solvent for a very long time. If you ask me, I think Watson may have had a sneaking suspicion that the counselors weren't being this successful all on their own, and that Joe was somehow being factored into the equation for all of their apparent success.

Frankly, the only time a client ever left a work placement was when he or she had the opportunity to trade up to something better.

Again, these upgraded work placements were usually a result of Joe's clandestine handy work, and had nothing to do with the fabricated stories that the counselors were spewing out to Watson at the Monday morning staff meetings.

For obvious reasons, Joe always stood back in the shadows when it came to taking the credit, and he was quite content in allowing the counselors to bask in the glory at the Monday morning staff meeting, because everyone in the room knew who was really "driving the bus."

As a rule, the counselors would generally tolerate Joe and his tinkering, and even though his constant meddling was a nuisance, it was never really a huge bone of contention with them.

After all, the counseling staff all knew that Joe was doing them a huge favor with his monitoring of follow-up services, and they also knew that they couldn't light a candle to Joe's expertise in maintaining placements as well.

In addition to that, the counselors all knew that nothing they could say or do would make a bit of difference in changing Joe's mind or his approach to the situation anyway, so why bother.

Now that being said, this is where the plot thickens and it gets really interesting!

The counselors all felt that as long as things were hunky-dory with all of their client placements, then they could generally put up with Joe's annoying antics and constant bull shit.

Then again…, if Joe's handy work went south, and hints of placement termination echoed through the hallowed halls of WEALTH, specifically…, Watson's office, then the counselors would show their true colors and go running down the hallway screaming to Watson.

I would characterize the counselor's behavior as, "rats jumping off of a sinking ship!"

Watson would then summon Joe into his office with the explicit intent of giving him a royal fleecing.

Now a royal fleecing was a step up from a tongue lashing, and it's generally what the Nuns used to call, "a good old-fashioned reprimand." I guess it's something that we all need from time to time. It was actually more comical than punitive when Watson fleeced Joe.

Typically, Joe would march right into Watson's office, and the counseling staff would all congregate out in the hallway and do our very best to keep the laughter down to a dull roar, so that we could listen to Watson take pot shots at Joe.

It was like having a "ringside seat at a heavyweight boxing match," and the only thing missing from the hotly contested showdown was a tub of buttered popcorn and the refreshing taste of an ice cold beer.

Hey, I loved Joe with all my heart, but even I found his routine fleecing to be nothing short of hilarious.

Joe would adamantly try to defend himself, and Watson would repeatedly interrupt him and say…, "No buts!"

When the fleecing was over, everyone in the hallway would scatter…, like roaches, so that Watson wouldn't catch any of us eavesdropping.

Well, now that you've gotten to know Joe a little bit better, I think it's fairly obvious as to why he is so missed around here. Joe made everybody's job a lot easier, including Watson's.

If it weren't for Joe, Watson would probably have nonstop traffic running in and out of his office all day long from counselors explaining why their job placements were floundering.

Sometimes I wonder just how much Watson really knew regarding Joe's shenanigans, but for the sake of convenience, he simply decided to look the other way.

The other day Mr. Watson reported to us that Joe had his quadruple bypass surgery, and that he is now recuperating at home. Although the surgery was a success, the doctor indicated that the surgery should have been done years ago.

In fact, the doctor actually characterized Joe's cardiovascular system by saying, "Joe's arteries were plugged up worse than a football stadium's toilets during halftime."

Anyway, it sounds like Joe may be out of the woods, and that's certainly good news to hear for all of us.

Joe occasionally calls, and when he does he emphatically says…, "Listen, my files better be up to date by the time I come back, and make sure my job bank doesn't get ice cold!"

We simply humor Joe and tell him what he wants to hear, so that we don't undo all of the painstaking work that the doctors just did.

The simple fact of the matter was that Joe's job bank was in shambles, and they were not being maintained in the meticulous fashion that he was accustomed to having them in.

Frankly, we were all pretty busy with all of the various responsibilities that Watson was throwing at us, and sorry to say…, but keeping Joe's job bank up to speed was not exactly a high priority with any of the counselors, myself included.

Lately, the talk around the water cooler is that Joe might not be returning to work. I wasn't sure if he had a minor setback, or had taken a severe and sudden turn for the worse.

Honestly, the news about Joe left all of us feeling somewhat hollow inside. As important as Watson is to the agency, Joe truly is the life force.

How will we function without him?

Chapter Four

One day while I was down on the contract floor, I saw Mr. Watson conducting a tour. As the group passed by me, I overheard someone on the tour make a rather disparaging comment to one of her colleagues regarding the caliber of work that we offered our clients.

Why must everyone be a critic?

In my opinion, the jobs on the contract floor were first rate, and a formidable challenge to the people working on them. Personally, I know that at least three-quarters of the jobs on the contract floor were well beyond my grasp.

Although the tasks that the clients work on are extremely monotonous and mundane, they seem to take a great deal of pride in their work, and you'd never know by the looks on their faces that they are working on tasks that the general public considers to be cruel and unusual.

As far as I'm concerned, the general public seems to perceive these types of jobs as being schlock work and well beneath them. The disabled are often looked upon by the manufacturing community as the prime work force for this type of grunt work.

So that being said, what makes the repetitive work our client's do any less important than the repetitive work that factory and mill workers do all across this great land of ours?

Well, it's been five months now working here at the agency and I was really beginning to hit my stride. I had a good handle on my caseload, some real solid contacts in the community, and best of all, I was finally on a first name basis with Ralph.

Ralph was the coordinating line supervisor of the contract floor, and he has been working here at the agency for over thirty years. From what I hear, Ralph is as close to being a legend in contract work as Joe Atkins is in job placement.

It's like having two "hall of fame" players on one agency team!

Any counselor that was on a first name basis with Ralph usually had the inside track in getting some of the prime jobs in the workshop for their clients. Many of the counselors on staff really didn't like Ralph. Ralph can be awfully stubborn and extremely set in his ways.

Now I know what you're probably thinking, - Ralph sounds an awful lot like Joe Atkins..., and in fact they are best friends.

Ralph took an immediate shine to me, not only because I was young and impressionable, but also because I was considered by most to be Joe Atkins' sidekick.

Although I was inexperienced, I portrayed an eagerness to learn and Ralph could sense this. I really like Ralph, and I have nothing but the upmost respect for him, although I will admit that much of what is said about him by the other counselors is pretty accurate.

Quite honestly, I think what really sets me apart from the other counselors on staff was that Ralph can sense my sincerity, as opposed to the other counselors who just wanted to use Ralph for their own personal gain, and really had no vested interest in him as a person.

Before Joe's illness, Joe and Ralph would have coffee and donuts together every morning out back. Although we were never privy to what they discussed, I'm sure that one of their main topics of conversation each day focused on the ineptitude of the counseling staff, and how much better the place would operate without us.

Every time I saw Joe and Ralph kibitzing together it made me chuckle. They just struck me as two frustrated old guys that felt they should be running the agency single-handedly.

Joe and Ralph wanted to run WEALTH as they saw fit, by cutting the excess fat..., presumably the counselors.

In a way, it might be interesting to see what Joe and Ralph could do if given the opportunity. Of course, they wouldn't admit it, but I think they'd have a pretty tough time operating this place without us.

If Joe and Ralph were in charge, I know for a fact that neither of them would give a rat's ass about regulations or protocol.

Department of Labor - who cares? Diplomacy - what's that?

Joe and Ralph were solely into the numbers game, and to be honest I really couldn't fault them for that. Although regulations are necessary, they can be a royal pain in the ass.

Now that Joe has been out sick I actually miss not seeing the dynamic duo together, as they sipped their coffee and complained about how inefficient the place was being run.

On the surface they appeared to be these two old curmudgeons, but I knew better..., because underneath that coarse exterior they were really teddy bears at heart. They both seemed to feed off of each other's energy, and together they truly were the power source that ran the agency. Mr. Watson may be the boss, but even he would kowtow to Joe and Ralph.

Well…, within reason of course!

Watson was quite aware of Joe and Ralph's exceptional abilities, and he would often permit them to showcase their talents by giving them some latitude in how they did their jobs.

Occasionally, Joe and Ralph would get a little too carried away with their unsanctioned enthusiasm, and Watson would be forced to reel them in and do some damage control.

Bur fear not!

Because Watson's damage control efforts would usually result in something positive happening for the agency.

Somehow Watson would be able to incorporate Joe and Ralph's misguided deeds as the basis for a new grant proposal. After writing the proposal, Watson would then conjure up some cockamamie title out of thin air and submit it as some sort of special program, which would usually result in WEALTH receiving federally appropriated funds in the form of a grant.

Upon receipt of the good news, Watson would then take Joe and Ralph out to lunch and they would all get a big laugh out of it. The counseling staff thought that it was nothing more than a staged performance between Joe, Ralph, and Watson.

Since Joe has been out with his heart attack, Mr. Watson's creative writing has fallen off, and Ralph, well…, he's just not the same old gunslinger without his partner in crime Joe.

Deep down inside, I think Watson really misses not being able to sort out the daily hi-jinx of Joe and Ralph. From Watson's perspective I think rectifying Joe and Ralph's misguided deeds brought him back to his early days in human services, when these types of shenanigans were common practice, and regulations were actually the exception and not the rule.

Ralph calls Joe once a week and fills him in on what's happening here at WEALTH. I'm sure Ralph tells Joe that the placement numbers are down and that the counselors are really not doing the job the way it should be done.

Although Ralph means well, he may be doing Joe more harm than good. I can only imagine how high Joe's blood pressure must be when he gets off the telephone with Ralph.

I'll ask Ralph from time to time how Joe is doing, and Ralph is usually very forthcoming in updating me. Ralph knows that I'm only asking out of concern, unlike my fellow counselors who only seem to ask about Joe so that they can get on

Ralph's good side for a future favor.

So here we are six months into the job and things seem to be going quite well. I think Mr. Watson is happy with my work, and the other counselors seem to have accepted me into the fold.

C.D. told me the other day over coffee, "Kid, you passed..., and you have nothing to worry about."

Well, perhaps..., but I still feel like I'm a bit of an outcast with the other counselors. I can't put my finger on it, but I often feel uncomfortable around them. I don't dislike them per se, but at the same time I don't want to stop after work and grab a beer with any of them either.

Frankly, I'm amazed at the amount of longevity that most of the staff at this agency has endured. Ten, fifteen, and twenty years is commonplace here. Look at Ralph and Watson for example, they have both worked here for over thirty years. The money is not that great, and the benefits are marginal at best, but people continue to work here anyway.

To tell you the truth, the staff could probably do as well if not better working somewhere else, but they continue to stay at WEALTH.

The bottom line is that the staff continues to remain here because they really enjoy the camaraderie that they share with one another, and the feeling that they are all in it together.

I sometimes wonder if I too might acclimate myself to this kind of thinking someday, and perhaps stay at WEALTH for many more years to come. Well..., I guess only time will tell.

For some reason, I began thinking back to a moment in time when I was in graduate school. It was a time when I had no disposable income whatsoever. So one day I decided to stroll over to the financial aid office and inquire as to what funds, if any, might be available to me, especially since I was so destitute. I thought perhaps I might qualify for some type of stipend, which is sometimes awarded to students who demonstrate financial need or hardship.

Often times, these stipend monies are buried deep within the bowels of the university's financial aid office.

In other words, colleges don't advertise having these funds, but if you demonstrate a little initiative and make a concerted effort at pleading your case, then maybe you'll get lucky.

Anyway, the financial aid officer told me that they couldn't give me anymore additional funds, however there was an urgent need for the university to fill a work-study position and would I be interested.

I then inquired, "Sure…, what's the job?"

The financial aid officer told me that the position was in the Secretarial Services Office, and that they were in dire need of assistance.

So after telling me about the position, she realized that a male student had never been placed in that type of work-study slot before, and then apologized for getting my hopes up.

I then curiously asked, "Is there a reason why it has to be a woman and not a man?"

She thought a minute, and then replied, "Actually, no…, it just never occurred to us to place a man in that particular work-study slot before."

Well, seeing how I was desperate, I asked her if I could interview for the position and the financial aid officer said with a coy smile, "Hey, I'm game if you are. I'll set up the interview."

The next day I met with the supervisor of the work-study position. She outlined all of the expectations of the job, and then asked me if I was still interested, to which I replied, "Well, I'm quite confident that I could do the job, ma'am," and then she hired me right on the spot.

I think about that little story from time to time because it reinforces to me that nothing is etched in stone. I never realized it then, but I was essentially on the cutting edge of breaking the stereotypical roles that society deems for the genders by taking the secretarial job.

At the time, I was only interested in making some extra money to help defray some college expenses, nothing more than that. But in retrospect, it really was a groundbreaking event.

When I think back on it now, I'm sure that I helped pave the way for more men working in the Secretarial Services Office. It proved to me that the unexpected can certainly take place, and yes…, even turn out quite well. This is something that I often think about when working with the clients on my caseload. Why can't they beat the odds, and rise up from the unexpected?

It's like playing the lottery. The odds might not be in your favor, but somebody has to win, and it might as well be me!

When I find myself having a tough day or mulling over a difficult case, I think back on my Secretarial Services adventure, and it really helps me put things into perspective.

Still quite immersed in my reflective thoughts about graduate school, I heard the intercom buzz and it was Dolly. She had laughter in her voice, as she light-heartedly conveyed to me that I had a telephone call, and that the person who wished to speak to me was my predecessor Allan Farnsworth, who apparently had a new referral that he wished to speak to me about.

As I waited for Dolly to transfer the call, I found it rather strange that Farnsworth would be calling me and not going through proper channels, that being…, Mr. Watson.

Usually Mr. Watson handles all new referrals, and then judiciously doles them out to the counselor who is "up" in the rotation.

Perhaps my imagination was getting the best of me, but I was beginning to think that the psychiatric tendencies of some of these clients that I work with on a daily basis were starting to rub off on me.

Although I had never met or spoken to Allan Farnsworth before, I'd certainly heard his name bantered about the break room a number of times, and frankly it was more in the context of good riddance than fond memories.

As I continued to wait on the line, I was becoming increasingly more intrigued about speaking with Allan Farnsworth. Not so much about the referral he wished to speak to me about, but more interested in knowing if he enjoyed working for the State Office.

Suddenly, I was gushing with curiosity in ascertaining his impressions, his workload, and most importantly…, if they were hiring.

Dolly then transferred the call, and Farnsworth and I immediately exchanged some light pleasantries. I think he was just as eager to speak with me as I was to speak to him.

Farnsworth asked me how things were going, and then made specific reference to some of the clients that he formerly worked with. He was careful not to ask me too many questions for fear of opening up a can of worms, and getting into a conversation that he just as soon not have.

There was a momentary pause in our conversation, and I found the courage to ask him about his State job. He was actually very forthcoming about it. He indicated to me that he really liked his new position, and if I wanted to talk further regarding State employment then he would be happy to meet with me for lunch sometime and discuss the matter at length.

Farnsworth then went on to say that the main reason he called me today was to talk about a man named Henry Josephson, whom he was hoping to sponsor at WEALTH. Farnsworth, who works for OVR, was in the process of referring this gentleman for vocational services, and he thought that Mr. Josephson could benefit greatly from our program.

As I hung up the phone, I found Farnsworth to be extremely engaging, and I couldn't understand why the WEALTH staff harbored so much resentment and acrimony towards him.

In my opinion, I thought Farnsworth was quite civil and cordial, and best of all, he may provide me with the opportunity I need in attaining my first solid lead to State employment.

It was probably a week later that I received another phone call from Allan Farnsworth, who engagingly said, "Jack, hi, Al Farnsworth here, how's it going? Say..., I was wondering if you had a chance to look over the referral packet that I sent you on Mr. Josephson? Oh, and by the way..., I haven't forgotten about us getting together for lunch."

I paused momentarily before responding to Farnsworth. I remember him telling me the last time we spoke that he was going to send me some information on Mr. Josephson, but I've been so damn busy these last few days that I haven't had a chance to check my mailbox.

At that point, I decided to do some fancy footwork, and then made up some lame excuse so that he wouldn't think that his new replacement at WEALTH was a total incompetent.

Upon hearing my excuse, Farnsworth's voice resonated with some disappointment. I then reassured him that I would look over the referral packet today, which seemed to satisfy him.

Farnsworth then wrapped up the conversation by saying, "So Jack, why don't you and I get together for an early lunch next Tuesday, say around eleven o'clock? We can talk about the Josephson referral, and then I can fill you in on all the particulars regarding State employment."

I replied, "Sounds great, Al. See ya, Tuesday."

As I hung up the phone with Farnsworth, I was feeling so exhilarated that I felt like I could take on my worst case, - like the Sampson's.

Yeah, bring 'em on..., nothing could break my spirits!

Well, I was wrong. Just as I was flying as high as a kite, the Sampson's wound up calling me later that morning, and of course they were very disgruntled. They once again needed me to pull a few bureaucratic strings for them, my "magic," as I often called it.

So after being stuck on the phone for over forty-five minutes, I finally finished up my gripe session with the Sampson's. When they hung up the phone they thought that all their problems were solved.

NOT!

Boy, I'll tell ya..., the Sampson's were so mentally fatiguing that every time I spoke with them on the telephone I felt like taking two aspirin and then lying down.

As I hung up the phone with the Sampson's, I wondered if my day could get any worse.

Well…, it did!

Just then Mr. Watson buzzed my office and instructed me to head over to the psychiatric center and interview a new referral, ASAP. I quickly informed Mr. Watson that I already had a new referral on the back burner, which was the referral from Allan Farnsworth.

Watson then told me that this was the referral from Farnsworth, and that the person in question currently resided in the local psychiatric hospital downtown.

Mr. Watson reiterated once again that he wanted me to look into the matter "ASAP," and that he was expecting a full report from me upon my return.

As I hung up the phone I thought to myself, "Farnsworth never mentioned to me that this guy resided in a psych center. How could he forget to tell me something like that?"

Of course, I haven't had a chance to look at the referral packet yet. I'm sure the case file has PSYCHIATRIC HOSPITAL written on it in big bold letters. I've heard some wild and crazy stories about the psych center, and frankly they weren't exactly warm and fuzzy.

Actually, I've had some prior experience working around psych patients before when I did my graduate internship at the VA hospital. But psych centers…, now that's another story, because those facilities are usually more hardcore.

Suddenly, I experienced a sinking feeling in the pit of my stomach about the way in which this whole referral was playing out. Not only was it starting to concern me, but I felt as if I was in way over my head.

As I sat at my desk, I was beginning to have some ruminating thoughts about Farnsworth.

I then asked myself, "How well do I know this guy? Huh…, not very well!"

Although it may sound crazy, but I was wondering if Farnsworth and Watson were in cahoots with each other. I started having all kinds of paranoid thoughts floating through my head, and I suddenly came to the conclusion that I was being taken advantage of.

For crissakes! I mean how do you not mention the simple fact that the man you're referring to WEALTH is living in a psychiatric center? This little piece of omitted information was not only a red flag, but it was really beginning to irritate the hell out of me as well.

I started to wonder if Farnsworth was playing some sort of practical joke on me, and sarcastically thinking to himself, "Hey, let's take the new guy for a ride!"

After all, Farnsworth has over ten years' experience as a counselor, so why wouldn't he mention to me that the guy he is referring to us lives in a psychiatric center. I was thoroughly convinced that this was more than just a simple oversight on his part.

So why do I feel like there are some puzzle pieces missing?

By now, I was beginning to get a tension headache, so I decided to get away from my desk for a few minutes and go grab a cup of coffee.

As I walked into the break room, I reached for the coffee pot and saw that someone had violated the "golden rule," which then prompted me to shout, "Great, no coffee!"

I then decided to swing by the reception area and see if the referral packet that Allan Farnsworth forwarded me was in my mail slot.

When I walked into the reception area, I saw that my mailbox was crammed with mail. Upon taking my mail out of the slot, I saw that there was a large manila envelope that had the words REFERRAL PACKET stamped on it in several places, and it was from Allan Farnsworth.

Apparently, Farnsworth had sent me a rather thick packet of information to read. I was thinking to myself, "Could all of this information be exclusively on Henry Josephson?"

Sure enough, as I opened up the envelope the name on the referral sheet read Henry Josephson. The packet that Farnsworth sent me must've been at least eight inches thick.

I then thought to myself, "Everything you wanted to know about Henry Josephson, but was too afraid to ask."

At that point, I felt so mentally exhausted that I tossed the referral packet over to the far side of my desk. I wasn't in any condition to start sifting through eight inches of ancient history right now because I had a splitting headache, and I needed to take a couple of aspirin and just chill out. Mr. Josephson will just have to wait until later…, much later.

The following day, one of the counselors on staff approached me in private and asked me whether or not I had a chance to review the Josephson referral packet yet.

I was wondering how he even knew about it in the first place?

Apparently, he heard through the grapevine that the psych center wanted Henry Josephson discharged ASAP, but one of the stipulations of his discharge plan was that he be involved in some type of work activity.

In other words, "Get him a job, and get him the hell out of here!"

I'm sure the psych center wasn't too fussy as to whom they could peddle him off to.

Then again..., maybe they heard about Watson's, "We take anybody policy," and with Farnsworth at the wheel, then this guy Josephson would be a cinch for enrollment at WEALTH.

Tuesday finally rolled around and I was feeling extremely anxious. I was all keyed up for a couple of reasons, both of which centered on my luncheon date with Allan Farnsworth today.

Not only was I a bit apprehensive about the Josephson referral, but I was quite anxious to hear all of the details that Farnsworth was going to impart to me regarding State employment.

My morning went by like a blur. The sign on my office door should read, "Jack O'Leary, Complaint Department."

Not only did I have to deal with a few nasty phone calls from the Sampson's, but there were also some problems down on the contract floor that needed my immediate attention as well.

When I looked at the clock on the wall it was almost eleven o'clock. Thank God the café that I was meeting Farnsworth at for lunch was only right around the corner.

As I approached the café, it suddenly occurred to me that I had no idea what Farnsworth even looked like. Well..., I wasn't going to worry about it, I'll just figure it out when I get there.

I walked into the café, and as I glanced around the premises, a tall stocky man then approached me from the side and smartly asked, "Excuse me, but are you Jack O'Leary?"

"Uh, yes..., I am." I replied.

He then amusingly said, "I thought so..., because counselors are always running late."

"So, I take it you're Allan Farnsworth?"

"Yeah, that's right. How's it going since we last talked?" Farnsworth asked, as we cordially shook hands and sized each other up.

"Well, um..., it's been interesting." I replied.

"Oh yeah, why's that?" Farnsworth asked, with some slight curiosity.

"Well, for starters..., I received your packet on Mr. Josephson, and come to find out that he's currently residing in the psychiatric center downtown."

Farnsworth nodded his head, and nonchalantly said, "Yeah, that's right. He's actually resided there for a long time. Multiple admissions, - you know how it is."

I then asked, "Well, um…, is he ready for this type of endeavor?"

"Who knows…, time will tell Jack. He's been in and out of the psych center more times than you can shake a stick at." Farnsworth said, as he quietly chuckled to himself.

"Huh, must be…, the packet was pretty thick." I sharply mumbled.

Farnsworth paused, and then inquisitively asked, "You seem rather agitated about his residential situation Jack. Is there a problem?"

"Well Al, as a rule, we usually don't receive any referrals from the psych center, and I guess it just took me a little off guard, that's all."

"I'm assuming that Watson talked to you about it, right?" Farnsworth asked, directly.

"Well…, no," I replied.

Farnsworth burst out into laughter, and then sarcastically blurted out, "Well, that sounds like the same old Watson that I know!"

So after having a good laugh at my expense, Farnsworth continued by saying, "Listen Jack, we don't expect you to turn this guy into a Rhodes Scholar. We just wanna refer him for some vocational services, so that he can be a more productive person and have a better quality of life. I hope you don't think we have some kinda hidden agenda going on?"

"No, not at all. That never entered my mind, Al." I replied.

Of course, I was lying. I knew there was something going on, I just couldn't figure out what it was yet.

"So have you had a chance to read through the referral packet yet?" Farnsworth asked, as he was sipping his coffee and perusing the lunch menu.

"Um…, no, not yet."

"Okay…," Farnsworth mumbled, with some obvious disappointment in his voice.

"Actually, I plan on reading through the packet this afternoon, and if I have any questions or concerns then I'll be sure to give you a call." I said, as I began scanning the lunch menu too.

"Sounds good, Jack. So what would you like to know about State employment?" Farnsworth asked, as he ordered up the blue plate special.

"Well, I'm just curious to know what's out there. I'm not really looking to switch jobs at the moment." I replied, as I ordered the blue plate special as well.

Farnsworth nonchalantly nodded his head, and then asked, "So are you thinking of applying for a job with the State in the future?"

"Yeah, I would consider State employment down the line." I casually replied.

Farnsworth then proceeded to tell me in general terms what the process was in applying for State employment. He informed me that there were more than just one or two State agencies that hired vocational counselors throughout the State system. Everything he told me was very useful, and I decided to just tuck it all away for future reference.

To be perfectly honest, I didn't want to say too much to Farnsworth regarding my interest in State employment, especially since I barely knew the guy. Plus, how do I know he isn't setting me up, or planning to tell Watson what my future intentions are.

Once again, I think Farnsworth and Watson have some kind of weird relationship going on, and for all I know…, they may be blood relatives. Farnsworth strikes me as one of those guys who seems friendly on the surface, but could you really trust him? I think not.

As I glanced at my watch, I saw that I needed to get back to WEALTH. The food at the café was good and the portions were quite generous. All and all, I was relieved to have finally met my predecessor. It was a bit of a strange encounter, but I'm glad we had the chance to meet.

The next day I passed by Mr. Watson in the hallway, who hastily inquired, "So Jack, where are we at in terms of that new referral I assigned you?"

Watson was a man of action, and he wanted to be apprised of his staff's every move.

As I stumbled over my words, I informed Mr. Watson that I was going to look into the matter today. I also told him that I touched base with Farnsworth, and that I was in possession of the referral packet.

Watson was then quick to say, "That-a-boy, Jack! I knew you'd get the ball rolling, ASAP!"

Yeah…, there goes the old, "ASAP" reference again. Why is it that whenever I'm confronted by an authority figure, I always seem to cower?

It must be my parochial school education coming into play!

In the deep dark recesses of my mind, I'll always be haunted by the Nuns. The "Sisters of Mercy," who rarely exhibited any…, and can certainly share in the credit with the Franciscan Fathers for making me the thoroughly neurotic man that I am today.

As I glanced at the clock on the wall, I saw that the day was quickly slipping away, and I didn't think that I'd have enough time to go out to the psych center to visit with Mr. Josephson.

Although I told Mr. Watson that I would, the staff around here is always telling Watson what he wants to hear anyway, you know..., just to keep him happy and safely off their backs.

So that being said, I thought I'd give the psych center a quick call and inquire if today was a good day to interview Mr. Josephson. Of course, I was hoping that they'd say no, but the great wave of Irish Catholic guilt was compelling me to make the ominous phone call anyway.

I picked up the phone and then punched in the number for the psych center. When the call rang through, a deep throated woman answered the phone by saying, "Ward 19, can I help you?"

This raspy voiced lady, who sounded like she was a two-pack a day cigarette smoker, was the ward charge, and her name was Stella.

At that point, I stated who I was and my reason for calling. She then indicated to me that today was not a good day to meet with Mr. Josephson because he had a couple of medical appointments scheduled this afternoon, so she suggested that I try back another day.

A reprieve! I just love it when I can slither out of doing something that I really don't want to do, but best of all, I didn't have to lie to Watson.

Well, since I had some time to kill, I thought that I'd browse through the referral packet that Farnsworth sent me, so that I could get to know Mr. Josephson a little better.

Uh..., not that I really wanted to mind you!

As I perused the various reports and summaries that were enclosed in the referral packet, I discovered that several of the reports that I was skimming through were from forty years ago.

I then surmised that this guy Josephson has been pretty messed up for a very long time, and then wondered if he was a product of parochial school education like me.

Anyway, much of what I was reading in the packet was meaningless information, but to play it safe, I thought I would jot down a few notes and highlight what I thought was pertinent.

Let's see..., paranoid schizophrenic, functioning in the borderline range of intelligence, and having a very spotty vocational history.

Hmm..., that sounds like most of the kids that I went to high school with.

Now ordinarily, you would think that the diagnosis of paranoid schizophrenia would be relevant, although from my experience I think it's nothing but a complete joke. This diagnosis seems to appear quite often in the case files. And take it from me, but if you hang around human services long enough, you'll definitely develop a diagnosis of paranoid schizophrenia yourself.

So after skimming through the referral packet, I was quite disillusioned with the lack of pertinent information that I managed to write down, which only amounted to one-half page of relevant information!

I mean, how bizarre is that? I have a case file in front of me that's at least eight inches thick, but yields only one-half page of what I would consider to be somewhat useful information.

Gee, I hope no one expects me to perform miracles with this guy!

At that point, I just kept staring down at the note pad in front of me. The three things that immediately jumped out at me on this man Josephson were, - paranoia, lack of motivation, and preoccupation with his thoughts.

Uh..., the more I thought about it, the more it seemed like it was describing me!

When I spoke with Stella the ward charge, she told me that Mr. Josephson was usually free between eight-thirty and ten o'clock every day, and that a scheduled appointment would not be necessary as long as I came to visit him within those specified times.

In addition to that, she also instructed me to check in with the psych center security office so that they could issue me a visitor's pass.

So I guess that means I'll be visiting the psych center tomorrow morning to interview Mr. Josephson. Unless of course..., I get hit by a bus, or find a way to weasel myself out of it.

The next day, to my chagrin..., I was shutting off my car engine in the parking lot of the psych center. I hadn't even had my first cup of coffee yet, and I was hoping to grab a cup inside.

Since I've never been to the psych center before, I was totally unfamiliar with the layout of the facility. Oh well, no worries..., I'll just ask someone for assistance.

As I locked my car door and approached the main entrance of the building, I thought as a friendly gesture I would ask the first patient I saw for some directions. I'm not really sure why I decided to do that. I guess I just wanted to do something nice, so that the patient would feel good about themselves, and then I would thank them profusely for helping me out.

Well, in theory…, my idea certainly sounded plausible, but in reality…, I was woefully mistaken, and whatever good intentions I had absolutely backfired on me.

As I approached a small group of patients who were milling about outside the front entrance, I arbitrarily asked, "Excuse me, but can anyone here tell me how to get to Ward 19?"

All of a sudden, this diminutive older woman began ranting and raving and screaming all sorts of profanities at me, and insinuating that I was harassing her.

She then began screaming for security, which was probably a good thing…, because I didn't know where the security office was located, and I needed them to issue me a visitor's pass. This way I figured security would find me, and save me the trouble of finding them.

Of course, this wasn't exactly the scenario that I had intended to have, and at that point my only thought was to get the hell out of there. However, the counselor in me decided to see it through and try to diffuse the situation, so I attempted to calm this distraught woman down.

Despite my best efforts, the woman continued to scream at the top of her lungs, and if anything, my futile attempts at calming her down were making things even worse.

Quite honestly, I had never seen anyone in my life this visibly disturbed before, well…, except maybe for Michael Wallace, the day that he attacked me in my office.

Finally, a security guard came on the scene and wanted to know what all the fuss was about. He then asked me who I was and if I had a hospital pass…, as if he were interrogating me.

I then calmly stated to the security guard who I was and my reason for being here today, and that I did not have a pass, but I was just simply asking the woman for directions to Ward 19.

Upon hearing my explanation the security guard lightly chuckled, and then conveyed to me that Ward 19 was the most secure and prohibitive living unit at the psych center.

He then amusingly quipped, "No wonder why she went off on you. When she heard you make reference to Ward 19, she probably had some kinda traumatic flashback."

I then made my apologies to the distraught woman, who just continued to spit and sputter, and then asked the security guard if he would point me in the direction to Ward 19.

So after issuing me a visitor's pass, the security guard wished me "good luck," to which I amusingly replied, "Thanks..., I think I'm gonna need it!"

As I ventured into the building, I walked down a long dark corridor. My head was on a swivel, as I kept a vigilant eye out for Ward 19. Although my gut was telling me that I was lost, I was afraid to ask anyone for assistance. I kept telling myself that I'd rather be stranded for days, then have another go around with any of these wacky patients again.

By now I was really beginning to panic, so I decided to approach a young woman, who I assumed was a nurse, because she had a stethoscope hanging around her neck.

In fact, she actually burst out into laughter when I asked her if she was a real staff person!

As I continued searching for Ward 19, it was becoming quite clear to me that nothing in this facility was laid out in any semblance of consecutive order. In my quest to find Ward 19, I passed by Ward 15, then it went to Ward 12, then Ward 27, and then finally to Ward 19.

Well, all I can say is…, if the floor plan of this place is any indication of the treatment being given, then I can fully understand why people are receiving such long term care here!

So after meandering through a sea of corridors, there it was, dead ahead…, Ward 19!

At that point, I was soundly convinced that I would never find my way back to the front door ever again. I only wished that I had left a trail of bread crumbs behind me, so that I could find my way back from whence I had come.

As I stood outside the massive steel door that had the number 19 boldly painted on it, I was thinking that the aesthetics of this place left a lot to be desired. It was simply the bare bones, and not exactly resembling the comforts of home.

Then again…, maybe they did this for a reason. Perhaps they didn't want people getting too comfortable around here, or else none of the patients would have any incentive to leave.

As I tried pulling on the door handle of Ward 19, the door wouldn't budge. I yanked on the handle a few more times, but then realized that the massive steel door was locked.

I then saw a buzzer to the side of the door handle, and above the buzzer I saw a tattered little sign that read, "Please press buzzer to alert Ward 19 staff."

So after pressing the buzzer, I heard a rattling of keys from the other side of the door, and then someone working the lock from the inside of Ward 19. The door then swung open and a rather brawny looking man stood in the threshold of the doorway with his arms folded, as if he was expecting a fracas. He was sporting a fresh buzz cut, and if I had to guess I would say that he may have been an ex-marine. I was almost tempted to shout out, "Semper-fi!"

He then asked with a bit of a wiseass cocky attitude, "Can I help you?"

I cordially replied, "Why yes…, I think you can. Is this the living quarters for a man named Henry Josephson?"

This large strapping man then said, in a rather snippy and suspicious tone, "So who wants to know?"

Although I was slightly miffed by his standoffish demeanor, I could see why he was so guarded. After all, this was a highly secure living unit and tight security needed to be enforced.

So at that point I indicated to this rather unfriendly guy who I was and why I was here today, and then flashed him my visitor's pass. I then informed him that Stella the ward charge told me that mornings were a good time to come by and meet with Mr. Josephson.

As soon as the strapping ward attendant heard me make reference to Stella, he seemed to let down his guard a bit and be less suspicious of me.

It was almost nine o'clock now, and I still hadn't had my first cup of coffee yet. I was becoming a little impatient, as the clock was ticking away on the available "free time" in Mr. Josephson's schedule.

I would later find out that this designation of "free time" that Stella had made reference to on the phone was a complete and utter joke, because "free time" is all that Mr. Josephson had.

The only things filling up Mr. Josephson's day were his coffee breaks, smoke breaks, meals, naps, his medication times, and of course…, - play time in his psychotherapy group sessions with Dr. Feelgood.

So after a slight stare down, the hulking ward attendant motioned me onto the unit. He then grunted, "follow me," where he escorted me to the visitor's lounge and instructed me to make myself comfortable.

Yeah right…, as if I could actually make myself comfortable in a deplorable place like this! The walls were completely embedded with brown nicotine stains, not to mention the putrid smell of lingering cigarette smoke that enveloped the entire unit.

Quite frankly, the air was so despicable that it was strong enough to choke an elephant!

The attendant then flippantly said, "I'll bring Mr. Josephson's social worker out to meet with you. Her name is Ms. Brown. Huh…, good luck with her," as he chuckled under his breath.

I remember seeing the name Ms. Brown on several of the reports in the referral packet that Farnsworth had sent me. Finally, a professional who will not only help me make sense out of all this chaos, but have the common courtesy of offering me a cup of coffee as well.

As I waited in the visitor's lounge, I found it to be an extremely small space. I sat as far back in the room as possible, so that I could avoid breathing in the toxic air that surrounded me.

This vile cigarette drenched air seemed to be permeating every square inch of the living unit, and it hovered over the room like a band of nimbostratus clouds, as if heavy thunderstorms were quickly approaching.

It's been twenty minutes now, and still no sign of Ms Brown.

As I continued to wait, I could feel my anxiety level climbing. All I could think about was all of the carcinogenic particles that I was breathing into my body, not to mention the clock that was ticking away on my available "free time" to interview Mr. Josephson.

Oh…, and did I happen to mention that I haven't had my first cup of coffee yet?

It's been forty-five minutes now, and there's still no sign of Ms. Brown.

Where the hell is she?

By now, I was getting extremely agitated, and my anxiety levels were completely off the charts. I hadn't anticipated waiting this long. I simply wanted to eyeball this guy, say a few patronizing remarks, and then be briskly out the door.

Yeah, I know that sounds pretty cynical, but I was way past rational at this point.

I hadn't breathed any oxygenated air in almost an hour, and I was fully convinced that parts of my brain were beginning to shut down due to anoxia.

As I looked up from my wristwatch, I saw a small man standing in the doorway. He was a very scrawny looking guy, as if he were extremely malnourished and hadn't eaten in weeks. He was about five-foot tall and barely weighed one hundred pounds soaking wet.

This tiny little man had very long fly-away hair, which was well past shoulder length, and he also had a rather long and scraggily looking beard. He then sent an icy chill down my spine when he addressed me in his quiet and quivering monotone voice, "Hello…, brother."

At that moment, the old Irish Catholic guilt immediately kicked into high gear, and it prompted me to say, "Good morning, sir."

He then said, with a deadpan expression, "Do you know Jesus loves you, brother?"

My mouth was agape, and I was absolutely spellbound. Not only by his looks, but by what he was saying to me too.

Well, seeing how I'm a Christian and a churchgoer, I tried to take it all in stride, so I simply said, "Yes..., I know he does, thank you."

This diminutive little man then decided to sit down in the adjacent chair next to where I was sitting and began staring at me. He was probably only staring at me for a few seconds, but it seemed like an eternity. He was making me feel even more uncomfortable than I already was.

As I glanced down at his hands, I noticed that the tips of his fingers had burn marks on them, and they were also thickly charred and covered in nicotine stains. Not to mention his general hygiene, which was certainly nothing to write home about either.

Although I didn't want to sound rude, I finally had to say to him, "Um..., you'll have to excuse me now because I'm waiting for someone, and she should be arriving very shortly."

Despite my rather direct tone, this diminutive little man seemed totally oblivious to my sharp words and standoffish demeanor. He then said, in a very spooky and eerie tone of voice, "That's okay, brother. I will wait with you, because it's all part of doing the Lord's work."

So after a few moments of uncomfortable silence, he then asked me in a real creepy sort of way, "Whom are you waiting for brother?"

Although quite annoyed at this point, I kept my cool and calmly said, "Ms. Brown..., do you know Ms. Brown?"

He quietly replied, "Yes brother, I know Ms. Brown. She is my sister."

"I see..., and may I ask what your name is sir?" I asked, half-heartedly.

In a trance-like tone, he mysteriously replied, "My name..., what is a name, a label, a fence. My name is Jesus Christ, and I love you brother."

"Okay...," I sarcastically said, as the bizarre little man continued to blankly stare at me.

This guy was definitely giving me the willies.

I then blurted out, "Well, it's been nice chatting with you Jesus, but you'll have to excuse me now because I need to go check on someone."

Needless to say, but I was absolutely furious. Not only have I been waiting for some wacky social worker to arrive, but now I find myself entertaining some crazy screwball too.

This seemingly deranged little man looked deep into my eyes, and in an eerie tone of voice he said, "What's the person's name brother? The person you're waiting to see with Ms. Brown. Maybe I can help you."

Well, as ridiculous as it may sound, but I actually took him up on his crazy offer, as I uttered, "Okay, well…, his name is Henry Josephson, maybe you could direct me to his room?"

The diminutive scary man then replied, "There's no need for that brother. Sometimes people refer to me as Henry Josephson."

"Excuse me….!"

Just then a large figure dashed through the doorway of the visitor's lounge. She briskly apologized for keeping me waiting, and then quickly sat down.

It was Ms. Brown…, Henry Josephson's social worker.

Ms. Brown was a rather large woman, who was completely out of breath, as she panted, "Hello Mr. O'Leary…, it's a pleasure to meet you…, I'm Ms. Brown…, Henry's social worker."

She then extended her large fleshy hand to shake mine.

"Yessss…, so I gathered," I said, incredulously.

"I'm so glad to see that you and Henry are getting acquainted with one another." She said, with a sickening syrupy smile.

"Well, um…, it's been very enlightening." I said, dumbfounded.

Ms. Brown then glanced at Josephson and scowled, yet she still managed to maintain her syrupy smile, as she sternly said, "I've been scouring the entire unit looking for you Henry."

Josephson was totally oblivious to Ms. Brown's sharp words or cutting tone of voice, and just sat there like a bump on a log in some sort of catatonic stupor.

I then decided to seize the moment by saying, "Ms. Brown, um…, I must say that I am a little taken aback by all that's unfolded this morning. Um, if you don't mind…, I'd like to reschedule this meeting with you and Mr. Josephson for another time."

Josephson then suddenly awoke from his brief hiatus, as he quietly mumbled, "I prefer to be called Jesus."

At that point, I glanced at Ms. Brown for some professional moral support, but she broke eye contact with me as she rummaged through her briefcase looking for her day planner.

I then explained to Ms. Brown that I didn't anticipate this meeting taking as long as it did this morning, and that I had a full day of meetings waiting for me back at WEALTH.

Of course, what I was telling Ms. Brown was nothing but a pack of lies. There were no meetings to get back to. I just knew that I needed to get the hell out of there and fast.

Conceivably, the only thing waiting for me back at WEALTH were most likely three or four nasty phone messages from the Sampson's, detailing their latest disaster, and Mr. Watson wanting to hear all of the gruesome details on how this "interview" with Josephson turned out.

So after hearing my convincing tale of woe, Ms. Brown then opened up her day planner so that she could set up another appointment with me.

I on the other hand was in no hurry to confirm a date with her. I conveniently made up another white lie stating that I had forgotten my appointment book back at the office, however I would be more than happy to call her later today so that I could set up another time to meet.

NOT!

I wound up giving her the old party line. I had no intentions of meeting up with either of these two whackos ever again. Not in this lifetime, or any other lifetime for that matter.

Anyway, there's a lot I could've said at that moment, but I opted to hold my tongue. I was 99.9% sure that I'd never see Josephson again.

I mean, c'mon…, who in their right mind would ever consider this guy for services!

Yeah, I was absolutely certain that my assessment of the situation was air tight and definitely a no-brainer, and that even a grade school kid could figure this one out.

While packing up my briefcase I glanced over at Josephson, who looked rather spaced out, as if he was floating on air. He didn't seem the least bit interested in what was happening around him, so I just nodded my head and grunted "good-bye" as I headed for the exit.

As I was walking towards my car, I was feeling rather confident that I could convince Mr. Watson that this guy Josephson was grossly unsuitable for the program, and most likely an accident waiting to happen.

Josephson really could be a potential liability to the agency, and mankind for that matter.

Life, as we know it, could be permanently altered if Henry Josephson were permitted to roam outside the four walls of the psych center.

Well..., maybe now I'm laying it on a little bit too thick!

Later that morning, Mr. Watson saw me working at my desk, so he decided to pop his head into my office and ask me how the interview went over at the psych center with Josephson.

Watson was quietly standing in the doorway, nonchalantly flipping through his overhead accounts sheets, as he patiently waited for me to give him the update.

Although I felt rather confident this morning that Josephson was not a suitable candidate for WEALTH, for some reason I was unable to convey those same exact sentiments to Mr. Watson, as I nervously stated, "Well Mr. Watson, um..., it was by no means a formal interview. Um..., there were some extenuating circumstances precluding me from doing my normal intake interview. Um..., in my opinion, Mr. Watson, um..., or should I say my professional opinion, um..., I feel that Mr. Josephson would not be a suitable candidate for our program."

Upon hearing what I had to say, Mr. Watson looked up from his overhead accounts sheets and he had a rather perplexed look on his face. He then sharply said, "Your professional opinion. So what do you mean that it wasn't a formal interview? Did you get a chance to ask him his goals or his interests, or what his dreams and aspirations are?"

I squeamishly replied, "Um, well, not exactly, sir. You see...," Watson interrupted me in midsentence and said, "Well..., what about his work history, his education, or even his hobbies?"

Watson had absolutely no idea what Josephson was portraying to me this morning in that "interview," because if he did he wouldn't be asking me all of these ridiculous questions.

I then began to backpedal a bit by saying, "Well, um..., actually Mr. Watson, we didn't get an opportunity to cover any of those points of interest either."

Watson looked totally bewildered, and simply uttered..., "Interesting."

So after a slight stare down, Watson calculatingly said, "Well, you're probably going to cover that in greater detail the next time you meet with him, right?"

I immediately thought to myself, "Jesus, I mean, Josephson, I mean, what...! Watson actually expects me to go back out to that crazy psych center again and interview that deranged little man. What am I..., a "used car salesman," having to pass every deal by the boss?"

It was quite apparent to me that Watson has absolutely no faith in my professional judgment whatsoever. Josephson is obviously psychotic, and clearly out of touch with reality.

At that point, I really wanted to say, "C'mon Watson…, you sent me out there to evaluate the situation and I did. I'm a trained professional, fully qualified in making a sound decision."

Well…, at least on paper anyway!

Watson kept staring me down and making me feel very uncomfortable. He then said, with great disappointment in his voice, "This is not what I was expecting to hear Jack."

I then thought to myself, "My opinion should be respected. Watson is nothing but a micromanager, who likes to scrutinize every decision that his counselor's make."

Well…, that's at least what I was thinking, as I was getting ready to say, "Mr. Watson, I will be setting up a follow-up interview with Mr. Josephson sometime this week, so that I can cover all of the areas of concern that you just outlined."

Oh, my God! I couldn't believe what just came out of my mouth. It was as if I was back with the Nuns again.

Watson smiled, because he essentially heard what he wanted to hear, as he jubilantly replied, "That-a-boy, Jack! I knew you were the right man for the job!"

"Thank you, sir." I quietly answered.

Watson then candidly said, "Ya know, most agencies wouldn't go within a country mile of the psych center because they possess certain…, biases toward psychiatric diagnoses."

"Well, that's very true Mr. Watson." I attentively replied.

Watson continued by saying, "In fact, it amazes me how some trained professionals have a tendency to prejudge individuals, even before they step into the interview room. Hahaha! I'm glad to see that you're not one of those close-minded professionals Jack."

"Thank you, sir." I replied, and then feeling as though the sensei had just taught his young grasshopper his first professional ethics lesson.

Watson then spiritedly said, "Okay, well…, keep me posted! Say Jack, if you want more information regarding vocational services for psychiatric populations, there's a wonderful article in last month's rehabilitation journal. Then again…, maybe you've already read the article, eh?"

"Well…, no, I, uh…, haven't had a chance to read last month's article yet Mr. Watson. Uh…, because I lent my copy to a friend." I replied.

I'm not really sure if Watson bought my little song and dance regarding last month's journal article, especially since we all know by now that I'm not a subscriber to the American Journal of Anything, but I didn't want to tell Watson that.

Thus far, my lying skills seem to be surpassing my counseling skills.

So before adjourning to his office, Watson conveyed to me that the federal government was in the process of appropriating millions of dollars to private agencies, so that individuals who reside in psychiatric facilities can have the opportunity to access some vocational services.

Watson then went on to say that he was putting the finishing touches on a grant proposal, which would enable our agency to potentially qualify for those proposed federal dollars.

So after hearing what Mr. Watson had to say, it didn't take me long to figure out why he's so hell-bent on having me go back out to the psych center again to re-interview Josephson.

Knowing Watson, I'm sure he's envisioning dollar bills flying right out of the psych center windows, and landing directly into the WEALTH coffers for the foreseeable future.

Also, it wouldn't surprise me one bit if Watson was in cahoots with Farnsworth. I'm sure that these two connivers have devised a plan in which Farnsworth takes all the credit for making the psychiatric referrals to WEALTH, and in return Watson gets to milk the cash cow.

I may have grossly underestimated Mr. Watson. I thought I'd be able to convince Watson that Josephson was unsuitable for services, and then he'd simply say, "Okay Jack, write up the denial of services report for Mr. Josephson, and have it on my desk first thing in the morning."

Yeah, right! So much for my no-brainer idea!

Watson has just lowered the bar for vocational referrals!

So now I find myself going back out to that wacky psych center again, so that I can re-interview that extremely impaired little man. Well, I better go call Ms. Brown and see what's available in her day planner. I'm sure her calendar is wide open.

"Jack," signaled Dolly.

"Yes Dolly," I replied, hastily.

She pointed to the telephone and said, "You have a phone call on line one."

"Thanks Dolly," I replied, as I was flipping through my Rolodex for Ms.

Brown's phone number over at the psych center.

"Hi, this is Jack O'Leary, can I help you?"

"Hi Jack, Al Farnsworth here…, how's it going."

"Oh, hi, Al. Watson and I were just conferring on Mr. Josephson."

"Ah…, that's great Jack! I'm glad you finally got the ball rolling on him." Farnsworth said, in a very condescending manner.

Listening to Farnsworth's smug remark really irritated the hell out of me, and even the mere sound of his voice was like hearing fingernails scraping across a blackboard.

Although perturbed by his rather snide comment, I managed to keep my composure and calmly say, "So anyway, Al…, I met with Ms. Brown and Mr. Josephson this morning, but due to some unforeseen circumstances, I was unable to secure all of the pertinent information that I needed. I'm planning on going back out to the psych center again later this week."

"Yeah, that's great! Listen Jack, I just got off the phone with Ms. Brown, and she informed me that Mr. Josephson's prospects for services at WEALTH are quite promising."

"Promising…," I muttered to myself.

As I listened to Farnsworth babble on about nothing, I was thinking to myself, "Why would Ms. Brown conjure up a crazy idea like that. I know I certainly didn't give her the impression that Josephson's prospects were promising."

Well, either she's a good liar, or destined to be living on the same unit in the psych center as Josephson.

Then again…, maybe she simply forgot to take her medication this morning!

Suddenly, Farnsworth stopped babbling for a moment, so I quickly interjected, "Well Al, as you know this is all very preliminary, and it's way too early to tell."

Farnsworth then flippantly replied, "Jack, I know what we're up against with referring Josephson to WEALTH. Social workers…, you know how they are."

I sarcastically thought to myself, "Yeah, and a certain OVR counselor that I know too!"

In wrapping up my conversation with Farnsworth, I then said, "Well…, like I said Al, I'll be going back out to the psych center sometime this week, and then we'll see what we can come up with. I'll keep you posted on any new developments."

"Thanks, Jack. I appreciate it, bye."

It seems like everybody wants a little piece of Henry Josephson. For now I'm keeping my thoughts and comments strictly to myself, especially with respect to the "three stooges," Ms. Brown, Farnsworth, and Mr. Watson.

So after my mentally exhausting telephone conversation with Farnsworth, my mind was absolutely reeling. As I tried to collect my thoughts, I heard the intercom buzz and it was Dolly, who nervously said, "Jack, you have a phone call on line two. It's Mr. Sampson, and he said that it's extremely urgent that he talk to you right away."

I then sarcastically mumbled, "Of course..., it's always urgent with Mr. Sampson."

Dolly must've heard my inadvertent slip of the tongue, because I could hear her giggling on the other end of the line.

So before Dolly could even transfer the call, I took a deep breath and then quickly said, "Hey Dolly, do me a favor, tell Mr. Sampson that I'll have to call him back, okay."

Dolly was a bit surprised that I was unwilling to take Mr. Sampson's call. She seemed to hesitate for a moment, but then cautiously replied, "Okay, I'll tell him..., but you owe me."

When I walked over to Dolly's desk, I could hear her finishing up her phone conversation with Mr. Sampson. Sampson was livid that I wouldn't take his call. He was yelling so loud on the other end of the line that Dolly had to pull the receiver away from her ear.

Dolly then hoisted the phone straight up in the air towards me, so that I could hear every foul word and indignant remark that Mr. Sampson was spewing.

As Dolly hung up the phone, that glaring look she gave me said it all. I felt really bad that she was subjected to Mr. Sampson's venom. So in an effort to pick up her spirits, I whimsically said, "Hey..., welcome to my world. I owe ya, "big time." Thanks, Dolly."

Unfortunately, I just couldn't deal with the Sampson's "flavor of the month" emergency right now. I had bigger fish to fry, such as getting a hold of Ms. Brown over at the psych center.

I went back to my office so that I could place a call over to the psych center. The call rang through, and then the switchboard operator patched me through to Ms. Brown's office.

"Hi, Ms. Brown. This is Jack O'Leary."

"Why hello, Mr. O'Leary. So what can I do for you?"

"Well, I'd like to schedule an appointment with you and Mr. Josephson this week, so that we can discuss what future endeavors might be available for him here at WEALTH Industries."

Ms. Brown was absolutely ecstatic with what I was proposing, and as I waited on the line I could hear her feverishly flipping through the pages of her day planner. She then indicated to me that she had a hole in her schedule for tomorrow morning, - surprise, surprise!

Hey, I'm sure her schedule is one big "crater!"

Anyway, I told Ms. Brown that I would take the available time slot, and she reassured me that she would be punctual and on time for our scheduled appointment tomorrow morning.

She then playfully said, "As a matter of fact, Mr. O'Leary..., I will make it a point to personally meet you at the front door of the main entrance tomorrow morning."

"Wow..., lucky me!" I thought to myself, as I listened to her drone on about nothing.

Well, I no sooner hung up the phone with Ms. Brown, and then who should come barreling into my office, but none other than Mr. Sampson.

"Where the hell did he come from?" I wondered.

Sampson got right up into my face, and then slammed his huge fist down on my desk, causing my coffee mug to tip over and spilling cold coffee all over my desk. He then began to pepper me with all sorts of accusations, and even accused me of deliberately ducking his calls.

Well..., I can't fault him there.

Then he accused me of being in league with the Social Security Administration, and that I was doing a "piss poor" job of representing him.

Again, from his perspective..., he may have had a legitimate gripe!

Oddly enough, but I actually found Mr. Sampson to be quite amusing, and I wasn't at all frightened by his vicious tone.

He then blamed me for all of his financial woes, and for the onslaught of correspondence that he has been subjected to by the Social Security Administration for the past nine months.

Sampson paused momentarily, and then shouted, "So what are ya gonna do about it?"

He then stood there with his eyes bulging wide waiting for me to cave into his demands, and then suddenly I had thoughts of Allan Farnsworth swimming through my head.

As I've stated before, Farnsworth neglected to tell the Sampson's that the meager amount of money that they were earning from their restaurant jobs would have a direct impact on their Social Security benefits, and thus reduce the amount of Social Security money that they were entitled to receive.

Farnsworth knew that he wasn't going to be around for this "train wreck" waiting to happen. And by the time the Sampson's finally figured it out, Farnsworth would've been long gone and settled into his new position with the State.

Sampson then resumed his yelling and screaming, and the only thing that I could do at that point was to remain quiet and permit him to just rant and rave and get it out of his system.

The next thing I knew Sampson picked up my desk with his mighty hands and began shaking it, as if it was a cardboard box. He continued to lambast me with all sorts of accusations, and I was now becoming a little more concerned for my personal safety.

At that point, I was praying that Dolly was summoning reinforcements, and instructing everyone on the counseling staff to start suiting up into their SWAT gear in the event that they needed to save me.

The new kid was once again under fire, except this time Sampson was about four times the size of young Michael Wallace!

Then, inexplicably and without any warning, Sampson abruptly ended his tumultuous tirade as quickly as it had started. He placed the desk down, folded his hands, and was patiently waiting for me to address him.

Sampson resembled a child, as difficult a concept as that might be. He had his little tantrum, and now he was expecting me to cave into his demands.

Well, at that point, I couldn't believe how composed I was. I just looked directly at Mr. Sampson and calmly asked, "So are you finished yelling now?"

He dutifully replied, "yes."

I then proceeded to tell him that although his Social Security money had been decreased, the money he was earning at his restaurant job was supplementing it. I then calmly said, "In other words, you're still making the same amount of money, but in two different checks."

All of a sudden, it's like a light bulb came on, and a look of relief washed over Mr. Sampson's face. That's all it took to turn him around.

It then occurred to me that this may have been was one of the few times in Mr. Sampson's adult life that someone has actually taken the time, or should I say had the courage to explain something to him.

He smiled, and then appreciatively said, "Okay, thanks Mr. O'Leary, I'll be good now."

We shook hands, and then Mr. Sampson turned for the door and walked directly out of my office.

I sat at my desk for a moment, and then reflected on my "counseling" session with Mr. Sampson. I then decided to stretch my legs a bit, and grab a cup of coffee out of the break room.

As I headed toward the break room, people began patting me on the back and commending me on my exemplary counseling skills. I just smiled, and humbly accepted their adulation and spirited compliments.

Even Dolly congratulated me. With a slight wink of her eye, she precociously smiled, and then whimsically said, "Way to go, Jack. I guess we're even now."

CHAPTER FIVE

It's Wednesday morning, and in a little while I'll be heading over to the psych center for my follow up meeting with Ms. Brown and the incomparable Henry Josephson.

I had some time to kill this morning, so I decided to go down to the contract floor and do some observations, and to also chat with some of the people on my caseload.

Scotty, who is one of the line supervisors on the contract floor, called me the other day and informed me that several of my clients were having some difficulty with a new assembly job that we just acquired, so I thought I would go down to the contract floor and assess the situation.

When I spotted Scotty out back, I informed him that I came by to see what the problem was with the new assembly job. Scotty not only explained the problem to me in great detail, but he also demonstrated the correct way that the assembly was to be put together as well.

So feeling somewhat confident, I told Scotty that I wanted to give the assembly a whirl, to which he humorously replied, "Are you sure, Jack? Because I've seen you in action."

I chuckled at Scotty's sarcastic remark, and then asked him if he would demonstrate the assembly for me one last time, but this time I asked him to go real slow.

Despite all of Scotty's valiant efforts at showing me the correct way that the assembly job needed to be done, when it was my turn to try, well…, I couldn't make heads or tails of it.

I felt as though I was trying to solve some sort of quantum physics equation!

And to add insult to injury, I couldn't seem to get past the first step of the assembly, which Scotty amusingly pointed out was the easiest part of the four part assembly.

At one point, I thought Scotty was going to literally fall off his chair in laughter because the client that I was attempting to help actually had to show me what I was doing wrong.

Anyway, I gave a few words of encouragement to the two clients who were struggling with the assembly job, and then said that I would check back with them in a couple of days.

Although I took a few blows to my ego this morning, Scotty appreciated the fact that I stopped by to see what the problem was and said that he'd keep me posted on their progress.

Before leaving for the psych center, I informed Dolly where I was going, just in case Mr. Watson was looking for me. When Watson hears where I've gone, I'm sure it will make his day.

So after parking my car, I headed toward the main entrance of the psych center. As I was approaching the building, I could see Ms. Brown pacing back and forth smoking a cigarette.

Upon seeing me, she quickly butted out her cigarette and then high-stepped her way towards me displaying a sickening syrupy smile. As she approached me, I didn't know whether I should be pleased by her promptness and cheery disposition, or be leery of an ensuing "con" job.

We exchanged a few light pleasantries, and then made our way into the building.

En route to Ward 19, I kept having some recurrent thoughts on how Ms. Brown greeted me this morning. She reminded me of some sort of shady realtor, who was trying to unload a piece of condemned property that has been sitting on the market for years. Josephson of course was the "property," and I was the "sucker" who was interested in buying.

As Ms. Brown went to unlock the door to Ward 19, I asked her if we could stop and chat for a moment. Before uttering a single word, I decided to choose my words very carefully.

I then said, "Ms. Brown..., I realize that Mr. Josephson has a lot of problems. I wasn't assigned to this case because of my vast knowledge of mental illness, I was assigned to this case because I have the least amount of seniority on the WEALTH counseling staff, and none of the other counselors were the least bit interested in coming over here."

Upon hearing my cutting remark, Ms. Brown had a very perplexed look on her face.

I then continued by saying, "Historically Ms. Brown, the psych center has never been considered a hotbed for viable work candidates. From what I understand, Mr. Josephson's case has been sitting on the shelf collecting dust for over a year and a half now..., maybe longer. Don't you think it's rather peculiar that his case file should resurface now after all this time?"

Ms. Brown seemed rather puzzled by my line of thinking, and then replied in a bit of a huff, "What is your point, Mr. O'Leary?"

"Quite honestly, Ms. Brown…, I'm not enthralled with being here today. I'm only here today because my boss is telling me to take another look at Mr. Josephson, "aka…, Jesus Christ, Our Lord and Savior." Well…, that's all I really had to say."

Ms. Brown didn't appreciate the point that I was trying to make nor did she make any attempt to add to the conversation. She probably thought I was going to be like all of the other "brain dead" clinicians that she's grown accustomed to working with here at the psych center.

In one last attempt to make my point, I said, "So Ms. Brown, Mr. Watson informs me that there is a lot of federal money available to individuals that are mentally ill, and that these monies are to be earmarked with the expressed intent of providing them with vocational services. What better place to tap into this reservoir of federal money than your local psychiatric center…, eh."

Ms. Brown scowled, and then defensively said, "Excuse me, Mr. O'Leary…, but we have some very capable people that reside here. They just need a chance to show what they can do."

"Well, that may be…, but what you fail to realize Ms. Brown is that the psych center is a veritable gold mine for exploiting the federal funds that are pending."

Ms. Brown's face began to redden. She looked totally pissed off and highly insulted. She then sternly replied, "We're not starting off on the right foot here Mr. O'Leary, and what's more…, I think you've totally misjudged the people that reside here."

Feeling quite frustrated, I attempted to say, "So Ms. Brown, to reiterate, Mr. Watson…,"

Ms. Brown interrupted me in midsentence, and then boldly said, "For your information, I know Mr. Watson and I've heard him speak at various social functions. He strikes me as a very fine judge of character and an asset to the community, which is why we chose WEALTH."

I immediately thought to myself, "No, WEALTH chose you…, because you have the potential for being a financial windfall."

Despite wanting to say more, I decided to hold my tongue because I didn't want Ms. Brown to think that I was trying to antagonize her. I said what I wanted to say, and although my efforts were in vain, I think I now have a truer picture of whom Ms. Brown really is.

I then concluded my conversation by saying, "Mr. Watson has instructed me to undertake a formal interview with Mr. Josephson, so that we can determine if he is a suitable candidate for vocational training. I will attempt to do so either with or without divine intervention."

Ms. Brown snarled, "I really don't see the need for sarcasm, Mr. O'Leary."

I replied, "You're right, and I apologize Ms. Brown. But just for argument sake, let's say that WEALTH does accept Mr. Josephson for services, as inconceivable as that might be…, you and I both know that his chances for success are somewhere between slim to none. Wouldn't you at least agree with that simple assessment, Ms. Brown?"

Ms. Brown abruptly stated, "I beg to differ, and I think you've totally misjudged Mr. Josephson altogether. In my view, Mr. Josephson is a work in progress."

I thought to myself, "A work in progress…, the man reminds me of the Mayan ruins."

This is exactly why I didn't go into the field of social work in the first place, too many bleeding hearts. I couldn't fathom Ms. Brown's unwillingness to see my point and call a spade a spade, or assess the situation for what it really was. After all, Ms. Brown had over twenty years' experience with this type of population. Why couldn't she see things from my perspective?

To my way of thinking, Ms. Brown seemed as delusional as Josephson, and for that matter…, Watson wasn't too far behind them.

I could see by the puss on Ms. Brown's face that there was really no point in talking with her anymore. I said what I wanted to say, and then told her that I was ready to meet with Mr. Josephson now. Ms Brown fumbled with her keys, and then she unlock the door to Ward 19.

As I walked onto the unit, I decided to take a nice deep cleansing breath. I thought taking a deep breath might be a good calming mechanism for me and help alleviate some of the stress that I just endured in speaking with Ms. Brown.

So after taking a nice long deep breath, I then suddenly went into a violent coughing jag. I had momentarily forgotten about the nasty smoke-filled air that permeates every square inch of this God forsaken living unit.

Given my psychic tendencies, I viewed this mishap of mine as a very bad omen for my upcoming meeting with Mr. Josephson. I was feeling quite alone in this interview this morning. I would have hoped that Ms. Brown would have been in my corner, and provided me with a little moral support. But sadly there would be no professional courtesies extended by her today.

Ms. Brown then instructed me to find a seat in the visitor's lounge, while she went to find "God," I mean…, Josephson.

Once again, I found myself retreating to the back of the visitor's lounge. I sat down and opened up my briefcase, and then removed all of the necessary forms and waivers that needed to be filled out for the meeting.

While I sat there waiting for Ms. Brown and Josephson to show up, I felt extremely anxious. I then decided to walk over to the doorway and survey the dayroom of Ward 19. I knew that I was taking my life in my hands by doing so, but my curiosity was getting the best of me.

As I stood there in the doorway of the visitor's lounge, I could plainly see that the entire living unit was engulfed in a sea of cigarette smoke. Everyone was aimlessly milling about, and they all looked to be in some type of zombie-like trance. The air quality was despicable, and the lighting was extremely dark and ominous, as if heavy thunderstorms were quickly approaching.

Even the fluorescent light fixtures were all covered in a filthy film of black soot from the lingering cigarette smoke that spewed everywhere.

At that point, I saw all that I wanted to see, so I quickly ducked back into the visitor's lounge and retreated as far back into the room that I possibly could. Although the visitor's lounge was by no means a safe haven for breathable air, it certainly beat the alternative.

As I was backing away from the doorway, it suddenly occurred to me that none of the other zombie-like individuals on the living unit seemed to be having any difficulty breathing.

It then dawned on me that perhaps the reason these patients resembled the walking dead was due to the lack of oxygenated air on the unit, and thus lacking the sufficient amount of oxygen flow needed to sustain healthy firing synapses for cognitive thought.

I must say that I was rather impressed by my line of deductive reasoning.

To tell you the truth, I had all sorts of erratic thought patterns going through my head as I waited for Ms. Brown to return with Josephson, and I'm quite sure that all of these off the wall thoughts that I was having were largely due to the onset of anoxia.

Don't ask me why, but I decided to take another peek into the dayroom. This time I took out my handkerchief and placed it over my nose and mouth, as if it were a homemade air filter.

As I scanned the dayroom, I spotted Josephson. He was going to town on a cigarette in the smoking lounge across the way. He was trying to get as many puffs off of his cigarette as he possibly could. It fascinated me as I watched him puff away on his cigarette in the smoking lounge. He was standing there in a fog of smoke, and I couldn't believe that the psych center actually had the audacity to designate that small room across the way as their smoking lounge.

As if that small six-by-eight foot room that they call a "Designated Smoking

Area" could possibly confine all of the carcinogenic particles permeating every square inch of that unit.

Once again…, the logic of the psych center thoroughly escapes me!

Josephson then butted out his cigarette and signaled to Ms. Brown that he was ready to leave. As Josephson approached the visitor's lounge, he extended his frail nicotine laden hand to me, while saying in his weak and quivering voice, "Hello…, brother."

As he continued to eerily stare at me, he mysteriously asked, "Why have you returned to me brother? Are you here to seek my forgiveness?"

In my opinion, Mr. Josephson was probably not accustomed to meeting with people for a second time. Most people aren't exactly reaching for their day planner to set up a follow-up appointment with him. Josephson probably thought that the next time he'd see me it would be on judgment day, in which he would help God his Father assess and sort out all of my many indistinguishable good works here on Earth.

We all sat down, and as crazy as it may sound, but I was beginning to re-think my position on being here today. I really didn't know what came over me, - an epiphany perhaps?

Of course, I did realize that I had a better chance of being struck by lightning six or seven times than Josephson had on being even remotely successful anywhere on the planet. The more we talked the more apparent it became to me just how psychiatrically impaired this bizarre little man was.

Throughout the interview Josephson was often incoherent, and his ability to differentiate fantasy from reality was virtually nonexistent. All of the conversations we had were highlighted by numerous inferences to Jesus. He continued to view himself as Jesus, and when making his many references to Jesus they were all stated in the first person.

As I continued to listen to Josephson, I was thinking to myself, "Either Josephson's medication wasn't absorbing directly into his bloodstream, or else the attending psychiatrist simply wasn't prescribing enough of a dose."

Josephson stated several times that he was the "Messiah," who was sent by God his Father to save mankind, and he actually referenced many of his good works and miracles that he performed here on Earth.

As I listened to him tell me one Bible school story after the next, it prompted me to chuckle, because if memory serves me correctly, Jesus never boasted about his greatness or chronicled his miracles to others, he simply let his actions speak for themselves.

Josephson's state of mind reminded me of wild surf crashing onto the shore of a rocky coastline. The more he spoke the less his chances were for success. It certainly goes without saying, but there was not a lot of relevant information being exchanged between us.

At one point in our discussion, I was tempted to make a preliminary recommendation to Ms. Brown that there was not a strong demand for "sheep herding" in our local job market. But then I'm quite certain that she would not have found my quipping remarks to be all that amusing.

Then again…, if not sheep herding, Jesus did perform some carpentry work.

Unfortunately, I think Mr. Josephson would have a tough time getting into the carpenters union, because I hear they're a pretty tight-knit bunch.

Well…, I guess I just earned myself another two weeks in purgatory for thinking such sacrilegious thoughts, but it was just too damn funny for my subconscious mind to suppress.

It's amazing how many things go through your mind when you're sitting down with a prospective client, and I use the term "prospective" quite loosely with regards to Josephson.

Josephson had me so rattled that I was seemingly more preoccupied with my own amusing thoughts than what it was that he was saying to me.

Now if I were a stand-up comedian, then my current frame of mind probably wouldn't be bad, but as a counselor, well…, it's not exactly the perspective that you should aspire to have.

Anyway, I couldn't focus on a single thing that Josephson was saying, or even determine if anything in this "interview" was the least bit useful in formulating a vocational plan for him.

Then again…, I can't believe I'm using the word plan and Josephson in the same sentence.

And then of course there was Ms. Brown…, what a joke she was!

She just sat there like a bump on a log, as she watched me struggle and try to make sense out of Josephson's many grunts, facial expressions, and hand gestures.

Quite honestly, there were so many comments that I wanted to make, but I was afraid of the potential consequences that might occur. After all, the bleeding heart was in the room, and she was hanging on my every word.

Despite Ms. Brown's large frame, I'll bet she could probably beat me in a foot race down to the Director's Office in lodging a formal complaint if she heard me ridiculing Josephson, or making what she construed to be a disparaging remark.

Of course, I couldn't take that chance, so I opted to let my witty snippets go dormant, and focus on being a more altruistic facilitator.

Well, after about an hour of interviewing Josephson, much of which became a staring match at the end, we reached a tentative agreement.

Honestly, I don't even know how we arrived at this agreement, but everyone in the gas chamber, or should I say the visitor's lounge, seemed to be nodding their heads in agreement.

Ms. Brown was grinning from ear to ear, and frankly I'm still not sure if Josephson knew why he was nodding his head.

Maybe one of the little voices that was hiding inside of his head told him that I was going to find him a sheepherder's job out in the middle of nowhere, with all the cigarettes that he could smoke while he tended his flock.

Anyway, Ms. Brown then presented her paperwork, scribbled her signature on a few forms, and thus making Josephson's vocational evaluation at WEALTH official.

Once again, I felt duped, as if I had just bought a piece of real estate that was condemned by the city, or at best…, a "fixer upper."

The "fixer upper," who was Josephson, could probably use a new poured foundation, because his present foundation was inundated with spider cracks. And the mortar that was holding it all together was so dried-out that it was quickly crumbling before my eyes.

Upon conclusion of the meeting, Josephson extended his frail nicotine laden hand to me. His handshake was as limp as a wet noodle. At that point, my only thought was getting to a sink as quickly as possible, so that I could thoroughly wash and sanitize my hands.

When I arrived back at WEALTH, I no sooner unlocked my office door when Mr. Watson broadsided me from behind and promptly asked, "So Jack, how did everything go over at the psych center this morning with um…, what's his name again?"

"His name is Henry Josephson, and it generally went well." I replied, as I tossed my backpack off of my shoulder.

"What do you mean that it generally went well? Were there problems again?" Watson asked with concern, as he sat down in the chair across from my desk.

I could tell that Watson didn't want to hear anything other than me saying that the meeting went well, and that a good time was had by all. I then nonchalantly said, "I secured all the pertinent information and we came up with a plan."

"You came up with a plan?" Watson replied, as his interest was definitely piqued.

"Yeah, he'll be starting with us in two weeks." I said, very matter-of-factly.

"Two weeks…, was that the best you could do?" Watson asked, disappointedly.

I just shook my head, and then dejectedly thought, "Where's my pat on the back and my resounding that-a-boy, Jack!"

For crissakes, here I thought I was doing something monumental. I was actually getting this deranged little man through the front doors of our agency in two weeks' time. This is something that no one else on the WEALTH counseling staff has managed to accomplish. Not even the great and powerful Farnsworth, who seems to be "God's gift" to vocational counseling.

So after taking stock of my rather contemptuous thoughts, I just brushed Watson's coarse comments aside and candidly said, "Yeah, two weeks…, that's the best we could come up with."

As I stood there staring at Watson, he probably expected me to throw Josephson into the backseat of my car and then plop him down on the contract floor, so that we could start the meter running on his vocational evaluation.

No doubt…, Watson will be agonizing over all of the federal money that he will be losing out on for the next two weeks. I'm sure that right after Watson leaves my office he'll probably be giving Farnsworth a call, and perhaps even attempt to influence somebody over at the psych center in moving Josephson's start date up for his vocational evaluation.

As I've said before, Watson and Farnsworth seem to be in cahoots with each other, and unfortunately I was smack dab in the middle of their little shell game.

Well the time is quickly approaching for Josephson to start his vocational evaluation, and as funny as it may sound, but I'm actually beginning to have a soft spot for the guy. I mean in the two times that I have met with him, he has never once said or done anything malicious to me.

Am I being homophobic?

He might not fit the mold, but then who made me judge and jury. I really don't have anything against the guy, I just don't think that he's a suitable candidate for vocational training.

Gee, is it possible that I'm starting to see Josephson in the same light as Watson, Ms. Brown, and Farnsworth.

Then again…, I don't wanna speak for Farnsworth, he doesn't strike me as the altruistic type. He probably went into counseling because there weren't any openings at the used car lot.

Of course, all of my apparent remorse and self-reflection could drastically change once Josephson starts his evaluation, and I get to see him up-close and personal on a daily basis.

But until then…, I'm willing to keep an open mind, so long as Josephson's parables don't interfere with productivity on the line, and cause the contract floor to come to a screeching halt.

Also, it probably wouldn't be a bad idea for me to brush up on some scripture passages, and to make sure that I have the King James Bible at the ready just in case. Maybe quoting scripture from time to time may help motivate Josephson when he goes off course.

To tell you the truth, I'm not really sure if I'm being proactive or feeding into his vast sea of delusions with having the Gook Book handy, but either way, I'm really going to try to put my best foot forward in making sure that this opportunity works out well for Josephson.

Josephson is slated to start his vocational evaluation at WEALTH today, and I'm praying that everything will go according to plan for Josephson.

Geez, there I go again, calling him Josephson. His name is Henry Josephson, and I need to start building a better rapport with him. I think I'll start by referring to him by his first name.

So to paraphrase…, I certainly hope that everything works out well for Henry today. I wonder what's going through Henry's mind right about now over at the psych center, and if he even realizes that he is starting a vocational evaluation with us today, well…, probably not.

As of Friday, I was still not sure how Henry was going to be transported over here. Henry was being treated more like a convict than a disabled person.

I know it must sound cruel to describe the psych center that way. After all, psych centers are in existence to help people. Deep down inside, I knew that some good was being done over there, I just didn't know what yet. Maybe Henry coming to us was part of that good being done.

As I glanced at my watch, I saw that it was almost nine o'clock. Henry should be arriving any minute now, so I decided to go outside into the parking lot and wait for him. I thought it might be a nice gesture for him to see a familiar face, and perhaps put his mind more at ease.

Yeah, I might be assuming a lot in thinking that Henry even remembers me, but I'm really trying to put my best foot forward, and be as optimistic as I possibly can.

In a way, Henry kinda reminds me of a distant relative that I just found out about, and after much anticipation, he has decided to come to my house for a long-awaited visit, or perhaps even stay with me for a couple of days.

Yeah…, I know that sounds like a pretty weird and scary thought, and perhaps now I'm getting a little too carried away with some of my insightful illustrations.

Anyway, I kept asking myself over and over again what my best approach was in dealing with Henry. As I pondered the question, I saw a vehicle pull up into the parking lot, and sure enough it was the psych center van.

I must say that I was rather impressed by their punctuality. It then got me to wondering if the psych center operated like a well-oiled machine, or were they simply on time this morning because they were overjoyed in getting rid of Henry for the day.

As I observed Henry through the windowpane of the vehicle, he looked rather dazed and confused. He was accompanied by two burly ward attendants and Ms. Brown.

At that point, the two burly attendants hopped off the van, hoisted up their britches, and then carefully surveyed the situation. They kinda reminded me of a couple of gun-slingers from the Wild Wild West, who just rode up into town, as they strung up their horses, strapped on their six shooters, and then moseyed into the saloon to wet their whistle with a couple of stiff drinks.

Then of course there was Ms. Brown, who looked quite pensive, as she gingerly negotiated her large frame off of the vehicle.

As I approached the psych center van to give a helping hand, who should suddenly arrive but none other than Allan Farnsworth. Farnsworth came barreling into the WEALTH parking lot in his sporty red convertible, as if he were the lead driver in the Indy 500.

Farnsworth jumped out of his car, combed his fingers through his hair, and then blew past me to assist Henry off of the van. Farnsworth barely knew Henry, yet that didn't seem to prevent him from making a big fuss.

Was Farnsworth really that dedicated? I thought not.

Personally, I think Farnsworth's efforts this morning was nothing more than a dog and pony show for Watson and the rest of the onlookers.

Well, so much for my resounding…, "Welcome to the agency Henry!"

Farnsworth took right over. He ushered Henry right off of the van, and then draped his long lanky arm around him, as if they were long lost friends.

Yeah, it was quite a sight. Farnsworth then waltzed Henry right through the front door of WEALTH, and everyone dropped what they were doing and followed closely behind.

It kinda reminded me of a Broadway production!

There was laughing and singing and all sorts of carrying on. I couldn't tell if people were following because of Farnsworth's magnetism, or because of Henry's mystique.

Nevertheless, I followed the crowd and decided to let Farnsworth run the show.

As I focused in on Henry, he had a look of sheer bewilderment on his face. He looked as though he couldn't process any of the information around him. Henry reminded me of a clump of seaweed…, that kept drifting back and forth at the mercy of the tides.

Suddenly out of the corner of my eye I spotted Mr. Watson. Watson was trying to catch up to Farnsworth and the rest of the entourage.

Watson was making his way through the crowd, as if he was an open field runner.

I then caught a glimpse of Ms. Brown, who was standing in close proximity to Henry. She looked a bit jittery, as if her clothes were two sizes too small. She didn't seem to appreciate all of the fanfare that was surrounding her. Her head kept bobbing back and forth, as she fielded all sorts of questions from the hordes of rabid staff.

Ms. Brown looked like she was at a press conference, as the staff peppered her with all sorts of questions about Henry. I'm sure the staff felt that they were entitled to know everything there was to know about Henry because they worked for the agency, but to their chagrin Ms. Brown would repeatedly say to them, "Sorry, but that's privileged information."

Meanwhile, Watson was smiling from ear to ear. He looked like he just won the lottery!

Watson has been waiting a very long time for this day, and the money that he'll be raking in from the psych center will certainly help pay a few of bills around here.

Yes, indeed…, Watson's ingenuity in knowing every state and federal law on the books is how he has managed to keep our meager budget in the black for over thirty years.

For all intents and purposes Henry was the litmus test, or better said…, the "sacrificial lamb," which is quite ironic, seeing how Henry resembled Jesus Christ, the "Lamb of God."

Watson was banking heavily on Henry being the unprecedented "Savior" of WEALTH Industries. I know it all sounds bizarre, but in a strange sort of way, it all made perfect sense.

By now, Watson finally caught up to the entourage, and they all ducked into the intake room so that they could get the ball rolling on Henry. There were forms that needed to be filled out before Watson could officially flip the meter on Henry's vocational evaluation.

If the truth be known, I was a little miffed that Watson had left me out of the loop, and I think it would be fair to say that I was feeling a little bit sorry for myself.

As I stood in the reception area checking my mail, I could see Watson scurrying around looking for all of the required paperwork needed to get the intake interview started.

Watson then happen to see me out of the corner of his eye, and emphatically called out, "Jack, where the hell have you been? I want you involved in that meeting on Josephson, ASAP!"

"Yes sir…, right away, Mr. Watson." I said, enthusiastically.

Watson handed me all of the necessary forms that needed to be filled out, and then I quickly high-tailed it down to the intake room.

When I entered the intake room, Farnsworth stood up and shook my hand. To my slight surprise, he actually asked me to conduct the meeting. Quite honestly, I wasn't sure if he did this out of professional courtesy, or because he's blatantly incompetent.

Nevertheless, I had the forms filled out in no time, and for what it was worth, I browsed through a few agency brochures with Henry and explain some of the finer points of the program.

Personally, I don't think Henry got much out of our little skull session, surprise, surprise!

Henry was drifting somewhere out in the middle of deep space, and the chances of radar picking up his weak transmitting bleeps were somewhere between slim and none.

We then engaged in some casual chitchat, and we were essentially killing time until Mr. Watson could join us for the meeting. I really didn't feel like making any small talk with either Farnsworth or Ms. Brown, and in terms of discussing anything with Henry, well…, we simply didn't have the luxury of accessing any satellite links to broadcast out into deep space where Henry usually spends the majority of his time.

Needless to say, but as we all sat around waiting for Watson to join us there was an awful lot of dead silence and a considerable amount of blank stares.

So after several more uncomfortable minutes, I felt a sudden sense of urgency, so I made up some lame excuse to Farnsworth and Ms. Brown that I needed to leave the room. It was my feeble attempt to see where Mr. Watson was and to find out what the hell was keeping him.

When I tapped on Mr. Watson's door, he was on the telephone. I signaled to him that we were all waiting for him to join us down in the intake room. Watson then placed his hand over the receiver and quietly said that he would join us as soon as he was finished up on the phone.

So after hearing what Watson had to say, I nodded my head and then reluctantly headed back into the intake room…, to rejoin the Three Stooges episode that was already in progress.

Upon re-entering the intake room, I immediately glanced over at Henry, who looked to be in some sort of bizarre catatonic state. He then suddenly snapped out of his hypnotic trance and began badgering Ms. Brown for a cigarette.

As Henry kept staring down Ms. Brown, he repeatedly harassed her by saying over and over again, "Please don't forsake me, sister. Please don't forsake me, sister. Please…"

In an effort to save Ms. Brown from Henry's clutches, I then asked if anyone would like some coffee. The minute Henry heard the word coffee, he immediately stopped badgering Ms. Brown and then turned his full-attentions toward me.

At that point, Henry then made some sort of weird primal grunt, and then raised his hand to his mouth, as if he were taking a drink. Apparently that was Henry's way of asking for coffee.

I on the other hand thought that an ice cold beer right about now might be the beverage of choice, even though it was only nine-thirty in the morning.

A few moments later, I returned with a tray of coffee. We all leisurely sipped our coffee, except for Henry, who guzzled his coffee down in two large gulps and then asked for more.

As I tried to comprehend what Henry just did, I then concluded that the lining of Henry's esophagus must be made out of PVC…, because there's no possible way that a normal person could have sustained drinking a scalding hot cup of coffee in two large gulps such as Henry did.

So after Henry drank his coffee and was told to wait for his second cup, he then sat there facing me in a catatonic stare, which I found to be quite unsettling.

Ms. Brown then attempted to divert Henry's attention by explaining some of the major points of interest in the WEALTH brochures. These were the same exact brochures that I had just showed Henry not more than ten minutes ago.

Apparently, Ms. Brown must have been napping when I did that little exercise in futility.

Henry could care less about the brochures!

I then glanced at Farnsworth to see what his reaction to the whole situation was, but as he caught my eye, he just casually smiled and seemed totally preoccupied in his thoughts, as he continued to leisurely sip his coffee.

Farnsworth finished his coffee, and then hastily excused himself from the room. About five minutes later, there was a tap on the door and in walked Mr. Watson.

Watson then nonchalantly asked, "So where are we at this point, Jack?"

I was thinking to myself, "Well…, we're about six hours away from getting a load on at the nearest gin mill!"

Instead I answered, "Well Mr. Watson, we've completed all of the necessary forms, and we've been familiarizing Henry with the program by reviewing some of our agency brochures."

"Splendid! Thank you for taking care of that Jack." Watson replied.

Watson then turned his attentions toward Henry and affably said, "So Henry,…welcome to WEALTH Industries. I really think you're going to like it here."

Henry was totally oblivious to Mr. Watson's gratuitous comments. Henry just stared out into deep space, as he kept slowly turning his head back and forth like a small kitchen fan.

Watson then continued by saying, "So Henry, we have been serving the community for over thirty years, and during that time we have employed thousands of people."

Mr. Watson spoke to Henry in very basic terms. This is a side of Watson that you don't see very often. Watson is usually very articulate and eloquent when he speaks.

Well…, except for when he addresses C.D. or Joe Atkins of course!

Despite Watson's best efforts, his informative little lecture with Henry went for naught. Henry was simply too far gone to appreciate the relevant substance of what Watson had to say.

Henry had an urge for another cup of coffee. So once again Henry made some sort of bizarre primal grunt, and then raised his hand up to his mouth, as if taking a drink from a cup.

Although Watson appeared to be somewhat frustrated with Henry, he glanced over at me and quietly said, "Jack, if you don't mind…, can you please get Henry another cup of coffee."

Watson was displaying an inordinate amount of patience with Henry. After all, there was a sizeable amount of money at stake, and Watson was going to make damn sure that nothing stood in the way of sealing the deal with Henry Josephson today and all those federal dollars that he has been dreaming about for months and months.

When I came back into the intake room, I placed the tray of coffee down on the table.

Just then Farnsworth half-heartedly knocked on the door and strolled back into the intake room. Farnsworth must have been hamming it up with some of his old crony friends from when he worked here, because he was all shit's and giggles when he re-entered the room.

I have really come to dislike Farnsworth, but as I've said before, I may need him for a future favor, so I swallowed my pride and asked him if he'd like me to pour him a cup of coffee.

Farnsworth declined the coffee, and then leaned over to Ms. Brown and asked her what he had missed while he was out of the room and could she please bring him up to speed.

Uh…, Farnsworth wants to know what he missed. Are you kidding me?

Now if Farnsworth had asked me what he had missed, I would have promptly told him nothing…, except for the fact that Henry has consumed most of the coffee in the agency.

It was getting close to ten o'clock now. Everyone seemed to be glancing at their watch and losing interest in the meeting. Watson had already left. He saw enough, well…, all that he wanted to see anyway, and he had me doing the mop up work in wrapping up the meeting.

I informed Ms. Brown and Farnsworth that I was going to take Henry down to the contract floor, so that I could familiarize him with his new program.

As Farnsworth and Ms. Brown were leaving the intake room, they both said "good-bye" to Henry and wished him "good luck." Henry seemed oblivious to their well-wishes because he was solely intent on smoking another cigarette, and he communicated this by using gestures, in which he proceeded to put two fingers up to his mouth and then pretended to blow smoke.

I actually found Henry's bizarre little antics to be quite amusing. As we all know by now, Henry is quite capable of speech, and he can certainly make all of his needs known verbally, yet he prefers to use gestures to express his wants and needs.

Then again…, maybe by using gestures Henry was simply trying to point out to us that he was bilingual, and fluent in two languages.

Henry smoked his cigarette right down to the nub, and I had to tell him several times to butt it out. I could see why his fingers were all charred and brown looking.

Once again, Henry put two fingers up to his mouth, which indicated to me that he wanted to smoke another cigarette.

Henry was a one-trick pony, and all he really wanted to do all day was smoke cigarettes and drink coffee, while professing to the world that he was Jesus Christ…, the Son of God.

I told Henry that he could smoke later, but for now we needed to get down to the contract floor so that I could introduce him to some of the people that he would be working with today.

As Farnsworth was coming out of Watson's office, he saw me heading up the hallway with Henry, and then shouted, "Hey Jack, keep me posted on Henry's progress, okay. Oh, and by the way…, we still need to finish discussing the application process for State employment."

At that moment, an icy chill went right down my spine by Farnsworth's completely unexpected and ill-advised comment, as I nervously thought to myself, "You idiot, keep it down, I don't want Watson to hear you!"

As I whisked Henry down the hallway toward the contract floor, I prayed to God that Farnsworth didn't spill the beans about State employment to Watson.

Ms. Brown, who was trailing Farnsworth out of the building, then acted like a real nosey-buddy, as she inquisitively asked, "Is Mr. O'Leary leaving WEALTH Industries?"

Damn social workers…, they like to know everybody else's business, but they won't breathe a single word to anyone about their own.

When we arrived on the contract floor, I introduced Henry to some of the clients that I considered "safe bets." These clients were extremely friendly and engaging, and I knew that they would welcome Henry with open arms, as only developmentally disabled people can do.

So after Henry met with some of his new coworkers, I then introduced Henry to Terry, who is the line supervisor that will be training him during his six-week vocational evaluation.

As Henry shook hands with Terry, Henry looked to be a million miles away. But then in an instant, Henry seemed to come alive, and eerily ask Terry if he believed in God his Father.

Terry, who is not only a good-natured guy, but someone who has the patience of a saint, simply smiled at Henry's rhetorical question and took everything that Henry said to him in stride.

I wound up staying with Henry for about an hour, and then Terry nonchalantly motioned for me to leave. As I quietly slipped away, I said a little prayer that Henry would settle in nicely, and more importantly…, that he would not start a Holy War.

When I turned the corner to leave the contract floor, who of all people should I collide into but Michael Wallace. As Michael caromed off of the wall, my adrenal glands kicked into high gear, and I was hoping that Michael wouldn't resort to violence due to my faux pas.

As I helped Michael up to his feet, he genuinely felt bad for bumping into me, and then took it upon himself to sign the word, "I'm sorry."

I quickly responded to Michael's olive branch by signing the word, "okay." We then smiled at each other, shook hands, and went our separate ways.

As I headed back to my office, I had a sudden thought of Richard Burroughs, Michael's OVR counselor. Burroughs was ecstatic the day we approved Michael for inclusion into the program, and he thanked me profusely for advocating so strongly for young Michael.

The day of Michael's determination meeting, I never mentioned to Richard Burroughs that Michael had assaulted me in my office. Watson knew that I was holding back information regarding the incident. And when the meeting was over, Watson pulled me aside and thanked me for using restraint, and no doubt…, for allowing the money train to remain on schedule.

When I arrived back at my office, I heard a light knock at my door and it was Mr. Watson. Watson had a big smile on his face, as he proceeded to say with some quiet enthusiasm, "We have had us one helluva day here, Jack."

"I guess so," I replied.

"You guess so? Jack today was a landmark day!" Watson exclaimed.

"Why's that?" I asked.

"Well, I just got off the phone with Ms. Brown. She was very impressed with the way you handled the Josephson referral, and said you were the consummate professional. She also told me how compassionate you were with regards to people with psychiatric challenges." Watson said, with a big smile on his face.

I couldn't believe my ears. The last time I checked, Ms. Brown and I were squaring off in a heated debate on the appropriateness of psychiatric referrals. Watson must know that I'm smarter than this. Why is Ms. Brown saying all these flowery remarks to Watson, or is she?

"In fact…," Watson hesitated a moment, and then continued by saying, "I've decided that I'm sending you back out to the psych center next week to evaluate more people."

"What!" I exclaimed.

Watson continued, "Well, it seems as though there have been some new developments. Ms. Brown has indicated to me that she might have some additional patients over at the psych center that might benefit greatly from our services. She sounded very optimistic."

"Optimistic! Well…, I think psychotic would be a better description." I shouted.

Watson chuckled at my biting remark, as he replied, "C'mon Jack…, Allan Farnsworth concurs with Ms. Brown's sentiments, and said that OVR would entertain any and all referrals."

"Oh, okay…, I feel much better now knowing that Farnsworth corroborates what a psychotic woman is telling him. I mean, c'mon Mr. Watson…, we don't even know if Henry Josephson is gonna work out or not." I said, whining like a spoiled and petulant young child.

Watson cracked a smile, and then soothingly replied, "Patience Jack, Rome wasn't built in a day. Besides, you must've known that it was only a matter of time before I'd send you back out there again, right?"

"No…, not really," I snarled.

"Listen Jack, we're in the business of enhancing people's lives, and from what I'm hearing there are quite a few patients out at the psych center that can benefit greatly from our services. For your information, Josephson was our test run."

"What do you mean Josephson was our test run?" I impetuously asked.

"Well, the reason why the Josephson case has been sitting on the shelf for over a year and a half now is because the politicians have been dragging their feet. The legislators have been trying to re-define certain laws in the mental health field, specifically the vocational training of individuals who reside in psychiatric facilities. Up until now, it's been nothing but rhetoric. We have been petitioning our local legislators for years to reduce the amount of red tape for people with psychiatric diagnoses." Watson stated pragmatically.

"So this is not a new initiative?" I inquisitively asked.

Watson chuckled at my naïve remark, and then replied, "Well, let's just say that the wheels of progress turn very slowly Jack, especially in the area of legislative law regarding human services. The general public gets very nervous when they perceive even the slightest change in social order. These new pieces of legislation that I and other committee members have been working on may help revolutionize the care that people receive in psychiatric facilities."

"So why on earth did they choose Henry Josephson as their designated test run? I mean, him of all people." I asked, in a dumbfounded tone.

Watson replied, "Well, they selected him because they wanted to show the legislators that if he could succeed, then virtually anyone with a psychiatric disorder could as well."

"Uh-huh…," I grunted.

"I'm sure you're not aware this, but Mr. Josephson was hand selected by a team of psychiatrists for this project, and based upon their clinical opinion, he was deemed to be the most psychiatrically impaired individual that they had at their facility." Watson said, and looking as though he was verge of laughing hysterically.

"I'm glad you find this so amusing Mr. Watson. Personally, I don't see the humor in it."

"Sorry Jack, but I do," Watson replied, as he began to laugh uncontrollably.

"So what you're telling me is that I have been coaching the "Mickey Mantle," no better yet, the "Babe Ruth" of mental illness all along."

"Well…, I guess you could look at it that way." Watson remarked, still laughing.

I then sarcastically said, "So this committee would rather bet all their marbles on their worst patient than on their best patient. Boy, that's convoluted thinking, and if you ask me I think mental illness is seeping into the minds of the administrators of that hospital."

"Yeah, I know…, and I would have to agree with you. I would much rather play to my strengths than rely on my weaknesses." Watson replied, understandingly.

There was a brief silence, and then Watson continued, "We'll need to come up with a contingency plan in the event that Josephson doesn't pan out. That is why we need to go back out to the psych center again and explore other avenues that may be available to us."

"So tell me…, who's we?" I asked curiously.

"Well…, we being, Ms. Brown, Farnsworth, and this agency, among others." Watson said vaguely, and doing a nice job at tap dancing around the question.

There was another brief pause, and then I asked the sixty-four thousand dollar question, "So which counselor is up in the rotation to go out to the psych center this time, Mr. Watson? I know from past experience that you're a big proponent in "Sharing the WEALTH," right?"

"Hey, nice pun Jack. But c'mon…, don't do this to me. I specifically sat down with you so that I could explain all of the details. I could've just as easily mandated you to go back out to the psych center again with no explanation whatsoever, but I didn't. Besides, you've built up such a solid rapport with the people out there and I'd hate to disrupt that." Watson said, smiling.

"A rapport, please..., who are you trying to kid Mr. Watson. I don't wanna seem out of line here, but are we doing this to enhance people's lives, or are we doing it for the money?"

Watson smiled, and then intriguingly said, "Well..., that's a very interesting point you're raising Jack."

Geez..., I hate it when Mr. Watson tells me that I've raised a very interesting point, because this tactic usually backfires on me, and then he uses my logic as ammunition against me.

Watson continued by saying, "Well Jack, you and I have had this conversation before, but perhaps we need to revisit it again, so that we can look at it in a whole different light."

"Okay...," I replied, reluctantly.

"So let me ask you something. Does the athlete play for the money, or for the love of the game? What about the rock star? Does he play for the money, or the artistry of the music? Something to think about. Wouldn't you agree, Jack?"

"Good point...," I said, concededly.

Frankly, I really didn't know how to respond to Watson's calculated analogy. Was he expecting me to counterpoint his argument, or merely fold up my tent and break camp in defeat?

Then again..., perhaps he was wondering just how far I would push the envelope with my convictions.

In any event, I think Watson saw that I portrayed a man who realizes that sometimes retreat is the better part of valor. I also think that I gained some respect from him today as well.

I wasn't a yes man..., but then I wasn't a six-inch thorn in his side either.

Watson continued by saying, "Jack, if you ask me athletes and rock stars would probably do what they do for a fraction of the money that they earn, but due to their exceptional talent they are compensated for their efforts, as we should be compensated for ours. Although, I will admit, that even I have been known to do some pro-bono work over the years."

"Really..., you mean to tell me that you've actually given out some freebies over the years Mr. Watson?"

Watson chuckled, and then replied, "Why, of course..., but not very often. After all, we need to generate enough revenue so that we can keep our doors open for business, and still provide Jack O'Leary with the champagne lifestyle that he has grown accustomed to having."

"Uh…, you're kidding me, right? I can barely afford to buy a six-pack of beer with the measly salary that you're paying me Mr. Watson."

Watson chuckled, and then amusingly said, "Jack, I just love your sarcastic wit. Anyway, I hope I've answered all of your questions with regards to client versus money. I think it's quite similar to answering the age old question of what came first, - the chicken or the egg."

"Ah, c'mon Mr. Watson…, that's not so tough, everyone knows it was the egg that came first."

Watson chuckled, and then quipped, "Oh yeah…, well then who laid the egg?"

We both laughed heartily, and for the first time since working here I can actually say that I saw a side of Watson that I had not seen before, and a side that I could really grow to admire.

So after chatting with Mr. Watson, I decided to stretch my legs a bit and go grab a cup of coffee from the break room.

When I entered the break room, C.D. was hard at work in brewing up another fresh pot. C.D. and I chatted for about twenty minutes. I then glanced at my watch and realized that it was almost quitting time for the clients down on the contract floor, and I was wondering how my psychotic little friend Henry Josephson was making out on his first day.

If you ask me, I'm sure Terry, Henry's line supervisor, will probably be stopping off at his favorite gin mill after work, so that he can tie one on after putting up with Henry all day.

As I headed down to the contract floor to see Henry, I was eager to see how he did today, and I wanted to give him a few words of encouragement before he went home.

I felt bad calling the psych center home for Henry. I certainly wouldn't want to work here all day, and then be subjected to living in a harsh and sterile environment like the psych center.

Then again…, I wonder if Henry even realizes how bad the living conditions are in the psych center, and that there might actually be a better quality of life somewhere else?

Anyway, as I walked onto the contract floor, Henry appeared to be as dazed and confused as ever. He had that usual faraway look in his eye…, his million mile stare, as I often called it.

Terry informed me that Henry hadn't done much of anything all day. He said that Henry was mildly disruptive and wouldn't attempt to do any of the tasks independently, and often required hand over hand assistance when performing even the simplest of tasks.

On a more humorous note, Terry did indicate to me that I had more mechanical ability in my little pinky than Henry had in his entire body.

I then amusingly quipped, "Gee Terry, I hope it didn't take you all day before you arrived at that conclusion."

Terry laughed, and then spiritedly replied, "Hey Jack, if your counseling career should ever go belly up, then don't worry..., because I've got a spot on the line for ya!"

Just then the psych center van pulled into the parking lot to pick up Henry. The same two strapping attendants that dropped Henry off this morning then lumbered out of the vehicle.

These two lunkheads sauntered into the building with a real smug look on their face, and seeing them prompted me to once again reflect on how bad I felt for poor old Henry and the meager existence that he was forced to endure back at the psych center.

I walked over to Henry as he was getting his jacket on to leave, and I encouragingly said, "Good-bye, Henry. I'll see ya tomorrow, okay buddy."

Henry barely made eye contact with me, but he did manage to make a slight hand gesture, which indicated some sort of acknowledgement to my words.

One of the psych center attendants was actually quite surprised to hear that Henry was coming back tomorrow, and then brashly said, "Hey mister, I was told that he was only coming over here for an evaluation, not that he was coming back tomorrow."

I then explained, "Well, Henry is involved in a six-week evaluation, and at the end of that time we will make a decision as to whether he should continue on in the program or not."

The brash attendant sarcastically replied, "What a waste of time and money that is. I can't believe you people need six-weeks to figure that one out. All it takes is five minutes at best."

I simply smiled, and then countered his rather harsh statement by saying, "Well, that's really not your concern is it. All you have to do is just keep bringing him here each day, and I would appreciate it if next time you'd keep your thoughts and comments to yourself. If you have any further questions, then you can take them up with Ms. Brown over at your facility."

"Ms. Brown, yeah right..., a lot of help she'll be. I'm sure she'll be coming over here next for an evaluation." The wiseass attendant commented, and then he and his side-kick buddy began laughing like two hyenas.

This guy was definitely getting my Irish up. I didn't like the way he was taking pot shots at Henry or Ms. Brown for that matter.

It made me think that only two short weeks ago, I was saying the same exact thing that this jackass was saying, and I suddenly felt quite ashamed of myself.

As I was packing up my belongings to leave for the day, I turned for the door and I saw Mr. Watson standing outside my office smiling.

Watson then piped up and vigorously said, "Jack, I think today went very well. I think we broke new ground today, not only with Josephson and future referrals from the psych center, but also our discussion regarding ideology and practices."

"Yeah, maybe…," I said, quietly.

Watson continued by saying, "Also, I heard from someone out back that you were defending your buddy Josephson this afternoon when the psych center came by to pick him up. I wish I could've been there to see you in action."

I replied, "Yeah, I wish you could have been there too. I could've used the moral support."

"Hey, not from what I heard." Watson quipped.

"Really…"

"Really…," Watson said, as he smiled like a proud father.

"So, uh…., is this the part when you tell me that my heroics will be reflected in my next paycheck Mr. Watson?"

Watson thought a minute, and with a cunning smile, he then blurted out, "Uh, no…, but nice try Jack."

CHAPTER SIX

Well, it's another Monday morning. I threw my backpack in the office and then hustled down to the break room, so that I could chew the fat with C.D. over a piping hot cup of coffee.

C.D. not only makes the best coffee on the planet, but he's also a big sports nut like me.

C.D. and I like to talk about the scores and highlights from the night before, and the discussions between us are usually quite spirited to say the least.

Hey…, most people usually dread Monday mornings, but not me. Because on Monday mornings, I get to cram three days' worth of sports watching into one sitting.

C.D. and I enjoy dissecting and analyzing every game that was televised over the weekend, and we usually like to hash it out before the Monday morning crowd shuffles in.

So after shooting the breeze with C.D., it suddenly occurred to me that I had forgotten to check my phone messages from last Friday, which was quite uncharacteristic for me to do.

Anyway, I walked into the reception area all charged up from not only my sports fix with C.D., but also having consumed three cups of C.D.'s high test coffee.

I then boisterously said, "Hi Dolly, do I have any phone messages from last Friday!"

Dolly flinched at the unexpected sound of my exuberance, and then sternly said, "Whoa Jack, you need to turn it down a notch. It's Monday…, remember. I'm barely awake."

She then reached across her desk and handed me a slew of phone messages, and was quick to point out that several of the messages needed my immediate attention, "ASAP."

I chuckled at her choice of words, and then amusingly said, "ASAP, gee Dolly…

, I think you've been hanging around Mr. Watson too long. You're beginning to sound like him."

Dolly then gave me one of her patented stares, and then snidely replied, "Jack, please…, I'm not in the mood."

As I walked back to my office, I was quietly chuckling to myself because everyone that calls me wants an immediate response to their phone calls.

So before scanning the messages, I thought I would draw on my psychic powers a bit, and see if I could guess who some if not all of the messages were from.

I guess you could say that this little psychic exercise of mine was my way of breaking up the monotony that the job sometimes poses, and was nothing more than an entertaining diversion to hone my psychic talents.

Before rummaging through the messages, I took a moment to think. On average, I usually get a couple right, but never a perfect score. Today I actually wasn't too far off the mark, and as it turns out four of the messages were from the Sampson's, and the rest but one was from OVR.

The one lone message that I received was from an old professor of mine that taught me in graduate school and his name was Dr. Stevens. Not only was Dr. Stevens my professor, but he was also my academic advisor as well. The message simply read, "Jack, please give me a call at your earliest convenience, thank you!"

Frankly, I didn't have a clue as to why Dr. Stevens would be calling me, but for now I just decided to put the message on the back burner and call him later in the week.

Well, it's been about a week now since Henry Josephson started his evaluation, and I wish I could tell you that he has made remarkable progress, but sad to say he really hasn't.

Everyone on the contract floor has been very supportive of him, and the unconditional regard that they have demonstrated toward him has been a source of inspiration for me.

I've been keeping Ms. Brown and Allan Farnsworth updated on Henry's progress, or should I say lack thereof. When speaking with them I try not to make it sound as bleak as it really is. I actually find myself being vague or even elusively optimistic, but not too optimistic, because I know from past experience just how easily swayed Ms. Brown and Allan Farnsworth are at misinterpreting information.

Of course, when updating Mr. Watson on Henry's progress I'm usually more reality based because Mr. Watson is only interested in the bottom line.

Well, another week has come to an end, and I can't believe where it has gone. Everyone has cleared out for the weekend. No machines, no clamor, and best of all, no client emergencies. The clients have collected their paychecks and happy faces prevail everywhere.

Sometimes I wonder how the clients spend the money that they earn here.

Oh, speaking of paychecks, Henry Josephson actually earned some money this week, a whopping sixty-seven cents. Can you believe that?

It actually cost more to write and process the check than the amount that was drafted!

Quite honestly, I was a bit suspicious when I heard that Henry earned some money this week. My initial thought was that Terry, his line supervisor, must have either made a mistake or cooked the books, and gave Henry credit for work that he didn't do.

Gee, if Henry keeps this up then he may need to contact an accountant, and be forced to file an income tax return just like the rest of us.

As I was packing up my belongings and getting ready to leave for the day, it suddenly dawned on me that I had failed to return Dr. Stevens' phone message from last Friday. I was planning on calling Dr. Stevens this week, but between my job placement duties, the Sampson's life disasters, and all the meetings that I'm required to attend, well…, it simply slipped my mind.

Boy, a whole week went by and I'm only thinking about Dr. Stevens' phone message now. I hope he doesn't think that I'm a total incompetent.

I slung my backpack off of my shoulder, and then picked up the phone and dialed Dr. Stevens' number. I surmised that his calling me must have been pretty important, seeing how he gave me his direct line and not his secretary's extension.

Despite the late hour on a Friday afternoon, I had a strong hunch that Dr. Stevens would still be in his office because the man is an absolute workaholic. He is so dedicated to his craft that he even has a small cot in an adjoining office, so that he can grab a quick catnap but still be accessible to his students. His work is his life. I'm sure that Dr. Stevens has a house or an apartment somewhere in town, but he always seems to be tethered to his office.

The phone rang twice, and then I heard the old familiar voice of Dr. Stevens say, "hello."

"Hello Dr. Stevens, this is Jack O'Leary…, I'm just following up on your phone message from last week. I'm sorry it took me so long to get back to you."

"Why hello, Jack. It's so good to hear your voice. I thoroughly understand, my boy. I know how busy it is working out in the private sector. It can get awfully hectic out there. I worked in the private sector when I first started my career. Hahaha! I won't tell you how many years ago that was, my boy. You may think I'm nothing but an ancient relic!"

At that point, Dr. Stevens and I both chuckled at his whimsical remark.

Stevens then said, "As a matter of fact, my dear boy…, I was such a pioneer when I first started out that no one even heard of a vocational rehabilitation counselor, and I can remember experiencing such consternation about ever going into the field in the first place."

"Well, I sometimes question my choice of professions too Dr. Stevens. I hope you don't think less of me for saying that."

"No…, not in the least, my boy. It's quite understandable. When I landed my first job, I had no idea what I was getting myself into. I worked three years at a small sheltered workshop that was out in the middle of nowhere. I believe the agency served about seventy-five clients."

"Wow…, that was a small workshop! WEALTH has a census of over three hundred!"

"Yes, well…, the field has certainly grown leaps and bounds since I first entered it. The truth was…, I didn't have a clue as to how I was going to help these people, but things got better. I eventually found my niche, and after some long deliberations I finally decided to go on for my doctorat because I discovered that the academic arena was where my true passion for the field was best suited."

"That's very interesting, Dr. Stevens. Thank you for sharing that story with me."

"Not at all, my boy. So I trust that everything is going well?" Dr. Stevens inquired.

"Yes…, I'm actually beginning to hit my stride, and feeling more and more comfortable each day. When I first started here, it was a little overwhelming."

"Well, as I try to convey to my students, it's an extremely arduous task to incorporate the theoretical concepts that you learn in school and then apply them on a day-to-day basis in the field. But that's all part of the challenge that we face as teachers, my boy."

"Well, you certainly prepared me quite well Dr. Stevens, and you made a definite impression on me!"

"Thank you, Jack. And you very much impressed me with your studies here at the university!"

"Gee Dr. Stevens, we sound like we're forming a mutual admiration society."

"Indeed…," Dr. Stevens said, with his usual vigor.

We both quietly chuckled, and then there was a brief moment of silence.

Although I can't speak for Dr. Stevens, but during that brief pause I was recalling some of the good times that he and I shared with one another back at the university.

Dr. Stevens then broke the silence, and hurriedly said, "Well, my boy, I'm a little pressed for time right now. I'm heading over to Simmons Hall to teach a class, you know the one…, that theories class that everybody dreads taking. Frankly, I don't understand why."

"Oh…, I think you know why Dr. Stevens," prompting both of us to laugh out loud.

"Yes, well…, it's a necessary evil. Anyway, perhaps we could talk more, or better yet, get together for a bite to eat next week. I would really enjoy that Jack."

"Um, sure, okay, that sounds like a great idea, Dr. Stevens!"

"Marvelous, now…, be sure to call me next week because I'd like to talk to you about an interesting proposition that I think you'd be quite suited for. Ta-ta, Jack!" Stevens said, with his usual splash of panache.

"Bye, Dr. Stevens. It was good talking to you."

As I walked toward my car, I wondered what it was that Dr. Stevens wanted to discuss with me. I must say that he had me rather intrigued.

On the drive home, I was reminiscing about my time in graduate school. I was very fortunate to have had several good professors, but I would have to say that Dr. Stevens was by far my most favorite. His whole professional life has been devoted to working here at the university, yet socially…, I really didn't know that much about him.

As far as I know, Dr. Stevens was in his late sixties, single, a little effeminate, and yes…, perhaps even a closet homosexual for all I know. But he's also compassionate, kind, and an innovative thinker. He possesses all the qualities that I aspire to have in order to be a good counselor, and what's more…, he's been able to successfully weave all of these fine attributes of his into our curriculum.

Dr. Stevens could have left the university a number of times to teach elsewhere, but he never did. He had offers for advancement to Chair Departments at prestigious universities all over the country, but declined.

In fact, I heard that he was actually en route to a new professorship at a very prominent university, when somewhere along the interstate he thought better of his decision and then headed straight back to Simmons Hall on our university campus, and he's been here ever since.

I guess one could argue the point either way…, Dr. Stevens was either very loyal or very apprehensive. But knowing Dr. Stevens, I'm sure he suffered through his decision.

Do I leave students behind that I have a vested interest in, or do I step out of the box and try a new endeavor.

Well..., I guess only Dr. Stevens knows the answer to that one.

In my opinion, Dr. Stevens should have been chairman of the department, but he was overlooked. The chairman of our department was Dr. Whiting. Dr. Stevens had almost twice as many years in the field as Dr. Whiting, but experience isn't always the deciding factor.

Dr. Whiting was this young political go-getter, who not only liked hobnobbing with the Chancellor of the university, but with anyone that could assist him up the almighty career ladder.

To his credit, Whiting was a very good professor, but the man was notoriously pompous and arrogant. Whiting was a very volatile man, and his students, as well as the professors for that matter, just wanted to stay on his good side.

Yeah..., as if he had one!

From what I understand, Dr. Stevens actually taught Dr. Whiting in graduate school, and then sponsored Whiting while he pursued his doctorate. It was common knowledge that Dr. Stevens always received a free pass from Dr. Whiting's unpredictable wrath, and on occasion, Dr. Stevens would intercede on a student's behalf when Whiting was being totally unreasonable.

Whiting was notorious for his temper, and his going off on tirades was common practice. Whiting was a stickler on how he wanted the curriculum to be taught, managed, and represented.

Although Whiting lacked social grace in and around Simmons Hall, he could certainly turn on the charm at cocktail parties, or when someone influential was touring the building.

Dr. Whiting was actually a very good instructor and administrator, but he lacked the charisma and easy country charm that Dr. Stevens possessed, and I think that deep down inside Dr. Whiting was quite jealous of Dr. Stevens.

But that being said, Whiting still had a soft spot for his old mentor, and held Dr. Stevens in very high regard.

Monday morning..., so after swapping scores and highlights in the break room with C.D., it was time to assemble for the Monday morning staff meeting. Once again, the Monday morning staff meeting consisted of Watson nitpicking about the same old issues and concerns.

Then again..., the Monday morning staff meeting was Watson's only opportunity each week to get us all together, so that he could refresh our memory as to what our jobs really were.

Hey, I'm not saying that his constant rehashing about the same old rhetoric wasn't justified, but his pep talks, and worse yet…, his reprisals, always seem to fall on deaf ears.

When it came right down to it, the counselors all knew that they were working for slave wages, so none of them were particularly fazed by Watson's constant reminders, reprimands, or needling criticisms.

Anyway, when the meeting finished up, Watson pulled me aside and quietly said, "Jack, can I talk to you in private, not here…, but down in my office. It will only take a few minutes."

"Sure Mr. Watson, but do I have time to call the psych center first and see how Henry Josephson did over the weekend?"

Watson replied, "Yeah, sure, that's fine. Why don't you go make your call, and then come by my office when you're done. I'll be in my office all morning working on the budget."

When I telephoned the psych center, I spoke with someone on Ward 19…, a John somebody. As a rule, I didn't like speaking with anyone at the psych center other than a supervisor because I wasn't too sure if I was getting accurate information, or if the person I was speaking with on the phone was even a staff person at all.

Hey, for all I know…, the patients are answering the phones over there!

Anyway, this guy John was not very helpful in telling me if Henry Josephson had a good weekend or not. In fact, everything John said were one word answers and completely vague.

Quite honestly, I was convinced that John was either a patient or soon to be one!

So feeling somewhat disillusioned, I hung up the phone, grabbed my clipboard, and then scurried down to Watson's office to meet with him.

When Mr. Watson saw me standing in the doorway, he waved me into his office and then instructed me to close the door behind me.

Suddenly, I experienced a bit of a strange sensation. Watson's body language and the intonation in his voice seemed all wrong. For some reason this meeting didn't seem natural.

Watson then casually asked, "So did you make your call over to the psych center?"

I replied, "Yes, but I wasn't able to get much information. The ward supervisor wasn't around, and the person that I spoke on the phone wasn't very forthcoming."

"Huh, well…, you should've asked to speak to Ms. Brown." Watson said, amusingly.

"Please…, spare me." I groaned.

Watson chuckled at my reaction, and then casually said, "Just give me another minute or so while I finish up these figures."

"Take your time, Mr. Watson. Hey…, if you happen to find any extra money kicking around in the budget, I could sure use a raise."

Watson looked up at me, took off his glasses, and then said with a straight face, "Extra…, believe me Jack, there isn't any extra."

Mr. Watson then slipped his glasses back on and resumed working on the budget.

While Watson crunched the numbers of the overhead accounts, I sat quietly panning his office. I don't get too many opportunities to camp out here, but I would sure love to have an office like this someday.

Watson's office is almost like a sanctuary for him. He's not a big subscriber to an open door policy, and as a rule he frowns on people who just waltz into his office and start engaging him in idle chitchat. Watson likes to conduct virtually all of his business away from his office. He prefers his office to be his own little private domain and exclusively just for him.

Frankly, I was very surprised when he asked me to meet with him down in his office instead of my office, or for that matter…, the parking lot.

To tell you the truth, I've been working here almost nine months now, and I can literally count on one hand the number of times that I have actually sat down in one of Watson's big cushiony leather chairs.

The times that I did drop by were extremely brief, such as to score a signature or hand deliver a pending report.

Anyway, as I looked around Watson's office, I was thinking back to the day of my job interview. I think I've grown quite a bit since then, and I would have to say that Mr. Watson has been the main reason for my professional growth and development.

Although Mr. Watson may incite me at times, he does seem to bring out the best in me, but then I guess that's the role of a good supervisor.

So as I waited for Mr. Watson to finish up with what he was doing, I just sat there marveling at the many plaques, awards, and photographs of him with famous sports stars, celebrities, and dignitaries.

He even had one with a past President!

Mr. Watson had autographed footballs and baseballs on display, and even a framed autographed jersey of a Hall of Fame hockey player. Wow!

As I continued to soak in the ambiance of the room, I had this incredible surge of pride gushing through my entire body because I was in the presence of such a great man.

I can honestly say that I would do just about anything for Mr. Watson, and yes…, even go back out to the psych center again and lock horns with Ms. Brown if I had to.

Watson quietly closed his accounts ledger book, took off his glasses, and then addressed me by saying, "So Jack, the reason I called you in here this morning is because I wanted to update you on Joe Atkins' condition. I spoke with Joe's wife Sarah over the weekend, and she said that Joe is really not doing very well. I know how much Joe means to you, and all of us for that matter, but he seems to have a particular influence on you."

"What do you mean that he's not doing well?" I asked, with grave concern.

"Well Jack," Watson hesitated a moment, and then continued by saying, "The doctor is saying that Joe has about a month to live."

"A month, that's all…, you mean there's nothing that the doctors can do?" I asked, alarmingly.

Suddenly, the tear ducts in my eyes were like two hot water pipes, bursting under extreme pressure, as the tears streamed down my face. I then reached for the box of facial tissues that were on Mr. Watson's desk, so that I could wipe away my salty tears.

Watson then addressed me by saying, "I'm sorry to break it to you like this Jack. I know you were hoping to hear more encouraging news."

"I can't believe it." I said, sadly.

"Well…, we're all pretty shook up about it." Watson said, with conviction.

"Did this just happen, because this is the first I'm hearing of it?" I asked, tearfully.

"Well, when I spoke with Sarah over the weekend, she indicated that Joe had taken a sudden turn for the worse. From what I can gather, it has something to do with a faulty valve, and some type of leakage around his heart. His condition is not only affecting his stamina, but he's experiencing some angina as well. He sleeps all day, due to the volume of medication that he's on. I've already told a few of Joe's close friends out back, like Ralph, Terry, and Smitty."

"I see...," I said, as I reached for another tissue to wipe my face.

Watson could see that I was jarred by the news. He looked like he wanted to say more, but what else was there to say. He then concluded by saying, "Joe would probably like hearing from you, and I would strongly encourage you to call or visit him, ASAP. It would not only mean a lot to him, but I think it would do you a world of good as well."

"Yeah, you're right, Mr. Watson. I'll call him later."

"Okay, well..., hang in there and I'm here if you need me." Watson said, consolingly.

At that point, the pit in the bottom of my stomach was like the size of Gibraltar, and I felt as though someone had just punched me squarely in the solar plexus.

Quite honestly, I had a hunch that Joe probably wouldn't be back to work, but I was optimistic that he might stay on with the agency in some type of consultant capacity.

As I got up from Mr. Watson's big cushiony leather chair, I felt dizzy. Apparently, the devasting news about Joe made me a little woozy. As I turned for the door, the picture of Watson and legendary baseball great Mickey Mantle of the New York Yankees seemed to catch my eye.

I then quietly asked, "Mr. Watson, what was it like having your picture taken with Mickey Mantle?"

Watson looked up at me, took off his glasses, and then softly said, "Jack, I just want you to imagine the best day of your life, and then multiply it by ten. That's how I felt when I had my picture taken with Mickey Mantle. He was my all-time favorite ballplayer, and as long as I live I don't think I'll ever be able to duplicate that feeling again."

"Yes sir..., I'm sure." I replied, and then I quietly exited his office.

When I went home that night, I told Mom and Dad about Joe. They were both saddened to hear the disappointing news and that Joe's prognosis was so bleak. Their kind words and sentiments eased my pain and helped prepare me for the inevitable. Mom and Dad both knew how much Joe meant to me, and the excitement that he generated in the workplace.

It then occurred to me that WEALTH would never be the same again. The agency with the loss of Joe would be severely compromised. Joe was never coming back. Our "power hitter" was going to be out of the "lineup" forever. How were we going to win without him?

Although there are many people feeling sad right now, I think the person feeling the saddest is Watson. Watson and Joe had an extraordinary relationship, although you might not think so, given the amount of tongue lashings that Watson has had to impose on Joe over the years.

Quite honestly, I think Watson knew that Joe's condition was far worse than what was being reported. When Joe first went out of work, he would drop by the agency once or twice a week and tell us that it was only a matter of time until he would be back. Meanwhile, Watson remained in the shadows, and permitted Joe to tell us what we wanted to hear.

Watson was maintaining a terrible burden, the burden of knowing that Joe was far sicker than any of us realized, and that in all likelihood Joe was never coming back to work again.

It'll be hard for Watson to replace a "hall of fame" placement counselor like Joe. People like Joe, well…, they just don't come along very often. We were all in the presence of a genius, as we all watched Joe integrate the business community with WEALTH's disabled population.

Over the years, Joe has been able to engineer some very interesting placements, many of which were extremely involved, and sometimes even mystifyingly convoluted.

As I sit here now, I'm reminded of one such placement that happened a while back in which Joe somehow obtained a job lead from an old friend of his, who just so happened to be the plant manager of a factory that Joe worked at many years ago.

In fact, this particular job lead ultimately led to Joe placing a client at the factory. But of course the story is not as simple as all that because nothing about Joe is ever that cut and dry.

Anyway, the way I heard it, several years ago Joe worked at a factory that was located downtown in the industrial section of the city. This is a part of the city that few ordinary people frequented, except for freight delivery or mercantile activity.

So even though Joe severed ties with this particular factory, he would still frequent them several times a month and talk about old times over coffee, because Joe and the plant manager were very close friends.

To play it safe with Watson, Joe maintained the factory on his "hit list," which of course was one of the little pet phrases Joe coined to identify businesses that he canvassed around town.

Joe would review his hit list every afternoon, and then jot down the day's events into his job bank, which was nothing more than a dinky little metal box filled with scratched-out index cards that he kept safely tucked away in a locked bottom drawer of his desk.

Quite frankly, Joe treated his job bank as if it was "Fort Knox!"

Joe wouldn't let anyone…, including Watson, come within a country mile of perusing the contents of his job bank unless Joe was present. Joe had some type of deep-seated paranoia with regards to his job bank. The counselor's on staff all thought that Joe was nuts, and at the very least that he suffered from some type of neurotic personality disorder.

So continuing on with the story. Joe would visit the old factory twice a month, and during the course of his visit he would hound his friend the plant manager repeatedly for an opportunity to place someone at the factory, and his friend would usually decline.

Actually, his friend wouldn't come right out and definitively say "no," but put it in a way that was vague or evasive enough so that he wouldn't hurt Joe's feelings. After all, they were very close friends, and the plant manager didn't want to jeopardize their friendship.

Joe would hound his plant manager friend month, after month, after month, and viewed this vagueness on the part of his friend as a way of fostering hope for a future placement at the factory. Joe probably thought that it was only a matter of time until he wore his friend down.

Well…, apparently Joe's persistence finally paid off!

One day Joe received a phone call from his plant manager friend, who asked Joe if WEALTH had anyone down at the agency that could proficiently utilize small tool instruments, so that they could insert these teeny-weeny screws onto this itsy-bitsy hinge.

Joe being the enterprising man that he was, simply wasn't going to let a golden opportunity like this slip through his fingers, and boldly told his plant manager friend that he had the perfect man for the job!

So after hanging up the phone with his plant manager friend, Joe immediately scratched his head and then wondered who this "perfect man for the job" was.

Obviously, Joe didn't have anyone at WEALTH who could fit the bill for the job, but he certainly wasn't going to reveal that little caveat to his plant manager friend.

Once again, Joe was forced to improvise!

So being the resourceful guy that he was Joe decided to make a few phone calls, and within a day or two, he managed to find someone to fill the position at the factory.

Was there ever any doubt?

Joe was able to commandeer the services of a former watch repairman, who decided to leave the job market due to personal problems.

Apparently the man that Joe found worked in a jewelry store downtown, and as a result of the day-to-day rigors of working in retail the man developed a social anxiety disorder, which not only forced him to leave his job, but it also deterred him from leaving his home as well.

Finally, through the help of counseling and medication, the man had his confidence restored, and this gave him the courage and the wherewithal to revisit the job market again.

The psychiatric social worker that was providing counseling services for the man took note of his tremendous progress, and eventually referred him to OVR.

Gee, I guess not all psychiatric social workers are as incompetent as Ms. Brown!

Anyway, what's really ironic about the whole story is that OVR had already been working with another private agency in town, similar to ours, but one which specializes in re-introducing individuals with occupational injuries back into the job market again.

Apparently, this particular agency that OVR initially contracted with was not having any luck in placing this former watch repairman back into the job market again. So when Joe decided to contact OVR to inquire if they had someone who might fit the bill for meeting the specific requirements for the factory job, OVR said that they did. OVR then decided to change vendors, and agreed to have WEALTH sponsor the former watch repairman instead of the other agency.

Needless to say, but this turn of events put a big smile on Watson's face because WEALTH was able to make money on the deal. And to add insult to injury, they were able to "hijack" a case from an agency that specialized in this type of clientele.

Yeah, it was a "win-win" situation for everybody involved, except of course for the agency that specialized in occupational injuries, who lost out on the sponsorship from OVR.

Joe pulled off the biggest "upset of the year!"

Well, that's how Watson characterized it at the Monday morning staff meeting anyway.

On a side note, the Director of the agency that we stole the referral from is a very close friend of Mr. Watson's and his name is Peter Samuels. The two men actually have a very good working relationship, and over the years they have constantly tried to outdo each other.

Of course, Watson was ecstatic that he was able to steal a referral from his old pal Samuels, especially since Samuels has stolen one or two referrals from Watson over the years.

As a testimony to their friendship, Samuels graciously called Watson and congratulated him on stealing the placement, but was quick to remind Watson that he was still ahead in their little head to head battle.

Watson being the classy guy that he is then treated Samuels to lunch and a round of golf. It was simply a friendly competition between two very good friends.

Samuels was so impressed with Joe's ability to pry the referral away from his agency that he actually offered Joe a job, and at double the salary that Joe was making at WEALTH.

Joe being the loyal guy that he was then graciously declined Samuels enticing job offer, and good-naturedly said, "Thanks for the generous offer, Mr. Samuels. You certainly know talent when you see it, but Watson needs me a helluva lot more than you do!"

So even after the placement was made, Joe would continue to visit the factory a couple of times a month, and enjoyed coffee with his plant manager friend.

Naturally, Joe would check on the former watch repairman to see how he was doing, even though we all know by now that it wasn't proper protocol, and certainly grounds for receiving a severe tongue lashing or maybe even a royal fleecing from Watson.

Over the years, Joe was able to finagle several other job placements at his friends' factory. Some were actually good placements, and others, well..., not so good, but all in all they were always quite entertaining.

Yeah, Joe will definitely be missed, and I can hear him now sarcastically bellowing to the other counselors on staff, "I've forgotten more than you'll ever remember!"

Then again..., maybe what Joe said was more truth than sarcasm.

To tell you the truth, every time I heard Joe utter that phrase it was like hearing it for the first time, and it usually prompted me to laugh out loud. Sometimes I would even hear Joe say it when I was in the middle of a serious counseling session with a client.

Gee, now that I think about it, I wonder if the clients thought I was laughing at them!

Then again..., my laughing out loud like that probably doesn't say much for my listening skills as a counselor.

The other day I was approached by a couple of clients, and clients who weren't even on my caseload. They were inquiring as to when they were going to start their new cleaning job.

This new cleaning job, which we were calling the transitional janitorial program, was slated to start when Joe returned to work. But now that Joe won't be returning to work no one seemed to know what the status of the new program was.

To be honest, I wasn't quite sure how to address the clients concerns regarding the new cleaning program, but reassured them that I would look into the matter for them and speak with Mr. Watson on their behalf.

The transitional janitorial program has been in the works for a while now, and Joe was the main architect of the program. Watson decided to put the program on hold until Joe came back to work, but quite honestly I don't understand Watson's logic. Watson knew that Joe was very sick, and that he would not be returning to work. So why would Watson say such a thing?

Perhaps Watson was in a little bit of denial himself regarding Joe?

Anyway, since none of the other counselors were taking any initiative in addressing the problem, I took it upon myself to approach Mr. Watson and get some clarification.

I walked down to Watson's office and knocked on his door. I poked my head in and casually said, "Excuse me, Mr. Watson…, but do you have a couple of minutes for me?"

Watson looked up from what he was doing, and nonchalantly said, "Sure Jack, c'mon in."

"Um…, I wanted to talk to you about the transitional janitorial program. A couple of the clients have been making some inquiries regarding its status, and they're getting a little antsy."

Watson replied, "Yeah, I know. Well, I've given the matter some thought, and I'm trying to come up with a solution. I'm hoping that it will be resolved very soon."

"Okay…," I said, in a somewhat deflated tone.

Watson sensed my frustration, and then candidly said, "Jack, I'm between a rock and a hard place. When you're the Director of a program someday, you'll know how it feels."

"Well, I'm sure that it's quite daunting Mr. Watson."

Watson continued by saying, "Anyway, as you know I've been canvassing for a placement counselor, but I really haven't had much luck. I even tried calling Dr. Stevens over at the university to see if there was any interest with some of the kids coming out of the master's program like you did, but thus far nothing."

I then said in jest, "Wow, you really are in desperate straits Mr. Watson. You mean not even a snot-nosed kid like me was interested in your generous offer to sign on with the agency."

Watson quietly chuckled, and then replied, "Well put, Jack."

Mr. Watson then continued by saying, "But all kidding aside Jack, I was really hoping on getting lucky again and recruiting another blue chipper like you. I must say that you've made quite an impact on this place, and the staff has really come to respect you."

"Thanks, Mr. Watson. So does this mean that I should expect to find more money in my next paycheck?"

Watson replied, "Hey…, nice try Jack, but the one thing I've learned in life is that you really can't put a dollar amount on sentiment." Watson then began to laugh uncontrollably.

"Ah…, very touching Mr. Watson." I said, smiling.

Watson then said, on the Q.T., "Between you and me, but I'm seriously thinking of eliminating a counselor position and designating someone on staff to head up job placement. I just don't have any other options available to me at the moment Jack."

"Well, for now that's probably you're only recourse Mr. Watson."

"Yeah…, I know," he said, as he pondered the situation.

I then piped up and said, "Personally, I think job placement is a lot more challenging than managing a caseload."

Watson nodded his head in agreement, and then replied, "You're right, and even if I did hire someone at this point, it would be a much easier transition for the person being hired to learn a brand new caseload, then it would be for them to figure out what our existing counseling staff already knows about job placement. Well…, with the exception of C.D., of course."

I chuckled at Watson's comment regarding C.D., and then affably said, "In the meantime, should I just keep stalling the clients when they ask about the new work program?"

Watson replied, "Yeah, why don't ya. I'm sure we'll get the ball rolling in a couple of weeks. Okay, well…, don't forget to call Joe, O'Leary. I know he'd like to hear from ya."

"Okay, I will Mr. Watson, thanks."

So after speaking with Mr. Watson, I went back to my office to telephone Joe. It's been a while since I called Joe, so I actually had to look up his phone number.

Even though Joe's last name begins with an "A," for Atkins, most of the counselors on staff actually have Joe's phone number listed in their Rolodex under "P," for "pain in the ass."

As I began dialing Joe's number, I experienced a sudden chill go through my body. I then looked down at my hand and saw that it was trembling. At that moment, I hung up the phone, took a couple of slow deep breaths, and then tried to compose myself.

Once again, I reached for the telephone to dial Joe's number, and even before my finger hit the keypad, I felt a rather sharp pain in my abdomen. It suddenly occurred to me that I was having some sort of panic attack. I've never had this type of sensation come over me before.

So not knowing what to do, I quickly hung up the phone, and then reached across my desk and shut my office door.

When I sat back down my abdomen was writhing in pain. The intensity of the pain was so sharp that it caused me to hyperventilate, and then I broke out into a cold sweat.

At that point, the muscles in my abdomen, that is to say the few that I have, began to ache and twitch. I kept rubbing my abdomen in hopes that the spasms would subside.

I then decided that phoning Joe might not be such a good idea right now, and like magic…, the intensity of my abdominal discomfort quickly dissipated.

The following week at the Monday morning staff meeting, Mr. Watson entered the room and he looked unusually happy. Watson took his place at the head of the table, and then proudly announced to the group that over the weekend he had been contacted by an anonymous benefactor, who has decided to donate a substantial amount of money to WEALTH.

In addition to that, this same benefactor is also bequeathing some showroom furniture, and the furniture will be used in upgrading the staff break room.

At that point, a rousing round of applause erupted, coupled with a few spirited remarks.

So after the fanfare subsided, Watson made it abundantly clear to everyone in the room that he didn't want to see people getting "too comfortable" in the break room. Watson reminded us that we had a job to do, and that he simply couldn't take time out of his extremely busy schedule to be policing the staff lounge all day long.

Watson then emphatically said, "I don't wanna see people lounging around the break room like it's their living room," which prompted everyone in the room to laugh, even Watson.

So after Watson made his sweeping announcement, all eyes seem to cast a shadow on C.D., who seemed oblivious to their stares, as he just sat there giddy as a schoolboy.

Suddenly, C.D. realized that all eyes were now riveted on him, which then prompted him to innocently say, "What…?"

Everyone in the room then burst out into laughter, as they watched C.D. squirm and turn red with embarrassment.

Even the mice in the agency know how much time C.D. spends in the break room!

Anyway, I'm glad that we're finally getting some new furniture in the staff lounge, because the furniture that we have in there now is simply deplorable. The cushions are all covered in coffee stains, and they have no support or definition whatsoever. And when you go to sit down on them, it feels like you're settling into a "sinkhole!"

Barry, who is one of the counselors on staff and weighs in excess of three hundred pounds…, is certainly a sight to behold when he tries to hoist himself up off of the couch.

Usually, Barry resorts to bouncing his large frame up and down several times, so that he can gain enough momentum to catapult himself up off of the couch and onto his feet.

Ironically, the new furniture couldn't have come at a more opportune time, especially after hearing Barry tell us the other day, as we were yanking him off of the couch yet again, "Either Watson buys new furniture, or else he needs to requisition a fork lift for me to continue working here!"

When the meeting finally adjourned, Watson approached me from the side and cordially asked, "So how was your weekend Jack?"

"Pretty good, but as usual it was way too short."

Watson replied, "Yeah, mine too. I really had a tough time dragging myself out of bed this morning."

I thought to myself, "Wow, I guess Watson is human, after all."

Watson then continued, "So have you had a chance to call Joe yet?"

"Um, well…, not yet. I tried calling him right after you and I spoke on Friday, but when I was dialing the number I experienced some sort of panic attack. I didn't get a chance to dial him up a second time, but I'll get around to it this week, I promise."

"Okay…, I spoke with Joe's wife Sarah over the weekend, and she said that she still hadn't heard from you. Have you ever met Sarah?"

"Um, no…, I haven't had the pleasure, but I hear she's the salt of the earth. I guess she'd have to be…, being married to Joe. After all, we only work with Joe, but

Sarah is cooped up with him for sixteen hours a day, seven days a week." We then both laughed.

Watson replied, "Well, their relationship isn't what you might think it is."

"Really…, why's that?"

"Well, Joe doesn't pull any stunts with Sarah. He's meek and mild in her presence, and never raises his voice or loses his temper with her." Watson said, with much assuredness.

I replied, "Huh, well…, maybe that's why he's such a maniac here at WEALTH."

"Without a doubt," Watson commented, as we both chuckled.

"I really miss him." I said, softly.

"Yeah, I know you do. So why haven't you tried calling him again. Are you afraid of having another panic attack?" Watson asked, with concern.

"I'm really not sure." I replied.

"Jack, Joe is failing, and he's going down hill fast. If you're gonna call him then I suggest that you do it right away, because time is of the essence."

"I understand, sir."

"Okay, well…, when you do talk to him just keep in mind that he's taking a lot of pain medication, and he may not come across as being too articulate, or even rational for that matter."

"Thanks, Mr. Watson. I'll get to it today. The thing is I've never had anyone close to me die before, and this is obviously more difficult than I realized."

"Well Jack, death is not an easy thing, and to this day I still struggle with it."

"Gee Mr. Watson, I was hoping that you'd have some words of wisdom for me, and provide me with a course of action for my unresolved feelings."

"Huh…, a course of action, I thought you took that course with Dr. Stevens over at the university. But all kidding aside Jack…, that deep dark journey you're referring to is something that you're just gonna have to figure out all on your own."

"Yeah, I guess you're right, Mr. Watson."

We shook hands, and then Watson spiritedly said, "All right, well…, get going O'Leary, and don't forget to call Joe today, okay!"

"Okay sir," I said, as I turned toward the door.

Watson smirked at my sir reference, and as I was exiting the conference room he balled up a piece of paper and threw it at me in jest. The paper ball grazed off of my shoulder, and as I looked back at Watson, I smiled and teasingly said, "Nice shot..., sir!"

Well, in the midst of all the excitement this morning at the staff meeting, Watson forgot to mention to us that on Friday we were going to have a catered luncheon.

Everyone in the agency, including the clients, would be enjoying each other's company over a nice meal. Apparently this was one of the stipulations that the anonymous benefactor had requested when pledging the endowment.

We haven't had a catered luncheon in a while, and I sure hope that Mr. Watson decides to order us some better food this time and not the crap we ate from "Super Burger" last time. The clients certainly had no trouble wolfing it down, but take it from me..., the food was pretty lousy.

As I was drinking my coffee this morning, I was thinking that I haven't heard from the Sampson's in a while.

Not that I'm complaining mind you!

Actually, I can't believe that I'm this concerned about not hearing from them. Nine months ago, I was ready to quit this job because of the Sampson's, and now I'm actually worried about not hearing from them.

Geez, this line of thinking defies reason!

Well, just to play it safe, I think I'll give the Sampson's a call this week and touch base with them. Although, if I was smart..., I probably should just let sleeping dogs lie.

Uh..., better make that sleeping bears lie, after all, we are talking about the Sampson's!

Well, I'm happy to report that Henry Josephson has been here for three weeks now, and not only has he earned a little bit of money, but there have not been any apocalyptic fires, floods, or plagues to befall the agency.

Of course, I'd be remiss if I didn't mention how young Michael Wallace was faring. Michael has made tremendous strides over the past six months, and I believe this is primarily due to the outstanding work that Jill Woodson has done with Michael.

Jill is the Speech Therapist that I recommended to Richards Burroughs to help Michael with his communication deficits. Jill has consistently showed up two to three times a week to work with Michael, and her diligent efforts have reaped valuable dividends for him.

As a matter of fact, Michael has been selected as one of the candidates that will be involved in the transitional janitorial program when it gets up and running, and from what Richard Burroughs tells me his family couldn't be happier.

That reminds me, but I haven't heard from Allan Farnsworth in a while. Although just the other day he mailed me a State employment application. He didn't have my home address, so he wound up mailing the application to me here at WEALTH.

When I opened up the envelope, I was shocked to see what the contents were inside, and extremely careful not to let anyone in the agency see what I had received in the mail.

After all, I wouldn't want any of the other counselors on staff to know that the "fair haired boy" was in possession of a State employment application. Because if they knew, well…, that would certainly get 'em talking around the water cooler.

CHAPTER SEVEN

I still haven't made that phone call to Joe yet. I seem to keep putting it off and putting it off. I really don't know how long I can stall Watson in telling him that I'm going to call Joe.

What if I have another panic attack when I pick up the phone!

Wait a minute, I know…, - maybe Dr. Stevens can help me out. I'm supposed to call him this week anyway. Perhaps he can give me some sound advice on what to do.

Why didn't I think about calling him in the first place?

I picked up the phone and dialed Dr. Stevens' number. The phone rang a couple of times, and then I heard his old familiar voice come over the line and say, "Good morning, Dr. Stevens."

"Good morning, Dr. Stevens…, this is Jack O'Leary. I hope I didn't catch you at an inopportune time, but I'm just following up on our phone conversation from last week."

"Why hello, Jack. It's so good to hear from you again, and so quickly, I might add. I'm glad to see that you're demonstrating some real initiative, and not out in the field dawdling."

I quietly chuckled to myself, as I listened to the animation in Dr. Stevens' voice. I wasn't at all surprised that he would be in his office. The man must spend anywhere between sixteen and twenty hours a day doing university business. Fortunately for his students he is never too far away from his telephone. He doesn't even have designated office hours. He simply has an open door policy of seeing students at their convenience.

Sure, I'm aware that some people may consider him to be a little flaky, and yes…, I've certainly heard a few risqué stories that I just as soon not repeat. But his altruism and his belief in the human spirit is what sets him apart from anyone else that I have ever known.

I'll admit that at times there does seems to be obvious hurt in his eyes, and pain that is firmly etched in his face, but it never seems to dissuade him.

Dr. Stevens sometimes reminds me of Pagliacci, smiling on the outside, but crying on the inside.

"So, Dr. Stevens…, I was curious as to what you wanted to speak to me about the other day."

"Well, I have an interesting proposition for you Jack."

"Oh, okay, well…, it sounds rather intriguing. So what is it?"

"Well, my dear boy…, I'm somewhat in a bind, and I was thinking that the time has come for you to sponsor an intern at WEALTH Industries. This person would be under your direct supervision. So, what say you lad…, are you game?"

"Wow! Do you really think that I'm up for the challenge Dr. Stevens? I mean… I wouldn't want to screw somebody up."

Dr. Stevens laughed heartily, and then summarily dismissed my reservations by saying, "Nonsense, my boy! You have a keen mind and you're very intuitive. Not to mention, but you're one of the brightest students that I have ever had the pleasure of teaching."

"Hey, you're not trying to butter me up now, are you Dr. Stevens?"

Dr. Stevens laughed once again, and then whimsically said, "Why, of course I am, my dear boy. But seriously Jack, just think it over. I know it's a lot to digest right now. Of course, there is the little matter of passing it by Mr. Watson first, but I'm sure he'll be quite agreeable. By the way, how are you and Bob Watson getting on?"

"Good, well…, we have our moments, but I have nothing but the utmost respect for him. I can't imagine there are any better agency director's than Mr. Watson."

"That's very perceptive of you Jack, and I completely concur. As far as I am concerned, Bob Watson is the cream of the crop, bar none. He and I have certainly had our differences over the years, but I wouldn't want anyone other than Bob Watson at the wheel."

"Well…, I've certainly learned a great deal under his tutelage." I remarked.

"Jack, I must say that it's very refreshing to hear one of my students lauding the praises of their supervisor. Regrettably, much of the feedback that I receive from students regarding their supervisors is quite negative. I would love to sit down and discuss your views sometime."

"Yeah, sure, that would be great Dr. Stevens."

"Excellent, my boy! By the way, I never did ask how you settled on choosing WEALTH from amongst all of your other job offers."

Before responding to Dr. Stevens' query, I quickly thought to myself, "Geez, if he only knew how many offers I actually had…, zero!" Lest we forget, but WEALTH was the only job offer on the table, and at the time I felt like Mr. Watson was doing me a big favor by hiring me!

"Jack, Jack, hello… are you there?" Stevens alarmingly called out.

"Yes, hi Dr. Stevens, I'm here, sorry.…, the phone slipped out of my hand." I said, and feeling guilty for concocting a white lie to Dr. Stevens.

Dr. Stevens then asked again, "So, my boy…, finish telling me how you decided on WEALTH Industries?"

So off the top of my head, I clumsily replied, "Well, um…, WEALTH has a great reputation, and uh…, I heard Mr. Watson speak at a symposium one time and thought that WEALTH would be a good fit for me in furthering my counseling skills."

Once again, I felt extremely guilty in conjuring up such an audacious cock and bull story to Dr. Stevens, but I just didn't have the courage to tell him the honest to goodness truth.

Dr. Stevens quickly responded, "Indeed, well…, you made a wise choice Jack. I know the salary is sparse there, but the experience you're gaining is absolutely priceless."

"Yes, well…, I'm very lucky Dr. Stevens."

"That's marvelous, Jack! Simply marvelous!" Dr. Stevens said, proudly.

Stevens continued by saying, "Okay, well…, just think it over and then talk to Bob Watson. If he's agreeable, and you're willing to take this supervisory role on, then give me a call and we can discuss the details over lunch, my treat."

"Okay, Dr. Stevens. And if I start screwing things up then I can call you, right?"

Dr. Stevens laughed once again, and supportively said, "Yes…, yes…, of course, my boy, that's my job, but I know it won't come to that."

"Um, well, okay. I'll speak with Mr. Watson and get his approval."

"Splendid, well…, it was good chatting with you, my boy. I'd really like to get a decision from you one way or another by the end of next week, so call me. Ta-ta, Jack!"

As I hung up the telephone, I was thinking that Dr. Stevens has a real knack for making you feel good about yourself. I was excited about the prospects of supervising an intern from the university. It made me feel like I just stepped up one more rung on my career ladder.

A career ladder, I might add…, that was a little shaky about ten months ago, but now seems to be on much firmer ground.

Suddenly, it occurred to me that I failed to secure Dr. Stevens' advice on calling Joe. Well, I guess I'm gonna have to figure this one out on my own after all.

It was about one-thirty in the afternoon, when Dolly buzzed me over the intercom and told me that I had a phone call on line one. Her voice sounded rather sad, as if she had been crying. I really wanted to say something to her, but I didn't want to pry or overstep my bounds. I then told Dolly that I was available to take the call, so she patched the call through to my office.

"Hello, this is Jack O'Leary, can I help you?"

"Hey kid, I heard you've been trying to get a hold of me. Sorry I wasn't able to take any of your phone calls. So how's it going?"

"Joe…, is that you?"

"Yeah, of course it's me, kid. So how the heck are ya?"

"Hey, I'm good Joe. So how are you doing?"

"Well, you know…, I have my good days and my bad days. Today is a good day, because I was able to eat breakfast with Sarah this morning without getting too tired or throwing up. So that's a good day, kid." Joe said, with labored enthusiasm.

"Hey, that's great Joe! So you heard I've been trying to get a hold of you, huh?"

"Why sure, Sarah told me that you've tried calling me several times, and so did the old penny pincher."

I chuckled at Joe's reference regarding Watson, and then replied, "Well, I didn't want you to think that I forgot about you Joe."

"Are you kidding me? I never thought that for a second!" Joe said, with a raised voice.

"Well, I knew we'd talk eventually…," Joe interrupted me, and excitedly said, "Sarah told me that you even stopped by the house too, but I was so out of it that she didn't have the heart to wake me up. I get real tired in the afternoon. Sorry you made a trip over here for nothing kid."

"Hey, don't worry about it. It was nice visiting with Sarah." I said, as the guilt was rising.

"Yeah, calling and visiting me the way you did, well…, that's what sets you apart from those other idiot counselors down at WEALTH. None of those bastards has even picked up the phone or dropped me a line to see how I'm doing, and they've known me a helluva lot longer than you have kid. I always knew they had a two-by-four shoved up their ass, but you, well…, you're different, and I really appreciate it kid."

"Thanks Joe…, but try to calm down. I don't want you having an angina attack, okay."

"Yeah…, okay…, you know how worked up I get kid." Joe said, gasping for air.

"So is there anything you need Joe?"

Joe replied, "Nah…, unless you can get a hold of a new heart for me kid."

I paused a moment, and then uttered, "Um….," I didn't know what to say. I was completely tongue-tied.

Joe piped up and said, "Kid, I'm only joking. Hey, when you get a chance Sarah and I would like you to stop by the house and visit with us, okay."

"Definitely Joe, you can count on it!"

"By the way…, where are we at with the transitional janitorial program that I was ready to start up before my illness?" Joe asked, and really struggling to finish his sentence.

"Well, the program is still on hold for the moment. Watson and I were just talking about it the other day. Watson thought maybe in a couple of weeks." I stated.

"Okay, good. So kid…, you probably heard that I'm not coming back to work, right?" Joe said, as he continued to fight for air.

"Yeah, I heard Joe." I replied, sadly.

"Listen kid, I don't have a lot of time left, so anytime you wanna come by the house and pick my brain about job placement then you're always welcome, okay."

"Okay, Joe. Thanks!"

"Hey kid, I've been giving it a lotta thought, and I think you should be the new job placement specialist." Joe said, as he sputtered into a coughing jag.

"Unh-uh, no way…, Joe. I'm not interested in being a full-time job placement specialist."

"Oh, c'mon…, kid! Watson already told me that he's planning on eliminating a counselor position, so that he can have a full-time placement specialist. I think you'd be the perfect man for the job! You're way better than any of those other idiot counselors that Watson has on his staff!"

"C'mon Joe, please settle down, I don't want you getting too worked up. You could spark an angina attack."

"Okay…, okay…, you're right. You know how fired up I get when I start talking about work kid." Joe said, wheezing and struggling to breathe.

In an effort to lighten the mood, I then humorously said, "So Joe, whatta ya saying…, that you want me to march right into Watson's office and tell him that I wanna be the next placement counselor?"

Joe quickly replied, "Yeah, that sounds about right. That's what I'd do if I were in your shoes kid. You're the logical choice. After all, I basically trained you to do the job, didn't I?"

"Well…, I can't argue with you there Joe."

"Jack, I think I'm gonna give Watson a call right now and recommend you for that job. In fact…," I interrupted Joe in midsentence and then frantically said, "Now just hold on Joe, you're getting too worked up about this, please don't call Watson. Watson is a very smart man, and I'm sure he'll make the right decision. Can you please do that for me, Joe?"

"But Jack, you're passing up a golden opportunity. You gotta make your own breaks in life." Joe said, and once again gasping for air.

"I know, but I really don't want you to call Watson on my behalf…, please Joe!"

At that point, the phone line went dead. I could tell that Joe was thoroughly disappointed by what I said to him, but he respected my wishes nonetheless.

Joe then gathered himself, and calmly said, "Okay, kid. I won't call Watson, but if he offers you the job then promise me that you'll at least consider it, alright."

"Okay Joe, I'll consider it."

Joe then tearfully said, "It's just that I don't want somebody screwing up my contacts and all of my job leads…, and what about my job bank! All of my hard work could go right down the drain in no time at all. You can appreciate that, right kid?"

"Hey Joe, I don't know who Watson has in mind for job placement, but I will personally guarantee that whomever he chooses, I will make sure that they don't screw it up…, I promise!"

"Thanks kid…, that really means a lot to me." Joe said, and starting to sound really fatigued.

"No problem, Joe."

"Listen kid, I'm getting a little tired now…, so I better let you go. Stay in touch…, and visit me when you can…, and give my regards to the boys…, out back." Joe said, as he was panting heavily, and barely able to finish his sentence due to his labored breathing.

"Sure Joe, it was real good talking to ya. Get some rest and I will definitely be in touch. Tell Sarah that I was asking for her, and I'll keep you both in my prayers. Good-bye, Joe."

"See ya, kid."

The minute I hung up the phone, I felt as if a thousand pounds had been lifted off of my shoulders.

Just then I saw Mr. Watson walk by my office door, and I quickly called out to him, "Mr. Watson, can I talk to you for a moment?"

Watson poked his head into my office, and then briskly said, "Yes…, what is it Jack?"

I excitedly replied, "Well, I just got off the phone with Joe Atkins!"

"Oh really…, so you got past your panic attack, eh?" Watson said, smiling.

"Yes, well, I don't know, maybe, anyway…, he actually called me!"

"Slow down, Jack. You remind me of a little kid on Christmas morning." Watson said, jokingly.

"Sorry sir, I guess I'm just a little wound up."

"Yes, I can see that. So is there anything new to report regarding Joe?" Watson asked, matter-of-factly.

"Well, let's see…, he basically told me that he has his good days and bad days, and that today was a good day, in terms of his health and spirits."

"Hmm…, well, I'm glad you spoke with him on a good day. I've witnessed some of his bad days, and trust me…, it's tough seeing him at those times."

"Yes, I'm sure it is sir." I quietly replied.

"So what else did Joe say?"

"Let's see, oh yeah…, he told me how much he appreciated all of the phone calls that I made to him, and the fact that I stopped by his house as well." I said, tongue and cheek.

"Oh really…, I was under the impression that you were having difficulty in that area." Watson answered, with a slight smirk.

"The truth is Mr. Watson, I wanna thank you and Sarah for telling Joe a few white lies on my behalf. That was very considerate of you both."

"Ah, well…, don't even give it a second thought Jack." Watson replied, modestly.

"Well, I'm quite indebted to both of you. Thank you, Mr. Watson!"

"Jack, Sarah and I may have technically told a few white lies on your behalf, but they really weren't lies. I know Joe is always in your thoughts, and has been since his illness."

"Yeah, you're right, Mr. Watson." I replied.

"Yes, well…, that's why I'm the boss Jack." Watson said, amusingly.

I smiled, and then quietly stated, "I think I'd like to give Sarah a call this week and thank her too."

"Well, that would be a very nice gesture. Sarah would like hearing from you. Joe talks about you quite often, and as I seem to recall he commonly refers to you as his young protégé."

"Really…?"

"That's right, you see Joe and Sarah never had any children, which is really too bad because I'm sure they would've made wonderful parents. Perhaps that's why Joe took such a shine to you. I think you were the son that he never had."

"Gee, Joe never mentioned to me about not having any children. I guess I just assumed he did. I'm surprised it never came up in any of our conversations."

"Well Jack, I'm sure it must've been an extremely painful subject for him to talk about, so try not to beat yourself up over it, okay."

"Yeah, okay. Thanks, Mr. Watson."

"Hey, don't mention it. Well, I'll see ya later…, I'm late for a meeting."

"Oh…, one more thing, Mr. Watson. I had a very intriguing telephone conversation with Dr. Stevens today. He was wondering if we would be interested in taking on an intern from the university. The intern would be under my direct supervision. He wanted me to discuss the matter with you, and then get back to him with our decision as soon as possible, you know…, ASAP."

Watson stared at me for a moment because he knew that I was busting his balls with my ASAP reference. He then cracked a wry smile, as he replied, "Hmm, well…, it sounds like it has some definite possibilities. Why don't you tell Dr. Stevens that we're interested, and ask him to forward you all of the pertinent information regarding forms to fill out…, etc."

"Great! I'll call Dr. Stevens today, and tell him it's a go!"

As Watson left my office, it then occurred to me that today I've had the opportunity to talk with three of the most influential men of my adult life. Well…, outside of my Dad of course.

Quite honestly, I can't think of three finer men then Dr. Stevens, Joe Atkins, and Bob Watson. The Lord has truly blessed me, and his divine plan has guided me to these three great men…, these "three wise men."

I grabbed a quick cup of coffee from the break room, and then beat it down to the contract floor so that I could convey Joe's warmest regards to Ralph, Terry, and Smitty.

Ralph, who misses Joe the most, was overjoyed in hearing the news about Joe, but I got the distinct impression that Ralph may have misinterpreted my heartfelt words into thinking that Joe was perhaps on the road to recovery, which we all know isn't the case.

So after updating the boys on Joe's condition, I decided to hang around the contract floor for a little while and talk with a few of the clients on my caseload.

It was quickly approaching three o'clock, and the clients were now getting ready to punch their time cards and call it a day.

As I glanced around the room, I noticed that Henry Josephson was nowhere to be found. Actually, I haven't seen Henry in a couple of days, and I wanted to see for myself if the meager paychecks that he has been earning over the last couple of weeks were warranted.

I then walked over to Ralph and inquired, "Hey Ralph, where's Henry Josephson? Is he on a bathroom break, or did he leave for the day?"

Ralph replied, "Gee, I haven't seen him today Jack, or yesterday for that matter. You probably should check with Dolly because she deals with the attendance and absences."

"Okay, thanks, Ralph."

I was somewhat perplexed as to why I wasn't notified by the psych center for Henry's apparent unscheduled absence. Perhaps it was nothing more than a simple oversight on their part, but at the same time I had this funny feeling inside of me that something wasn't quite right.

Well, I'm sure that Dolly can sort it all out for me when I talk with her.

As I walked toward the reception area, I saw Dolly reaching for her jacket and getting ready to leave for the day.

I then quickly asked, "Excuse me, Dolly. I know you're on your way out, but can you tell me why Henry Josephson hasn't been here for the last two days?"

Dolly replied, "Well, all I can tell you is that I received a phone call yesterday morning from a supervisor at the psych center saying that he wasn't going to be into work. I didn't think it was unusual, so I simply said, "okay," and hung up. I wasn't aware that he was absent today."

"Do you happen to remember if the person you spoke with on the phone yesterday was named Stella?"

"Stella, hmm…, come to think of it her name was Stella. Does that help you Jack?"

"Yeah, that helps. Thanks, Dolly. I'm sorry I detained you."

"That's okay…, good-night, Jack. I'll see ya tomorrow."

I hustled down to my office so that I could telephone the psych center. I've been calling the psych center so often these past few months that I had the number resigned to memory.

So after dialing the number, the operator connected me to Henry's living unit. A man answered the phone, and I hastily asked him if I could speak to Stella the ward charge. He then informed me that Stella wasn't available, and he wouldn't specify as to her whereabouts.

I then identified myself, and for what it was worth, I decided to ask him why Henry Josephson has been absent from WEALTH Industries for the past two days, which prompted him to say that he wasn't at liberty to divulge such information to me over the phone.

"Shit! I knew he'd say that…, damn psych center." I mumbled to myself.

The young man then said, "Perhaps Ms. Brown can help you. Do you know Ms. Brown?"

"Yes, I know Ms. Brown, please connect me." I replied, rather abruptly.

After a minute or so the young man came back on the line and courteously said, "I'm sorry, sir…, but Ms. Brown does not seem to be in her office. Would you like me to page her?"

"Yes…, thank you," I replied, in a rather snippy tone.

Another brief moment passed by, and then the young man came back on the line and said, "I'm sorry, sir…, but Ms. Brown doesn't seem to be answering her page either. Would you like to call back or perhaps leave a message?"

"Um…, can you please tell Ms. Brown to give Jack O'Leary a call at WEALTH Industries, she knows the number. Please tell her that it's of the utmost importance that we speak, and that it's in regards to Mr. Josephson."

"Okay, sir. I'll give her the message."

"Yeah…, thanks." I replied, in total disgust.

As I hung up the phone, I felt bad that I took all of my frustrations out on the young man like that. I know that he was only doing his job, but it's not easy dealing with the psych center.

Dealing with the psych center is like being sucked into a black hole, and then spiraling downward into complete nothingness.

"Where the hell is Henry Josephson," I muttered to myself.

The next day I arrived to work totally exhausted. I wound up tossing and turning all night and didn't get a wink of sleep, because my mind was consumed with thoughts of Henry.

A month ago, who would've thought I'd be worrying about Henry Josephson like this?

As I walked into the building, I thought I would call the psych center around eight o'clock because that's when Ms. Brown gets into work. Hopefully Ms. Brown can shed some light on the mysterious disappearance of Henry Josephson, and maybe set my mind at ease.

C.D. beat me into work today. Gee, maybe he couldn't sleep either. Perhaps he was dreaming about all that coffee he was going to consume today, and every day for that matter.

As I was unlocking my office door, I could hear C.D. down in the break room humming a catchy little tune. He had the water running full-bore, and as he rifled through the silverware drawer, the clattering noises that he was making sounded like a Caribbean calypso band.

So after stowing my belongings, I walked down to the break room and joined C.D. for a cup of coffee. I needed a cup of his high test, so that I could try to wake up and face the day.

When I entered the break room, I saw C.D. perusing the newspaper, as he patiently waited for the coffee to finish brewing.

I shuffled toward the coffeepot and mumbled, "Morning C.D., how's it going?"

"Good morning, sonny boy…, I'm doing swell. Say, you look a little tired this morning." He said, as he glanced up from his newspaper.

"Yeah, I'm really tired. Hey, is that coffee almost ready?" I asked, yawning.

"Almost, kid. So how come you're so tired? Were you and the little lady out till the wee hours of the morning last night?" C.D. asked, and then giggled like a schoolboy, as he ambled over to the coffeepot and poured two cups of coffee.

"Nah…, you'll only laugh if I tell you." I said, as I took a big gulp of his black gold.

"Oh yeah…, well try me kid!" C.D. exclaimed.

"Well, it's Henry Josephson. He hasn't been at work for the last two days, and I can't seem to get a hold of anyone over at the psych center to find out why."

"Josephson…, hey kid, listen, my worries about this place stop as soon as I walk out the front door at four o'clock, and I'll have you know that I sleep like a baby. Anyway, I didn't know that the "spaceman" was absent for the past two days. I'm sure there's a perfectly good explanation for it." C.D. said, as he chugged down his first cup of coffee.

As I listened to C.D. give his two cents worth regarding Henry Josephson, I was thinking to myself, "Hey C.D., how would you know what's going on around here? You spend virtually every minute of the day down here in the break room."

I then answered C.D. by saying, "Well, I left a message for the psych center to call me back, that is…, if they remember to take their medication," and we both laughed heartily.

C.D. sarcastically replied, "Yeah, you're right kid…, I hear they dispense medication over there like its penny candy," as we both continued to laugh.

It was now eight o'clock, and Ms. Brown should be waddling into her office right about now. I said "good-bye" to C.D., and then went down to my office to call the psych center.

When I dialed the number, the operator informed me that Ms. Brown was going to be out of the office all morning.

"Shit…," I mumbled to myself.

I then asked the operator to have Ms. Brown give me a call, and I made it a point to say that it was imperative that I speak with her as soon as possible.

The operator then robotically replied, "I'll see that she gets the message…, sir!"

By now, it was eleven o'clock and there was still no word from Ms. Brown. I was now beginning to think that it was time for me to pull Mr. Watson into the equation.

I ran down the hallway towards Mr. Watson's office, so that I could apprise him of the situation. I was praying that Watson wouldn't blow his stack, due to the fact that I waited so long to inform him of the three unaccounted absences of Henry Josephson.

When I knocked on Watson's door, he was working at his desk on the overhead accounts. He looked up and saw me standing in his doorway, and then pleasantly said, "Oh, hi, Jack. C'mon in…, what can I do for ya?"

"Well Mr. Watson, I'm a little troubled and I think I need your help."

"Oh really, well…, sit down and tell me all about it." Watson replied, as he took off his glasses and then gently leaned back into his sleek leather chair.

"Um, well…, I'm a little worried about Henry Josephson. He hasn't been here for the past two days, and from the looks of things maybe three…, because he's not here today either."

Suddenly, Watson's friendly disposition instantly vanished, and in an agitated tone of voice he shouted, "What do you mean that he hasn't been here for the past two days? You mean to tell me that we have lost funding on him for the last two days…, maybe three?"

"That's right, sir. I've been trying to ascertain his whereabouts since Tuesday, which is the last day he is accounted for on the books."

"This makes no sense Jack!"

"Yes, I agree. I've called the psych center several times to speak with someone in authority, but nobody seems to be around. I've even tried to get in touch with Ms. Brown on numerous occasions, but she's not returning any of my phone messages either."

"Well, believe you me…, we'll certainly get to the bottom of this dilemma that I assure you." Watson stated, with adamant conviction.

"I mean, what could it be? Ahhh…, he's probably sick with the flu. But then why don't they tell us, or at the very least make up some half-assed excuse." I bemoaned.

"No Jack, it's not the flu, something really stinks here. The psych center is like the "FBI." They don't like to divulge any information, and they're a little too security minded for my taste."

We both sat quietly for a moment, and then Watson perked up and decisively said, "You know what…, I'll bet Allan Farnsworth might know something. Call the psych center one more time, and if you don't get anywhere with them then call Farnsworth. He is definitely worth a call. He may very well be the linchpin in figuring out this little conundrum of ours."

"Wow! That's a great idea, Mr. Watson. I never thought about contacting Farnsworth. I'm starting to realize that there's a lot more to Allan Farnsworth than meets the eye."

"Yeah, I taught him well…, maybe too well." Watson said, and sounding like a loving father whose child went awry. Watson then said, "Okay, go make that call O'Leary."

"I'll get right on it, sir." I replied, and feeling a helluva lot better now that Watson was involved.

So after beating it down to my office, I punched in the number for the psych center and I asked the operator if I could speak with Ms. Brown.

Once again, Ms. Brown was still out of the office and could not be reached by phone or page. I then tried calling Stella the ward charge, but she was nowhere to be found either.

So given the fact that nothing was panning out at the psych center, my only recourse now was to give Allan Farnsworth a call over at OVR.

I dialed Farnsworth's number, and after several rings I heard his extremely irritating and smug voice come over the line and say, "Hello, Allan Farnsworth."

Wincing from the sound of his voice, I then said, "Hi Allan, this is Jack O'Leary."

"Oh..., hi, Jack. What can I do for ya?" He replied, with some hesitancy in his voice.

"Well, I need to talk to you about Henry Josephson."

"Okay..., but before we get into that, did you receive the State employment applications that I sent you in the mail?" He cunningly countered.

"Um, yeah..., I did. Thanks for sending them out to me so quickly, Al." I said, as I was forced to swallow my pride, and take a healthy bite of humble pie.

"So how can I help you with regards to Henry Josephson?" He inquired.

As I listened to the tone of his voice, I had the distinct impression that Farnsworth knew more than he was willing to let on. I then stated, "Well, for starters..., I was wondering if you knew why Henry has not been at work for the past couple of days."

"Yeah, right. So did Ms. Brown ask you to give me a call?" Farnsworth asked, rather suspiciously.

"No, why..., should she have?" I quickly countered.

"No..., no..., I was just wondering how much she might have told you with regards to Mr. Josephson, that's all."

"So Al..., is there something I should know about?"

"Um, well..., we seem to have a bit of a situation with Mr. Josephson." Farnsworth said, and sounding quite aloof.

"A situation, what exactly do you mean a situation. Is he ill, or under house arrest, or did he relapse into a catatonic stupor..., what?" I asked, in frustration.

"Well...," Farnsworth chuckled on the other end of the line, and then flippantly said, "If only that were the case, but apparently Mr. Josephson has absconded from the psych center."

"What..., you mean he's missing!"

"Apparently so. They have people out looking for him as we speak, such as Ms. Brown and that flaky ward charge Stella, as well as a modest detail of security officers. But so far they haven't been able to ascertain his whereabouts."

"So when were you going to notify us, Al?"

Farnsworth immediately fired back by saying, "Hey Jack, I'm sorry you were left out of the loop. It's a very sensitive situation. The psych center is extremely hush-hush when it comes to these kinds of matters. Their primary objective is to circle the wagons, and concentrate all of their efforts on damage control. They're not exactly forthcoming when it comes to divulging information to outside agencies."

"Okay, well…, you're an outside agency, and you seem to be up to speed on the situation." I stringently pointed out.

"Well, that's only because I've got a friend who works over there and he gave me the heads up." Farnsworth said, defensively.

"Uh-huh…, so does the news media or the police know yet?"

"I really don't know, possibly." Farnsworth answered, vaguely.

"So I thought he was on a highly secure unit, and closely supervised around the clock?" I asked, sharply.

"Hey Jack, I really don't wanna argue with you. We have a problem and we need to be working together to resolve it." Farnsworth said, as he tried to downplay the situation.

"Oh…, are we arguing, I thought we were having a conversation between two colleagues. Secure unit, my ass! Don't they have bed checks over there?" I shouted.

"I don't know, I guess so. They discovered he was missing Tuesday night." Farnsworth replied, and sounding exasperated.

"All right, well…, I guess what's done is done." I said, backpedaling.

Sure, at that point, I could have thrown Farnsworth under the bus, but I really didn't want to complicate the situation any further by antagonizing him and possibly pissing him off.

I'm not proud to admit it, but in the back of my mind I was thinking that Farnsworth was still my only real solid lead to future State employment hopes.

Yeah, I knew I was selling out, and yes…, severely compromising my integrity, but I was afraid of what might happen to me if I landed on the wrong side of the "Prince of Darkness."

Just then I saw Mr. Watson standing in the doorway. I motioned for him to come into my office so that I could bring him up to speed on my conversation with Farnsworth.

At that point, I placed the telephone receiver against my chest so that Farnsworth couldn't hear what I had to say to Watson. Needless to say, but Watson was appalled at what I conveyed to him, and he couldn't wait to get on the phone to speak with Farnsworth personally.

When I told Farnsworth that I was putting Watson on the line, you can only imagine his reaction, as he quietly mumbled, "oh brother," under his breath.

As I handed Watson the receiver, he decided to put the conversation on speakerphone, so that I could listen in on all of the gory details that were going to be discussed.

"Allan, hi…, Bob here."

"Morning Bob," Farnsworth nervously answered.

"Listen Allan, somebody dropped the ball on this Henry Josephson situation. I don't appreciate being left out of the loop by a couple of State agencies that are trying to cover their asses, especially when these same two State agencies pleaded with me to take this Josephson fella in the first place."

"Well Bob, you knew what you were getting yourself into when you signed on to accept Mr. Josephson into your program. You signed on for a shit-load of state and federal money."

"Now just hold on Allan, don't try to change the subject!" Watson bellowed.

"Bob, you're right…, and I'm sorry it all came down like this. It wasn't intentional. As I tried to convey to Jack, it was an oversight on my part and a breakdown in communication."

At that moment, I quietly chuckled to myself on how quickly Farnsworth changed his tune. Farnsworth knew that he was no match for Watson, and now he was trying to come across like some innocent bystander who was caught in the switches.

"Allan…, you of all people." Watson said, disappointingly.

"What Bob?" Farnsworth innocently blurted out.

"C'mon Allan…, you worked for me for over seven years, and I would've expected some sort of loyalty, or at the very least the common courtesy of a heads up phone call. Don't you trust us?"

"Sorry Bob, it won't happen again."

"Gee whiz, Allan! I can't believe you've kept us in the dark with this guy Josephson for the past three days! That really irks me to no end!"

"I know…, I know…," Farnsworth said, and sounding rather pathetic.

Watson continued his verbal onslaught by furiously saying, "Listen Allan, I've lost three days of funding because of this! I need every penny that I can get my hands on in order to keep this place afloat! You better find a way to dip into some sort of slush fund down there at OVR, so that you can settle my cash flow problems for the lost time on Josephson!"

"Don't worry, Bob. I'll make sure you get paid for the lost time on Josephson, I promise." Farnsworth said, in an effort to appease Watson.

I quickly thought to myself, "With the mere stroke of a pen, Farnsworth can do anything he wants in that job!"

"All right, now we're talking Allan." Watson said, in a much calmer tone of voice.

"Listen Bob, you have my personal guarantee that I will keep you abreast of any further developments with Josephson. Trust me, he will eventually surface and everything will be back to normal again, you'll see."

"Yeah, all right. Just make sure you keep us in the loop, okay. Good-bye, Allan."

"Bizarre," I said, as Watson hung up the phone.

"My, my, my..., Josephson has flown the coop, and they don't stand a prayer of finding the poor bastard." Watson stated, amusingly.

"What makes you say that Mr. Watson?"

"Why..., because they have Ms. Brown and a bunch of keystone cops out looking for the poor son-of-a-bitch, that's why. He couldn't be found even if he wanted to." Watson quipped, and we both lightly chuckled.

"Well, I just hope he's okay. I wonder how he's managed to elude the posse thus far. He's been missing for three days now, and Farnsworth didn't lead us to believe that they had any solid leads in finding him." I said, with grave concern.

"Yeah, you're right. It just doesn't add up Jack."

So after a brief moment, Watson continued by saying, "Jack, I wanna commend you on the outstanding job you did in getting to the bottom of this whole dilemma."

"Thanks, Mr. Watson. Although I probably should've involved you sooner, but I really thought I could resolve the situation on my own."

"Nonsense, you took calculated steps, and you were very decisive in your actions. Plus, OVR is reimbursing us anyway." Watson said, with a look of satisfaction on his face.

"Hey Mr. Watson, I gotta say that I really liked the way you gave it to Farnsworth on the phone. He's a little too arrogant for my taste, and I think he needs to be knocked off of his high horse every once in a while."

"You're right, although if memory serves me correctly, I think some people have said that about me on more than one occasion." Watson commented.

"Oh, well…, I wouldn't know anything about that sir." I said, with a sheepish grin.

"Is that right?" Watson replied, with a slight smirk.

Watson then headed back to his office, and I remained at my desk deep in thought, as I reflected on the day's events. Although we added a few more brush strokes to the canvass today, the true picture of what really happened to Henry Josephson was still quite baffling.

Either no one knows, or no one's talking.

The only plausible explanation is that Henry probably made a wrong turn at the stairway, and then aimlessly wandered out the front door of the psych center and just kept walking.

What really frightens me however is that Henry has no means and no direction, and he's certainly an easy target for being victimized by some unsavory characters out on the city streets.

But what astounds me even more is that no one has reported the sighting of a bizarre and pathetic looking little man wandering the streets of their neighborhood to the local authorities.

Let's face it…, Henry is not exactly inconspicuous, and he's definitely someone that sticks out like a sore thumb.

It's Monday morning, and instead of making a beeline down to the break room to discuss the scores and the highlights with C.D. over a hot cup of coffee, I decided to head straight over to Mr. Watson's office and see if he heard any news about Henry Josephson over the weekend.

Mr. Watson was on the telephone when I tapped on his office door, and upon seeing this I could feel my heart begin to race. I surmised that since Watson was on the telephone this early in the morning that perhaps he might have some late breaking news about Henry, but to my chagrin it wasn't the case at all. Mr. Watson was merely speaking with his wife Anna, who was simply reminding him to pick up a few assorted items at the grocery store on his way home tonight.

When Mr. Watson hung up the phone, he saw me standing in his doorway, and then simply said, "Sorry Jack, but I have no further news to tell you on Mr. Josephson."

Although disappointed, I was glad to hear that there was nothing catastrophic to report about Henry.

"So do you think we'll hear any news from Farnsworth today Mr. Watson?"

"I don't know Jack, I hope so." Watson said, as he was totally preoccupied in flipping through some papers on his desk.

"Yeah, me too…, but I still think that Farnsworth is holding back information. I guess deep down inside I wanna believe that Farnsworth has some shred of human decency. After all, he's in the business of helping people, right?"

"Well, not necessarily…," Watson said, as he glanced up from his work.

"What do you mean by that Mr. Watson?"

"Well, it's been my experience that not everyone in human services has good intentions. There are some people like Farnsworth that have their own personal agenda, and the quicker you figure that out than the better off you'll be."

"Okay, I see what you mean." I replied.

Watson continued, "Not everyone in this field belongs to the church choir. The vast majority do, but be advised that there are "snakes in the field," the field of human services that is…, and Allan Farnsworth may be the first snake that has slithered across your path thus far."

"So even you see Farnsworth as a snake, huh…, Mr. Watson?"

"Absolutely! Clinically speaking, Farnsworth is a narcissist, but in layman's terms, he's nothing but a snake who's only out for himself. I've encountered his kind many times slithering out in the fields. In time, you'll learn to walk among the snakes, and even side-step a few so that you don't get bit. But be advised…, you may need to arm yourself with a whip and a sturdy pair of steel tongs. Oh…, and don't forget to wear some high leather boots as well."

Hahaha! "Well…, thanks for providing me with all the cold blooded facts Mr. Watson!"

Watson chuckled in appreciation of my descriptive play on words, and then replied, "So anyway, how was your weekend? I hope you had a chance to relax."

"It was okay, but I seemed to be focused on worrying about Henry Josephson."

"Well, some cases will do that to ya, but you'll figure it out. Listen Jack, until we hear something more definitive about Mr. Josephson then you need to put him behind you, so that you can focus all of your energy on your caseload. Your clients are all counting on you Jack, so try not to sell them short because you're all wrapped up in worrying about Mr. Josephson."

"You're right…, thanks, Mr. Watson."

Watson continued, "I know the Bible talks about the shepherd leaving his flock so that he can find the one stray, but at the risk of sounding like an agnostic…, I'm more concerned about managing the day-to-day operations here at WEALTH than what the "Good Book" has to say."

"Right again, Mr. Watson..., I understand."

"Okay, well..., why don't you go grab some coffee and catch up with C.D. down in the break room. He's probably wondering where you are. I know how much his company means to you first thing in the morning, especially Monday mornings..., right." Watson said, smirking.

"Oh, you know about that, huh?"

"Jack..., I thought you knew?"

"Knew what?" I asked, innocently.

"That I know everything that goes on around here..., everything." Watson said, smiling.

I quietly nodded my head, and then replied, "Huh..., I'll keep that in mind Mr. Watson. See ya at the eight-thirty staff meeting."

The Monday morning staff meeting proved to be uneventful and consisted of the same old rhetoric. When the meeting concluded, I went straight down to my office to give Dr. Stevens a call so that I could tell him that Mr. Watson has approved the intern placement.

So after dialing the number, the call rang through and I heard the old familiar voice of Dr. Stevens eloquently say, "hello."

"Dr. Stevens, hi, it's Jack O'Leary. Sorry I didn't get back to you last week, but I've been in the middle of a situation here at work."

"A situation, well..., that sounds quite ominous Jack. You wouldn't be referring to the Henry Josephson situation, now would you?" Stevens inquired.

"Well, yeah...," I replied, and dumbfounded that he even knew about it in the first place.

"Yes, well..., we here at the university were quite saddened to hear that the poor man has disappeared. Are you the counselor of record Jack?"

"Well, yes..., but I was under the impression that it was a highly confidential matter, and that only a few people in the immediate circle were privy to the information."

"I see, well, my dear boy..., how do you know I'm not in the immediate circle?" Dr. Stevens said, in jest.

"Well..., because if you were then you wouldn't be talking about it. You have too much integrity for idle gossip." I replied, smartly.

"Touché, my boy! You know me quite well, and I'm ecstatic that you're adhering to the cannons of confidentiality. Bravo, Jack!"

"Thank you, Dr. Stevens. But to tell you the truth, the details regarding the disappearance are so sketchy that I'm not too worried about breaching any of the cannons of confidentiality."

We both then lightly chuckled.

"Well, my boy…, you're in the middle of a high profile case, and that can be very disconcerting."

"Yeah…, you're right, Dr. Stevens."

"Hmm…, do I detect some trepidation in your voice Jack?"

"Well, Mr. Watson has been very helpful, but I thought perhaps you could give me a different perspective on what my course of action should be."

"Ah…, a course of action, I thought you took that course as one of your core requirements here at the university." Stevens quipped, and we both light-heartedly chuckled.

"Nice pun, Dr. Stevens. But to be honest with you, I feel a little bit frustrated. I've tried calling the psych center repeatedly, but the two supervisors that I have been dealing with are never available. Consequently, with it being a highly secure unit, I can't seem to get a shred of information from anyone over there."

"Well, have you attempted to make your inquiries in person?" Stevens quietly asked.

"Um, well…, no. Mr. Watson has made it abundantly clear to me that it's not our problem at this juncture, and he doesn't want me sticking my nose where it does not belong."

"I see…, so what's the problem Jack? You seem to have resolved your dilemma. Or is there something else that's troubling you?"

"I don't know. I just think I should be doing more, that's all."

"I see, well…, getting an ulcer certainly won't help the poor fellow."

"Hey Dr. Stevens, what you and I are discussing is being held in the strictest of confidence, right?"

"Why, of course it is my boy. You and I have a teacher/student relationship, which I value to be very sacred." Stevens said, staunchly.

"Good, I'm only asking because I don't want you to think that I'm spilling my guts to everyone who makes inquires with regards to Mr. Josephson, that's all."

"Spilling your guts, my, my, your feelings are very deep-seated. For a minute there I thought you were teaching the teacher the tenets of confidentiality. A course, I might add…, that I've taught a few times over the years here at the university."

"Yeah, as a matter of fact, I took that course from you in my second semester."

"Indeed…, but try not to internalize everything Jack. This is your first serious incident since leaving graduate school. You're doing just fine, my boy. So just stay the course!"

"Thanks, Dr. Stevens. I'll keep that in mind."

"Now, if you'll permit me to change the subject. Do you have any news with regards to placing an intern at WEALTH Industries?" Dr. Stevens asked, with great anticipation.

"Well, yes…, Mr. Watson has approved the placement."

"Splendid! Great job, Jack! Well done!" Stevens exclaimed.

"Yeah, thanks. I must admit, I'm pretty excited too Dr. Stevens."

"So the intern that I am placing in your care is a young lady named Lenore Richards. Lenore is a lovely girl, and in my opinion…, quite a scholar." Stevens said, admiringly.

"Yeah, okay, but is she good looking and available?" I asked, playfully.

"Now, now, Jack…, what would your fiancée say about that?" Dr. Stevens quipped.

"What fiancée?" I replied.

Dr. Stevens paused a moment, and then humorously said, "Jack, I hope I won't be dealing with any sexual harassment allegations while Ms. Richards is in your care."

We both laughed heartily, and then I replied while still laughing, "I don't think you have anything to worry about in that regard Dr. Stevens."

"Yes, well…, in any event, Lenore will be a wonderful asset to WEALTH. She is personable, kind, and possesses exceptional counseling skills. I really think that the two of you have the makings for the perfect formula for success!"

"Well, I certainly look forward to the challenge Dr. Stevens."

"Let's see, today is Monday…, perhaps later this week you can come by my office and we can chat about Lenore. Afterwards, we can dine at the commissary, my treat of course." Dr. Stevens said, with his usual animated flare.

"Sounds like a plan, Dr. Stevens."

"Now be sure to call me this week, so that we can set up a time to meet. Oh, and one last thing Jack, Mr. Watson was right in what he was telling you with regards to Mr. Josephson."

"Watson was right? Right about what?"

"Well, he was right in telling you to leave the Josephson matter alone until further developments come to light." Stevens said, gently.

"Yeah…, I know Dr. Stevens." I quietly replied.

"Do you…? Jack, you need to focus all of your energy on your caseload, because the people on your caseload are depending on you." Stevens stated, in dramatic style.

"Wow, that's exactly what Mr. Watson said!"

"Yes, well…, don't be so hard on yourself, my boy. Focus on the things that you have control over, and let God worry about the rest."

"Thanks, Dr. Stevens. I think I needed to hear that."

"No thanks needed, my boy. I'll talk to you later in the week. You know where to find me, if you need a reflective ear. Ta-ta, Jack!" Stevens said, with his usual panache.

I decided to take the stellar advice of Mr. Watson and Dr. Stevens to heart. The people on my caseload do need me, and I'm re-dedicating myself to make a more concerted effort in dealing with the challenges that they present to me head on.

Well, Henry has been missing for almost two weeks now, and although there is no new news to report, I'm happy to say that I've been feeling a lot less anxious regarding the matter.

Hey, don't get me wrong, I'm still quite concerned for Henry's safety and well-being, but his mysterious disappearance is not totally consuming me like it was.

So that being said, I let my curiosity get the best of me the other day after the Monday morning staff meeting, when I asked Mr. Watson if he had anymore additional news on Henry.

Watson took a noticeably abrupt tone with me, as he curtly replied, "Jack, I have no further news to report on Mr. Josephson, and I wish you'd stop asking me about it all the time."

Mr. Watson then gathered up his papers and shoved them into his folder. Obviously he was perturbed about something, and I think it was more than me just asking him about Henry.

I then quietly said, "Actually, I seem to be doing much better regarding the Josephson matter, and I think a lot of it has to do with the conversation I had with

Dr. Stevens last week."

Watson glanced at his watch, and then hastily replied, "Oh really..., and what did the good doctor say to make you feel so much more at ease?"

"Well, nothing that you haven't already said. He simply echoed verbatim what you have been telling me all along."

Watson glanced at his watch again, and then impatiently asked, "What exactly are you driving at Jack?"

"Well, Dr. Stevens told me that I should be focusing all of my energy on the things that I have control over, like you've been telling me to do all along." I said, clumsily.

"I see..., so essentially you're complimenting me. Is that the gist of this conversation Jack?" Watson asked, rather abrasively.

"Well, yes..., that's what I'm attempting to do, but obviously I'm not doing a very good job of it." I replied, and feeling quite hurt by his rough edge.

Watson stared at me for a brief moment, and then sarcastically said, "Jack, did you need someone with a PhD to convince you that what I've been telling you to do all along was right?"

"No..., I'm just simply saying that things are much clearer to me now, that's all."

Watson hesitated a moment, and then took a more apologetic tone by saying, "Hey listen, I'm sorry, I'm not trying to give you a hard time. I didn't have a very good weekend. I don't wanna get into it right now, but maybe later we can talk."

"Okay, well..., sorry your weekend was so difficult. Sure, we can talk later. I'll see if I can pencil you in. I have an extremely tight schedule." I said, in an effort to lighten the mood.

Watson quietly chuckled in appreciation of my humorous comment. He then patted me on the back and headed directly toward his office.

Four o'clock, where did the day go. As I sat at my desk, my mind was consumed with thoughts of Mr. Watson. I kept wondering what threw him into such a tailspin over the weekend.

Well, since I was all caught up on my work, I thought I would go down to Mr. Watson's office and see if he was out of his doldrums.

Hey, I'm a trained counselor..., maybe I can say something that will make him feel better.

Yeah, I know it's a stretch, but perhaps the grasshopper can teach the sensei a thing or two.

When I tapped on Watson's door, he was diligently working at his desk, crunching the numbers of the overhead accounts. Watson was punching the keys of his desk calculator so fast that it looked as though sparks were flying everywhere.

As Mr. Watson glanced up from his desk, I casually said, "Hi, Mr. Watson. I had a few minutes, so I thought I would come by and assess your spirits."

"Oh, hi, Jack…, c'mon in. So you were actually able to squeeze me into your extremely tight schedule, eh?"

"Well, of course. But let's make it snappy, because I'm a very busy guy. So what are you working on over there?" I asked, as I slid into one of Watson's big cushiony leather chairs.

Watson replied, "Just give me another minute or two Jack, I'm almost done."

As I waited for Watson to finish up, I was certainly in no hurry. As I've stated before, sitting in Watson's office is like spending the day at the museum.

And then, at closing time…, when everyone has been ushered out of the front door, having one of the security guards you know grant you exclusive private access to a secret inner sanctum that is ordinarily closed to the general public.

Watson then put down his pencil, and casually said, "So…, what's up?"

"Oh nothing…, I just wanted to come by and check up on ya, and see if you were okay. This morning when we spoke you seemed awfully dejected."

"Yeah, well, I'm doing better. Once I get immersed in my work, it seems to thoroughly occupy my mind."

"Well, I don't know what's troubling you Mr. Watson, but if there's anything that I can do to ease your burden, then please don't hesitate to call on me."

"Thanks, I appreciate that Jack. It's Joe, he's not doing very well. I dropped by his house yesterday and paid him a visit. He's failing Jack, and although I've tried to accept it, well…, sometimes it gets the best of me."

"You're a great humanitarian, Mr. Watson." I said, boldly.

"No, not really…, I'm nothing special." Watson replied, modestly.

"Mr. Watson, I can't think of a better man to emulate my career after than you. It is a privilege and an honor to work for you."

"Thank you, Jack. However, I'm not quite sure if those are your exact sentiments when you're perusing the paltry dollar amount in your paycheck each week." Watson quipped.

I laughed heartily at Watson's witty remark, as I panned his office in absolute awe.

Watson then took a more serious tone by saying, "Ya know, Jack…, you're the only one on my staff whoever comes down to my office to check up on me."

"Really, well…, I just came by to see if you needed any help, that's all."

Watson smiled momentarily, and then humorously interjected, "Hey O'Leary, this sudden concern of yours…, you wouldn't be playing the sympathy card so that you can weasel more money out of me each week, now would ya?"

"Well…, the thought did cross my mind Mr. Watson."

Watson quietly snickered, and as he leaned back in his sleek leather chair, he amusingly commented, "You're pretty cagey, O'Leary. I may have grossly underestimated you."

I chuckled at Watson's humorous reply, and then inquisitively asked, "So besides Joe, does Sarah have any immediate family?"

"Well, yes…, she has me." Watson said, with utter surprise.

"Yeah, she has you…, you're a friend of the family, right?"

"No…, not as a friend of the family. Sarah is family, she's my sister."

"Holy cow! You mean to tell me that Joe is your brother-in-law?"

"Yeah, didn't you know that?"

"No…, now I see why this is so difficult for you."

"Exactly!" Watson said, sadly.

"Wow…, Joe is your brother-in-law! What about all those tongue lashings you've given him over the years? Didn't it bother you?"

"No…, not in the least," Watson emphatically said, as a slight grin adorned his face.

"Huh…, Joe is your brother-in-law," I quietly mumbled to myself.

"Actually, I'm heading over there now. Hey, would you like to follow me over in your car?" Watson asked, as he reached for his sports coat.

"Yeah, sure, I'd like that."

"Great, let me give Sarah a call. Hey, do me a favor, will ya. Can you go out back and make sure that all the lights are turned off?"

"Sure, Mr. Watson. And then I'll meet you out in the parking lot."

So after checking the back area of the building, I then shot out to the parking lot so that I could wait for Mr. Watson.

A few moments later, I saw Mr. Watson scurrying out the front door and heading toward his car. As Watson was approaching me, I suddenly realized what a dashing looking man he was.

Watson had a full-head of salt and pepper hair, which was never out of place…, and the custom-made suit that he was wearing accentuated his tall and slender physique. He had his car keys in one hand, while his beige overcoat was draped across his other outstretched arm.

As Watson continued to walk towards me, he had the look of a thoroughbred racehorse, gliding effortlessly through the air. He looked like something right out of a fashion magazine.

Watson then gestured for me to come over to his car.

As Watson was unlocking the driver's-side door, he casually said, "Jack, let's take my car, I just remembered that Joe and Sarah's house is a little out of your way. I have to come back this way to go home anyway, plus you'll be good company for me on the ride over."

"Sure, Mr. Watson." I replied.

I was ecstatic to be climbing into Watson's luxurious Lincoln Town Car. I have always admired his car in the parking lot, but I never dreamed I'd be a passenger in it someday.

So after fastening my seatbelt, I immediately inhaled the intoxicating aroma of leather upholstery, or as Dad would say, "new car smell."

Watson's car was equipped with a sun roof and power everything…, seats, windows, and locks. As opposed to my rundown jalopy, which had none of the aforementioned accessories.

Mr. Watson's radio had surround sound, with eight high-fidelity speakers strategically positioned in perfect symmetry. I felt like I was sitting in a symphony hall, because classical music is the only music that Mr. Watson enjoys listening to.

As Mr. Watson turned up the volume on his car stereo, he glanced at me and quietly said, "I hope you don't mind my taste in music? I find classical music to be soothing for the soul."

I smiled at Watson, and pleasantly said, "Classical music is great, I listen to it all the time."

Of course, I was lying. I would have preferred listening to some kick-ass rock'n roll, but I wasn't about to tell Watson that.

Watson looked at me in a rather surprised way, and then replied, "Really? I thought a young guy like you would be more inclined to listen to that rock and roll music."

I just smiled and nodded my head. I thought perhaps Watson was a mind-reader, and then followed up his rather astute remark by saying, "Actually, I like all varieties of music."

"Ah..., you're eclectic, eh." Watson shrewdly said, as he was pulling out of the WEALTH parking lot.

At that point, I opted not to say anything more about my taste in music. Instead I was praying that Watson wouldn't start quizzing me on my favorite classical composers or concertos, because if that had happened then I would've undoubtedly been in uncharted waters.

Beethoven and Mozart, well..., they all sounded the same to me!

My ineptitude for lying about classical music would surely come back to bite me in the ass if I didn't change the subject fast, so I was hoping that Watson would not further explore the not so deep waters of my classical music knowledge, and thankfully he didn't.

Every so often, I felt compelled to compliment Mr. Watson on how beautiful and luxurious his Lincoln Town Car was. Although my sentiments were genuine and heartfelt, I guess I felt a sense of obligation to overstate the obvious because Watson was my boss.

There was a momentary lull in the conversation, which then prompted me to say, "Mr. Watson, I didn't get a chance to tell you, but I'm getting together with Dr. Stevens tomorrow for lunch over at the university. He wants to discuss the intern placement with me."

Watson replied, "Good, it will be nice having another pair of hands around the place. I like to refer to it as "Sharing the WEALTH," if you catch my drift Jack."

"Ah, yes, well..., I believe you've used that clever little pun of yours before Mr. Watson. In fact, I'm sure you consider me to be a "WEALTHY" man for working here."

Watson replied, "Indeed, I do Jack. And the time you spend here will be a "WEALTH of experience" for you," prompting both of us to lightly chuckle.

Mr. Watson then asked, "So do you know anything about the intern that you'll be supervising?"

"Um, well, I know a few things about her....,"

Watson interrupted me in midsentence and commented, "ooh, her, great! It'll be nice to have a female counselor intern. Maybe she can teach all of you male counselors how to be more sensitive," prompting Watson to quietly snicker to himself.

I countered Watson's witty remark by saying, "Yes, I agree..., and perhaps she can even teach you a thing or two, Mr. Watson."

Watson then glanced in my direction and cracked a wry smile, as he amusingly retorted, "Well, perhaps she can. I pride myself on having an open mind."

"So anyway…, the intern is a young lady named Lenore Richards. Dr. Stevens says that she is very smart, "a scholar," I believe he termed it, and that she'll be graduating at the end of the semester." I said, as I ran my hand along the plush leather trim of the passenger-side door panel.

"Good, I like getting interns that are ready for graduation." Watson brashly replied.

I then amusingly interjected, "Yeah, then you can smooth-talk 'em into working for you at slave wages, just like the rest of us. Right, Mr. Watson."

Watson took his eye off the road for a split second, and replied, "Uh…, now that will be quite enough of that Jack, or else I'll be forced to fill your position with our budding new intern."

On that humorous note, we then pulled into Joe and Sarah's driveway.

At first glance, Joe and Sarah's home was very quaint. It was a small ranch style house, and it actually reminded me of an oil painting. It had a traditional white picket fence encircling the perimeter of the yard, with some well-manicured shrubbery, and an attached one-stall garage. The lawn was a brilliant shade of green and it looked to be well-cared for.

As we made our way up the front walkway, I could see Sarah in the house. She was in the kitchen darting from one place to the other, as she was busy preparing something for our visit.

We stepped up to the front door and Mr. Watson rang the doorbell. We could see Sarah making haste toward the entryway, as a radiant smile swept across her face to greet us.

As Sarah rushed for the door, her glide was similar to that of Mr. Watson's glide, which I had taken notice of not even ten minutes ago in the WEALTH parking lot. I guess it only stands to reason that their glides should be similar, after all…, they are brother and sister.

Sarah opened the front door and gave her "baby" brother a big hug. Sarah had beautiful blond hair and blue eyes and she was quite petite. She had on a pair of light blue slacks, a pastel blouse, and a cute frilly apron that she wore snugly around her meager waistline.

Mr. Watson then stepped aside and introduced me to Sarah, as he proudly said, "Sarah, I'd like you to meet Jack O'Leary, my young protégé."

Sarah then warmly said, "It's very nice to make your acquaintance, Jack. I've heard so many good things about you from Joe and Bob. I'm so glad we have finally gotten the chance to meet." Sarah then gave me an unexpected embrace.

"Thank you, Sarah. It's a pleasure to meet you too."

Sarah then eagerly said, "Well…, why don't you two boys c'mon into the house! I've got some homemade chicken noodle soup simmering on the stove!"

Watson began rubbing his hands together like a little kid, as he excitedly said, "Sounds good to me Sarge, I'm starving!"

Sarah turned toward the kitchen and we followed directly behind her. I then gave Watson a slight tug on his arm and whispered, "Did you just call your sister Sarge?"

Watson quietly replied, "yeah."

"So why do you call her Sarge?" I inquisitively asked.

Watson seemed a bit puzzled by my question, and then replied, "Can't you figure that out? She's my older sister, and as kids she loved ordering me around all the time, so I would accuse her of bossing me around like a sergeant. What can I say, it's a nickname that stuck."

I then commented, "Oh, okay. I thought maybe you called her Sarge because the first three letters of the name Sarah matches the first three letters in the name Sarge."

Watson sarcastically replied, "You gotta be kidding me, right? Sarge is simply short for sergeant, and there's no other explanation than that. Ya know Jack, if you ask me I think you're tapping into areas of the brain that we humans don't ordinarily use."

Mr. Watson smiled, patted me on the back, and then turned toward the kitchen as he resumed inhaling the intoxicating aroma of Sarah's homemade chicken noodle soup that was simmering away on the stove.

As we stepped into the kitchen, Watson nonchalantly draped his arm around my shoulder, which not only took me by surprise, but seemed totally out of character for him to do as well.

Watson wasn't the touchy-feely type like me, but maybe under different surroundings I was seeing a different side of him, and a side that I'm really not accustomed to seeing.

This was actually the first time that Watson and I have socialized with each other outside of the workplace. I was gaining a better appreciation for him. I was honored to be here today, but I was even more honored that he considered me to be his "young protégé."

When Sarah saw us enter the kitchen, she pleasantly smiled and then directed us where to sit down. The aroma in the kitchen was heavenly. Although the kitchen was small, the décor was homey and perfectly designed to a fault. The cupboards, the counters, and the lace curtains were all pristine and exact. The place settings on the kitchen table were exquisitely arranged, and it looked like something right out of a home and garden magazine.

Sarah ladled each of us a large bowl of chicken noodle soup, and to go along with our soup she had some mouthwatering tuna melt sandwiches that were grilling on top of the stove.

I marveled as she kept darting around the room making sure that everything was perfect for her guests, and what's more…, she seemed to find absolute joy in doting on us hand and foot.

When I glanced at Watson, he wasn't at all fazed by Sarah's attentiveness. I'm sure he's grown quite accustomed to this type of red carpet treatment every time he comes over to visit.

As I scanned the place settings that were laid out on the table, I noticed that there were only three settings and not four. Sarah informed us that Joe was lying down in the bedroom, and that he would not be joining us for supper.

Although I was disappointed that Joe would not be joining us, it didn't seem to prevent us from enjoying a nice meal, or preclude us from engaging in laughter and some pleasant repartee.

During the course of our conversation, I thanked Sarah for all the "white lies" that she told Joe on my behalf. Although she down-played her efforts, I could tell that she appreciated my words and sentiments nonetheless.

So after our tasty meal, Sarah put on a pot of coffee and insisted that we stay for dessert. She continued to be at our beck and call, and when we attempted to clear the table she told us not to because we were her guests and that she would clean up later.

Honestly, I really wasn't expecting all this fuss on the part of Sarah. If anything, we should have been serving her, but that would not have been Sarah's way.

Joe was truly a blessed man to have a wife like Sarah. She had beauty, charm, and an unbounding heart. What a magnificent blend to have in a wife!

When we finished dessert, we adjourned to the bedroom to check on Joe. Although I was a bit nervous to see him, I was hoping to at least catch a glimpse of him and maybe say "hello."

Sarah went over to Joe's side of the bed to see if he was sleeping. Sarah noticed that the slits of his eyes were slightly open and that he was beginning to stir. Sarah then bent down and whispered to Joe that Watson and I had stopped by to say "hi," and to see how he was feeling.

Joe quietly smiled, and then gestured for us to come over to his side of the bed.

Watson extended his hand for me to go first and so I did. Watson sensed that I was a bit nervous, so he gently put his hand on my shoulder to help guide me through the darkened room.

As Joe saw me approach his side of the bed, he groggily said, "Hey kid…, thanks for stopping by again to see me. How's it going?"

"Good Joe, real good…, everything is smooth." I replied, cheerfully.

Suddenly, I could hear Sarah quietly chuckling in the background when I made my colorful reply to Joe, because she knew that "smooth" was Joe's patented little expression.

Joe then said, "I'm a little tired today kid. I'm not much of a conversationalist right now. Maybe you could stop by again when I feel a little more spunky, okay."

"Sure, Joe." I replied, with my hand resting gently on his shoulder.

As I listened to Joe, his eyes were real heavy and his voice was trailing off considerably. He then fought to open his eyes again, but this time he directed his comments toward Watson, as he struggled to ask, "Bob…, do you have that placement counselor lined up yet?"

"Not yet, Joe. I'm still working on it, but don't worry…, I'll sort it all out this week. Right now you need to get some rest, and we'll talk about it later, okay."

"Yeah, okay, but call me if you have any questions. Just remember Bob, Jack would be perfect for the job." Joe said, in a struggling shallow voice.

"I'm sure he would Joe, but I need to weigh all of my options first before I make a decision. Don't worry, I'll keep you posted." Watson said, as he was fighting back the tears.

At that point, all I could think about was the movie "Brian's Song," in which Gale Sayers is telling Brian Piccolo, who was lying on his death bed with cancer, that everything was going to be okay. The love that those two men had for each other in the movie closely paralleled what was unfolding before me now, and I saw a side of Watson that I never thought possible…, and I was deeply moved.

As I stood there watching this tender moment, I began wondering if anyone else on the WEALTH staff had ever seen this side of Watson before. I then vowed to myself that there was absolutely nothing that I wouldn't do for Bob Watson…, nothing.

Sarah bent down to give Joe a kiss on the cheek, as she affectionately said, "Joe, my darling, I'm just going to show the boys out. Get some rest and I'll be in later, dear."

Tears were in Sarah's eyes as she turned toward us. Her eyes resembled reflecting pools of aquamarine water, as they radiantly glistened in the low lighting.

Sarah was careful not to let Joe see her tears. As she retreated into the shadows of the room, she took out a tissue from her hip pocket and then daintily wiped her watery eyes. Watson and I remained completely still, so that Joe could not detect the sadness in the room.

As Joe fell off to sleep, Sarah took a deep breath, smiled at us comfortingly, and then we all proceeded out of the bedroom. Sarah closed the bedroom door behind us, and then we all walked over to the front door in absolute silence.

Watson and I then grabbed our coats. As we said our "good-bye" to Sarah, we each gave her a tender embrace, and once again thanked her for her warm and gracious hospitality.

Although I felt compelled to do something for Sarah, Watson and I just walked out the front door and headed straight for the car without uttering a single word.

As we backed out of the driveway, Sarah was standing in the dimly lit doorway waving "good-bye" to us. Although she managed to smile, I could readily detect the heart wrenching sorrow and pain that was firmly etched on her face.

On the car ride back to WEALTH, Watson and I barely uttered a word to each other. There was no light-hearted banter or laughter, vis-à-vis our visit, or even any compunction on my part to give Watson any gratuitous compliments regarding his luxurious car.

When we reached WEALTH, Watson pulled up next to my car and quietly said, "Well, tonight meant a lot to me Jack. Thanks for making the effort."

"Well, thanks for inviting me to come along with you Mr. Watson. You and Sarah really helped me make it right with Joe, and I'll always be indebted to both of you for that. Thank you."

We shook hands and then I reverently said, "good-night."

When I arrived home, it was close to midnight and Mom and Dad were wondering where I was. I had failed to notify them that I was stopping by Joe's house with Mr. Watson after work.

As a rule, I generally let Mom and Dad know my plans, especially Mom…, so that she doesn't worry needlessly or wear down her rosary beads, as she prays for God to keep me safely in the "Palm of His Hand."

So after telling my parents the sad news about Joe, Mom suggested that we say a few prayers. When we were done praying, Mom said that she would offer up a novena for Joe this week along with lighting him a candle at weekday Mass tomorrow morning.

In addition to that, Mom also said that she would speak to Father Sullivan, the pastor of our parish, and ask him to have the congregation pray for Joe at Sunday Mass.

Well..., it looks like we have all of our bases covered. So I guess that means Joe is now "officially" in God's Hands.

Chapter Eight

"C'mon…, c'mon…," I mumbled to myself, as I waited for the traffic light to turn green.

Since starting at WEALTH I haven't been late for work, but I guess today my streak is officially over because Mom had to call me three times this morning to pry me out of bed. I think visiting Joe last night was so emotionally draining for me that it zapped me of all my energy.

Quite honestly, I wasn't planning on starting my day thirty minutes late today. I've got a million things to do, plus I'm scheduled to go over to the university later and meet up with Dr. Stevens for lunch, so that he and I can discuss plans for the intern placement.

Before tackling the laundry list of things that I needed to do this morning, my first order of business was to grab a cup of C.D.'s high test, so that I could try to wake up and face the day.

I grabbed my coffee mug off of my desk, and en route to the break room I was praying that C.D. hadn't drained the first pot dry yet.

As I proceeded down the hallway, I found it extremely odd that I couldn't detect the intoxicating aroma of coffee being brewed. I stepped into the break room, but to my surprise it was dark and empty, and there was no sign of life.

I quickly thought to myself, "Where the hell is C.D., and why isn't there any coffee made?"

Although I was half-asleep when I arrived to work this morning, I could've sworn that I saw C.D.'s car out in the parking lot.

Well…, maybe I was mistaken and Watson gave him the day off.

Anyway, I grabbed the coffee out of the cupboard, shoved a filter into the basket, and then decided to throw an extra scoop of coffee grounds in for good measure. I hit the switch on the coffee maker, and then began flipping through a magazine as I waited for the coffee to brew.

For a fleeting moment I felt as if I was a young C.D., as I lazily hung around the break room waiting for the coffee to brew, and the sheer thought of it caused me to laugh out loud.

When the coffee was finished brewing I poured myself a cup, and since C.D.

wasn't around to chew the fat with I decided to go back to my office and work on a few pending reports.

As I proceeded to exit the room, I stopped rather abruptly, so that I would avoid bumping into C.D., who at this point had just stormed into the break room with a big scowl on his face.

In the midst of avoiding a collision with C.D., I wound up spilling coffee all over my new trousers, and to make matters worse, C.D. didn't seem the least bit remorseful about the mishap nor did he have the common courtesy to apologize.

I immediately placed my coffee mug down on the counter, and then reached for the roll of paper towels to wipe the spilt coffee off of my new khakis. C.D., who seemed oblivious to my plight, went directly over to the coffeepot and poured himself a cup of coffee, and as he was adding his cream and sugar, he began mumbling a steamy string of expletives under his breath.

As I finished dabbing the remaining split coffee off of my trousers, I glanced at C.D., who was still pissing and moaning about something. Although I was somewhat miffed by what just happened, I decided to let the incident go and ask C.D. why he was so late this morning.

I then calmly said, "Morning C.D., where were ya? I thought you might've had the day off. How's the coffee this morning? Is it strong enough?"

"What, yeah…, it's fine. Hey kid, you didn't happen to make any "Irish" coffee this morning did ya, 'cause I could sure use a little extra "bite"?"

"Hey, that's pretty funny. So you're running late today too, huh…, C.D.?"

"I wish," C.D. snapped.

"Boy, I just couldn't get my ass out of bed this morning, and then I wound up hitting every red light coming in." I said, yawning.

"Oh yeah, well…, isn't that ducky. I've been here since seven o'clock. I guess that's the thanks I get for coming into work early. I'm sure Watson probably decided to dump on the first counselor that he saw this morning."

"C.D., why are you in such a bad mood this morning?"

"Well, I'll tell ya kid, I think I was in the wrong place at the wrong time. I no sooner pulled into the parking lot this morning, when all of a sudden Watson catches me directly in his crosshairs and summoned me into his office. And then when I asked him if I could at least grab a quick cup of coffee first, he screamed, "No…, the coffee can wait!" Do you believe the nerve of that guy?" C.D. remarked, as he once again mumbled a string of fiery expletives under his breath, while pouring his second cup of coffee.

"Is everything okay? Hey, it's not Joe, is it?" I asked alarmingly.

"What, Joe, who, Joe Atkins? No, but funny you mention Atkins, because guess who the next job placement counselor is gonna be?"

"You! Watson picked…, you?" I replied.

"Yeah, thanks a lot for being late today kid!"

"Wow! Well, who's gonna do your job?" I asked, even though I really didn't know what C.D. did around here, except drink gobs of coffee all day long.

"I don't know…, I guess Watson will just have to look into his crystal ball ASAP to figure that one out." C.D. snarled.

It was quite apparent to me that C.D. was not enthralled with his new work assignment, because C.D. has grown quite accustomed to sitting in the break room all day doing nothing.

C.D. was not happy with the prospects of having new expectations placed upon him, and that he might actually have to do something constructive around here besides make the coffee.

And worse yet…, be more accountable to Watson!

Although I felt bad for C.D., I found it quite humorous listening to him bellyache about his new work assignment, and it took every fiber in my being not to burst out into laughter.

"Well C.D., if there's anything that I can do to help you out in your new work assignment then just let me know, okay." I said, reassuringly.

C.D. ambled over to the coffeepot and poured himself another cup of coffee, and then flippantly replied, "Thanks kid, I'll keep that in mind. I know you spent a lot of time with Atkins, and there may be a time or two that I need your help."

I patted C.D. on the back, and encouragingly said, "Anytime C.D., just hang in there."

As I exited the break room, I could hear C.D. once again mumbling a string of profanities under his breath, while slamming a few of the utensil drawers out of sheer frustration.

Actually, I was thinking that C.D.'s predicament was some sort of poetic justice. He's so accustomed to sliding by and having things essentially fall his way, but now he'll be forced to start earning that meager paycheck that Watson begrudgingly doles out to him each week.

As the morning dragged on, I could hear C.D. taking up shop outside the break room, as he vehemently complained about his new work assignment to whomever would listen.

Occasionally, I would stop working at my desk so that I could hear him tell every passerby his tale of woe. I was praying that Mr. Watson wouldn't catch wind of all the hot air that C.D. was spewing because it could potentially turn ugly.

Hey, I really like C.D., and I'll do everything in my power to help him out. But at the same time he has to help himself, and ultimately realize that it's Watson's way or the highway.

As I resumed working at my desk, I couldn't seem to focus on what I was doing. It then occurred to me that I only had one cup of coffee this morning instead of my usual two cups.

Boy, I really wanted a second cup of coffee, but I didn't want to run the risk of bumping into C.D. again. If I go back down to that break room, he will surely corner me and start up with his incessant bellyaching again, and I really wasn't up for round two in listening to him whinge and whine about his new assignment. So I guess I'll just have to lay low, and wait until the coast is clear down in the break room to get that second cup of coffee.

Well, it's been almost an hour since I left C.D. in the break room, so the coast should be clear by now. I grabbed my coffee mug off of the desk, and then slowly made my way down the hallway toward the break room.

In a humorous sort of way, I felt like I was conducting some sort of covert operation, because I decided to inconspicuously cradle my coffee mug in the palm of my hand and then tuck it behind my back. I did this in the event that I saw C.D., because if he saw a coffee mug in my hand then he would surely usher me back into the break room again and continue to rehash the misery of his new assignment.

"Yikes," I said to myself, as I walked past the break room.

C.D. was sitting at the break room table reading the newspaper. I should've realized that he'd still be in there. Other than the bathroom, the break room is the only place that I ever see him around here.

Well…, I probably won't be having a second cup of coffee anytime soon!

As I turned to make my getaway, I saw Mr. Watson up the hallway and he motioned for me to come down to his office. As I walked into Mr. Watson's office, he closed the door behind me and then pleasantly said, "Good morning, Jack. So did you sleep well?"

I replied, "Actually…, too well. I was thirty minutes late for work this morning, although I don't know if I should be telling you that or not."

Watson just smiled, and then casually said, "No…, no…, I appreciate your candor, and I'll be sure to make a mental note of your tardiness so that I can dock your pay. Thanks, Jack!"

I chuckled at Watson's witty remark, and then replied, "Hey listen, thanks again for last night. You and Sarah really made me feel at home, and I'm glad I got the chance to see Joe."

"Yeah, last night was nice. But there's really no need for you to thank me. I enjoyed it immensely myself, and Sarah appreciated us stopping by too."

"Well, that's good. So I hear we have a new placement counselor. C.D. told me the big news this morning down in the break room. He didn't appear to be too happy about it, and he wound up having a bit of a meltdown in the process."

Watson replied, "Yeah, well…, I know he's not a happy camper, and I also know that he's no Joe Atkins either, but then again…, who is?"

"Well, no one at this agency, that's for sure, or any other agency for that matter. I tried being supportive to C.D. this morning, but there was just no talking to him."

"I know…, I've already heard his less than favorable opinion on the matter." Watson said, as he gently leaned back in his sleek leather chair.

There was a momentary pause, and then Watson interjected, "Jack, I just don't think that C.D. can do anything constructive around here other than making the coffee."

"Well…, he does make exceptionally good coffee." I humorously replied.

"Very funny…, but what really concerns me is how am I going to break the news to Joe. When Joe hears that I've selected C.D. to head up job placement, well…, I'm afraid it will do him in. I seem to remember Joe wanting young Jack O'Leary to take over the reins of job placement." Watson light-heartedly stated.

"Yeah, I seem to vaguely remember hearing that too." I said, chuckling.

"Actually, I did consider it, but it wouldn't be practical."

"Really…, you actually considered me?"

"Sure, why not. I mean with all the time you logged out in the field with Joe, you probably learned a thing or two about job placement. That, or else you learned where every donut shop and fast food restaurant was in town." Watson said, and we both laughed.

"Well…, most of 'em, anyway." I replied, still chuckling.

Watson continued by saying, "I've directed C.D. to get job placement up and running immediately. It's been sputtering since Joe left. No offense…, to you or the other counselors."

"Hey, none taken…, and you're absolutely right." I answered.

"I've been telling Joe that everything is copasetic, when in actuality…, it's not. Now that we have designated someone to head up the program, I'm hoping that things will get back to normal again." Watson stated, with conviction.

"Well, I think it will all come together." I said, agreeably.

"Yeah, well, I hope so. But let's not forget…, we've got C.D. heading up the program. I'll be sending out a memo this week outlining the new appointment of C.D. to job placement along with the new client distribution list from C.D.'s caseload to the rest of the counseling staff."

"Hey, the counselors all have seventy clients on their caseload now, so what's another ten or twenty to be responsible for, right?" I humorously quipped.

Watson flashed me one of his patented sarcastic stares, and then jokingly remarked, "Uh…, now that will be quite enough of that. There will be no dissention in the ranks O'Leary."

"Yeah, I know…, just playing devil's advocate Mr. Watson. After all, labor needs to shake management's cage every once in a while, right." Prompting both of us to quietly chuckle.

"So what's on your agenda for today O'Leary?" Watson asked, as he opened up his accounts ledger book.

"Well, I thought I'd spend a little bit of time down on the contract floor this morning. Procurement just received a new job."

"Yes, I'm aware." Watson nonchalantly replied, as he perused his work.

"Well, I thought that while I'm down on the contract floor I would see how the new job is done, and then try my hand at it." I stated with confidence.

Watson looked up from his work, and then amusingly said, "Uh…, no offense Jack, but I hear you have some major challenges when it comes to working on anything mechanical, which is what most of the jobs entail down on the contract floor."

"Oh, is that right." I replied, brashly.

"Hey, the way I hear it, your mechanical abilities are not quite up to snuff. Maybe you should just stick to what you do best, which is counseling. You wouldn't want to discourage our clients, would ya? You might wind up shaking their confidence." Watson said, and then he burst out into uncontrollable laughter.

"Now was that really necessary…, to point out my shortcomings like that?"

Watson paused a moment, and then exuberantly shouted, "Yes, I think so." Watson then began to laugh even harder, and I joined in on the laughter as well.

As I got up from Watson's big cushiony leather chair, I casually said, "Well, on that note, I think I'll go down to the break room and see if the coast is clear, so that I can grab a second cup of coffee. Oh, don't forget…, I'm heading over to the university later to meet with Dr. Stevens."

"What, yeah…, I remember. Hey, let me know how you make out over there. Oh…, and give my regards to the old guy, will ya." Watson said, as he was busy scanning his ledger book.

"The old guy…, you mean Dr. Stevens, don't ya. I'll tell him you were asking for him."

Watson looked up, and then contritely replied, "Oh yeah, right…, I meant, Dr. Stevens."

When I left Watson's office, I peeked into the break room only to discover that it was a good news bad news scenario. The good news being that C.D. had vacated the premises, but the bad news was that the coffeepot was as dry as a bone.

Once again, someone had violated the "golden rule" of the break room!

I was beginning to wonder if it was the same person neglecting the sanctity of the "golden rule," or was it a conspiracy.

Well, it was like "déjà vu" all over again, as I dragged out all the fixings to make a fresh pot of coffee. It wasn't so much making the coffee that concerned me, but the time required for it to brew. I didn't want to run the risk of bumping into C.D. again.

As I waited for the coffee to brew, I was thinking that the break room wasn't exactly the safest place in the world for me to be avoiding C.D., especially since the break room was essentially "home base" for C.D., and he should really consider moving his desk in here.

So when the coffee finally brewed, I hastily poured my long awaited second cup, and as I turned to make my getaway, who should I see standing directly behind me but none other than C.D., with his trusty coffee cup in hand and a grimaced look on his face.

C.D. then said, "Jack, sit down and talk to me. You ran off so quickly earlier that I didn't get a chance to tell ya about my meeting with Watson. You wanna hear all about it, don't ya?"

I replied, "Of course…, sorry about earlier, but I had to make a quick phone call to OVR."

Obviously, I was lying to C.D., but what other choice did I have.

C.D. took a big slug of coffee, looked me straight in the eye, and then said, "Jack, I've been thinking, I may need your help in getting the ball rolling on this new assignment after all."

"Sure C.D., whatever you need." I replied.

C.D. then said, "You were like Atkins sidekick, and I'm sure he told you things about job placement that he would never dream of sharing with any of the rest of the counselors."

"Well C.D., I don't know about that." I answered.

"As a matter of fact, I'm sure Atkins probably told you a few juicy stories about me and the rest of the sorry staff that works here too, right?" C.D. said, smirking.

"Ah…, c'mon C.D., you're exaggerating."

Once again, I was forced to stretch the truth, because many of the stories that Joe conveyed to me about C.D. and the rest of the counselors on staff weren't exactly too flattering.

"So kid, since Atkins isn't around you're probably the only one in this whole goddam place who can figure out that damn job bank of his, right?"

"What do you mean figure out?" I asked.

"I mean the damn thing is all written in code, like it's the CIA! Does Atkins really think that anyone around here gives a shit about his sacred job bank? Huh…, I know I don't!"

"Gee C.D., I don't think the job bank is written in code. Joe may have used some abbreviations for his own personal cataloguing, but I don't think it was done with the explicit intent of preventing someone from tampering with it."

"Listen kid, I've known Atkins a helluva lot longer than you have, and I'm telling you that his damn job bank is written in some kinda cockamamie code and I'm gonna need your help in breaking it!"

"Well, like I said C.D., whatever you need. I'm a little booked up today, but tomorrow we can attempt to decipher the cryptic inferences of Joe's job bank."

Upon hearing my whimsical reply, C.D. had a very perplexed look on his face, as he scratched his head and wondered what the hell I was babbling on about.

C.D. paused a moment, and then in a desperate tone of voice he said, "Kid, you're the only one around here that I can trust. The other counselors on staff can't make any sense out of that blasted job bank either, and even if they could they wouldn't help me out one iota. I'm in a real tight spot here kid, and I'm really counting on your help."

"Hey C.D., don't worry. We'll work it out, you'll see. I know my way around Joe's job bank pretty well, and I know exactly how he indexed everything."

"Okay, thanks kid, tomorrow…, right?"

So after chatting with C.D., I decided to head down to the contract floor. Even though I was trying to avoid C.D. like the plague this morning, I'm really glad we had a chance to talk.

I'm hoping that my reassurances will help C.D. turn the corner with respect to his new assignment, and give him the confidence he needs to succeed.

In addition to that, I'm sure Mr. Watson would've been proud of the way that I handled the situation too, and that helping C.D. out will be one less thing that Watson has to worry about.

While I was making the rounds on the contract floor, I touched base with several of the clients that were targeted for the transitional janitorial program. I told them that they would be starting their new cleaning job next week, and of course they were quite elated to say the least.

When the clients heard that C.D. would be overseeing the janitorial program, well…, their cheers turned to jeers.

Even the clients knew how incompetent C.D. was!

At that point, the clients started moaning and groaning and taking all sorts of pot shots at C.D., and asking me why I wasn't heading up the program instead. I tried to be very diplomatic with their concerns, and did my best to reassure them that things were going to work out fine.

I must admit that some of the off-color comments that the clients were saying about C.D. were pretty damn funny, and although I may have taken a few extra liberties in permitting them to say more than they should have, well…, their comments were just too hilarious to resist.

The university was only about a ten minute drive from WEALTH. As I drove down the main artery of the campus, I felt like I was a student again. The street was dotted with old stately looking brick architecture, which housed the various "Schools of Knowledge."

I smiled when I drove by the old fraternity house, and seeing the "old girl" again certainly brought back some fond memories…, and memories that are better kept untold.

When I pulled into the parking lot, I saw Dr. Stevens' little sports car nestled in its' usual spot. The designated parking space had a sign that read, Dr. James Stevens, Professor and Student Advisor of Rehabilitation Counseling.

It was a distinction that he was quite proud of and had deservedly earned!

I walked up a small flight of steps that led into the building, and then three doors down on the left was Dr. Stevens' office. As I approached his office, the door was ajar. I lightly knocked, and as I glided through the door, I casually uttered, "hello."

When Dr. Stevens saw me enter the room, he promptly stood up. As I walked toward him with my hand extended, I noticed a young lady out of the corner of my eye that was sitting in a chair off to the side of the room.

Dr. Stevens was beaming, as he shook my hand and exuberantly greeted me by saying, "Why hello, Jack. It's so good to see you again, my boy!"

"The pleasure is all mine Dr. Stevens."

Dr. Stevens then turned in the direction of the young lady, and proudly said, "Jack, permit me to introduce Lenore Richards. Lenore is the student that I spoke to you about."

Ms. Richards then stood up, and her presence was nothing short of breathtaking. She was an extremely attractive young woman, and she seemed to possess a look of radiance about her.

At the risk of sounding dramatic, but if I didn't already have a fiancée I think it might have been love at first sight.

She then walked toward me, and as we shook hands she eloquently said, "It's a pleasure to finally meet you, Mr. O'Leary. Dr. Stevens has told me so many good things about you."

"Likewise, Ms. Richards. Dr. Stevens has spoken quite highly of you as well, although I must confess that I didn't expect to meet with you today."

Dr. Stevens then jumped into the conversation, and spiritedly said, "Yes, well Jack…, sorry for the sneak attack, but I thought it might be a good idea to get the ball rolling. Lenore is slightly behind in her contact hours for the semester. I thought if we met today we might be able to jump start the process, and give Lenore the opportunity to begin her training at WEALTH by Friday. Well…, that's only if it's convenient for you that is."

"Um, sure. So, shall we get to know each other a little better Ms. Richards?" I asked.

We all sat down and Dr. Stevens facilitated the meeting. It didn't take long for a lively conversation to ensue, and there was much give and take amongst us. Dr. Stevens then handed me a folder, which outlined all of the goals and objectives of the program, along with some evaluation forms that needed to be filled out periodically throughout the internship.

Ms. Richards then told me a little bit about herself, such as her background, her goals, her interests, and most importantly…, her reasons for entering the counseling field in the first place.

As I continued to listen to Ms. Richards, I was acquiring a good sense for who she was as a person, and I was beginning to understand why Dr. Stevens was so impressed with her.

When the meeting finally concluded, we all felt pretty good about what was discussed.

Dr. Stevens then whimsically said, in his light-hearted southern drawl, "Well..., I don't know 'bout you two young folks, but I'm famished. What say we mosey over to the commissary and have us a little bite to eat, and just remember..., it's my treat!"

We all took a leisurely stroll over to the commissary. Not only did we enjoy a tasty meal, but Dr. Stevens entertained us with a few amusing tales from his thirty years in the classroom.

When I glanced at my watch, I couldn't believe how quickly the afternoon had slipped away. Despite all of the enjoyment I was having, I really needed to get back to WEALTH.

As I was saying my "good-byes," I gave Ms. Richards WEALTH's telephone number in the event that she needed to get a hold of me before Friday, and then she reciprocated by giving me her home telephone number in the event that I needed to contact her.

Dr. Stevens was quite pleased with how the day turned out, and as I headed toward my car, he capriciously called out, "Tutaloo, Jack. Thanks again for coming to our rescue, my boy!"

As I was driving back to WEALTH, I was thinking of all the different catch phrases that one could use in describing WEALTH Industries for the first time. Phrases such as, a "WEALTH of knowledge," or "sharing the WEALTH," or even simply..., a "WEALTHY experience."

These witty little snippets that I was creatively conjuring up in my mind could be useful in serving as an effective ice breaker for Lenore Richard's orientation on Friday.

Then again..., maybe I'm trying too hard to impress her, and if I were really smart then I should probably leave the clever stuff up to Mr. Watson, because he has had thirty years of experience to hone his creative juices.

When I arrived back to WEALTH, the first thing I saw was C.D. bellyaching to several of the staff outside of the break room. I was disappointed to see C.D. engaging in such juvenile behavior because I thought that C.D. had gotten all of that venom out of his system this morning when he and I had our little heart-to-heart talk, but apparently I was mistaken.

So given the fact that C.D. was still on a roll, I didn't want to come within a country mile of him right now. I then decided to slip past the break room and duck into the reception area, so that I could check my mail slot.

Dolly saw that I was back from my meeting at the university, and as she handed me my phone messages, she also informed me that Mr. Watson wanted to see me, ASAP.

As I flipped through my telephone messages, I saw that one of the messages was from Allan Farnsworth. I was a bit puzzled as to why Farnsworth would be calling me. I can't say that it was unusual because I did have several of his clients on my caseload, but they were all low maintenance clients, and they were nothing like Michael Wallace or the notorious Sampson's.

Why was Farnsworth calling me?

I'm always quite suspicious when I get a phone call from Allan Farnsworth.

Then again…, maybe the message had something to do with Henry Josephson.

Anyway, my curiosity was piqued, so I picked up the phone and dialed Farnsworth's number. The minute I heard, "Good afternoon, Allan Farnsworth…," my whole body cringed.

At that point, I managed to find the intestinal fortitude to say, "Al, hi…, it's Jack O'Leary. I'm just returning your call from earlier."

"Jack, hi, how's it going? It's really good to hear from ya. It's been a while since we last chatted." Farnsworth replied, like a coiled snake getting ready to strike.

"Yeah, I know. So what can I do for you, Al?"

"Oh nothing…, I'm just keeping you updated on Henry Josephson's case, that's all."

"Are there any new developments?" I asked, eagerly.

"No, no news…, but I told Bob that I would keep you in the loop."

"Okay, well…, no news is good news, I guess." I replied, in a deflated tone.

"Jack, don't worry, I've had these types of cases before, and they usually turn out just fine. Oh, by the way…, I sent you several job vacancy announcements that periodically come across my desk. I thought you might find them interesting, and maybe one or two may even catch your eye. Okay, well, give my regards to Watson, bye."

"Okay, thanks for the update…, and the vacancy announcements too, bye."

It was almost quitting time. Before heading out for the day, I thought I would go down to Watson's office and find out what he wanted to see me about. I lightly knocked on his door, and then quietly asked, "Excuse me, Mr. Watson…, but you wanted to see me?"

"Hi Jack, c'mon in. Hey, it could've kept till morning. I just wanted to know how you made out over at the university with old what's his name, oh yeah…, Dr. Stevens." Watson quipped, as he smiled and then eagerly waited for my reaction.

"Well…, old what's his name sends you his warmest regards, and as far as the new intern goes, I think you'll be quite pleased with Lenore."

Watson replied, "Lenore…, so you're already on a first name basis with the young lady. I'll bet she's very attractive, am I right?"

"Well, yeah…, but she's also very smart and quite personable too." I said, backpedaling.

"Yes, I'm sure she is…, but I'm sensing that you might be a little infatuated with her too, am I right?"

"No, not at all…," I said, defensively.

"Jack, don't worry, your secret is safe with me. Well, for a price…, of course." Watson stated, with a sly grin.

At that point, I was completely tongue-tied by Watson's unexpected yet rather astute comment, and I must admit that he really seemed to get my goat.

Watson then eased up on me a bit by saying, "I really had you going there, didn't I? So were you expecting to meet with the young lady today?"

"Actually no…, I was quite surprised to see her there. Dr. Stevens indicated that he's very anxious for her to start the internship as soon as possible. That's ASAP…, if you catch my drift."

Watson knew that I was busting his balls with my ASAP comment, but he never flinched, as he simply replied, "ASAP, yes…, well put, and I would have to concur with the good doctor."

I quietly chuckled in appreciation of Watson's gamesmanship in not taking the bait.

Watson then casually asked, "So when is the young lady slated to start with us?"

"Um, Friday…, if that's okay with you."

"Sure, Friday works for me, although I thought you said, ASAP. Friday is not exactly ASAP in my book, but I guess I'll be flexible as usual. Right, Jack?"

"Right! So did I miss anything interesting while I was gone?" I casually asked.

"Not really…, although I did hear through the grapevine that a certain young counselor will be involved in some sort of espionage mission in "breaking the cryptic code" of a certain job bank." Watson said, smirking.

"Oh…, you heard about that, huh."

Watson quietly replied, "I have my sources. So it sounds like C.D. isn't smart enough to figure out Joe's job bank, huh. My guess is that he probably wasn't breast fed as a baby."

I laughed at Watson's sarcastic remark, and then inquisitively asked, "So tell me Mr. Watson, was C.D. ever a good employee?"

"No, well…, let's just say that he's always been able to stay one step ahead of the law. I've been putting up with his shenanigans for over twenty-five years, but for some reason I still manage to keep him on."

I then stated, "What's really ironic is that C.D. actually thinks that he's doing you a big favor by working here."

Watson commented, "Well, that's because C.D. has a warped perception. I like C.D., but he's just not very reliable. Well…, except for making the coffee of course."

I replied, "Yeah, I like C.D. too, but I wouldn't wanna be stuck in a fox-hole with him."

Watson chuckled, and then quietly answered, "Well put, Jack!"

So after a brief pause, Watson continued by saying, "Jack, when you work with people for as long as I have, it's as if you're married to them. You'll see what I mean someday when you're in charge of a program."

"Yeah, but even some marriages end in divorce. Right, Mr. Watson."

"You're right, and if C.D. continues to demonstrate an unwillingness to accept his new work assignment, then he and I may be headed for divorce court."

"Gee, it sounds like you're drawing your line in the sand and daring C.D. to step over it."

"Essentially, that's what it's come down to." Watson said, sadly.

"But if he can turn it around and accept his new assignment, then he'll be okay…, right?"

"Maybe, but at this point I can't give you a definitive answer Jack."

"I'm sure you realize this Mr. Watson, but you're asking C.D. to abandon his comfort level, and take on an assignment that he hasn't the faintest idea on what to do."

"Comfort level, please…," Watson said, with a sarcastic chuckle.

I then pleaded with Watson by saying, "Just give me the chance to point C.D. in the right direction. We'll start by figuring out Joe's job bank and then go from there."

Watson replied, "Gee, I didn't know you had all this extra time on your hands O'Leary. Maybe I need to re-evaluate your duties, and take a closer look on how you spend your day around here."

I laughed heartily, and then answered, "Well Mr. Watson, I just want you to get your monies worth out of me each and every day, so that you'll sleep better at night."

"Uh-huh, well…, that's very considerate of you Jack." Watson said, smiling.

I chuckled.

"Actually, I'm not surprised that C.D. came crawling to you. He seems to have a real knack for getting people to bail him out of tight spots. I've seen this type of behavior in him before time and time again." Watson said, sternly.

"Well, maybe so…, but I have a soft spot for the guy." I quietly replied.

"For crissakes, Jack! I can't even get C.D. to go down to the contract floor, which is right here in the building! So how in the hell am I going to get him to do job placement out in the business sector!" Watson shouted.

"Alright…, now just simmer down Mr. Watson. Don't get all in a flap. You just finished telling me that you're gonna let me work with him, right?"

"Well, I don't know if I actually agreed to that, but for the sake of argument you can give it your best shot, and I hope you prove me wrong." Watson stated, with a little more composure.

"Okay…, good." I said, with a much greater sense of relief.

Watson continued by saying, "Jack, I'm not at all confident that C.D. can tuck the ball under his arm and run with it. He'll most likely want to lateral the ball off to you, so that you can do all of the fancy footwork for him, while he has the luxury of drinking coffee and reading the newspaper all day in the comfort of the break room. Let's face it, he's already got you breaking down Joe's job bank for him, and the next thing he'll want you to do is make the rounds for him too. That's the way C.D. operates."

"Perhaps, but I still wanna help him out." I replied.

"Listen Jack, I don't want you going off on some wild goose chase with C.D. because you feel sorry for him. Just remember, I have an agency to run. However, if it means that much to you then I'm willing to give you some leeway. But I better see some results, agreed?"

"Agreed, but I'm not just doing this for me, I'm also doing this for Joe. I made him a promise and I intend to keep it." I said, with unwavering conviction.

Watson quietly replied, "Well, since you put it that way…, a promise is a promise. Jack, you continue to impress me. Maybe you'll make a good counselor someday after all."

"Well, thanks for the backhanded compliment Mr. Watson. Coming from you, well…, that really means a lot to me."

"Hey, don't mention it O'Leary. Well…, it's past quitting time, so why don't you get the heck out of here before I'm forced to pay you overtime! I'll see you in the morning."

On the drive into work this morning my mind was racing with all of the things that I needed to accomplish today. Lenore Richards will be starting her internship in two days, and I still need to come up with a plan to orient her.

Watson was right…, Lenore did dazzle me with her beauty. I was desperately trying to convince myself to stay focused on being her mentor and not her admirer.

In addition to Lenore, I also need to get together with C.D. sometime today so that he and I can attempt to crack the secret code of Joe's job bank, and thus ease his mind about his new assignment. I just hope that he's in a much better frame of mind today than he was yesterday.

As I pulled into the parking lot, I didn't see C.D.'s car yet. I really wasn't too concerned about it because it's usually a horse race between C.D. and me as to who makes it into work first.

Well…, after Watson of course.

C.D. and I generally arrive to work around the same time every day, and whoever makes it down to the break room first usually gets the coffee going.

So after brewing up the coffee there was still no sign of C.D., so I decided to pour two cups of coffee and then stroll down the hallway toward Watson's office.

As I approached Watson's office, I could see him working at his desk. I then promptly said, "Morning boss, can I interest you in a freshly brewed cup of coffee?"

Watson replied, "Sure, I could go for a cup, even if it's coffee that you made."

"Very funny, Mr. Watson. You'll eat those words once you take a big gulp of the "black gold" that's sitting in your cup. Anyway, how do you know I made the coffee, maybe C.D. did?"

"Well, he didn't because he called in sick today." Watson stated, very matter-of-factly.

"Oh really…," I replied, as I sat down in Watson's big cushiony leather chair.

Watson took a sip of his coffee, and then sarcastically said, "Not bad…, for a rookie."

I chuckled, and then quietly asked, "So is C.D. sick, or is he pouting?"

Watson took another sip of his coffee, and then replied, "The latter, he always pulls these types of stunts when things don't go his way. He's nothing but a big cry baby."

"So what did he say when he called?" I inquired.

"Just that he wanted me to put him down for a sick day, that's all." Watson replied.

"So did he get testy with you on the phone?" I asked, sipping on my coffee.

"No…, but I could tell that he was in one of his sulking moods, so I just said "okay," and then hung up the phone." Watson stated, nonchalantly.

"It sounds like a classic case of passive-aggressive disorder if you ask me." I remarked.

In a raised tone of voice, Watson said, "Oh…, he's a classic all right, a classic pain in the…," I interrupted Watson in midsentence and calmly said, "Hey, don't go there Mr. Watson."

"Yeah, you're right, O'Leary." Watson replied, as he used some restraint.

In a soothing tone of voice, I quietly stated, "C.D.'s wounds are still raw, and he hasn't fully accepted his new assignment yet."

Watson snarled, "There you go again…, defending him! His wounds, his comfort level, it's nothing but a bunch of malarkey O'Leary!"

"Malarkey! How do you know a word like that, you're not Irish." I said, smiling.

Watson replied, "Why, because I work with a bunch of hooligans, that's why. And in order for me to get their attention, then I need to speak their lingo."

"So am I one of those hooligans that you're referring to?" I innocently asked.

"You? No…, you're more like a Leprechaun, because in you there's luck. I just wish I had another five or ten like ya." Watson said, in a wee bit of an Irish brogue.

"Thank you, sir. That really means a lot to me." I casually replied.

"You're welcome, but I thought we had that "sir" thing cleared up. In fact, I think the time has come for you to start calling me Bob. I think you've earned the right."

"Whoa…, I don't know if I'm ready for that. I mean even some of the old timers around here still call you Mr. Watson."

"Yeah, I know…, but with you it's different. Wouldn't you agree?"

"Well, you did refer to me last week as your young protégé."

Watson chuckled, and then replied, "Yes, I did. So my young protégé, what's on tap for today?"

"Um, well…, I guess whatever it is that you want me to do Bob."

"Good answer, Jack," as Watson chuckled at my rather witty comeback.

Watson continued, "I wanted C.D. to get the ball rolling today on the janitorial program. I know it may seem like an imposition, but I've already made some arrangements for us to clean an office building in town, and I was really hoping that you'd oversee the cleaning crew today?"

"Sure, Bob."

"That's the spirit, Jack." Watson said, smiling.

"Well, I'm ready for a second cup of coffee. Would you like a refill, Bob?"

"No thanks…, maybe later. Keep up the good work, O'Leary. You're on the right road to making a solid cup of coffee."

"Gee, thanks for the vote of confidence Bob. Oh, by the way…, I forgot to tell you, but Farnsworth called me yesterday. He had nothing new to report, and only called to say that he was keeping us in the loop, but personally I think he was just snooping around for some information."

"I see that it didn't take you long to size up Allan, did it Jack?"

"Is it that obvious?" I replied.

"I can detect some animus in your voice when you speak of him." Watson stated.

"Well, I know that you and Farnsworth are friends."

"Really…, and what makes you say that?" Watson replied, with a slight chuckle.

"Well, I thought it was quite evident the day that Henry Josephson started his evaluation. Both of you appeared to be pretty chummy, at least that was my impression anyway."

"Yeah, well…, looks can be deceiving. Hey, I like Allan, and we do schmooze each other from time to time, but our relationship is strictly business." Watson said, candidly.

"Well, I just thought you had a personal relationship with him outside of work, that's all."

Watson replied, "Frankly, I try to have as little to do with Allan as possible. Allan is a very self-centered man, and I can only tolerate him in small doses."

"Yeah, well…, I can certainly attest to that Bob. Well, I'm gonna grab a second cup of coffee, and then I'll touch base with you later in coordinating the cleaning crew."

"Sounds good, Irish." Watson said, as he opened up his overhead accounts ledger.

When I entered the break room, I discovered that the "golden rule" had once again been violated. Apparently, no one around here knows how to make coffee except for C.D. and me.

As I was throwing the coffee together, I was thinking back to the day that I started here. I remember C.D. distinctly telling me about upholding the "golden rule" of the break room, and that whoever drinks the last cup of coffee makes the next pot. I was wondering if C.D. gave that little pep talk to anyone else on staff, or was it something that he just made up out of thin air.

Then again…, maybe I'm the only one around here who is stupid enough to even listen to C.D. in the first place.

So after slugging down my second cup of coffee, I headed over to Watson's office so that he could brief me on the transitional janitorial program.

Watson then handed me an instructional sheet, and he made it quite clear to me that I follow his directives to the letter, so that we could make a good impression on the business that we were cleaning today.

So with my instructions in hand, I then hustled out back to the loading dock where the clients and staff were all waiting for me on the WEALTH cargo van. When the staff saw that it was me hopping onto the vehicle instead of C.D. they were pleased beyond belief, because in their mind, having C.D. along for the ride was comparable to having another client to supervise.

The day went off without a hitch. The clients did a fabulous job and the proprietor of the business couldn't be happier. He was so impressed with the work we did that he said he would mention our name to several of his business associates around town and highly recommend us.

On the ride back to WEALTH, everyone was laughing, singing, and just plain whooping it up. I was proud of the work that I did today, and I knew that Bob would be proud of me too.

When we pulled up to the loading dock, Watson gave each of the clients a "high five," as he cheerfully said, "I guess I don't have to ask how things went over at the worksite today, especially with all of these smiling faces I see. Good work, everybody!"

It's Thursday morning, and Lenore Richards will be starting her internship at WEALTH tomorrow. I've been so busy of late that I still haven't given any thought as to how I'm going to orient her. This will definitely be the number one priority on my "to do" list for today.

Late yesterday afternoon, Bob informed me that he wouldn't be in the office this morning because he had some pressing business to attend to in town, so he asked me to keep tabs on the place in his absence. Boy, I sure hope that doesn't get the other counselors "nose out of joint."

Quite honestly, if I were in their shoes and Watson asked someone with less seniority than me to supervise the place in his absence, well…, it would certainly bother me.

As I pulled into the WEALTH parking lot, it was strange not seeing Watson's car nestled in its usual parking space. I didn't see C.D.'s car either, but as I've stated before, he and I were usually neck and neck at getting into work at the same time every morning.

So after putting the coffee on, I headed over to the reception area to check my mail slot and to sift through my many phone messages from yesterday. In the midst of rummaging through my messages, I heard the telephone ring so I walked over to Dolly's desk to answer it.

"Good morning, WEALTH Industries…, how may I help you?"

"Hey, sonny boy. What are ya buckin' for Dolly's job now? Well, forget it…, 'cause her legs are way better than yours. Is the old man there?" C.D. asked, in his usual gruff tone of voice.

"Hey C.D., how are ya? Watson isn't here right now, but he'll be in later. Is there anything that I can do for ya? You're coming in today, right?"

"Nope, I don't think so, kid. Not today, and maybe never again. I've had it, and I'm sick and tired of putting up with all of Watson's bull shit!"

"But C.D., the new assignment will work out fine, you'll see."

"Hey Jack, it doesn't matter, I'm eligible for retirement and I just might pack it in!"

"C.D., Watson said that it's okay for me to help you figure out the new assignment. In fact, I took the cleaning crew out yesterday for the first time and they did really well. The crew practically ran itself."

"Kid, Watson doesn't need me, he's got you doing two jobs!"

"No…, it's not like that at all. I only went with the work crew yesterday to kick off the program. I'm telling you, it went very well…, and if you give it a chance I think you'll agree."

"Why the hell can't we just go back to the way we did it when Atkins first went out sick?" C.D. grumbled.

"C.D., it's too hard doing our job full-time and placement once a week, you know that."

"Nah…, it's no good, kid. I just can't do the job anymore. Tell Watson to mail me my retirement papers, and tell him to do it ASAP, right Jack!" C.D. bellowed, and then he began laughing hysterically, like a mad man.

C.D. hung up the phone and I just sat there in quiet disbelief.

Gee, what a turn of events we have had today. Watson is out of the office, C.D. is threatening to quit, and Lenore Richards is starting the first day of her internship tomorrow and I still haven't the faintest idea as to how I'm going to orient her.

Well, I guess I have no other choice but to tag-a-long with the cleaning crew today, which means that I'll just have to put my regular full-time job on hold again and do C.D.'s job.

Hey, don't get me wrong, I really enjoyed the cleaning crew yesterday, but the program really eats up your day, especially when I have meetings, reports, and phone messages to return.

Perhaps I'm feeling a bit sorry for myself, but here I am the least senior member on the counseling staff, yet I feel like the little Dutch boy, who is desperately trying to plug up every leak in the dike with no help from anyone whatsoever.

I'm either stupid, or the only counselor on staff who has a conscience!

Well, I'm sure if Mr. Watson were here right now he would want me to supervise the janitorial crew again, and continue to help solidify that program. So I guess I'll just have to leave Watson a note and inform him of what has transpired.

Also, when Dolly comes into work I'll just have to tell her that C.D. has called in sick for the rest of the week, and that I will be overseeing the janitorial crew for the day. And if she needs to get a hold of me, then she can just give me a call over at the worksite.

It's three-thirty, and once again the clients on the janitorial crew did a fabulous job today. Although I enjoyed the day, my heart just wasn't in it today like it was yesterday.

Quite honestly, I just had too many things on my mind today, what with C.D. and Lenore, and all of the many phone messages and reports that were pending for me back at the office.

So after finishing out back, I hustled over to Watson's office so that I could update him on my day. When I knocked on Bob's door, the first thing out of his mouth was, "You've had quite a day, O'Leary. So what's up with C.D.?"

I sarcastically replied, "Yeah, quite a day Bob! Hey, you don't have any ice cold beer stashed away in this man cave of yours, do ya? I could sure use a frosty one right now."

Watson lightly chuckled, and then sat back in his sleek leather chair.

I then dejectedly said, "Well Bob, the note I left you pretty much says it all. C.D. said that he's gonna quit, and he wants you to mail out his retirement papers, ASAP. There was really no talking to him this morning."

Watson shouted, "Retirement papers…, yeah right! I've been down this road with C.D. before! I've been carrying his ass for over twenty-five years, and I'm sick and tired of his bull shit! He should be more worried about me firing him than his threatening me with retirement!"

"So you're not too concerned, Bob?"

"To be honest with you, if he quits…, he quits. I'll send him a can of gourmet coffee as a retirement gift. I think we've gotten every last "drop" out of that "pot" he calls a career anyway!"

"Nice imagery, Bob. So what are you planning on doing?"

"Nothing! I'll mail out his precious retirement papers and call his bluff. I've already told you that I'm not playing his little game anymore."

Quite honestly, I couldn't fault Watson for feeling the way he did. Watson really didn't do anything to provoke C.D.'s sudden march into retirement. It sounds like Watson and C.D. have been playing their own little private game of chicken for a very long time.

I really couldn't justify defending C.D. anymore. I still didn't want C.D. to quit, but I'm finally seeing a side of him that Bob Watson has had to put up with for over twenty-five years.

Watson was right…, he said that C.D. wouldn't make it past the first week of his new work assignment.

Once again…, that's why Watson is the boss!

Watson then said, "Jack, I need you as my job placement specialist, temporarily…, that is, until I can make other arrangements. You're the most equipped counselor I've got."

"What about Lenore Richards…, she's coming tomorrow. Won't that mess up our plans?"

"How? In what way? She's still gonna follow you around regardless, right?"

"Well, yeah…," I muttered.

Watson continued, "Listen, this is what I'd like to propose. I want you to manage all of the placement duties, which also includes the transitional janitorial program, plus one-quarter of your caseload, and I will pick up the remaining three-quarters. What do you think of that idea?"

"All right..., that sounds fair Bob. That way I can still instruct Lenore Richards on all aspects of rehabilitation counseling instead of just job placement."

"Gee, I wish things could've gone this smoothly with C.D., but then you and C.D. are like comparing apples and oranges. Well..., make that apples and coconuts." Watson said, and we both quietly chuckled.

Watson paused a moment, and then decisively said, "Now Jack, I have one further stipulation for our little deal. I still want you to continue working with some of the more difficult clients on your caseload, such as, the Sampson's, Michael Wallace, and that Randy character, who's always getting into mischief down on the contract floor. You have a much better rapport with those people than I do, and I really don't wanna disrupt that."

"Well, that's very considerate of you Bob. In other words..., you want me to continue working with all the pains in the asses on my caseload, so that you don't have to be bothered with any of their day-to-day disasters. Would that be a more accurate assessment, Bob?"

Watson paused momentarily, and then said with a big smirk on his face, "Well, if that's the way you wanna look at it Jack. Clinically speaking...,"

I interrupted Watson in midstream of his convoluted rationale and said, "Bob, please..., don't give me any of your clinical bull shit. I'll do it, because you still have a building to run."

"Okay, sounds good!" Watson hastily replied, and sealing the deal before I could change my mind.

"Well, its five o'clock..., I better shove off. I'll see you in the morning Bob."

"Yeah, okay. Hey O'Leary, make sure you get a good night's sleep tonight. Hahaha...! I think you're gonna need it." Watson said, as he quietly chuckled to himself as I walked out the door.

CHAPTER NINE

"Bob's here, phew…, that's good," I mumbled to myself, as I pulled into the parking lot.

Yesterday was a very stressful day, and although I'm happy that yesterday is over, I must admit that yesterday's experience has now given me a better understanding as to what Bob has had to contend with around here for the past thirty years.

But that was yesterday and this is today!

I've got Lenore Richards starting her internship this morning, and I still have no idea as to how I'm going to orient her.

Well, maybe I can throw a few ideas together before she arrives, that is, providing there are no unexpected surprises or emergencies waiting for me when I enter the building.

I stowed my backpack in the office, and as I grabbed my coffee mug off of my desk, I thought to myself, "I've got a very busy day today, so I better make that coffee extra strong."

As I trudged down the hallway to make the coffee, I thought I detected some noise coming from the break room, and then I experienced the sudden aroma of coffee being brewed.

When I walked into the break room, who should I see making the coffee but none other than Bob Watson, and I was shocked beyond belief. Since working here I've never seen Bob in the break room, let alone making the coffee.

"Good morning, Bob."

Watson turned in my direction, and then nonchalantly said, "O'Leary, good morning…, the coffee is almost ready."

"So what got into you this morning, Bob?" I asked, as I pulled up a chair.

"Well O'Leary, I knew you were gonna have a busy day, so I thought I would help you out. Listen, I was thinking that after we have our coffee, we can map out our strategy for the day down in my office."

Bob then grabbed the coffee urn and poured two piping hot cups of coffee.

As Watson handed me a cup of the freshly brewed coffee, I amusingly said, "Boy, I could sure use a cup of coffee…, even if it's from a pot that you made."

Watson countered my whimsical remark by saying, "For your information, you haven't had a good cup of coffee until you've had some of mine O'Leary. Who do you think taught C.D. how to make the perfect cup of coffee?" Watson then took a savory sip of his coffee and smiled.

I then took a sip of the freshly brewed coffee, and amusingly said, "Not bad, but I've had better."

"In a pig's eye you have! That's the best cup of coffee you'll ever have in your lifetime, or any other lifetime you go traipsing through." Watson adamantly said, as he hid his sly grin behind his coffee mug.

"Actually, on second thought Bob, this coffee isn't half bad. Maybe we should get you in here more often to whip us up a pot or two every day."

"Well, that's not gonna happen O'Leary. I want my staff spending less time drinking coffee, and more time with the clients down on the contract floor. If I start making the coffee, I'll never get any work out of the bunch of ya." Watson said, as he took one last gulp of his coffee.

"Yeah, I see your point, Bob."

"Why don't we go down to my office and figure out the day. Oh…, help yourself to a donut, they're over on the counter."

"Oh, okay…, don't mind if I do Bob." I replied, as I reached for the gooiest one I saw.

As Watson was rinsing out his coffee cup, he casually said, "I stopped by this little Italian bakery on the other side of town this morning called Migliori's. His donuts are really good."

"Gee, what a coincidence…, my parents buy from Migliori's bakery all the time. I've known Mr. Migliori since I was a little kid. It's amazing that with all the bakeries in town you should buy from there." I stated, and feeling the psychic energy in the room.

Watson grabbed another donut out of the box and said, "These might be the best donuts that I've ever had. Take two, O'Leary…, we might be down in my office for a while. And make sure you bring enough napkins with ya. I don't want you dropping crumbs all over the place."

"Yes…, mom." I amusingly quipped.

Watson and I spent the better part of an hour discussing and coordinating the day. We talked about our plan with Lenore Richards, in terms of the logistics of her internship, and also how we might be able to utilize her with regards to the transitional janitorial program.

In addition to that, Bob said he would attend the two determination meetings that I was scheduled to attend this morning because he knew that I would be all tied up for most of the day.

He then indicated to me that after careful review of the data, he is recommending that both people at the determination meetings are suitable candidates to continue in our program.

Wow…, what a surprise that was!

So after hearing Bob's recommendation, I sarcastically said, "Gee Bob, I can tell you put a lot of thought behind that decision, eh."

Bob just smiled, and opted not to say anything incriminating.

It was almost eight-thirty, and Lenore Richards should be arriving any minute now. Although I haven't spoken to her since our initial encounter, she did indicate to me that she knew where WEALTH was located, so I wasn't too concerned about getting any last minute phone calls from her stating that she was lost.

When I swung by the reception area to check my mail, I informed Dolly that I was expecting a young lady this morning around eight-thirty, and that I would appreciate it if she notified me when she arrives.

Dolly sensed that I was a little on edge, however she couldn't resist having a little fun at my expense, as she humorously said, "Okay Jack, I'll let you know when Ms. Richards arrives, but does your fiancée know about this?"

Suddenly, the old Irish Catholic guilt seemed to get the best of me, as I clumsily tried to explain to Dolly who Ms. Richards was and her reason for seeing me today.

Dolly let me squirm for a minute or two, and then interrupted me in midstream of my tongue-tied explanation by saying, "Jack, I'm only teasing you. Mr. Watson already filled me in on Ms. Richards."

"Oh…, okay Dolly. I guess I'm just a little nervous this morning, but I'll be okay." I said, with some embarrassment, as Dolly lightly snickered and then reached to answer the telephone.

When Watson and I had our little powwow this morning, he suggested that Lenore Richards tag-a-long with me on the work crew today. He thought that involving her with the cleaning crew would not only be educational, but provide me with an extra pair of hands as well.

Watson humorously said, and I quote, "While you're busy instructing Ms. Richards on the goals and objectives of the agency, you can both be cleaning windows over at the worksite."

As I was finishing up some work at my desk, I heard a light knock on my office door and it was Dolly. Dolly was smiling like a Cheshire cat, while saying in a very sultry and provocative voice, "Excuse me, Mr. O'Leary…, but there's a young lady here to see you."

"Thanks, Dolly." I replied, and sounding a little bit jittery.

Dolly kept staring at me with a very precocious smile. I must admit that she was doing a pretty good job at busting my balls, and she knew that there was nothing that I could do about it.

As Dolly stepped away, I could see Lenore Richards standing in the hallway. She looked absolutely stunning, and at the risk of sounding overly dramatic…, she took my breath away!

At that moment, I felt as though I had just lost all of my objectivity as her supervisor. I was literally spellbound by her natural beauty, and as crazy as it may sound, but Lenore Richards seemed to have me right where she wanted me, even though that wasn't her intent at all.

Ms. Richards was totting a canvas backpack, which was draped over her left shoulder, and to my slight surprise, she had her bicycle in tow that she wheeled right into my office.

Her eyes were wide, and her face was beaming with anticipation. I then jumped up from my desk, and walked toward her with my hand extended to greet her.

"Good morning, Mr. O'Leary. It's great to be here today."

"Hi, Ms. Richards. Well…, it's great to have you."

"Um…, I hope it's not too much of an inconvenience, but is there a place that I can stow my bicycle? It's my sole means of transportation."

"Sure, we'll find a home for your bike. So, um…, welcome to WEALTH Industries! I know you must have a million questions, and hopefully I can answer most of them for you. My job is to make you feel comfortable, well…, at least for the first day anyway. Just kidding…, I think you're going to really like it here." I said, awkwardly.

"Yes, I'm sure I will." Ms. Richards replied, quite eloquently.

"Um…, before we get started, I probably should warn you that I possess a rather off-beat sense of humor. Harmless really, but I hope you find my humor as funny as I perceive it to be."

Ms. Richards quietly giggled, and then said, "I'm sure I'll find your humor quite enchanting."

"Uh…, I don't know about that, but I think you'll find my humor quite original." I replied, chuckling.

"Well, I'm up for a little originality." She quipped.

"Great! Well…, I think we have a full day planned for you today, and it should prove to be not only very informative, but hopefully fun as well. Before we begin our little adventure, I thought I would introduce you to Mr. Watson, who is our Executive Director of the agency. His office is right down the hall. Why don't you follow me?"

"Lead the way…," Ms. Richards replied.

We walked down the hallway towards Mr. Watson's office, and as usual he was busy at his desk. I tapped on Watson's office door, and then heard him promptly say, "Come in."

As we stepped into Watson's office, he looked up to see who it was. I then introduced Lenore Richards to him by nervously saying, "Um…, hi, Mr. Watson. Um…, I would like you to meet Lenore Richards, who…, um…, will be interning with us for the next, um…, six weeks. Um…, Ms. Richards, this is Mr. Bob Watson, um…, the Executive Director of the agency."

Upon hearing my rather shaky introduction, Watson momentarily glanced in my direction and then quietly shook his head. Under normal circumstances, Watson may have offered up an amusing quip on my less than stellar introduction, but for now he just decided to let it go.

Watson stood up, and with his hand extended he walked toward Lenore Richards.

As Watson and Lenore Richards cordially shook hands, Watson said with noticeable ease, "It's very nice to make your acquaintance, Ms. Richards. Welcome aboard!"

Watson then glanced over at me, as if to say, "Now that's how it's done rookie!"

Ms. Richards meekly replied, "Thank you, sir. It's very nice to make your acquaintance as well. Thank you for agreeing to sponsor me, so that I can fulfill my course requirements."

Watson graciously responded, "Not at all, Ms. Richards. It's our way of giving back to the academic community."

"Um, excuse me sir…, but I prefer to be called Lenore instead of Ms. Richards. Well…, if that's okay with you." She asked, innocently.

Watson smiled, and then warmly said, "By all means…, Lenore it is."

I then interjected, "Hey Lenore, why don't you and I dispense with the formalities and keep it on a first name basis as well," which prompted her to quickly say, "Sounds great, Jack!"

Watson then casually said, "So Lenore…, Jack has a full day planned for you, and I think you'll come to appreciate some of the innovative things that we do here at WEALTH Industries."

Lenore replied, "I'm very much looking forward to the experience, sir."

I quietly chuckled to myself because that's about the third or fourth time now that Lenore has called Watson "sir," but for now he seems to be letting it go.

"Well Jack, you have about twenty minutes before the cargo van is ready to take off with the work crew. That should be just enough time to give Lenore a quick tour of the place."

"Okay…, I'm right on it, sir." I replied, causing Watson to do a slight double-take, and then quietly smile in appreciation of my "sir" reference.

We left Watson's office and then I proceeded to give Lenore the cook's tour of the building. I showed her all of the major points of interest, such as, the offices, the break room, the restrooms, and finishing up on the contract floor.

As we went from place to place, Lenore appeared to be quite impressed with what she saw, and noticeably more at ease then when she first arrived.

Although Lenore didn't say much, I could tell that she was soaking everything up like a sponge, and I was beginning to see why Dr. Stevens was so taken by his eager young student.

When we were done touring the building, we went out back and joined the others who were already assembled on the WEALTH cargo van.

On the ride over to the worksite, I introduced Lenore to the clients and staff that she would be working with for the day. It goes without saying, but the clients were swooned by Lenore's beauty, and they seemed to be falling all over her left and right.

As I listened to the bevy of "sweet nothings," and witnessed the number of affectionate stares that were being cast in Lenore's direction, I thought to myself, "The clients may be slow, but they're certainly not stupid…, because they sure know a pretty face when they see one!"

Even Scotty, who was driving the van, had a pretty tough time keeping his eye on the road because he seemed to be more preoccupied with sneaking a peek at Lenore in the rearview mirror then he was on the road ahead of him.

Yeah, everyone on the van was captivated by Lenore's natural beauty, and who could blame them.

In general, the clients are usually quite shy when meeting people for the first time, yet this morning they were anything but shy, almost brash…, and definitely uninhibited in making some rather bold inquiries into Lenore's personal life.

They especially wanted to know her marital status and if she had a boyfriend.

I must admit that I was rather curious in knowing the answer to that particular question myself, and I struggled to hear Lenore's quiet response over the oohs and ahhs of the crowd.

As we continued to ride along, the clients were starting to get a little too carried away with some of the questions that they were asking Lenore, and I had to remind them several times that their curiosities were getting a little too personal and even teetering on crossing the line.

Upon hearing my reprimands, the pendulum would then swing to the other extreme, and the clients would then profusely apologize to Lenore and ask for her forgiveness. Lenore was really good at handling these awkward situations in a delicate, yet effective manner.

I found Lenore to be very friendly, courteous, and quite adept at making small talk, and she knew just how to laugh at the right moments. I was very impressed with all of her little subtleties, which for me spoke volumes about her character.

In an effort to acclimate Lenore to her new surroundings, I jotted down some background information on each of the clients that she would be working with today.

From time to time, I would quietly chuckle to myself as I watched Lenore studiously read and assimilate the information that I gave her, and the cute little way that she kept referring back to the sheet when she wasn't quite sure of the correct approach to take with each of the clients.

Throughout the course of the day the clients took to Lenore like a fish to water, and in no time at all both Lenore and the clients were settling into a very workable routine.

Lenore was agreeable to anything that I asked her to do, but best of all she was very constructive in her approach, and wasn't at all afraid to correct the clients when needed.

We arrived back to WEALTH at approximately three-thirty. Lenore hopped off the cargo van first, and then proceeded to assist each of the clients off of the vehicle one-by-one.

As I watched Lenore give each of the clients a helping hand, I seemed to be rather amused. Especially with regards to some of the more capable clients, such as young Michael Wallace, who as we all know by now is quite strong and very athletic.

Michael was signing the word "help" so that Lenore would assist him off of the vehicle. Although Michael only needed to step off of the van a mere six-inches, he acted as if he was scaling the great abyss, and pleaded with Lenore to take his hand so that he wouldn't fall down.

Hey, Michael is no fool…, and he sure knows a pretty face when he sees one. So why not take full advantage of the situation.

So after all the clients were helped off of the cargo van, it was then my turn to climb down. Lenore extended her hand to me, but I was quick to decline her generous offer.

Once everyone was off of the cargo van, the clients all said "good-bye" and then proceeded to walk in the direction of the time clocks, so that they could punch out for the day.

As I glanced back over my shoulder, I noticed that the clients couldn't stop taking their eyes off of Lenore. As they continued to gawk at her, they sheepishly giggled like giddy young schoolboys, and I'm quite sure that each of them will be thinking about Lenore all weekend long.

While en route to my office, I turned to Lenore and calmly said, "Lenore, helping the clients off the van was a very nice gesture, but they'll expect that type of preferential treatment from you all the time. Next time, why don't you let them get off of the van on their own, okay."

Upon hearing my suggestion, Lenore looked at me like a scolded child, as she contritely said, "Sorry Jack, I was only trying to be nice."

I quickly replied, "I know that…, and I'm not trying to sound like an ogre, but the clients need to be more independent and we need to have more of a mindset not to do for them. I realize that sometimes it's a very fine line."

At that point, I felt bad coming down on Lenore like that, especially on her first day. I tried to be as sensitive as I possibly could. I didn't want her to think that I was being a real jerk, but what I said to her was the correct thing to say. I wasn't trying to be mean or a killjoy. I was just trying to provide Lenore with what I refer to as a "teaching moment," - no pain, no gain!

We went back to my office to rehash the day, and I casually asked Lenore, "So was today what you thought it would be?"

"Better…," she said, without hesitation.

"Oh really, well…, maybe we didn't challenge you quite as hard as I thought we did."

Lenore laughed out loud, and then replied, "Actually, I think it was the incredible level of supervision that you provided me today Jack!"

"Oh, yeah…, I'm sure that's exactly what it was." I said, with a tinge of sarcastic humor.

Lenore chuckled.

"Well Lenore, I must say that you're everything that Dr. Stevens said you'd be and more."

"Thank you, Jack. And you're everything that Dr. Stevens said you'd be as well."

"Okay, well…, I'm glad we've got that all cleared up." I amusingly quipped.

"Um…, so same time on Monday, right?" Lenore inquired, as she was hoisting her backpack over her shoulder so that she could head out for the day.

"Yep, same time. Hey listen, I have some forms that we both need to fill out and sign every day. It's similar to a daily log. It basically keeps track of your hours, and verifies that everything is on the up and up. I'm gonna leave them in this folder on top of my filing cabinet, so that you have easy access to them."

"Okay Jack, sounds good." She replied.

"Now just remember…, we're operating on the honor system here, so there'll be no fudging on your hours." I humorously remarked, and we both laughed in unison.

"Well, I can see that I won't be pulling the wool over your eyes Jack. See ya, Monday." Lenore said, as she wheeled her bicycle out of my office.

"Okay Lenore, see ya Monday." I replied, and then wondering what she would be doing for the next two days and with whom.

Despite the fact that I've only spent one day with Lenore, it was quite evident as to why Dr. Stevens was so impressed with his eager young student. Although Lenore was a free spirit, she was laser focused, incredibly smart, down to earth, and an extremely kind person as well.

Before leaving for the day, I decided to swing by Watson's office. I knocked lightly on his door and exuberantly said, "Hey Bob, how's it going?"

Watson, who had his head deeply buried in a mound of papers, then replied very matter-of-factly, "Good, Jack. So how did our budding intern do today?"

"Um, good, real good…, and not only does she possess a great personality, but she's not afraid to roll up her sleeves and pitch right in as well."

"Really, well…, that's quite refreshing to hear. I want you to keep me posted on her progress." Watson said, as he continued to work feverishly at his desk.

"Yeah, okay, well…, I can see that you're busy, so I'll let you finish up. It's Friday, and the weekend is beckoning. See ya Monday, Bob."

"Okay, O'Leary. Hey, sorry I'm so preoccupied here, but I'm doing my job and your job too." Watson said, as he looked up at me with a coy smile.

I quickly countered, "Hey, wait a minute Bob, don't expect any sympathy out of me. I'm doing my job and C.D.'s job. So tell your tale of woe to someone who really cares, okay."

We looked at each other for a split second, and then we both burst out into hysterical laughter.

Chapter Ten

"Bob's not here yet, huh…., that's strange, he never runs late unless he tells me ahead of time." I thought to myself, as I pulled into the WEALTH parking lot.

As I was walking into the building, I was wondering if Bob's tardiness this morning was in any way related to his swinging by Migliori's bakery again to buy the staff another two dozen donuts like he did on Friday. But then quickly realizing that treating the staff to donuts for two consecutive days in a row was completely out of character for Bob to do.

So after stowing my backpack in the office, I then made my way down to the break room so that I could get the coffee going. As I was waiting for the coffee to brew the telephone rang, and to my surprise it was Bob on the other end of the line.

"Jack…, hi…, it's Bob. Listen…, I won't be coming into work today." He said, in a somewhat incoherent tone.

"Is everything all right Bob? What do you have a twenty-four hour bug."

"Well…," he said, and then a sudden pause.

As I waited for Bob to respond, it sounded like he was crying on the other end of the line.

Bob then blurted out, "Jack, there's no easy way to tell you this, but Joe died in his sleep early this morning."

"What! No! No! Oh my, God! No!" I exclaimed.

"Jack, listen, I've only just found out about this within the past forty-five minutes. I'm at Sarah's house right now, and she's pretty shaken up."

"No! No! No!" I screamed.

"Jack, pull yourself together. I need you to be strong and handle things for me in my absence today." Watson said, in much the same way as Knute Rockne pleaded for the Fighting Irish to win one for the "Gipper."

"No, I can't believe it." I said, and continuing to be stunned by the news.

"Listen Jack, I want you to cancel the staff meeting this morning and straighten up the back room, and then break the news of Joe's passing to the others. Tell Dolly to take all of my phone messages, and that I'll get back to whoever calls, ASAP. You're welcome to stop by Sarah's house this afternoon after work. Okay, well, I gotta go…, thanks again, bye."

As I hung up the phone, the tears that I was desperately trying to hold back began streaming down my cheeks like two broken water mains. I was so overwhelmed with emotion that I just sat at my desk sobbing uncontrollably.

So after having a good cry, I thought of all the good times that Joe and I shared with one another. As I sat there alone with my thoughts, I found comfort in knowing that Joe and I had experienced some very memorable moments together, which were private and known only to us.

I then decided to walk down the hallway so that I could catch the pedestrian traffic going in and out of the break room, and convey the sad news of Joe's passing to the rest of the staff.

Other than Dolly and Ralph, no one seemed to shed any visible tears for Joe, and I found that to be very disconcerting and it saddened me greatly.

I then glanced at the clock and saw that it was almost eight-thirty, and Lenore Richards should be arriving any minute now.

To tell you the truth, I wasn't in any mood to go gallivanting with the janitorial crew today, even if it meant that I'd be in the all-day company of a beautiful woman like Lenore.

Anyway, I'm sure that sending Lenore out on the janitorial crew today will be all right. She seemed to be quite comfortable in that role on Friday, plus she'll have a couple of senior staff with her so it should work out just fine.

It's probably not a good idea for me to be out of the building today anyway, especially if Bob happens to call and needs me to attend to something for him.

As I sat at my desk waiting for Lenore to arrive, my mind then plummeted into a sea of memorable recollections of Joe. I thought about the fatherly way that Joe took me under his wing and taught me everything there was to know about job placement. Joe never cared that I had more education than him, or that I made more money than he did. He never felt threatened by me, unlike some of the other small-minded characters that work here.

Suddenly, I found myself getting deeper and deeper in reflective thought, and then in an instant, I was jarred back into reality by the sweet sound of Lenore's voice, "Jack…, Jack…, hello…, is there anybody in there? It's time to come out and play now."

Although seemingly trapped in the deep dark recesses of my subconscious mind, I managed to catapult myself back into reality. I then looked up at Lenore, and in a bit of a glassy daze, I nonchalantly said, "Oh…, good morning, Lenore.

How's it going?"

I was pretending like everything was okay, even though it wasn't. And on top of the heart wrenching sadness that I was feeling right now about Joe, I was mortified to know that Lenore had exposed a side of her supervisor that I would've rather she not see.

Lenore then said, with an innocent smile, "I'm fine, but I'm more concerned about you Jack. Your eyes were as wide as saucers, and you looked like you were in some deep dark trance, as if someone had just hypnotized you."

"Yeah, um…, sorry about that. You kinda caught me at a bad moment."

"Is everything okay, Jack? The place seems awfully quiet."

"Well, Mr. Watson just called a little while ago, and informed us that one of our staff passed away in his sleep early this morning. Everyone is pretty shaken up about it."

"Oh dear…, I'm so sorry to hear that." Lenore replied.

"Yeah, thanks. The man who died was our job placement specialist, and his name was Joe Atkins. Joe was the best goddam job placement specialist in the city, and maybe even in the whole goddam world! Geez, I'm sorry Lenore…, that was very unprofessional of me to say, but I'm just so upset right now."

"Hey, don't apologize…, you're entitled to your feelings. It's not easy losing people that we care about. I lost my father several years ago, and I'm still trying to come to terms with it."

"Thanks, Lenore. Hey, I'm sorry to hear about your dad."

"Yeah, well…, not to change the subject, but what's on the agenda for today Jack?" Lenore asked, pensively.

I could tell by the mere mention of her dad's passing away that it was very painful for Lenore.

"Um…, well, in the "wake" of. Oh, pardon me, Lenore. I guess that was a poor choice of words, let me rephrase that. Um…, Mr. Watson asked me to be in charge of the building today, so I'd like you to go with the cleaning crew and I'll stay back."

"Oh, okay, Jack. So are you in charge of the building when Mr. Watson isn't here?"

"Well…, not ordinarily. I really don't know who assumes responsibility when Mr. Watson isn't here because he hasn't missed a single day of work since I've been here. So I guess the situation really hasn't presented itself before."

"Is Mr. Watson a friend of the family? Is that why he's not here today?" Lenore asked.

"Actually, Joe was Mr. Watson's brother-in-law."

"Oh, I see." Lenore quietly replied.

So looking to change the subject, I then said, "Okay, well…, you have just enough time to grab a quick cup of coffee out of the break room, and then this afternoon you can fill me in on all the details of the janitorial crew."

"Okay, Jack. It's a date!"

Lenore went down to the break room to grab a cup of coffee, and I headed toward the reception area to see Dolly.

When I swung by the reception area, I saw that Dolly was quietly sitting at her desk and she appeared to be deep in thought. I could tell that Dolly was still quite jarred from hearing the news about Joe.

I then asked Dolly if she saw my note regarding the canceling of the staff meeting and she indicated that she had. She then asked me if I knew when the calling hours were for Joe, or if any funeral arrangements had been made yet. Sadly, I didn't have any details to give her.

So after a brief pause, I then asked Dolly if she would do me a favor by canvassing the building and taking up a collection for Joe, and that I would use the money she collected to purchase a flower arrangement on behalf of the WEALTH staff. Dolly said that she would be happy to make the rounds, so I reached into my pocket and got the ball rolling by giving her five dollars toward the flower arrangement. She then stood up and gave me an unexpected embrace.

After chatting with Dolly, I walked out back so that I could assess the general tenor of the contract floor. It goes without saying, but the mood was very somber. Although people were working steadily, there wasn't the usual zeal or enthusiasm that typically prevails throughout.

Yeah…, I guess you could say that the back room was in mourning, and it felt as though we should be flying the flag at half-mast. The USS WEALTH, paying tribute and homage to one of its most revered and esteemed officers', Mr. Joe Atkins.

Several of the clients approached me and expressed their sadness and grief about Joe, and others simply asked me "why?" Sadly, there was nothing I could say to put their minds at ease.

Ralph, Smitty, and Terry were all huddled together drinking coffee and looking quite melancholy. They asked me how I was holding up, but all I could do was shrug my shoulders and continue to mingle with the clients. They all could tell that I was barely holding it together.

So after about two hours of milling around the contract floor, I went back to my office and saw a note on my desk that read, "Jack, please see me when you get a chance, Dolly."

I walked down the hall toward the reception area and saw Dolly at her desk. I approached her and quietly said, "Hi Dolly, I saw your note. You wanted to see me?"

"Yes Jack, I was able to collect seventy-five dollars. I didn't want to leave it on your desk because…, well…, you know." She said, as the tears glistened in the corners of her eyes.

"Thanks, Dolly. I'll be stopping by the florist after work, and then I'm going over to meet Mr. Watson at Sarah's house." I explained, as Dolly softly smiled.

At three-thirty, I walked out to the loading dock so that I could wait for Lenore and the janitorial crew to arrive back from the worksite. I kept glancing at my wristwatch and anxiously hoping that Lenore and the gang would be pulling up soon, so that I could touch base with her and then proceed over to Sarah's house to meet up with Bob and convey my condolences.

Just then I saw the WEALTH cargo van pull into the parking lot. The occupants didn't look as jovial this time around as they had on Friday.

No doubt…, their hearts were heavy due to Joe's passing.

Lenore hopped off of the van first, but this time she opted to have the clients exit the vehicle on their own accord. Her actions brought an immediate smile to my face because I could hear the client's pleading for her assistance, but Lenore held firm. I was pleased to see that she heeded my advice, and it reassured me that I really was her mentor.

When everyone climbed off of the van, I approached Lenore from behind and tapped her on the shoulder. As she wielded toward me, her smile was bright enough to light up a city block.

I then asked Lenore how things went over at the worksite today, and she energetically replied, "Everything went very well. I took notes on the client's progress, and, oh…, a Jill Woodson came by to work with Michael Wallace on some sign language training. I also took your advice about having the client's be more independent, especially getting off of the van."

"Yes, I saw that. Thank you, Lenore." I replied, and trying to sound cheerful.

"So how are your spirits Jack…, any better?" Lenore asked, with concern.

"Slightly, but I'll be fine. I don't mean to cut you short, but I'm in a bit of a hurry. I'm going over to meet Mr. Watson at his sister's house, and I need to make a stop along the way."

"Okay, so will I see you tomorrow Jack?"

"Yeah, sure, but if anything should change I'll give you a call. I'm pretty sure I have your number written down in my office, right?"

"You should, I remember giving it to you at our first meeting with Dr. Stevens, and then you placed it in your folder."

"Um…, aren't the last four digits, 8753?"

"Wow, that's right! Boy, you have a good memory Jack." Lenore replied, smiling.

"Well Lenore, I make it a point never to forget a pretty girl's phone number," which prompted both of us to laugh.

"It's good to see you laughing Jack. It certainly becomes you."

"Well…, thanks, Lenore. I think you bring out the best in me. Listen, I'd love to chat, but I really gotta go. I'll call you if anything changes, bye."

"Okay, bye, Jack."

"Oh, say Lenore…, don't forget to sign out on one of those verification forms that are in the folder on top of my filing cabinet." I said, as I was scurrying away.

"Okay Jack, don't worry, I will. I have to go back to your office to get my bicycle anyway. I'll see ya, when I see ya!"

As I was leaving the back area, I asked Ralph if he wouldn't mind making sure that all of the lights were turned off and that all of the doors and windows were secured for the night.

Ralph just held a sarcastic stare at me, and quietly said, "Uh…, Jack, I always do."

I felt funny asking a guy who has worked here for over thirty years to attend to such trivial matters. But Mr. Watson entrusted me to look after the place in his absence, and come hell or high water, I was going to make damn sure that I followed his directives to the letter.

So after leaving WEALTH, I drove over to Williams Florist, which just so happens to be the most popular florist in town, and a florist that my mother often frequents.

When I walked into the shop, I was fortunate to have Mr. Williams, the proprietor of the florist, wait on me…, especially since I didn't have a clue as to what I needed to buy.

Mr. Williams has known my parents for years, and yes…, you guessed it - the florist is on Dad's truck delivery route as well.

To tell you the truth, I don't frequent the florist all that much, and my fiancée will certainly attest to that. But knowing that Mr. Williams was waiting on me certainly put my mind at ease, and I knew that he would fix me up with a very nice floral arrangement.

As I approached the counter, Mr. Williams casually asked, "Say…, aren't you Winnie O'Leary's boy?"

"Yes…, that's right, Mr. Williams."

"So what can I do for you today?"

"Well, I need a floral arrangement for a coworker of mine, who suddenly passed away in his sleep early this morning Mr. Williams. Can you help me out?"

"Why sure…, in fact I've got just the perfect floral arrangement for you. Jackie, is it?" Mr. Williams inquired, kindly.

"Yes…, Jackie." I said, and feeling like I was ten years old again.

"Well Jackie, seeing it's you, and I know your Mom and Dad, I'm going to sell this floral arrangement to you for only forty-five dollars. How does that sound?"

"That sounds great, Mr. Williams! I'll take it, and thank you!"

Mr. Williams smiled and then nodded his head in appreciation of my gratitude. He then carefully took the flower arrangement out of the refrigerated display case, and then proceeded to wrap it up in pretty tissue paper.

So after paying Mr. Williams the forty-five dollars, I was thinking that I still had thirty dollars left over and I wanted to spend it.

It then occurred to me that it might be nice to bring some baked goods over to Sarah's house, so I decided to swing by Migliori's bakery and pick up an assortment of pastry, rolls, and a large tray of Italian cookies with the remaining funds.

When I entered the bakery, Mr. Migliori was standing behind the counter. Upon seeing me, he enthusiastically blurted out in his melodic Italian accent, "Jackie boy, bon giorno! Where-da-heck-have-a-you-been-a-hiding-you-self-a?"

"Hi, Mr. Migliori. You're right, it's been a long time, but I still know where to go to get the best baked goods in town." I replied, and trying to sound cheerful despite my heavy heart.

"So Jackie, what's-a-been-a-go-in-on-with-a-you,-Pisano? Are-you-a-here-to-pick-up-some-a-bake-a-goods-for-a-dinner-ta-night?" Mr. Migliori asked, with a big smile.

"No…, no…, Mr. Migliori, I'm bringing the baked goods over to a friend's house. Her husband passed away in his sleep early this morning, so I thought I'd pick up an assortment of rolls, pastry, and a large tray of Italian cookies."

"Oh…, I'm-a-so-sorry-to-a-hear-that-Jackie boy. Okay…, okay…, now-don't-a-you-worry, I'll-a-fix-a-you-up-a. Jackie, not-to-be-a-nosey, butta-who-a-died?"

"Actually, he was a coworker of mine. His name was Joe Atkins. Did you know him?"

"No…, the name doesn't ring-a-da-bella. Listen, you sit, and I'll-a-put-a-da-order together. Help-a-you-self-to-some-fresh-a-coffee, capisce!"

I watched Mr. Migliori throw my order together in no time at all. Mr. Migliori looked like a "maestro," as he danced around the bakery counter snagging baked goods left and right, and then placing them ever so carefully in the bakery boxes that were all lined up on top of the counter. He then boxed them up and tied the string like a craftsman, and watching him actually picked up my gloomy spirits a notch.

When Mr. Migliori finished filling my order, I attempted to hand him the thirty dollars, which was balance of the collection money.

Mr. Migliori then said, in his beautiful Italian accent, "Whatta-ya-doin-a-Jackie-boy-a, keep-a-you-money, this-is-a-my-a-treat. Tella-da-Atkins-family-that I'm-a-so-sorry-for-their-loss, and please-convey-my-a----come si dice…., how-a-you-say-a----oh yeah…, my-a-sympathies."

"But Mr. Migliori, I can't take all this stuff for free! Please…, take the thirty dollars, which I'm sure is still not enough money for all of the stuff that you've given me!" I pleaded.

"Jackie, please, letta-me-do-this, and say-a-hello-to-your-Mama-and-Papa-for-me, yes! Hey…, and-don't-a-wait-a-so-long-to-come-back-here-and-a-see-me, capisce. Okay, arrivederci, and bon appetite!" Mr. Migliori said, with a warm smile.

To tell you the truth, I wasn't too happy about walking out of Migliori's bakery without paying him any money, but Mr. Migliori's actions didn't surprise me one bit. Mr. Migliori is a very kind and generous man. One way or another, I'll make sure that I make this up to him, but for now I've got to get over to Sarah's house so that I can pay my respects.

When I arrived at Sarah's house the street was literally dotted with parked cars on both sides of the street. Presumably everyone was here to pay their respects to Sarah. I actually had to park my car two full blocks away in order to get an available parking space.

As I got out of my car, I decided to leave the flowers and all of the baked goods in the backseat and go knock on the front door first. I didn't want to be juggling all these items so far away from the house on my own. As I rang the doorbell, I was hoping that Bob would answer the door and thankfully he did.

"Hi, Bob. It's good to see ya." I said, somberly.

"Likewise, Jack. C'mon in," he said, with a faint smile.

When I entered the home, Bob surprised me by giving me a warm embrace, and I responded by embracing him back. Bob then quietly said, "Thanks for stopping by, Jack."

"Yeah, you're welcome. Hey Bob, I brought over a few items that are sitting in the backseat of my car. Do you think you could help me bring them in?"

"Sure, Jack. I've been cooped up in this house all day, and I could use a little fresh air."

When we reached my car, Bob noticed that the backseat was completely buried. He then humorously remarked, "Geez O'Leary..., what the heck did you do, rob a bakery?"

I chuckled at Bob's remark and then replied, "Well, actually Bob, you're not too far off the mark. I robbed Migliori's, you know..., that little Italian bakery over on Andreano Avenue."

"Yeah, sure, Migliori's..., it's a great little bakery." Watson said, as he shut the back door of my car, and then helped me lug the items toward the house.

"Well get this Bob, Mr. Migliori gave me all this stuff for free, as a way of conveying his condolences to the Atkins family. Can you believe it? He doesn't even know Joe or Sarah, but that's the kind of man Mr. Migliori is."

"Huh..., I'll have to remember that." Watson said, as he opened up the front door.

We entered the house and managed to find an empty space on the counter for the flowers and all of the baked goods.

As I glanced around the house, it was jammed packed. I guess I wasn't expecting such a large turnout this afternoon, but seeing all of these people made me feel a little more insulated.

Bob walked into the kitchen, reached into the refrigerator, and then handed me an ice cold beer while saying, "Here ya go, Irish. You look like you could really use one of these."

"Thanks, Bob." I replied, as I twisted the cap and then took a healthy guzzle of my beer.

Bob then said, "Jack, c'mon this way..., I wanna introduce you to my wife Anna."

"Oh, okay...," I answered, and then I took one more healthy guzzle of my beer and polished that "bad boy" off in two hearty swigs.

As Watson side-stepped his way through the crowd, I followed closely behind him.

We seemed to be walking in the direction of a tall, slender, and very attractive woman, who noticeably stood out in the crowd. This very striking woman was holding a beverage in one hand, and a small dish of hors d'oeuvres in the other. She was engaged in a quiet conversation with another woman, but one who was much older than her.

Watson waited until there was a pause in their conversation, and then quietly interrupted his wife Anna by saying, "Excuse me, Anna…, but I'd like you to meet the young man that I was telling you about earlier. This is Jack O'Leary. Jack, this is my wife Anna."

We cordially shook hands, and then greeted each other by simultaneously saying, "It's a pleasure to meet you."

At that moment, the exactness of our words, and the precise cadence by which we said it, prompted both of us to quietly chuckle. We then held an admiring stare toward each other.

Anna then pleasantly said, "Bob has told me so much about you Jack. I'm so happy to finally make your acquaintance. I'm only sorry it had to be under these circumstances."

"Yes, I agree, Anna."

As I chatted with the Watson's, I was keeping an eye out for Sarah because I wanted to convey my condolences to her. Other than Bob and Anna Watson, I really didn't know anyone else in the room. Thus far, none of the WEALTH staff had dropped by to pay their respects yet.

While continuing to converse with Bob and Anna, I kept thinking to myself, "Boy, another ice cold beer would sure taste good right about now," but I thought better of it…, because I didn't want Bob to think that his young protégé had succumbed to the "Irish curse."

I then quietly asked, "So have you made any arrangements for the calling hours yet, Bob? Several of the staff down at work were making some inquiries."

"Well…," Bob hesitated a bit, and then glanced at Anna, who seemed to catch his eye. Bob then cautiously said, "Today, right now…, these are the calling hours."

"Oh…, I see." I replied, somewhat surprised.

Bob quietly said, "Sarah decided against having any calling hours at the funeral home. She preferred to have a small gathering of family and friends in the comfort of her own home, with plenty of food and drink."

"I understand," I said, respectfully.

Anna was quietly listening to the conversation, and she smiled at me each time I glanced her way. I sensed that she and Bob both knew that these were unusual circumstances. I'm not saying that it was the wrong to do, but I guess I'm more accustomed to having the calling hours at the funeral home, with people parading past the body and saying a few gratuitous words, or quietly praying on the kneeler, as they reflect on some tender moments about the deceased.

"So when is the funeral Bob?" I asked, with some uneasiness.

Bob replied, "Tomorrow…, and I have decided to cancel programming for tomorrow as well. Joe was an icon at our agency, and closing WEALTH in his honor is the right thing to do."

"What church is Sarah affiliated with?" I asked, with interest.

"Saint Luke's, however the service tomorrow will be celebrated at Saint Stephen's because it is a much larger church, and we're expecting a huge turnout. Do you need directions to Saint Stephen's?" Bob asked, casually.

"Um, no…, I know how to get to Saint Stephen's. It's a magnificent church, and it must hold several thousand people." I stated, with utter assuredness.

"Yes, you're right. Sarah knows the pastor of Saint Stephen's quite well. I think they may have gone to high school together." Bob commented.

"Um…, I don't know if I mentioned this to you Bob, but I was an altar boy as a kid, and I've actually served Mass in every Catholic Church in the city. In fact, I almost went into the seminary."

"Is that right," Bob said, as he popped a luscious hors d'oeuvre into his mouth.

"That's right, Bob. You see…, growing up I was a good little Irish Catholic altar boy, and not only did I serve on the altar every day at weekday Mass, but I also served Mass two to three times every Sunday morning in our home parish of Saint Patrick's as well."

"Huh, Saint Patrick's…, I should've guessed." Bob said, chuckling.

"Well Bob, my mother is very pious, and she enjoys attending Mass every day, and two to three times on Sunday. And not just at our parish, but she's also been known to jump in the car and hit one or two other churches in the same day as well."

"Really now…," Bob said, with a slight smirk.

"Yep, that's right! My Mom loved dragging me along with her, and then dropping me off at the sacristy so that I could help serve Mass up on the altar with the priest. I think seeing her little "Jackie boy" up on the altar gave her a great sense of joy, and I truly believe she thought I was some sort of emissary to God. To this day, I still don't know how she managed to finagle a way to get me up on all those different altars around town, but she did."

Bob then began to laugh uncontrollably, as he commented, "Gee, now I see where all of that Irish Catholic guilt of yours comes from O'Leary!"

"Yeah, well…, you don't know the half of it Bob." I said, snickering.

"Jack, you're very funny." Anna said, as she placed her hand over her mouth, and then quietly chuckled.

"Well…, thanks Anna, but unfortunately this is my life we're laughing about." I quipped, as we all laughed once again.

Just then I saw several of the WEALTH staff filing into the house, most notably, Ralph, Smitty, Terry, Dolly, and even C.D. showed up. Then out of the corner of my eye I saw Sarah.

I turned to Bob, and quietly said, "There's Sarah, I should go over and pay my respects to her."

Bob hastily replied, "No…, not yet, Jack. Let her mingle, she just woke up from a nap. There'll be plenty of time for you to talk to her later, okay."

As Sarah made her way through the crowd, she appeared to be putting up a pretty good front. She was smiling and conversing and telling people to help themselves to food and drink.

I then saw Ralph give Sarah a hug. As I watched that tender moment between them, I could see tears streaming down Sarah's face, and for the first time today I felt incredibly sad.

Sarah then began hugging each member of the WEALTH staff, as they were all lined up in a row to offer their condolences. Sarah was knocking them off one-by-one, as she gave each of them a firm hug, while valiantly saying, "Thank you for coming, thank you for coming…."

So after hugging Dolly, who was the last person in line, Sarah quickly turned and spotted me standing next to Bob and Anna. Sarah smiled and then walked directly over to me.

Sarah proceeded to give me a big hug, and then bravely said, "Jack, thank you for coming over to the house. Did you get something to eat? Please…, help yourself. There's plenty of food out in the kitchen. People have been so generous. Please eat something because I really don't know what I'm going to do with all of this food."

As I listened to Sarah ramble on, I could tell that she was very shaky, and that she was barely holding it together. Her voice was quivering, and her thoughts sounded quite scattered.

"Thanks, Sarah. I'll get something to eat in a little while."

"Okay…, but make sure you help yourself to anything in the house." She said, adamantly.

"I know, I will. Thanks, Sarge."

Sarah then clasped her hands in mine, and with tears welling up in her eyes she earnestly said, "Jack, I just wanted you to know that Joe absolutely loved you. He spoke of you quite often, and wished that everyone on the WEALTH counseling staff could've been more like you."

"Thank you, Sarge. That really means a lot to me." I said, as tears ran down my face.

Watson was listening intently, and then comfortingly placed his hand on my shoulder.

Sarah then fought to be strong, as she mustered the courage to say, "Now c'mon…, I want you to get something to eat out in the kitchen. Bob, why don't you go with Jack and get something to eat as well, and make sure you bring something back for Anna."

"Yeah, okay…, that sounds good Sarge." Bob replied.

Bob and I then headed toward the kitchen, and en route we saw a small contingency of WEALTH staff that were all huddled together in the far corner of the living room.

As the WEALTH staff chatted amongst themselves, they were all helping themselves to a plate of hors d'oeuvres. Upon seeing Watson, they "wolfed down" whatever food they had on their plate, and then looked guiltier than a kid in a candy store.

Although I found their actions to be utterly amusing, I knew that this was not the time or the place to be saying anything funny, so I just decided to keep my thoughts and comments to myself.

We stopped and chatted with the WEALTH staff for a few minutes, and Bob actually cracked a few jokes, which seemed to take the WEALTH contingency by surprise.

Apparently, Bob's sense of humor was quite foreign to them, but not to me. Ironically, here I am the least senior member on staff, yet I seem to know more about the boss than they did.

In my short tenure with Bob, I have gotten to know him better than people who have known him for ten, twenty, or even thirty years. I only wish that the WEALTH staff could have a similar appreciation for Bob as I do.

Bob once again reminded the staff that WEALTH was going to be closed tomorrow, and yes…, - according to "Ebenezer" Watson, the staff would all be paid for the day and the time would not be charge against their accruals. Watson also stated that the funeral Mass was at ten o'clock, and that the service was going to be held at Saint Stephen's Church.

Watson then humorously said, "If you all expect to be paid for the day, then I expect to see you all in attendance at Saint Stephen's Church tomorrow morning…, and on time."

So after making his grand announcement, Bob then cordially invited everyone into the kitchen for some food and refreshments.

When we walked into the kitchen, the room was wall to wall people. I saw C.D. across the way conversing with someone and he had a cup of coffee in his hand, surprise, surprise. I then caught his eye and motioned for him to come over and chat with me.

As C.D. and I shook hands, he glumly said, "Hey kid, how's it going? Boy, it sure is tough about Atkins."

"Yeah, it sure is. So I think you have some unfinished business to attend to with Bob, wouldn't you agree, C.D.? So why don't you go over there and patch things up with him?"

"Ah…, Bob is it, sounds pretty chummy. So are you two on a first name basis now?"

I chuckled at C.D.'s sarcastic tone, and simply said, "Could be, but I don't kiss and tell."

C.D. smirked at my whimsical remark, and then commented, "Uh…, you mean kiss ass, don't ya?"

I quietly snickered at C.D.'s wisecrack, but then took a more serious tone by saying, "Listen C.D., you and Bob go way back. I don't think you want some silly squabble to stand in the way of doing something that you might regret, don't you agree."

C.D. replied, "Maybe…, but things got real ugly between us this time, and I don't think it can be fixed."

I then interjected, "Well, as an old professor of mine would often say, "You'll never know how cold the water is unless you get your feet wet," which I think applies in this case, wouldn't you agree, C.D.?"

"Hey…, what the hell is that supposed to mean kid? Are you trying to throw that college mumbo-gumbo at me again, because it won't fly?" C.D. exclaimed, and sounding really scared.

"Shhh…, simmer down, you know exactly what it means. So I suggest that you elbow your way through the crowd, and go over there and talk to Bob. At the very least, you should make your condolences known to Bob about Joe." I said, adamantly.

"Yeah, you're right. Thanks, kid. Talk to you later."

C.D. made his way over to Bob, and I made my way over to the refrigerator, so that I could crack open another ice cold beer.

It then suddenly dawned on me that I had neglected to phone home and inform Mom and Dad of Joe's death, and to also tell them that I was stopping by Sarah's house to pay my respects.

Well, since I was halfway towards the refrigerator, I figured first things first. I'll grab my beer, and then I'll make my call.

Suddenly, I felt like a "salmon running up river," as I negotiated my way through the dense crowd of people. I managed to snatch a beer out of the refrigerator, and then made my way towards the telephone so that I could call Mom and Dad.

When I telephoned home, Mom wondered where I was. She was sad to hear the news about Joe, and said that she would certainly keep Sarah in her prayers.

Before hanging up the phone, Mom felt compelled to remind me, "Jackie, make sure you drive carefully on your way home tonight, your eyes…, remember."

I thought to myself, "My eyes…, how could I forget that albatross hanging around my neck? My eyes are the reason I'm fielding four to five phone calls from the Sampson's every day, and not up in the broadcasting booth where I should've been destined to be."

As I made my way back toward the kitchen, I noticed that C.D. and Bob were engrossed in a very serious conversation, and by all accounts it appeared to be civil.

When their conversation concluded, they smiled and shook hands. I was happy that they were able to resolve their differences, and even happier that no punches had been thrown.

As the afternoon wore on I noticed that I was becoming more and more comfortable in my surroundings. Initially, I was quite nervous about being here today, but now I seem to have acquired an unexplained feeling of contentment that's come over me.

Could this contentment be due to all of the familiar faces I see, or is it simply the four bottles of imported beer that I've managed to guzzle down in the course of an afternoon?

Then again…, maybe it was a little of both.

People kept streaming into the house at a steady pace. I saw members of the business community that Joe networked with along with several OVR counselors, including Farnsworth.

To be honest, I'm sure that Farnsworth saw me, but he didn't bother to go out of his way to even acknowledge me. The OVR counselors that dropped by all knew Joe from their early days of working at WEALTH, so naturally they stopped by the house to pay their respects.

When it came right down to it, all of the OVR counselors knew that Joe was the best placement specialist in the city, and they also knew that with him being gone then their chances of placing clients into meaningful work slots just got a lot tougher.

It was starting to get late and many of the guests were heading toward the door. C.D. and Ralph were reaching for their jackets, and I told them that I would walk out with them.

When I said "good-bye" to Sarah, she looked absolutely exhausted. I gave her a gentle hug, and then told her that I'd see her at the church service tomorrow morning. Despite her best efforts, all Sarah could manage to do was muster a faint smile and quietly nod her head.

As I turned for the door, Bob extended his hand for a parting handshake and said, "Jack, thanks again for everything, including talking some sense into C.D. tonight. Although, if you ask me, I think you may have had some ulterior motives in coaxing him back to work."

"Oh really..., and what exactly would those motives be Bob?"

"Well, let's see..., probably because your coffee is lousy and you don't have anyone to talk in-depth sports with in the morning." Bob said, chuckling.

"Yeah, well..., I guess that just about covers it Bob." I replied, with a slight grin.

"Yes, well, that's why I'm the boss Jack. But all kidding aside, thanks again for everything. So I'll see you at the church service tomorrow, right?"

"Oh yeah, I'll be there. See ya in the morning, Bob. Good-night."

When I arrived home, I shared the events of the day with Mom and Dad. They truly felt my pain, and were so emotionally moved by my words and heartfelt sentiments that they asked if they could accompany me to the funeral Mass at Saint Stephen's Church tomorrow.

Naturally, I told them "yes," but then quickly remembering that Mom never misses an opportunity to commune with the Lord.

So after Mom and Dad went to bed, I quietly sat on the living room couch and reflected on the events of the day. It was going toward eleven o'clock now, and it suddenly dawned on me that I had failed to notify Lenore Richards that the agency would be closed tomorrow.

Ordinarily, I'm not one to make phone calls after ten o'clock, but these were unusual circumstances, so I dialed Lenore's number and hoped that she hadn't gone to bed yet.

The phone rang once, and a soft voice quickly answered, "hello."

"Oh…, hi Lenore, this is Jack O'Leary. I'm sorry to be calling you so late, but I needed to tell you that WEALTH Industries will not be in operation tomorrow."

Lenore, realizing that it was me, then perked up and inquisitively asked, "Oh really…, why's that Jack?"

"Well, as you know, one of our staff members passed away in his sleep early this morning. Anyway, the funeral is tomorrow, and we're closing the agency in his honor so that everyone at WEALTH can attend the service."

"I see. Well, I think it's quite admirable that the agency is going to be closed in his honor tomorrow." Lenore staunchly replied.

"Yes, I agree. Joe was not only an icon at our agency, but he was a pillar of the community as well. He was a great man." I said, very respectfully.

"So is it a closed service, or can the public attend?" Lenore sweetly asked.

"No…, it's open to the public. As a matter of fact, they're having the service at Saint Stephen's Church, which is the largest Catholic Church in the city. From what I understand, they're anticipating a large turnout tomorrow."

"What time is the service tomorrow?" Lenore quietly asked.

"Ten o'clock, at Saint Stephen's Church."

"Um…, would it be okay if I attended the service?" She asked, innocently.

"By all means, Lenore. However, I don't want you to feel obligated."

"No…, I'd really like to go Jack. May I sit with you?"

"Certainly, Lenore. Do you need a ride to the church?"

"No thanks, the church is pretty close to where I live. I'll just walk, I love the fresh air."

"Okay, well…, I'll see you tomorrow morning. Good-night, Lenore."

"Good-night, Jack. Thanks again for calling."

The following day Mom, Dad, and I drove over to Saint Stephen's Church to attend Joe's funeral. Although there were not many parking spaces to be had, we were very fortunate to find a prime spot close to the church. Apparently, Mom knows the caretaker of the church, and he waved us into a restricted parking lot that is reserved for only clergy and church personnel.

Gee, I guess churchgoing has its rewards after all!

The funeral service was slated to begin at ten o'clock, but we arrived at nine-fifteen. We decided to get there a little bit early because not only were we anticipating a large turnout, but also because Mom enjoys praying the Rosary and having some quiet time with the Lord.

We walked into the church, splashed ourselves with holy water, and then proceeded to make the "Sign of the Cross." Mom then walked directly over to the elegant marble statue of the Blessed Mother, which radiantly stood in the front vestibule of the church.

Once again, Mom made the "Sign of the Cross," and then stood there gazing at the elegant statue of Our Blessed Mother, as she marveled at all of its beauty.

I then gently leaned into Mom, and whispered, "C'mon Mom, we gotta find a seat."

Mom replied, "Okay…, but look Jackie, isn't Our Blessed Mother beautiful?"

"Yes Mom, she's beautiful, but you say that every time you come to Saint Stephen's."

We made our way up the center aisle, and then sat in the pew directly behind Bob Watson and the immediate family.

As we filed into the pew, I reminded Dad to make sure that we had enough room for Lenore. I then knelt down and said a few prayers, and when I was done praying I tapped Bob Watson's shoulder and quietly said, "good morning."

Bob turned around and smiled, which then prompted me to say, "Hi Bob, I'd like to introduce my parents. This is my Dad, Jack O'Leary Sr., and my Mom, Winnie O'Leary."

My parents and Bob Watson cordially shook hands, and then exchanged a few light pleasantries with one another. Bob then introduced his wife Anna to my parents.

I waited for a pause in their conversation, and then I asked Bob where Sarah was. Bob informed me that she was over in the rectory with Father O'Malley having tea, and deciding on what scripture passages would be recited for the funeral service.

So while Bob and Anna conversed with my parents, I kept a vigilant eye out for Lenore. Hordes of people kept filing into the church at a steady pace. I started to get a little concerned that Lenore wouldn't find us in the dense crowd, so I gave

Dad a gentle nudge and told him that I was going to walk to the back of the church and wait for Lenore.

And in terms of saying anything to Mom, what was the point? Mom was already knee-deep in reciting the Rosary, and praying for God to keep us all safely in the Palm of His Hand.

Well, I no sooner reached the back of the church, when suddenly I felt a light tapping on my shoulder. When I turned to see who it was, it was Lenore.

Lenore gently smiled, and then I informed her that we were all sitting in the front of the church with my parents and the Watson family.

We walked up the center aisle, genuflected, and then joined Mom and Dad in the pew. I then introduced Lenore to my parents, and they exchanged a few light pleasantries.

While Lenore turned to compliment Mom on her dress, Dad leaned over to me and boldly whispered, "That Lenore is quite a looker, Jackie boy. Just remember…, you have a fiancée."

I gave Dad a sarcastic stare. And before I could even respond to his totally unexpected and startling remark, Bob Watson then turned around and acknowledged Lenore by saying, "Good morning, Lenore. It was very considerate of you to join us…, thank you for being here."

I too echoed Bob's sentiments and admired Lenore for attending the service today. When you think about it, here she is a brand new intern in a totally new situation, yet she opted to attend a funeral service of a man that she didn't even know.

Quite honestly, most young people in Lenore's situation would have preferred a leisurely day off, such as a day at the beach or shopping at the mall, but not Lenore.

Just then Sarah exited the sacristy and joined us in the congregation. Before sitting down in the pew next to Bob, she acknowledged me and warmly smiled. I then introduced Sarah to my parents and Lenore. Sarah thanked all of us for attending the service today, and then she quietly sat down next to her "baby" brother, who then lovingly placed his arm around his big sister.

It was now time for the service to begin. I don't think you could've squeezed one more person into the church, even if you tried. The community really came out in droves to honor Joe.

Father O'Malley, who is the pastor of Sarah's home parish, which is Saint Luke's, helped officiate over the funeral service with Father Sheridan, who is the pastor of Saint Stephen's.

It was a lovely service, with poignant scripture passages recited by Bob and

Anna Watson, and also by Ralph…, who provided the congregation with some inspiring insights and heartwarming stories on how Joe lived his life.

To my surprise, Ralph had a wonderful public speaking voice. He captivated the crowd with his emotionally charged words, and he also shared a few humorous and zany tales regarding his best friend Joe and the amazing forty year friendship that they enjoyed with one another.

So after all of the thought provoking readings and heartfelt testimonials, the Benediction part of the service was held.

Suddenly, the church became engulfed in an aromatic smell of incense, and a sense of sorrow seemed to loom over the entire crowd. The congregation was quite moved by the prayers and actions of Father O'Malley and Father Sheridan, as they blessed the casket with incense and then solemnly prayed over the body. Needless to say, but there wasn't a dry eye in God's House.

When the service concluded, we all congregated outside on the church steps. Bob then informed us that there would be a luncheon for family and friends over at Flaherty's restaurant.

Bob was quite insistent that we all attend the luncheon, and then he turned to Lenore and quietly said, "Lenore, you're certainly welcome to join us, if you feel so inclined."

Lenore then proudly replied, "I would be honored to join you. Thank you, Mr. Watson."

Bob then turned toward my parents and cordially asked, "Mr. and Mrs. O'Leary, would you care to join us at Flaherty's? It will give us an opportunity to get to know each other better."

"Yes, we'd love to join you Mr. Watson." Mom graciously replied.

Flaherty's restaurant was only about a five minute car ride from the church, and it was considered to be one of the finest restaurants in town. Although I've never had the pleasure of eating there before, it was known for its elegant fine dining and specialty dishes of Irish cuisine.

Mr. Flaherty, who is the owner of the restaurant, was a very rich and highly successful businessman and restaurateur.

Apparently, Joe Atkins and Mr. Flaherty had a solid business relationship, and given the fact that they were both from good Irish stock, well…, that certainly didn't hurt matters either.

Mr. Flaherty bought into Joe's ideas about hiring the disabled, and over the years Joe had successfully placed well over a dozen workers at Mr. Flaherty's restaurant.

On the short drive over to the restaurant, Dad mentioned to me that he knew Mr. Flaherty personally, and that he was actually on a first name basis with him as well.

In a very magnanimous gesture on Mr. Flaherty's part, he decided to reserve the back room of his restaurant for the luncheon today, free of charge…, which was his way of honoring his good friend Joe Atkins.

So after everyone was assembled, Mr. Flaherty went around to each of the tables and told his guests to order anything they wanted to off of the menu, and made it a point to say in his elegant Irish brogue, "Please don't be shy…, it's on me!"

Mr. Flaherty then spotted Dad from across the room, and gave him a big smile and a hearty wave. Flaherty then exuberantly called out, "Jack O'Leary, we'll talk later…, boy!"

So after everyone was seated at their tables, Mr. Flaherty reached for the microphone so that he could address the crowd, and at that moment a hush fell over the entire room.

Mr. Flaherty cleared his voice, and then said in his exquisite Irish brogue, "May I please have your attention? First and foremost, I wanna t'ank you all for being here today. Today is a day of celebration for our dear friend Joe Atkins, so let's all have a good time in his memory. As a token of my appreciation, I'd like you to order whatever you want off of the menu, and I want you all to eat to your heart's content. Oh…, and please don't forget to help yourself at the bar, because the drinks are on the house!"

When Dad heard that the drinks were on the house, it was like music to his ears!

Dad then looked me straight in the eye, and excitedly said, "C'mon…, Jackie boy! Let's get up there and have us a drink! You certainly don't have to tell me twice!"

To put it bluntly, Dad has as the Irish would say…, a "wee bit" of a drinking problem, and sometimes the "drink," as they also say…, can get the best of him.

So without hesitation, Dad made haste for the bar and ordered up his favorite beverage before the magnanimous gesture on the part of Mr. Flaherty was rescinded.

That being said, I thought I would follow Dad up to the bar, not only for company, but to also serve as his conscience as well. Before joining Dad up at the bar, I asked Mom and Lenore if they would care for something to drink.

Mom perked right up and quickly said, "Yes Jackie, I'd like a nice gin and tonic, please."

I then turned to Lenore, who quietly said, "Um..., a glass of white wine would be lovely. Thank you, Jack."

So by the time I made it up to the bar, Dad had already quaffed down an ice cold beer, and he was looking to get the attention of the bartender, so that he could order up another.

When Dad realized that I was standing right next to him, he exuberantly shouted, "C'mon..., Jackie boy! Get in here and enjoy an ice cold bottle of beer with your old man!"

I calmly replied, "Okay Dad, but first I promised to bring some drinks back to the table for Mom and Lenore. Tell ya what..., why don't ya order me up any bottle of German import beer that they have, and I'll be right back to join ya, okay."

Dad looked at me rather cockeyed, and then boldly said, "A German import! Jackie boy..., the Germans don't know shit about beer! Why don't I order ya up a good old Irish Stout?"

"Okay Dad..., that'll be fine."

To tell ya the truth, I didn't want to leave Dad up at the bar any longer than I had to. For all I know he may be knocking back his third or fourth bottle of beer by the time I get back from bringing the ladies their drinks.

After all..., Mr. Flaherty said, "don't be shy," and believe you me that's all the encouragement that Dad needed to hear.

So after handing the ladies their drinks, I then casually asked them, "Would you ladies mind if I stayed up at the bar and chatted with Dad and the guys for a little while?"

Of course, what I was asking them was merely a smokescreen, because my main reason for going back up to the bar was to keep a steady eye on Dad, but I certainly didn't want to convey my true sentiments on the matter, especially with Lenore sitting right there at the table.

Mom took a sip of her gin and tonic, and then blurted out, "That's a good idea, Jackie. That way you can keep an eye on your father. You know how he gets when he drinks too much."

Well..., so much for discretion!

Obviously, I would've preferred keeping Lenore in the dark with regards to all of the O'Leary skeletons, which up until now were safely tucked away in the back of the family closet.

When I finally made up to the bar, the first thing I asked Dad was, "So Dad, how many soldiers have reported into camp?"

That was my subtle way of asking Dad how many beers he's already consumed thus far.

But to be honest with you, I don't even know why I bothered asking him that question, because I knew I wasn't going to get a straight answer out of him anyway.

Dad replied, "Oh this, um…, it's my second beer, and I took the liberty of ordering you up an ice cold Irish Stout, Jackie boy! So whatta ya say we drink one for Joe Atkins, eh boy!"

So after hoisting our glasses in the air, Dad guzzled down his "second" beer, and then asked the bartender to set him up with another. His "third," I believe.

Yeah right!

Dad must be living in a time warp, because he's still treating me like I'm ten years old! By my calculations, Dad has already had at least three beers by now…, maybe even four!

I then leaned into Dad, and whispered on the Q.T., "C'mon Dad, you gotta pace yourself. It's not even noon yet, and you've already drank more beer in one hour than Mom allows you to have in a whole month."

When Dad drinks, he likes to speak in an Irish brogue, whether he's home or at the local pub. So in his best made up Irish brogue, Dad whimsically said, "Jackie boy, don't worry about your mother or your coworkers. This is a day for celebration in the swankiest Irish restaurant in town. The Irish sure know how to throw a party when you die. Wouldn't you agree, Jackie boy?"

"T'at I would, t'at I would," I replied, in a "wee bit" of an Irish brogue of my own.

By now, Dad had hoisted two sheets into the wind, and he was on the verge of hoisting his third and final sheet up the mast. He was downing the beer like there was no tomorrow, as he kept slurring his words, and speaking in his cockamamie Irish brogue to everyone along the bar.

Dad looked up from his beer, and then whimsically said, "There's an old Irish expression that maybe you've heard before Jackie boy, and it goes like this, "Perhaps no one lives better than the Italians, but certainly no one dies better than the Irish." May God bless ya, Joe Atkins!"

At that moment, Dad raised his glass up to the heavens, and then quaffed down his beer in one full gulp.

I then echoed Dad's sentiments by saying, "I'll drink to that Dad, but try to keep it down, okay."

Dad caught the eye of the bartender, who then handed Dad another bottle of Irish Stout. So after taking a hearty slug of his ice cold beer, Dad panned the room and said in his slurring Irish brogue, "This is a real swanky joint. Wouldn't you agree, Jackie boy?"

"Yeah, it's really nice Dad," as I ran my hand across the smooth oak finish of the bar.

"Well Jackie boy…, I've been in this restaurant many times making my deliveries, but I never thought I'd have the pleasure of being a guest in here. Mr. Flaherty is a real stand-up guy, especially for someone who is as loaded as he is. Well, speak of the devil, will look who it is." Dad said, as he saw Mr. Flaherty approaching the bar to say hello to some of the fellas.

Mr. Flaherty, who was en route to the kitchen, was all smiles as he passed by the bar.

When Flaherty spotted Dad, he pleasantly said, "Jack O'Leary, how are ya…, boy!"

Dad shook Mr. Flaherty's hand, and then replied in his cockamamie Irish brogue, which by now was quite embarrassing to listen to, "Hello Kevin, we were just speakin' of ya, lad. I'd like to introduce me son, Jackie. Jackie boy, this is the founder of the feast, Mr. Kevin Flaherty."

"It's a pleasure to make your acquaintance, Mr. Flaherty." I cordially said, as we firmly shook hands.

"The pleasure is all mine Jackie!" Mr. Flaherty replied, exuberantly.

"Kevin…, Jackie worked with Joe Atkins down at WEALTH, and they were very close friends. Isn't that right, Jackie boy?" Dad said, as he guzzled down his beer, and prayed that it wouldn't be his last.

It was becoming quite obvious that Dad was starting to feel the effects of all that Irish Stout he was drinking. His speech was noticeably slurred and his balance was quite unsteady.

Dad was definitely out of practice because Mom keeps him on a fairly short leash. Mom knows what Dad is capable of when he gets tipsy. When Dad drinks, he has a tendency to be boisterous. Not in an obnoxious way, but in a way that would still be characterized as being socially unacceptable. To my way of thinking, I would classified Dad as a happy drunk.

Flaherty then staunchly said, in his elegant Irish brogue, "Joe was a great man, and this celebration that we're having today in his honor is only a small token of my appreciation!"

"Yes…, I wholeheartedly agree Mr. Flaherty, and I'd like to thank you once again for your abundant generosity." I said, respectfully.

Flaherty replied, "T'ank you, Jackie. Now, if you gentlemen will please excuse me my presence is required in the kitchen. If there's anything you boys want then be sure to ask for it."

Now Flaherty's Irish brogue was the real McCoy, and not a phony made up brogue like Dad's

As Mr. Flaherty headed toward the kitchen, Dad hoisted his glass in the air and replied, "Now there goes a great man, Jackie boy. A great "Irish" man…, and he sure takes care of your old man at Christmas!"

Just as I was about to order up another Irish Stout, I heard Bob Watson's voice come over the loudspeaker and say, "Excuse me, everybody…, but can I please have your attention."

Bob raised his glass in the air, and then reverently said, "I would like to propose a toast. Here's to Mr. Kevin Flaherty, who we would like to thank for hosting this celebration today in honoring our dear friend Joe Atkins."

Upon hearing Bob's toast, there was the sound of glasses clinking and people echoing the words, "Hear! Hear!"

Everyone took a sip from their glass, and then looking skyward Bob said in jest, "Yeah, I'm sure Joe is giving God a few tips on how to run things more efficiently up there. To Joe!"

The crowd roared with laughter, including Father O'Malley and Father Sheridan, as we all raised our glass once again to pay tribute and homage to our dear friend Joe.

Well, the afternoon festivities were absolutely wonderful. The crowd was happy and the mood was light and carefree. There were all sorts of reminiscent stories being bantered around the room regarding Joe and all of his zany hi-jinxes over the years.

The food was simply out of this world, and no one was holding back when it came to ordering off of the menu. Steak, lobster, and all sorts of exquisite Irish dishes were being served.

Flaherty even went to the expense of hiring a quartet, which not only entertained the crowd with an array of toe-tapping Irish music, but with an assortment of traditional Gaelic melodies as well. People sang and danced, oh yeah…, and they "bloody well" drank too!

Dad's drinking had slowed down dramatically as the afternoon wore on because Mom was now keeping a pretty steady eye on him. Mom was so preoccupied in watching Dad that she didn't see me knock back beer after beer throughout the course of the afternoon.

The highlight of the day was watching some of the old-timers teaching the youngsters how to dance the Irish jig.

The fiddles were screechin' and the hands-were-a-clappin', as the banquet hall was engulfed in all sorts of melodic Irish sounds.

Even Mr. Flaherty got out on the dance floor. He kept the beat of the music going with his oak shillelagh, as he proudly showcased his Irish step-dancing talents.

In truth, the afternoon festivities resembled more of a St. Patrick's Day celebration than it did for the passing of a great friend.

I was glad that we were not consumed with feelings of grief or sorrow about Joe, or even realizing the main reason why we were all assembled there in the first place.

Today was truly a day that placed more emphasis on celebrating a life than mourning a death.

When the glorious affair was over, we all hugged and said farewell to each other. We managed to clear out the restaurant by five o'clock, which was just in time for Mr. Flaherty to welcome in the dinner crowd.

We dropped Lenore off at her house, and as she exited the car she thanked me for the ride home. She then peered into the back seat and graciously said, "It was very nice meeting you Mr. and Mrs. O'Leary."

Mom cordially said, "Likewise…, dear," and Dad was quietly dozing in the back seat half-asleep.

Well, I guess you could say that the "drink" finally caught up to him.

CHAPTER ELEVEN

"Jack..., Jackie..., for the last time, wake up! You're both gonna be late for work!" Mom shouted, as she stood at the bottom of the stairway.

As I staggered out of bed, I suddenly realized that my head was pounding like a drum. I guess all of that Irish Stout that I drank at Flaherty's yesterday wasn't such a good idea after all, because as the Irish commonly say, "I woke up with a "wee bit" of a hangover this morning."

Still half-asleep, I poked my head into Dad's bedroom and sluggishly grunted, "C'mon..., Dad. Mom just called for the last time, so you better get up."

In a muffled tone, Dad replied, "I'm not going into work today Jackie boy. Be a good lad and close the door for me, will ya." Dad then hiked up the covers and rolled over on his side, and began snoring like a foghorn.

"Okay Dad, but I sure hope you know what you're doin'..., 'cause Mom's not gonna be too happy with ya."

So after popping a couple of aspirin out of the medicine cabinet, I took a quick shower, threw on some clothes, and then beat it downstairs.

When I walked into the kitchen, Mom had her coat on and she was getting ready to leave for weekday Mass. She then asked me if Dad was up yet, and if he was dressed for work.

So not knowing what to say, I decided to make up some half-assed excuse as to why Dad was still in bed, which of course did not please Mom in the least.

As I reached for my car keys, Mom remarked that I smelled like a distillery. I was then quick to point out to her that the alcohol she smelled was that of my after shave, and although I've had some luck in using that line on her before, today, well..., she simply wasn't buying it.

I then gave Mom a quick peck on the cheek and ran for the door, before she could even say another word on the matter.

When I pulled into the WEALTH parking lot, I was happy to see not only Bob's car parked, but my old pal C.D.'s car parked as well. I'm glad that Bob and C.D. were able to patch up their differences, and I was hoping that maybe now things could get back to normal again.

The minute I walked into the building, I could immediately smell the intoxicating aroma of fresh brewed coffee. I tossed off my backpack, grabbed my coffee mug off of my desk, and then beat it down to the break room because C.D. and I had a lot of catching up to do.

When I entered the break room I immediately saw C.D., who was totally engrossed in perusing the morning newspaper, with a freshly brewed cup of coffee nestled by his side.

Despite the four piece percussion band that was playing in my head, I was able to muster up enough strength to say, "Good morning C.D., so were you able to find everything in the break room this morning?"

C.D. looked up from his newspaper and gave me a cutting glance, as he sarcastically replied, "Hey, I haven't been gone that long sonny boy. I still know where everything is in here, thank you very much!"

To which I replied, "Okay, just checking. I guess you have it all resigned to memory, right? After all, you've spent the better part of your adult life in here."

"Just go on…, coffee's ready!" C.D. barked, in his usual gruff but friendly tone.

I poured myself a cup of coffee, and then walked down the hallway towards Bob's office so that I could say good morning to him. As I approached Bob's office, I could see a glimpse of him at his desk. Bob was leaning back in his sleek leather chair with his hands cupped behind his head, as he aimlessly gazed out the window. He seemed to be totally preoccupied in his thoughts, as if he were a million miles away.

I lightly knocked on his door, and then pleasantly said, "Good morning, Bob."

Bob then swiveled his chair around in my direction, as he quietly said, "Oh…, good morning, Jack." Bob seemed a bit distraught, and I could tell that he wasn't his usual self.

"So how's Sarah doing?" I asked, with great concern.

"Pretty good…, it's gonna take some time for her to heal, but I think her conversation with Father O'Malley yesterday helped." Bob said, softly.

"Good, Bob. Well…, I know she's not out of the woods yet, but it sounds like she's on the mend."

Bob then decided to change the subject by saying, "So your parents were very nice, and they certainly had a lot of good things to say about their "Jackie boy" yesterday."

"Oh…, right, I guess you did spend some time talking to them." I replied, and we both lightly chuckled.

"So did you happen to see C.D. in your travels?" Bob nonchalantly asked.

"Yeah, he's here. So what are your plans with him Bob?"

"Well, I guess I'll just reassign him back to his old caseload. I know he can't screw that up. That caseload practically runs itself." Bob said, sarcastically.

"So I guess in his mind he won, right?" I remarked, as I sat down across from Bob.

"Well, I guess you could look at it that way. Our little game of chicken actually lasted a lot longer than usual this time. Maybe next time he'll quit for good. One can only hope." Bob said, in a very agitated tone of voice.

I quietly snickered at Bob's quipping remark in the hope that it might break the tension in the air, but Bob looked rather serious. I could see that Bob was in no mood for frivolous chitchat. Bob was definitely troubled, and I'm sure it was more than just having C.D. back to work today.

"So can I get you a cup of coffee, Bob?" I asked, as I rose from his comfy leather chair.

"No thanks..., why don't you go and catch up with C.D., and I'll grab some coffee later." Bob said, as he opened up his accounts ledger book.

So after leaving Bob's office, I headed back down to the break room to grab a second cup of coffee and to catch up with C.D. on some lost time. As I reached the break room, I saw C.D. exiting the room with his coffee in one hand and a big raspberry danish in the other.

I then hastily said, "Hey C.D., where are you going? I thought we'd catch up over coffee."

C.D. replied, "Sorry kid, no time for idle chitchat, I've got some work to catch up on. I'm sure that none of you bozos bothered to do any of my paperwork while I was gone. Hey kid, there's some donuts over on the counter so help yourself. I went to a new bakery this morning. I think it's called Mig something or other. It's a little Italian bakery over on Andreano Avenue. Have you ever heard of it?"

"Yeah, sure, it's called Migliori's, and it's the best bakery in town. My mother frequents that bakery quite regularly. How do you think I managed to acquire this little pot belly of mine?"

I then reached into the box and helped myself to a big jelly donut.

"Yeah, well, dig in..., and don't say I never did nothin' for ya. See ya later, kid." C.D. said, as he whisked toward his office.

Well, how do you like that..., the tables have been turned. Here I am looking to chew the fat with C.D., only to have him fleeing the scene so that he can go and catch up on his work.

So, C.D. is at his desk, Watson is at loose ends, and I have a splitting headache from all that Irish Stout I drank at Flaherty's restaurant yesterday. I then decided to grab a second donut out the box, and head back to my office to do some paperwork.

It was now eight-thirty, and as I looked up I saw Lenore strolling into my office with a big smile on her face, as she enthusiastically said, "Hi Jack, I've got a lot of energy today because I didn't work yesterday."

Lenore was certainly quite cheery, as she parked her bicycle in the far corner of my office and then slung her backpack off of her shoulder. She then signed herself in on one of the daily attendance sheets, and seemed quite eager to start the day.

"So Lenore, you looked like you were really getting the hang of that Irish jig yesterday."

Lenore laughed, and then light-heartedly replied, "Yeah, yesterday was fun. Your Mom can sure cut a mean rug. So what are we doing today Jack?"

"Well, I think I'm gonna ride over to the worksite with you and the work crew today, and then I need to follow up on a few appointments." I said, matter-of-factly.

"Sounds good," Lenore answered.

Lenore has certainly been quite amenable to anything that I have asked her to do, and thus far she is making me look like a pretty good supervisor. Maybe that's why Dr. Stevens was so keen on placing her with me in the first place. Dr. Stevens wanted to make sure that my first supervisory experience would be a successful one, and having someone like Lenore as my first intern to supervise would certainly be just the ticket in ensuring that success.

We walked out back to board the cargo van, and en route Lenore was curious to know what types of appointments I was following up on today. I indicated to her that I had to check on a couple of job leads that were pending with some of the local businesses in town.

I then explained to Lenore that Joe had a system, which to the normal person may have seemed somewhat convoluted, but to him it made perfectly good sense. Although Lenore was trying to understand what I was saying to her, she seemed to be a bit lost in my explanation.

Anyway, I told Lenore that after flipping through Joe's job bank the other day, I noticed that he had highlighted some question marks next to the names of several businesses, and I was intending on visiting these businesses today so that I could get some further clarification as to their status. These notations that Joe highlighted were just simple reminders for him to make future follow-up visits.

In other words, this was Joe's subtle way of reminding himself that he needed to go back and "hound the daylights" out of these businesses, and to see whether or not he could convince them to buy into the concept of hiring the disabled.

Lenore found my explanation to be quite amusing, and then poignantly said to me, "Gee, now I see why you miss your friend Joe so much Jack."

So after dropping the cleaning crew off at the worksite, I then made my way over to my first appointment. I felt a little funny carrying an attaché case with me on my visits, especially since this was the same exact attaché case that Joe used on his visits.

I kinda felt like a "Fuller brush man," going door to door…, peddling my wares!

Yeah, doing this gig we called job placement was something that none of the other counselors on staff wanted to do, even if it meant that they'd be out of the building all day, and far, far away from the all-day scrutiny of Bob Watson.

My appointments finished up earlier than expected, and I caught up with Lenore and the work crew about one-thirty in the afternoon. I thought I would put some smiles on all of those tired and hungry faces, so I stopped off at the pizzeria and picked up a couple of large pizzas.

Lenore struck me as the vegetarian type, so I decided to get one large cheese pizza and one large pepperoni.

When I came waltzing into the building with two piping hot pizzas under my arms everyone was quite surprised, and needless to say, but the pizza was devoured in no time at all.

Hey, even a staunch Irishman like me can appreciate a good pizza pie when I taste one!

So after we ate our pizza, we finished cleaning the remaining offices and then headed straight back to WEALTH. I could tell that the clients were pretty tired because they weren't their usual chatter-boxes on the ride home. Lenore seemed tired too, and her quiet demeanor was certainly a far cry from the unbridled enthusiasm that she displayed in my office this morning.

When we arrived back at WEALTH, Lenore and I said some quiet good-byes to the clients, and then went directly back to my office so that we could record our data for the day.

Lenore sat for a few minutes to collect her thoughts, and then she began chipping away at her paperwork. When she was all done, she filed the work and then signed out for the day on one of the daily attendance sheets that were kept in the folder on top of my filing cabinet. Lenore was certainly getting to know her way around my office pretty well, yet I couldn't help notice how tired she looked, especially since she barely said two words all afternoon.

As Lenore was maneuvering her bicycle around my desk so that she could leave for the day, I felt compelled to ask her, "Lenore, are you okay? You look really tired."

She quietly replied, "Yeah, well…, I suffer from anemia. I'm dragging right now, but I'll be okay. Once I take my iron pill and have something to eat then I'll be as good as new. At my last medical check-up the doctor recommended that I need to put on about fifteen pounds."

"Wow, that's a novel idea! A doctor who actually wants his patient to gain weight!"

Lenore chuckled at my whimsical comment, and then bashfully said, "Yeah, well…, I guess I'm unique, or weird, or whatever comes to mind first."

We both laughed in unison at her cute little remark.

I then asked, "Are you sure you're gonna be okay to bicycle home? I can drive you…, it wouldn't be any trouble."

She quickly replied, "Nah…, that's okay, Jack. I think the fresh air will do me good. Thanks, anyway."

"Okay, hey Lenore…, not to hold you up, but I wanted to applaud you for yesterday. I mean going to the funeral the way you did, well…, it was exceptionally thoughtful on your part."

"Gee whiz, Jack…, it's not necessary to thank me. It was simply the right thing to do."

"Well Lenore, I think it's that type of spirit and enthusiasm that is going to make you an outstanding counselor someday," which prompted Lenore to quietly giggle and then say, "Jack, now you're starting to sound like Dr. Stevens."

"Maybe so…, but I think if Dr. Stevens was here right now he would be applauding your efforts as well. In fact, I just might have to make mention of this commendable deed of yours in your final evaluation." I remarked, with a splash of panache.

Lenore chuckled, and then replied, "Jack, you're funny, but seriously…, I wanted to go and I really had an enjoyable time. Yesterday was truly a celebration for your friend Joe."

"You're right, it was." I quietly said.

"Jack, I hope you don't mind me saying this, but you seem to have reconciled Joe's death rather quickly, and you've been able to find some sense of closure."

Lenore was absolutely right, - I have reconciled Joe's death, and in record time…, but I really don't know why. Could I possibly have some sort of deficit, or weird mental quirk?

I thought about what Lenore said for a moment, and then quietly replied, "Well, it still hurts…, but maybe I'm doing a good job at concealing it."

The next two weeks at WEALTH were relatively uneventful. Lenore was becoming more and more comfortable in her role and quite adept at learning the ropes. She was now attending the Monday morning staff meeting and finds the experience to be quite rewarding.

I must say that I get a big kick out of watching her take copious notes during the meeting, and then afterwards, trying to assimilate what was discussed.

Watson really hasn't said too much to me about Lenore, but I know he's quite impressed with her. I'm sure he'll be looking to groom her as his next recruit on the counseling staff, or should I say…, his next "victim."

Well, it's been about a month now since the mysterious disappearance of our old friend Henry Josephson, and believe it or not, but I still haven't heard a single word from Ms. Brown.

That woman actually has the audacity to call herself a social worker?

Huh, well, if you ask me…, I think she's more like an "asocial" worker. I don't think one lousy phone call from her is asking too much!

Has she not heard of the term professional courtesy?

Initially, when the incident first occurred, I could understand Ms. Brown's reluctance in not wanting to divulge any information to me regarding the investigation. But it's been a whole month now since Henry's disappearance, and I still haven't heard a peep out of her.

Yeah, I know I shouldn't let it bother me, but it just seems to gnaw at me like a giant toothache!

Every so often, Henry seems to pop into my head. I'm not really sure how staunch the efforts have been in locating him.

I seem to reflect on Henry the most when I'm sitting in church, probably because Henry envisions himself as being Jesus Christ, who was sent by God his father to save mankind.

As crazy as it may sound, but sometimes I wonder if Henry groomed himself to look like Jesus on purpose, or is he just so out of touch with reality, that it simply doesn't occur to him that he needs to visit the barbershop every once in a while for a fresh haircut and a nice clean shave.

In a funny sort of way, the subject never came up in any of our conversations, which is somewhat surprising to me, especially since I tend to have a rather off-beat sense of humor.

Then again…, if I had the misfortune of being delusional, such as Henry Josephson, then I too might delude myself into thinking that I'm Jesus Christ, especially since Jesus Christ just so happens to be the greatest man that has ever walked the Earth.

If you're in for a penny…, then why not be in for a pound!

Well, it's been six weeks now and Henry is still missing. Believe it or not, but Henry has been receiving a lot of media coverage of late. Shocking as it may sound, but Henry has been the focus of several newspaper articles, and even our local television station has mentioned his name on the evening news. I'm not quite sure what is prompting all of this sudden notoriety.

Perhaps some high ranking mental health official out at the State Capital has just found out about the incident, and the investigation has resulted in some finger pointing.

I've actually heard through the grapevine that one of the major television networks is planning on picking up the story, and broadcasting a nationally televised news segment featuring Henry and the alleged security mishap at the psychiatric center.

As a matter of fact, I even received a phone call from our local newspaper, in which they were attempting to dig up some dirt on Henry's involvement here at WEALTH, but I declined to comment. I told them that any disclosure on the matter would be a breach of confidentiality.

I'm sure that Dr. Stevens would have been proud of the way that I handled the situation, and applauding me for not opting to sell out my integrity for a mere fifteen minutes of fame.

The police, the FBI, and even the community action league have all been involved in attempting to solve the mysterious disappearance of Henry Josephson. There are flyers and posters of Henry plastered all over the city.

All of a sudden, Henry has become a "civics lesson!"

Even the psych center managed to pony up some reward money…, to the tune of one thousand dollars, to anyone who might have information leading to the whereabouts of Henry.

Well…, all I can say is good luck to anyone who tries to contact the psych center, and I pray that your call doesn't get routed to Ms. Brown.

From what I understand, Henry has now been classified as a missing person, and I for one can certainly attest to that. I knew that Henry was a missing person the minute I laid eyes on him.

But all kidding aside…, every available resource is being utilized to locate

Henry, and I pray to God they do.

Our local television station ran a news segment on Henry last night. They broadcast updates from time to time in hopes of jogging people's memory, but unfortunately last night's broadcast had nothing new to report.

When they flashed the photograph of Henry on the television screen, it looked more like a caricature drawing by a sketch artist than an actual photo. His features were very pronounced, such as his deep sunken eyes, chalky complexion, and his long scraggily hair and beard.

Quite honestly, Watson hasn't said too much regarding the sudden notoriety, but I know he's been quite active behind the scenes. Mr. Watson has been doing everything in his power to convince the legislators that Henry's disappearance had nothing to do with his grant proposal.

As a matter of fact, Bob just recently attended a special hearing at the State Capital, and the hearing was televised by our local news affiliate. Throughout the hearing Bob was poised and articulate, and I thought he made a very compelling argument to salvage his proposal.

Despite being peppered by an onslaught of questions and accusations, Bob managed to hold his ground, and adamantly stated at the hearing, "There is no direct evidence to support or link that future referrals from the psychiatric center will result in another elopement."

By day's end, Bob's efforts went for naught, and the legislators did not seem to buy into his impeccable logic. Bob's worst fears were realized, and the State Legislature decided to pull the plug on Bob's grant proposal and rescind their previous decision, as they categorically stated, "We, the members of the Legislature, as of today are halting all funding for individuals being referred from all statewide psychiatric centers. However, we may at some point revisit the proposal upon any further developments in the Josephson case."

Upon hearing the Legislature's decision, Bob was completely devastated, and I have never seen him look so glum before…, not even at Joe's funeral.

For the past two weeks, Bob has literally barricaded himself in his office, and Dolly told us the other day on the hush-hush that Bob has been burning the midnight oil, all in the hopes of rewriting a new grant proposal and one which may help circumvent the Legislature's decision.

Well, Lenore is now in the fourth week of her internship. As a token of my appreciation for all of her hard work and dedication, I decided to stop by Migliori's bakery on the ride into work this morning and splurge for some baked goods.

When I walked into the bakery, I saw Mr. Migliori working behind the counter. He turned in my direction when he heard the bells on the front door jingle, and when he saw it was me, he instantly smiled and said, "Jackie boy…, bon giorno!

How are your Mama and Papa?"

"Good, good, Mr. Migs, thanks for asking." I replied, as I scanned all of the baked goods in the display case.

"Bravo! Now Jackie, what-can-I-a-do-a-for-you-a?"

"Well, let's see…, I'll take two dozen assorted danish, please?"

"Bravo! Sounds-a-good, I'll-a-fix-a-you-up-a. Sit, and-a-be comfortable, Jackie boy. There's-a-fresh-a-coffee-on-a-da-counter, so please-help-a-you-self-a!"

"Thanks, Mr. Migs." I replied.

I've been calling Mr. Migliori, Mr. Migs…, ever since I can remember, and I think he likes hearing me call him that.

So as Mr. Migliori was filling my order, he and I engaged in some casual small talk. He asked me how the Atkins family was holding up, and I told him that it was day-to-day.

I then conveyed to him that the Atkins family wanted me to extend their appreciation for his show of generosity regarding all of the baked goods that he had given them, and upon hearing what I had to say, Mr. Migs was so overcome with emotion that he shouted out…, "Bravo!"

As I watched Mr. Migs fill my order, I noticed that he looked a little tired. I then asked him if he was feeling okay, and he proceeded to tell me that he has been pulling double duty of late because his bakery helper of twenty-five years had to quit the bakery due to health reasons.

At that point, I asked Mr. Migs if there were any special skills needed to be a bakery helper. So after telling me what the expectations of the job were, I told Mr. Migs that we might have someone down at WEALTH Industries who might be perfect for the job.

I also mentioned to Mr. Migs that we provide cleaning and janitorial services as well, and at cut rate prices! Mr. Migs said that he would definitely think it over and then get back to me.

So after filling my order, Mr. Migs told me what I owed him. I then gave him the amount, plus an additional twenty dollars.

When Mr. Migs realized that I overpaid him, he had a look of sheer panic on his face. He then said, in his melodic Italian accent, "Jackie boy, you-a-pay-a-me-too-mucha, twenty dollars, a-too-mucha!"

I replied, "Hey, think of it as a tip Mr. Migs. I'll see you soon, Pisan. Arrivederci!"

As I was walking out of the bakery, I could tell that Mr. Migs felt very uneasy about taking the extra money, but he decided to let it go.

He then smiled and said, while shaking his forefinger at me, "Yeah, okay..., this-a-time, butta-next-a-time, it's-a-my-treat, capisce!"

"Capisce," I said, as I headed out the door.

As I drove away from Migliori's bakery, I quietly chuckled to myself because I was finally able to put one over on good old Mr. Migs. He hates it when someone outfoxes him.

When I arrived at work, I walked down to the break room and placed the danish on top of the counter. As I turned to make the coffee, I spotted C.D. whisk into the break room.

I then said, "Good morning C.D., I brought in some danish, so please help yourself."

C.D.'s eyes lit right up, as he spiritedly said, "Don't mind if I do, sonny boy. I hope you have a raspberry danish in there, 'cause it's my favorite."

"Don't worry..., it's in there, it's in there." I said, with a touch of sarcastic humor.

I then walked down to Bob's office to say "good morning" and to let him know that I brought in some danish, and if he wanted any then he better get down to the break room quick before C.D. goes through the whole box."

Bob then affably said, "Great, I'll be right down."

When I re-entered the break room, I stopped dead in my tracks as I watched C.D. devour a whole raspberry danish in two bites. He was cramming the danish into his mouth like there was no tomorrow. He looked just like a little kid because he had splashes of raspberry jelly smeared all over his mouth, and crumbs hanging off of his cheek and chin.

As I handed C.D. a napkin, he excitedly remarked, "That was a great danish, kid! I'll bet you went to that little Italian bakery over on Andreano Avenue, Mig something or other, right?"

"Yep..., Migliori's, it's the best bakery in town." I replied, as I took a sip of coffee.

Bob then walked into the break room and poured himself a cup of coffee. He then peeked into the pastry box and helped himself to a plump apple danish, as he casually asked, "So what's the big occasion in you springing for the danish this morning, O'Leary?"

I was then quick to say, "C'mon Bob, do I really need a reason to display such generosity?"

Upon hearing my rousing response, Bob and C.D. both chuckled.

Bob replied, "Well O'Leary, it's just that you're always crying poverty, and constantly telling me how little I pay you. I wouldn't want you to squander your pittance on us, that's all."

C.D. roared with laughter.

I then interjected, "Very funny, Bob. But since you asked, I brought in some danish today because it's Lenore's one-month anniversary with us. I just thought it would be nice to show her how much we appreciate all of her fine efforts thus far."

"Geez Bob…, I think the kid is sweet on her." C.D. said, laughing uncontrollably.

Bob then quickly countered, "Now just hold on C.D., I think Jack has a good point there. Lenore seems to be everything I'm looking for in a new counselor and more."

Watson then quietly glanced in my direction and nonchalantly winked his eye.

So after chatting with Bob and C.D. for a little while, I went back to my office so that I could finish up a few reports that were pending. About twenty minutes later, Lenore arrived and she was wheeling her bicycle through the threshold of my office door.

"Good morning, Lenore!" I excitedly said.

"Hi Jack, how's it going?" Lenore replied, rather blasé.

"Hey, everything is great! Listen…, I don't know if you're aware of this or not, but today is your one-month anniversary with us here at WEALTH! I thought we might celebrate this epic event by enjoying some coffee and danish this morning!"

"Oh…, well thanks, Jack. That was very thoughtful of you, but I'm gonna have to pass on that because my stomach is a little queasy this morning. Um…, is there any milk down in the break room? That might help settle my stomach." Lenore said, squeamishly.

"Sure, just make yourself comfortable and I'll be right back Lenore."

So after grabbing some milk out of the refrigerator, I hustled back to my office where I discovered Lenore hunched in a ball and doubled over in pain. She was clutching her abdomen with both of her hands and moaning considerably.

I quickly placed the glass of milk down on my desk, and then frantically said, "Lenore, are you okay? You're in no condition to be here today. C'mon…, I'm gonna drive you home."

At that point, I helped Lenore to her feet and then escorted out of the building. I sat her in the front seat of my car, and then ran back into the building to retrieve her backpack and bicycle.

As I was driving Lenore home, I looked over at her demure frame and noticed that her complexion was pasty white, and that her whole body was trembling.

I then quietly said, "This is not how I intended to celebrate your one-month anniversary."

"Sorry, Jack." Lenore replied, with noticeable discomfort.

"Hey Lenore, I'm only kidding with you. Anyway…, you know what they say about the best laid plans. When you feel better we'll celebrate, okay." I said, reassuringly.

"Thanks, Jack. That was awful sweet of you to think of me like that. I've been nauseous all weekend. I was hoping that it would've subsided by now. I was so looking forward to, ooooh that hurts…, attending the Monday morning staff meeting. Ooooh…, sorry, Jack."

"Hang on, Lenore…, we're almost there!"

I pulled up in front of Lenore's house. I then carefully helped her out of the car and assisted her up the porch steps, which led to her front door.

"Thank you, Jack. I'm sorry for the inconvenience."

"No problem, Lenore. Wait here and I'll go grab your bicycle."

"Okay, thanks. You can leave the bike on the porch. No one will bother it."

I carried Lenore's bicycle up the steps, and then placed it on the porch. She thanked me once again, and then optimistically said, "I'll see you tomorrow, Jack."

As I hustled down the porch steps, I turned back at Lenore and replied, "Yeah, okay…, but only if you're feeling better. See ya, Lenore."

I jumped into my car and then beat it back to WEALTH, just as fast as my rickety jalopy would allow. Not only was I running thirty minutes late for the Monday morning staff meeting, but I had also neglected to tell Bob that I was leaving work so that I could take Lenore home.

When I finally made it to the staff meeting, I tiptoed my way into the room and then carefully slid my chair out from under the table without creating too much of a stir.

As I quietly scooched my chair into the table, Mr. Watson decided to have a little fun at my expense, as he sarcastically said, "Good morning, Jack. It's so nice of you to join us today."

At that point, the entire room erupted into hysterical laughter, most notably C.D., who could barely control himself.

Even Dolly was quietly giggling behind her steno pad.

I've come to the realization that the counseling staff loves it when the "fair haired boy" is singled out, and made an example of by the boss.

So after everyone had a good laugh at my expense, all I could manage to say was, "I'm sorry for being late, Mr. Watson."

When the meeting was over, Watson extended his hand and apologized for embarrassing me in front of the whole group by saying, "Sorry Jack, but I just couldn't resist the temptation."

Which then prompted me to say, "No problem, Bob. You know what they say about paybacks."

Watson smiled in appreciation of my gamesmanship, and then simply said, "Indeed…, so where is our budding intern? Did she enjoy her danish?"

I replied, "Well, that's why I was late for the meeting Bob. I wound up driving Lenore home. She was experiencing all sorts of stomach cramps and nausea. Apparently she was sick all weekend, and she was obviously in no condition to work today."

"Huh…, that's too bad. She must've contracted some sort of stomach flu. So can you go with the janitorial crew today?"

"I've got a full schedule today Bob."

"Well, I guess Terry and Smitty can handle it. I'll just need to tell Ralph." Watson said, apprehensively.

"Uh-huh, well…, good luck with that Bob. Then again…, you are the boss and what you say goes, right?" I said, tongue and cheek.

"Well, yes…, in theory, but this is reality we're talking about. Don't worry, I'll work it out."

"Thanks, Bob. I'd say that I owe ya, but seeing how you just "tarred and feathered" me in front of that pack of hyenas this morning, well…, I'd say that we're even."

The following day Lenore managed to make it into work. Although she didn't possess her usual vim and vigor, it was still good to see her nonetheless. She said that she was feeling a lot better today and that all she really needed was a good days' rest.

She then asked me what she had missed in the Monday morning staff meeting, and I proceeded to fill her in on every little detail, except of course the little practical joke that Bob Watson decided to play on me in front of the entire counseling staff.

Lenore looked somewhat pensive as I was speaking to her, so I asked her if there was something on her mind. She indicated to me that she was quite nervous about graduating and losing the security blanket of school. She also said that she didn't know where to begin in terms of job hunting, and that a lot of her friends already had jobs lined up after graduation.

As I listened to Lenore's concerns, it was strangely reminiscent to what I had experienced coming out of graduate school myself. I then tried to reassure her that what she was feeling was completely normal, and that I too had experienced the same fears and apprehensions as well.

She then dejectedly said, "Ya know…, I wouldn't be surprised if all this nausea that I've been experiencing lately is directly related to stress, and the uncertainty of looking for a job."

Once again, I tried to reassure Lenore that everything was going to work out fine. So in a last ditch effort to pick up her spirits, I then whimsically said, "Hey, between me, Dr. Stevens, and your stunning good looks…, we'll get you a job with very little trouble, by gosh!"

Lenore held an admiring stare at me for a brief moment, and then light-heartedly replied, "I swear Jack…, you're definitely sounding more and more like Dr. Stevens every day."

We then walked out back to meet the cargo van. Although I managed to pick up Lenore's spirits a notch, I was still a bit apprehensive as to whether she was up for the challenge of working on the cleaning crew today, but she was rather persuasive in reassuring me that she was.

Lenore then climbed up onto the cargo van, took a deep breath, and squeamishly uttered, "Okay…, I think I'm good, Jack." And then they all drove off to the worksite.

As I was watching the cargo van pull away, Bob approached me from behind and then casually said, "I see that Lenore is here today. So how is she feeling?"

"Well, she looks a little green around the gills, but she says that she's feeling better."

"Good! So has Dr. Stevens contacted you at all with regards to her progress?"

"Oh yeah, we've chatted…, and he's very delighted."

"Good, good, I'm glad we were able to land such a "blue chipper." I'm seriously thinking of offering her a job when the time comes. Do me a favor, will ya…, try to keep it under your hat. I'm only telling you this as a courtesy because you're her supervisor, and her confidant…, no doubt." Bob stated, with a sly grin.

"Her confidant…, I don't know what you're implying Bob. I'm her supervisor, not her parish priest. I'm sure she'll be entertaining many job offers." I said, cagily.

I was absolutely elated to hear Bob's intentions of hiring Lenore, but I didn't want to let on to Bob that Lenore has trepidations about entering the job market. I didn't want Bob to think that he held the upper hand, or that he had an unfair advantage on the poor girl.

After all, Bob has been at this game for a very long time, and my nondisclosure to him regarding Lenore's fears and apprehensions was my feeble attempt at leveling the playing field. I was simply trying to look out for Lenore, as any good supervisor would do.

Essentially, I wanted Bob to think that Lenore had options, and that in order for him to secure her services then he might have to open up his wallet.

Bob then candidly said, "Well, if Lenore does agree to an interview then I don't want you coaching her, okay."

"Coaching her?"

"Yes, coaching her! I'm sure you haven't forgotten how you financially skinned me alive in your job interview…, a good little Irish Catholic "guilt ridden" altar boy like you. You should be ashamed of yourself. In fact, I hope you said three Our Father's and ten Hail Mary's as penance for your sins of deception." Bob said, with a big smirk on his face.

"Please Bob…, let's not drag God into this, shall we."

Bob chuckled.

I then continued by saying, "So you think I skinned you alive, huh. Why…, because you had to fork over an additional five hundred dollars a year more. Well, I did the math Bob, and the measly amount of money that you coughed up to me works out to less than an extra ten dollars a week, better yet…, an extra twenty-five cents an hour more. If you ask me, you're the one who should be dropping to his knees and begging for God's forgiveness, not me."

All of a sudden, Bob began laughing hysterically, as he light-heartedly replied, "Well…, on second thought, you might be right O'Leary."

Bob then threw his long lanky arm around my shoulder, as we both lightly chuckled and headed back toward the offices.

Although Lenore managed to make it through the day without getting sick, she looked pretty exhausted as she was wheeling her bicycle out of my office at the end of the day.

As I said "good-bye" to Lenore, I was busting at the seams to tell her about Bob's intentions of giving her an interview, but I knew it just wasn't the right time to tell her. Lenore will just have to hang in there a little while longer, but it will certainly be worth the wait.

That night after dinner, I chewed the fat with Mom and Dad for a little while, and then decided to plop myself down on the living room couch and watch some television. As I bounced the channels around, I couldn't find anything good to watch on TV.

As I kept clicking the remote control from one channel to the next, I stumbled upon something that caught my eye, which just so happen to be a news segment on Henry Josephson.

At first, the news broadcast seemed to be rehashing the same old rhetoric on Henry, but as I continued to watch the telecast something extraordinary occurred.

Suddenly the composite head shot of Henry Josephson appeared on the screen, and remained superimposed, while news teams had cameras zeroing in on a man resembling Henry Josephson being escorted into the main entrance of the psych center by an entourage of law enforcement personnel, one of which I instantly recognized as being Ms. Brown.

And trust me…, there was certainly no mistaking her!

At that point, I immediately turned up the volume on the television set and frantically called out, "Mom, Dad, come into the living room, quick!"

Mom and Dad rushed into the living room, and in a startled voice Mom asked, "What is it dear?"

I then excitedly said, as I was pointing toward the television set, "Look, its Henry Josephson, they found him! He's alive, I can't believe it!"

"Who dear," Mom asked, in a quandary.

"You know…, the guy from WEALTH Industries, who's been all over the news! They found him! They're escorting him into the psychiatric hospital right now, holy shit!"

"Watch your language, dear!" Mom snarled.

Dad then chimed in and said, "Wow! He looks pretty scary, Jackie boy. You actually work with that character?"

"Yeah, he's pretty scary all right." I replied, with some nervous laughter.

"Where did they find him?" Mom inquired.

"They didn't say, but I'll bet Bob Watson might know. I think I'm gonna give him a call right now." I hastily said, as I darted for the phone.

I dialed Bob's number, and after one ring I heard Bob come on the line and light-heartedly say, "Hi Jack, I'll bet you're calling about Henry Josephson."

"Geez Bob…, are you psychic? How did you know it was me?"

Bob laughed, and then replied, "Because I have caller ID, and when I saw your name and number come up I surmised that you saw the news footage about Josephson on the television."

"Gotcha! So Bob…, do you know anything more than what's being reported on TV?"

"Why, of course…, you know how resourceful I am. I made a few phone calls and I got the real dope. Oh…, pardon the pun, I mean all of the details on what happened to Mr. Josephson. I still can't believe it myself."

"So what's the latest, Bob?" I asked, eagerly.

"Well…," Bob momentarily chuckled, and then continued by saying, "From what I hear, Henry Josephson has a brother named Simon. This Simon fella is pretty limited, and like Henry he's not playing with a full deck either. Anyway, on the night in question, Simon must have slipped past security over at the psych center and waltzed right out the front door with Henry."

"Wow, that's incredible! I don't remember reading about a brother in the case file. I wonder if Henry even recognized Simon as being his brother."

"Who knows? I think Henry Josephson would've done virtually anything if he heard the word cigarette or coffee used in a sentence." Bob sarcastically replied.

"Yeah, you're right, Bob. So then what happened?" I asked, chuckling.

"Well, like I said…, this guy Simon is pretty limited, and he must've concocted this hair-brain idea to have his brother Henry come live with him."

I quickly interjected, "Geez…, only God knows what type of squalor that was."

Bob continued by saying, "Anyway, Simon devised a plan to become Henry's custodial guardian, which certainly wasn't done out of brotherly love that I assure you."

"Boy, Simon sounds like a real sleaze ball." I stated, candidly.

"You're right…, Simon was trying to bilk the system by getting his grubby little hands on Henry's social security disability money. Simon was looking at Henry as some sort of "cash cow," and hoping that Henry would be the answer to all of his immediate cash flow problems. If you ask me, this type of scenario happens more often than you think." Bob replied.

I then quickly pointed out, "So Bob, didn't Simon realize that he couldn't gain immediate access to Henry's funds? There are forms that need to be filled out, not to mention a paper trail that would ultimately lead the authorities right to his doorstep."

Bob quietly chuckled, and then replied, "Yeah, I know…, but like I said Simon is not playing with a full deck, and in all likelihood he should've been living on the same ward over at the psych center with his brother Henry. The Josephson gene pool is apparently quite shallow."

I laughed at Bob's amusing metaphor, and eagerly asked, "So then what happened Bob?"

"Well, Simon put the wheels into motion, but then realized that his little scheme wasn't working out according to plan."

"Well, yeah…, hello Simon! So what happened next Bob?"

"Apparently, Simon hears on the news that the psych center is posting a reward for any information leading to the whereabouts of Henry. So seeing how Simon's original plan wasn't panning out, he opted for plan B. Simon called the psych center saying that Henry mysteriously showed up on his doorstep one night. The psych center knew that he was lying, but they decided to play along with the story anyway. The truth finally came out once the investigators questioned Simon, and did a thorough background check on him." Bob stated.

"Wow, what a conniver that Simon is." I said, dumbfounded.

"Yeah, it's pretty far-fetched. I wonder what it was like being cooped up with Josephson for all that time." Bob commented.

"Uh…, which Josephson are you referring to Bob?" I quipped, and we both laughed.

Bob then humorously remarked, "Yeah, I'm sure it was no picnic for either one of 'em."

"So what will happen to Simon now Bob? Is he looking at any jail time?"

"Apparently not…, Henry would have to press charges, and you know that's not going to happen. It's complicated, but as long as Simon forfeits the reward money and signs a few legal documents, then he is free to go on his own recognizance."

"It's just not right, Bob. There should be some type of consequence, or at the very least, Simon should be mandated by the court to undergo a thorough psychological evaluation."

"You're right…, but given the fact that Simon is a blood relative, coupled with the extensive amount of cognitive deficits that Henry possesses, then nothing can be substantiated."

I then asked, "So do you see Henry returning to WEALTH?"

"No…, I don't think so Jack. He's too much of a liability."

"Yeah, I would have to agree with you Bob."

Bob then piped up, and adamantly said, "However, I still haven't changed my views with regards to providing vocational services to the mentally ill."

"Really...?"

"That's right, as a matter of fact, I'm very optimistic that I can change the Legislature's decision. I'm still quite convinced that there are some patients over at the psych center that can benefit greatly from our program, just not Josephson." Bob adamantly said.

"Perhaps..., but in my view the psychiatric clientele is still very dicey." I stated.

Bob then staunchly replied, "True, but that still doesn't negate the fact that the federal government is willing to hand over an exorbitant amount of money, so that agencies such as ours can provide vocational opportunities for the mentally ill."

"Once again, it's all about the money. Right, Bob?"

"On the contrary, it's all about the services. And in light of the new developments in the Josephson case, I plan on making a few phone calls tomorrow so that I can petition the State Legislature and the Commissioner of Mental Health to convene a special caucus, so that we can re-address the WELL initiative." Bob said, boldly.

"The WELL initiative..., what's that?" I asked.

"You know, the WELL initiative..., the name of my grant proposal. I thought you knew." Bob said, with utter surprise in his voice.

"No..., I don't believe so. What does WELL stand for Bob?"

Bob proudly stated, "WELL stands for Work Evaluation and Life Liberties."

"Wow..., that's a pretty catchy phrase Bob. Did you think it up?"

"Why, of course. You know I have an affinity for catchy phrases. Listen Jack, when the time comes for you to be a grant writer just remember one thing..., that every new program needs a name, and the catchier the name the better it may sound to the people doling out the dough." Bob said, enthusiastically.

"I'll keep that in mind, Bob. Well..., I'll let you go, and I'll see ya in the morning."

"Okay, Irish..., good-night!"

The next day the rumor mill was running at full-bore, and it was churning out all sorts of wild gossip about Henry. The WEALTH staff was flocking to me in droves, all in the hopes of gaining additional information other than what was being reported on the news station.

Even C.D. was trying to pry some information out of me.

Maybe someone on the counseling staff promised to buy C.D. a canister of gourmet coffee, in exchange for any juicy tidbits of information that he might be able to get his hands on.

At one point, C.D. amusingly stated, "Hey kid, what kinda cock and bull story are they trying to peddle on the television about that Josephson fella?"

I then asked, "What do you mean by that C.D.?"

C.D. replied, "Well, they're saying that Josephson found his way over to his brother's house. Who the hell are they trying to kid. That guy couldn't find water if he jumped straight out of a boat and landed smack dab into the middle of the ocean!"

Before heading out back to join the work crew, Lenore made a few inquiries regarding Henry, but asked more out of concern than out of idle gossip.

Well, the minute that Bob got into work this morning he was on the telephone with every legislator who was willing to take his call. I'm sure that Bob will be calling in some pretty hefty markers this week, all in the hopes of influencing some votes when the Legislature reconvenes.

Take it from me, Bob can be relentless when he's on a mission, especially when there's money at stake, because Bob knows exactly what limbs to shake on the money tree. Now that the WELL initiative has new life, Bob is going to make damn sure that every legislator knows that his grant proposal had nothing to do with the unfortunate disappearance of Henry Josephson.

So now that Henry is back in the fold, Bob has a legitimate shot at lifting the moratorium off of the WELL initiative. The federal faucet is now ready to be turned back on, so that the flow of federal dollars can come pouring in and be funneled directly into the WEALTH coffers.

Yeah, I can see Bob now…, rubbing his hands together and yelling from the rooftops, "Boys, we're back in business!"

As I was getting ready to leave for my afternoon appointments, I looked up and saw Bob standing in the doorway. He looked quite pleased with himself, as he stood there gazing at me.

Bob then spryly said, "Hi Jack, are you getting ready to make the rounds?"

I casually replied, "Yeah, I'm just on my way out. So how's it going Bob? I haven't seen you all day. Have you been making productive use of your time today?"

Bob confidently said, "I always make productive use of my time, you of all people should know that. But since you asked, I'll just say that things are moving along quite "WELL," Jack."

"Ah…, nice pun Bob."

Bob gave me an appreciative smile, and then proudly said, "In fact, I've been able to convince the State Commissioner of Mental Health to convene a special hearing next week, so that we can re-address the WELL initiative."

"Um…, did you say convince or coerce, I didn't quite catch that Bob?" I asked, smiling.

"Ah…, very funny Jack. I'm quite sure that I said convince, but I'll remember that snide little remark of yours when I'm tallying up your paycheck this week."

"Oh…, I'm sorry, Bob. I must've misspoke, I meant to say convince," which prompted both of us to laugh out loud. I then gazed at Bob in appreciation of his great sense of humor.

Bob then nonchalantly asked, "So how is our budding intern doing?"

"Quite well," I said, confidently.

"Good, good, and is she completely over her illness?"

"Oh yes, she's recuperated nicely."

"Excellent, so tell me…, how long before her internship is over?"

"Um…, she has less than two weeks left." I replied.

"Good, okay. Well, as you know, I'm very interested in hiring her, and I'll probably be making my pitch to her sometime next week. She's good…, and I'd hate to lose her."

I then replied, "Well squeaks, you better open up your wallet, and don't even think about offering Lenore the same meager starting salary that you gave me. Just remember one thing Bob, when you're sitting across from Lenore in the interview room, think about all that federal money that will be pouring in when the Legislature overturns their decision on the WELL initiative. You'll be "rolling in dough," so I think you can spare a few extra dollars for Lenore. Don't you agree, Bob?"

"Uh Jack…, you're her supervisor not her agent, but I do see your point." Bob replied, with a wry smile.

"Good," I said, with a look of contentment.

"Okay, well, carry on…, and try to drum me up some business out there O'Leary, will ya. I've got a payroll to maintain." Bob said, as he whisked himself back to his office.

The following day I received a phone call from my arch nemesis…, Allan Farnsworth. Farnsworth was his usual nauseating self, as he laid on the bull shit by saying that we should get together real soon for lunch.

He then mentioned to me that he saw me at Joe Atkins' house last week, and apologized for not getting the chance to chat with me, but he had trouble negotiating the dense crowd.

As I listened to Farnsworth ramble on and on about the crowd and the people that were there, I quietly thought to myself, "Is this guy for real?"

I then opted to take the high road, and conveyed to him that I fully understood the situation and that I too had trouble battling the crowd at Joe Atkins' house as well.

There was a momentary lull in our conversation, and then Farnsworth deceptively said, "Well Jack, the reason I called you today was to talk about Henry Josephson. I know you haven't known Henry for very long, but Bob has indicated to me that you've been able to establish some type of rapport with him."

I quickly thought to myself, "A rapport..., who in the hell are you trying to kid?"

Suddenly my instincts were telling me that Farnsworth was posturing for some type of favor, so I just decided to answer him in a vague sort of way by saying, "Well Al..., I find Henry to be a pretty interesting guy, and I guess I've grown quite fond of him."

Once again, I tried playing it very cool with Farnsworth, especially since he was my only real solid lead to State employment.

Farnsworth then cunningly countered, "You're right..., Henry is an interesting guy, and I think he needs to continue his work evaluation at WEALTH. Don't you agree, Jack?"

"Well Al, that's really not my decision, that's Bob's decision." I stated, cautiously.

"Listen Jack, I'm aware of Bob's efforts in lobbying the State Commissioner on Mental Health, as well as the State Legislature, and I'm quite certain that he won't have any trouble swinging enough votes in his favor to get the WELL initiative back up and running."

"Well Al, I really don't know. Bob doesn't discuss such matters with me. Anyway, shouldn't you be talking to Bob about this? After all, he has the final say on everything that goes on around here." I said, and keeping my cards very close to the vest.

"Yeah, I know..., but I just thought you could try to convince Bob to reinstate Henry back into the program again that's all." Farnsworth replied, in a very cagey way.

"Gee, I don't know what to tell you, Al."

"Actually, it's my understanding that Bob is not real keen on having Henry resume his work evaluation at WEALTH. I just thought that if you spoke to Bob and put a good word in for Henry that perhaps Bob would listen to you." Farnsworth said, as he turned up the heat.

"Boy, you must think I carry a lot of clout with Bob, Al."

Farnsworth snidely chuckled, and then in a sarcastic tone of voice he replied, "Oh, I know you do, I still hear things that go on down there."

"Evidently...," I thought to myself.

It was quite obvious to me that Farnsworth had a stool pigeon at WEALTH, and whoever it was they were certainly providing him with some pretty good inside information.

I then stated, "Well Al, I don't know if I can be of any assistance to you. Bob sees the big picture a lot better than I do. I really don't know if my recommendation would carry that much weight with him."

There was a moment of uncomfortable silence on the line, and then Farnsworth perked up and said, "Hey Jack, I'll tell ya what..., if you scratch my back then I'll scratch yours."

"So what are you proposing, Al?" I asked.

"Well, if you help me get Henry reinstated at WEALTH, then I might be able to "grease the wheel" in securing you a State position. In fact, I know of at least one position that might be available within the next month or two." Farnsworth mentioned.

"Um, well..., let me think it over and I'll get back to you, okay." I said, diplomatically.

"Sure, sounds good. Well, I'll talk to you later Jack, bye."

As soon as I hung up the phone with Farnsworth, I knew that I had just made a pact with the devil. I then began to wonder how I was going to pull this little arrangement of ours off.

When Bob and I spoke on the phone the other night, he was quite adamant about Henry Josephson not returning to WEALTH. Although Farnsworth is aware of Bob's intentions of not wanting to reinstate Henry, I'm inclined to believe that Farnsworth wouldn't be going out on a limb like this unless getting Henry reinstated back into the program was a real feather in his cap.

Then again..., Bob knows how I feel about Henry, so maybe I can try to persuade Bob to reconsider his decision, and have Henry reinstated back into the program again after all.

I mean it's definitely worth a shot, and when push comes to shove, I can certainly schmooze with the best of 'em. I'm sure that I can present my argument in a way so that Bob won't even suspect that Farnsworth put me up to it.

Yeah, I'm pretty sure that I can make this work, and I'm also pretty sure that State employment is definitely within my grasp. Yahooooo!

So after taking stock of my rather deceptive thoughts, I decided to strike while the iron was hot, so I went straight down to Bob's office to see if he was available to talk with me.

When Bob saw me standing in the doorway, he quickly said, "C'mon in, Jack."

I walked into Bob's office, and casually said, "Hi Bob, how's it going?"

Bob replied, "Things are good. So are you getting ready to make the rounds?"

"Yeah, I'm leaving in a few minutes Bob, but I just wanted to run something by you first before I head out the door."

"Sure, fire away." Bob replied, as he leaned back in his sleek leather chair.

"Well…, I've been giving it some thought Bob, and I think it might be a good idea to reinstate Henry Josephson back into the program after all."

With a coy smile, Bob responded, "Allan Farnsworth got to you, didn't he?"

My heart skipped a beat, as I replied, "What do you mean he got to me?"

"You know…, him convincing you to convince me. I've seen this tactic with Allan before. I like to refer to it as the "old back door play." So what exactly did Allan promise you Jack? He must've really sweetened the pot for you to approach me on such a delicate matter, eh."

"Well Bob, since you brought it up, we did have a conversation, but I think you're reading too much into it. Farnsworth simply stated that OVR has invested a great deal of time and money into Henry, and that they would like to salvage the placement." I said, defensively.

"Salvage the placement. Is that what Allan Farnsworth said to you?"

"Well, yeah…," I replied, and wondering how I was going to climb out of this ten foot hole that I was digging for myself.

The fact that I was lying to Bob really turned my stomach, especially with everything that Bob has done for me these last couple of months. But I simply couldn't tell him the real reason why I was advocating so strongly for Henry.

Let's face it…, nothing good ever comes from lying, and with the way my luck has been running lately, I was really afraid that this deceptive ploy of mine was ultimately going to backfire on me and bite me in the ass.

"Well Jack, I'll admit that you do have a soft spot for Josephson. Although, if you ask me, I think the soft spot that you have for him is not necessarily in your chest cavity, but somewhere in the vicinity of your temporal lobe." Bob said, amusingly.

Despite feeling riddled with guilt, I chuckled at Bob's amusing quip and replied, "Well, I just think that Henry Josephson deserves another shot Bob, that's all."

"Uh-huh, well…, a little word of advice Jack, Allan Farnsworth has a history of making promises that he can't keep. He likes to use people over and over again, until the well runs dry. The man has no conscience, and I was ecstatic the day he left WEALTH for his State job."

Suddenly, I could feel my blood beginning to boil, and I was soundly convinced that Farnsworth was using me just like Bob said. This little partnership that I was entering into with Farnsworth was beginning to smell as rotten as three day old fish.

Although I was selling out, my only saving grace at this point was that I actually had Henry Josephson's best interest at heart, and that Farnsworth was asking me to do something that I probably would have done anyway.

Farnsworth's inducements about State employment may have been an incentive for me to advocate for Henry, but now these promises…, whether empty or not, almost seem meaningless to me now because it's compromising my integrity with Bob.

As I was leaving Bob's office, I casually commented, "Well Bob, that's all I wanted to say. I really don't think that Henry would hurt us, if he was reinstated back into the program."

"Uh-huh, so now you're a fortune teller too…, huh, Jack?" Bob sarcastically quipped.

I chuckled at Bob's witty remark, and then quietly said, "Well Bob, I know that our conversation is a bit premature because everything still rests in the hands of the State Legislature, but I just wanted to express my opinion on the subject that's all."

"Okay, well…, I'll take what you said under advisement. Let's just see how everything plays out next week at the State Capital, shall we."

"Okay, Bob. Well, I'll catch you later. Thanks for your time."

When I walked out of Bob's office, I was not a happy camper. The fact that I was not being completely honest with him really bothered the hell out of me, and it seemed to reignite any smoldering acrimony that I harbored for Allan Farnsworth.

It never seems to fail, but every time I have dealings with Allan Farnsworth I get very irritated and thoroughly worked up. It's almost like having an allergic reaction to some type of addicting food that I just can't resist eating over and over again.

With any luck, maybe I won't have to deal with Farnsworth much longer.

Then again…, with the way my crummy luck has been running lately, the State job that I do eventually land, well…, I'll probably have Allan Farnsworth as my office mate.

Now wouldn't that be poetic justice!

CHAPTER TWELVE

Well, here it is…, Lenore's last week of her internship, and I can't believe how fast the time has gone. Lenore has been everything that Dr. Stevens said she'd be and more.

She'll be arriving any minute now, smiling, singing, and embracing life. She still has no idea that Bob wants to hire her, and when she hears the news I'm sure she'll be utterly ecstatic.

It was just about eight-thirty, and I was getting ready to head down to the Monday morning staff meeting. I kept glancing at my watch and hoping that Lenore would come strolling through the door at any second now, so that she and I could walk down to the meeting together.

As I sat there waiting for Lenore to arrive I felt a little bit tense. I'm sure that all of this uneasiness that I was feeling was due to the fact that it was Lenore's last week, and I wanted everything to work out for her according to plan.

Just then the telephone rang, and Dolly pleasantly said, "Jack, you have a phone call on line one, it's Dr. Stevens."

"Thanks Dolly," I replied, as I reached for the phone.

"Good morning Dr. Stevens…, how are you?"

"Jack, my boy…, it's so good to hear your voice." He said, in his own inimitable way.

"Likewise, Dr. Stevens. As a matter of fact, I was just thinking of you earlier because this is Lenore's last week, and I've been doing some introspective thinking on how satisfying the experience has been for me." I said, in a very high brow sort of way.

"Introspective thinking…, my, my, you sound like you should be teaching a graduate course here at the university. I thought you would simply say that a good time was had by all." Dr. Stevens quipped, and we both laughed.

"Well Dr. Stevens, I paid quite handsomely for a good college education, so I may as well put it to good use."

"Touché, Jack! That's the spirit!" Dr. Stevens said, with his usual zeal.

I then light-heartedly asked, "So what can I do for you Dr. Stevens?"

"Well Jack, I simply wanted to touch base with you and see whether you had any last minute questions before submitting Lenore's final paperwork to me."

"Actually Dr. Stevens, I think I'm all set. Although I am glad you called because I have something of extreme importance that I'd like to discuss with you."

"I see, and prêt ell…, what might that be?"

"Well, Lenore doesn't know this yet, but Mr. Watson is planning on interviewing her this week in hopes of offering her a position here at WEALTH."

"Splendid," Dr. Stevens remarked.

"Yeah, it's terrific. Anyway, Lenore has expressed to me that she has been experiencing a great deal of anxiety over the prospects of looking for a job, and I'm quite sure that she'll be seeking your counsel on the matter."

"Ah…, I see. Well, I am her academic advisor, and you're probably right in your assessment. So were you looking for me to steer her in WEALTH's direction?"

"No, well yeah, I mean…, I'm just worried about her that's all. She was experiencing some physical ailments last week, such as stomach cramps and nausea, and she confided in me that these illnesses might be the result of her leaving school and entering the work force."

"Oh dear," he remarked.

"Anyway, I just thought you should be aware of the situation. I'm not trying to sway you one way or the other. Bob is fully aware of the fact that Lenore is a "blue chip" recruit, and he certainly doesn't want to lose her."

"You're right, Bob Watson certainly does know a blue chipper when he sees one. After all, he hired you…, didn't he?"

"Thanks, Dr. Stevens." I said, modestly.

"Yes, well…, having Jack O'Leary and Lenore Richards on the same counseling staff, now that would be quite a formidable lineup indeed for Bob Watson. I liken it to say, "Ruth and Gehrig," if you don't mind my sports metaphor."

I chuckled at Dr. Stevens' whimsical analogy, and then replied, "Well, I think it could prove to be a very effective one/two punch."

Just then Lenore came strolling through the door with her bicycle in tow. She saw that I was on the telephone, so she simply smiled and gave me a slight wave of her hand. I smiled at Lenore, and then motioned for her to sit down in the chair adjacent to my desk.

I then wrapped up my conversation with Dr. Stevens by saying, "Well, it was very nice chatting with you Dr. Stevens."

Lenore then piped up, and excitedly said, "Oh, is that Dr. Stevens? Please tell him I said, "hi," okay."

Dr. Stevens then said, "Jack, my dear boy…, I've been meaning to ask you something."

"Yes, what is it Doctor?"

"Well, are you finally relieved that Mr. Josephson has been found?"

"Most definitely! In fact, the word relief may be an understatement Dr. Stevens."

"Indeed, as a matter of fact, I hope to incorporate your experience into my curriculum. I'll have you know that you're making me a much better instructor Jack. I just love it when my students can teach me a thing or two!"

"Well, I'm glad I could be of service Dr. Stevens."

As I glanced at Lenore, her beautiful lavender blue eyes then jogged my memory to say, "Oh, Dr. Stevens…, Lenore wanted me to say "hi," and she looks forward to seeing you very soon. Oh yeah…, and that she misses you very much," prompting Lenore to gently smile.

I no sooner hung up the phone with Dr. Stevens, when Lenore impetuously asked, "So what were you and Dr. Stevens discussing on the telephone Jack?"

As much as I wanted to come clean with Lenore, I decided to have a little fun with her instead by saying, "Now Lenore, you wouldn't want me to kiss and tell, would ya? I mean, hasn't Dr. Stevens taught you anything about the cannons of confidentiality?"

"Yes, he has…, but I still wanna know anyway Jack, please…," she pouted.

"Hey, I'm still waiting to hear the magic words." I said, teasingly.

"Magic words," she questioned.

"Yeah, you know…, that you're willing to do anything for me to tell you."

"Jack, what kind of a girl do you think I am?" Lenore said, with a sheepish grin.

"Well, let's see, I think…,"

Lenore interrupted me in midstream of my amusing quip, and decisively said, "Don't say it Jack, I can see that you're not going to tell me anything, anyway…, are you?"

"Don't worry, Lenore. You'll find out soon enough, and trust me…, it'll be worth the wait. Now c'mon, let's go…, we're late for the Monday morning staff meeting?"

We headed down to the conference room and found our usual places at the table.

At one point during the meeting, I turned to Lenore and devilishly whispered, "I hope you're taking notes."

In a bit of a panic, Lenore then reached into her backpack and took out a pad of paper and a pen and began jotting down every word that was streaming out of Bob Watson's mouth.

As I watched Lenore try to keep pace with Bob, I sat back in my chair and quietly chuckled, because Lenore had no idea that I was playing a practical joke on her.

There was no need for Lenore to take such copious notes, because Dolly always records the minutes of the meeting and then distributes them to the counselors. It was nothing more than a friendly prank that a supervisor was playing on an unsuspecting intern.

Before adjourning the meeting, Bob made an unexpected announcement by saying, "I'd like to thank Lenore Richards for helping us out these past six weeks. Lenore has done an outstanding job at managing the transitional janitorial program, and at the risk of sounding bold, I think she did an even better job than Jack O'Leary could have possibly done."

Upon hearing Bob's cutting remarks, the counseling staff all roared with laughter, most notably C.D., who was not only bellowing uncontrollably, but he was making some rather snide remarks to the person sitting next to him as well.

Once again, it never fails how utterly amused the counseling staff is when the "fair haired boy" is the brunt of the boss's punch line.

As the crowd continued to laugh, Lenore came rushing to my defense, as she emphatically stated, "Jack, you're the force behind the janitorial program."

At that point, I just smiled and quietly nodded my head. When the laughter subsided, I just stared at Bob and addressed him by saying, "Thanks for the vote of confidence, Bob."

Bob sheepishly grinned, and then playfully bowed his head for forgiveness.

When the meeting was over, Bob extended his hand and then good-naturedly said, "Hey Jack, thanks for being such a good sport in the meeting. I hope there are no hard feelings."

I cheerfully replied, "Not at all, Bob. You know I'm a team player," prompting Bob to lightly chuckle, as Lenore stood by as a quiet onlooker.

So once the conference room cleared out, Bob turned toward Lenore and casually asked, "So Lenore, what are your plans after this week?"

Lenore innocently replied, "Well, I don't have anything lined up at the moment Mr. Watson. I guess I need to get cracking on that. Perhaps Jack can give me a few ideas."

At that point, Bob took the opportunity to say, "Well, maybe we can convince you to come and work for us. Just think it over and I'll get back to you on it, okay."

Bob then excused himself and headed back toward his office.

Once Bob was safely out of earshot, Lenore turned to me, and in a low excited voice she screeched, "Jack, it sounds like Mr. Watson wants to offer me a job! Holy crow…, I can't believe it! You and I need to talk about this right away!"

"Oh, we will…, trust me." I said, as a sinister smile swept across my face.

"Great!" She exclaimed.

"Now c'mon…, the cargo van is waiting. We'll talk more about it this afternoon."

"Okay, Jack. Thanks, I really owe ya one."

"Oh yeah…? Well, uh…, what do you have in mind?" I asked, precociously.

"Well, not that…, but maybe dinner." She replied, and we both laughed heartily.

We parted company, and as I watched Lenore walk toward the loading dock, she turned back at me and smiled. I was happy to see that Lenore was in a much better frame of mind, and the fact that I may have contributed to picking up her spirits a notch gave me a great sense of joy.

As I walked back to my office, I began to set my sights on how Lenore and I would attack Bob in terms of the upcoming job interview. Bob was casting his line a little earlier than I had anticipated, and I was somewhat surprised that he broached the subject in my presence.

I must admit that Bob wasn't trying to be sneaky about it, but at the same time I thought he'd play his cards a little closer to the vest, and not be as transparent as he was.

At approximately three-thirty, Lenore came charging into my office and almost startled the daylights out of me. She barely said "hello," as she got right down to business in filling out all of the required documentation for the day.

So after finishing her paperwork, Lenore plopped herself down in the chair adjacent to my desk and then quietly folded her hands. She then took a deep breath, and in one fell swoop she anxiously said, "Do we have a strategy lined up yet for my job interview with Mr. Watson?"

At that moment, I just looked at Lenore in utter astonishment. I then decided to have a little fun with her by amusingly saying, "We, as in…, you and I?"

"Jack, c'mon…, you know what I mean. When I said we, well…, it was just a figure of speech. Why are you teasing me? Do you have any idea how nervous I am right now?" Lenore groaned, in her cute little whine.

"I'm sorry, Lenore. I'm just having a little fun with you. Don't worry, I'm working on a strategy for your interview, and Bob won't know what hit him."

"Sorry Jack, I know that I'm over-reacting, but I'm just really nervous."

"It's all right, I know you have a bad case of the jitters. Tell ya what, why don't you call it a day, and we'll talk more about it tomorrow. I'll map out a little strategy for us, and then we'll both go over it together. How does that sound?" I said, reassuringly.

Lenore replied, "All right, that sounds like a plan. I have a bit of a tension headache anyway. Thanks for all your help Jack."

"You're welcome, Lenore. Hey, would you like me to drive you home? We can throw your bicycle in the back of my car. It's no trouble."

"No thanks…, the fresh air will probably do me good. I'll see you tomorrow, Jack."

"Okay Lenore, good-night. I hope your headache goes away." I said, as she wheeled her bicycle out of the office.

Tuesday morning, boy…, I have a lot to do today. I'm sure that C.D. is down in the break room right now wondering where the hell I am, but I'm totally swamped with work.

I don't wanna talk ill of C.D., especially since he's my friend, but he never seems to do anything around here except drink coffee and read the newspaper.

Meanwhile, I have more irons in the fire than a blacksmith shop!

Well, maybe I'm feeling a little bit sorry for myself because I'm pretty overwhelmed at the moment, yet C.D. has the luxury of lounging around the break room all day doing nothing.

To tell you the truth, I've never seen C.D. attend a determination meeting nor have I ever seen him visit with a single client down on the contract floor.

He doesn't even swing by the reception area to check his mail!

Well, C.D. certainly won't die of stress, that's for sure. Unless of course, the coffeepot breaks, or he runs out of coffee grounds or filters.

As I was driving into work this morning, I was thinking that I need to call Migliori's bakery this week and order up a sheet cake for Lenore.

Then again…, maybe I should wait until Lenore interviews with Bob because I'm not really sure what the cake should say. It will either say, "Good Luck" or "Welcome Aboard."

At precisely eight-thirty, I looked up and saw Lenore wheeling her bicycle into my office. She was brandishing a big smile on her face, as she effervescently greeted me by saying, "Good morning, Jack. Do you think we can work on my job interview strategy today?"

"Absolutely, Lenore. In fact, I gave it some thought this morning and I came up with a few ideas. Just to let you know Bob is a brilliant negotiator, and as funny as it may sound, but he enjoys a formidable challenger to go toe to toe with." I said, excitedly.

"Really…," Lenore replied, pensively.

"That's right, especially when he lures you into the part about salary and bonuses!"

"Sorry Jack, but I don't find this as amusing as you do." Lenore said, with grave concern.

"You're right…, I'm sorry, Lenore. I'm not trying to make light of the situation, I was just reflecting back on my job interview with Bob a year ago. But hey…, I made it through that day and so will you, my dear."

"I'm sorry I snapped at you, Jack. I guess I'm just a little bit nervous. I'm grateful that you're going to coach me through it. I know it sounds weird, but I'm actually worried about hurting Mr. Watson's feelings when I start dickering with him."

"First of all, get that notion right out of your head Lenore. When it comes to negotiating in a job interview you simply, "take no prisoners." Bob won't have any respect for you if you cave in on his first offer. You need to portray value. He doesn't want to lose you…, trust me. He'll make it look as though he's doing you a big favor with his first offer, but that's all part of the game." I staunchly said.

I paused a moment, as I reflected back on Dad's eleventh hour advice, when he adamantly stated, "Jackie boy, whatever you do…, don't take their first offer!"

Lenore then said, in a frightened tone, "Jack, I don't know if I have the stomach for this."

"Nonsense Lenore…, you'll be fine. There's only gonna be a few stickling points that will be open for discussion, and I'm gonna coach you through it." I replied, confidently.

"Well, if you say so Jack, but it's still very nerve-racking for me." She stated, anxiously.

I then reached across my desk and handed Lenore a piece of paper. On the paper were a set of questions to ask Bob in the job interview. I also took the liberty of jotting down some suggested responses as well.

In addition to that, I wrote down some figures, such as, salary, bonuses, professional fees, time off, and other incentives that I felt were reasonable expectations and solid bargaining chips for Lenore to use at her discretion.

As Lenore perused the sheet of paper, she quietly said, "Wow, this is really good!" I could see the wheels in her head turning, and a sense of calm come over her entire body.

So after Lenore finished reviewing the handout that I gave her, I then adamantly stated, "Lenore, you need to hold your ground in the interview. Because if you don't, then not only will you come up short, but Bob will be very disappointed that you caved in too early!"

"Okay…, I'll try Jack." She replied, hesitantly.

I then took a much softer approach by saying, "Listen Lenore, just look over the handout tonight. When you feel confident that you have fully digested all of the information that I gave you, then you and I can do some role-playing tomorrow, okay."

"Yeah, okay, thanks Jack. I feel much better already. You're a great supervisor!" Lenore exclaimed, and then she leaned across my desk and gave me a kiss on the cheek.

I looked at Lenore, and then amusingly said, "Uh…, is that the best you can do?"

Lenore erupted into a fit of uncontrollable laughter, and then precociously said, "Well…, for now. After all, you haven't gotten me the job yet."

"So tell me Lenore…, have you had a chance to mention your job interview to Dr. Stevens yet?" I asked, in a rather sly way.

She replied, "Yes, we spoke briefly about it. I basically told him that Mr. Watson wants to meet with me and discuss employment possibilities."

"I see…, and did the good doctor have any helpful words of advice for you?" I asked, with noticeable interest.

"Well, like I said…, we only spoke briefly about it because he was in a bit of a rush to get to class, but he did have one solid piece of advice for me." She replied.

"Okay, I'll bite. What did Dr. Stevens say?"

"He said that I should do whatever Jack O'Leary tells me to do." Lenore stated, proudly.

My mouth was agape, and all I could manage to say was, "Really?"

Just then and right on cue, Bob appeared in the doorway of my office, and energetically said, "Good morning…, eager young minds. How's it going?"

"Good, fine," we both light-heartedly answered.

"Excellent!" Bob replied, robustly.

Bob then continued by saying, "Lenore, I hope this isn't being too presumptuous of me, but I've taken the liberty of scheduling an interview with you for Wednesday afternoon."

"Oh, tomorrow…, okay." Lenore replied, with some trepidation in her voice.

Bob then turned to me and asked, "Jack, I hope this doesn't pose a problem for you."

"No…, not at all, Bob. We can certainly work around that." I said, with aplomb.

"Good, thank you, Jack. Well, I'm off to the State Capital today, and I'll be gone all day. Jack, be a good lad and watch the store in my absence, okay?" Bob requested.

"Sure, Bob. So are they discussing the WELL initiative out there today?" I asked.

"Yes indeed…, things are going quite "WELL" for the WELL initiative." Bob quipped.

"Nice pun, Mr. Watson." Lenore remarked, as we all chuckled in unison.

"Thank you, Lenore. As a matter of fact, the State caucus will be voting on the WELL initiative next week. Maybe you can accompany me for the vote Jack, and if all goes "WELL," I'll even buy you lunch." Bob said, with a big smile.

"Buy me lunch! That sounds too good to be true, and an opportunity that I can't pass up. I'd love to take a road trip with ya, Bob!"

Bob smiled, and then hurriedly said, "Okay, well…, I'll see you later," as he dashed out the door.

Lenore turned to me and then nervously stated, "Jack, I just wish Mr. Watson would ask me point blank if I want the job or not, so that I don't have to go through the rigmarole of an interview. I just want it to be over!"

"Yeah, I know, but where is the adventure in that Lenore. Believe me, come Wednesday afternoon when the interview is all over, you'll look back on this and laugh, and then wonder why you ever got so worked up about it in the first place."

"I guess so, but I have knots in my stomach just thinking about it." Lenore replied.

"Well, like I said Lenore…, just read over the information tonight, and then tomorrow morning we can go over everything in greater detail. That way it will be fresh in your mind."

"Okay, Jack. Well…, I'll see ya this afternoon when I come back from the work crew."

Although Bob asked me to keep an eye on the building today, I was unexpectedly called out of the office and wound up being gone all afternoon. I met with a businesswoman in town who was very interested in hearing about the types of services that we offered at WEALTH. She apparently heard about us through our local Chamber of Commerce, and the appointment lasted a lot longer than I had anticipated.

So after spending almost three hours talking to this businesswoman, I wound up walking out of her office with a signed contract in my hand and a big smile on my face.

Not only did she agree to terms with our janitorial services, but she was also quite intrigued about our sub-contracting services as well.

She explained to me that she was having a lot of difficulty securing a reliable work force, due to the tedious nature of her product. Consequently her company has been falling behind in meeting their deadlines for her online business orders, and if this trend should continue then she was afraid that her company was headed for bankruptcy.

I then conveyed to her that we specialize in what it was that she needed, and suggested that she might want to set up an appointment with us, so that she could take a tour of WEALTH and see first-hand if our program could meet all of her operational needs.

When I finally returned back to WEALTH, it was about five-thirty in the afternoon, and everybody had cleared out for the day. I swung by my office to drop off the signed contracts, and to check my phone messages.

Among the many messages that were piled on my desk, I saw a rather dire note from Lenore that read, "Jack, I waited until four-thirty, where the heck are you? I hope you're still planning on being here tomorrow for our dry run. I'm really counting on you! Thanks, Lenore."

I lightly chuckled after reading Lenore's note of desperation, and then cunningly said to myself, "Don't worry, Lenore…, you'll be ready, and Bob won't know what hit him."

So after rifling through the remaining messages, I saw a message from Allan Farnsworth, who wanted me to give him a call, "ASAP." I found his choice of phrases to be quite comical, because I thought only Bob Watson had exclusive rights to that patented little expression.

As I was driving home, my mind was preoccupied with thoughts of Farnsworth. For some reason Farnsworth reminds me of a "CIA operative," very secretive..., in his words and in his actions. One never knows what to expect when getting a message from Allan Farnsworth.

Anyway, I still need to play it very cool with Farnsworth because he's still my best and only hope right now in securing a State job.

Quite honestly, having Farnsworth as my "ace in the hole" is not exactly reassuring, and for that matter, - it's probably not ethical either.

It's Wednesday morning, and I arrived so early this morning that I actually beat Bob into work. I threw on a pot of coffee, and while it was brewing I decided to give Mr. Migliori a call over at the bakery, so that I could reserve one of his delicious sheet cakes for Lenore.

When I dialed the bakery, Mr. Migs answered the phone in his beautiful and melodic Italian accent, "Good-a-morning, Migliori's-a-bakery. How-a-can-I-a-help-you-a?"

"Hi, Mr. Migs. It's Jackie O'Leary..., how are ya?"

"Jackie boy, it's-a-so-good-to-a-hear-from-you,-Pisan. Why-you-a-calling? You-should-a-stopped-in-a-da-shop-to-a-see-me..., capisce!"

"Yeah, I know Mr. Migs, but I had to get into work early today."

"Okay, this-a-time,-butta-next-a-time,-you-come-in-a-here-to-see-me..., yes. Now, what-can-I-a-do-for-you, Jackie boy?"

"Well, I wanted to place an order and then pick it up domani."

"Bravo! So-whatta-you-like, Jackie boy?"

"Well, I'd like to order a full sheet cake, but I'm not quite sure what it's going to say yet. I was wondering if you could make the cake ahead of time, and then when I pick it up domani you can put the finishing touches on it for me, capisce."

"Why yes, of-a-course-I-a-capisce, that's-a-not-a-problem, Jackie boy."

"Bravo!" I said, which prompted Mr. Migs to laugh.

Mr. Migs warmly said, "Jackie boy, your Italian..., she's-a-notta-too-bad for an Irishman, keep-a-practicing. Is-a-there-anything-else-a-thatta-you-need, Jackie boy?"

"Um, well..., I'll probably get some assorted cookies and baked goods, but I can grab that out of the display case domani."

"Bravo! I'll-a-talk-a-to-you-domani, Jackie boy. Arrivederci!"

"Arrivederci, Mr. Migs..., and grazie." I said, in return.

When I turned for the door, I saw Bob standing in the hallway. He had a big smile on his face, as he curiously asked, "Did I just hear you say arrivederci? I hope you're not placing calls to Italy? I don't think the budget would allow for such an extravagant expenditure like that."

I chuckled at Bob's witty remark, and then casually replied, "Oh that, well..., I was just ordering a cake from Migliori's bakery. Sometimes I talk a little Italian to Mr. Migliori. I only know about five or six words in Italian, but Mr. Migliori gets a big kick out of listening to me."

"Hmm, I see, well..., that's very worldly of you Jack. So will you join me for coffee?"

"Sure Bob, don't mind if I do."

When we walked into the break room, we saw C.D. already sitting down to his first cup of coffee. Upon seeing us, C.D. looked up from his newspaper and nonchalantly grunted, "Morning, gents!"

Bob and I poured ourselves some coffee, and then joined C.D. at the break room table.

C.D. turned away from his newspaper again, and in a bit of a whiny voice he said, "Geez kid, I was really hoping that you were gonna bring in some fresh danish today from that little Italian bakery over on Andreano Avenue."

"Uh..., sorry to disappoint ya C.D.," I replied, as Bob and I leisurely sipped our coffee.

"Man, I've got a real taste for a raspberry danish." C.D. whined again.

Bob then reached into his pocket and pulled out a ten dollar bill, and quietly said, "Here C.D., why don't you head over to Migliori's bakery? I've got a sudden urge for an apple danish."

"Bob, you're springing for danish? Are you feeling all right?" I asked, jokingly.

"Hey kid, don't look a gift horse in the mouth. Let's see that ten spot, Bob!" C.D. exclaimed, as he snatched the bill from Bob's hand and then whisked out the door.

As Bob watched C.D. high-tail it out of the break room, he said in a very deflated tone, "Boy, I wish C.D. could get half that excited about his job."

Prompting me to say, "Yeah, I'm sure it must frustrate the hell out of you, Bob."

Bob took a sip of his coffee, and then casually asked, "So is Lenore ready for her job interview today?"

"Yeah, I think so." I replied, matter-of-factly.

"Hey, you haven't been coaching her, have you? Wait, don't answer that. I don't think I wanna know." Bob stated, with a grimaced look on his face.

"Well Bob, I think the role of a good supervisor is to foster growth and learning at all times, wouldn't you agree?" I replied, with a faint smile.

"Yeah, well…, I guess you just answered my question Jack. It sounds like you've given Lenore the combination to the safe." Bob said, wide-eyed.

"C'mon Bob, look at it this way, you've already started the day off right by springing for the danish. So let's carry that magnanimous gesture of yours straight through to this afternoon's job interview with Lenore."

"Jack, you know my generosity abounds." Bob said, as he smiled behind his coffee mug.

"Yeah, I know that Bob, but I think you've really mellowed over the past year. When I first started here, I was actually quite intimidated by you."

"And now you're not? Well…, I just might have to do something about that O'Leary. I don't want you getting too comfortable around here, or else you're liable to start shirking your duties," prompting both of us to laugh heartily.

Just then C.D. rushed into the break room, and he was completely out of breath. C.D. had two pastry boxes tucked securely under each arm, which he was holding like a football.

C.D. placed the pastry boxes down on the break room counter, and then exuberantly shouted, "Dig in, boys!"

Bob gave me a gentle nudge with his elbow, and then inquisitively asked, "Hey C.D., where's my change?"

C.D. had a very nervous look on his face, and then replied in a panic, "They were four seventy-five a dozen Bob, so I told the old Italian guy to keep the change."

"Okay…, just checking." Bob said, as he quietly glanced at me, and then winked his eye.

So after chitchatting with Bob and C.D. for a little while, I went back to my office and returned Allan Farnsworth's phone call from yesterday. I was curious to see what he wanted, although common sense told me that it probably had something to do with Henry Josephson.

I dialed the number, and after several rings, I heard the familiar smug voice of Allan Farnsworth come over the line and nauseatingly say, "Good morning…, Allan Farnsworth."

So after grimacing from the mere sound of his voice, I then calmly replied,

"Good morning, Al. This is Jack O'Leary. I'm just returning your phone call from yesterday."

"Oh, hi Jack..., thanks for calling me back so quickly. How are ya?" He asked, in a real syrupy manner.

My instincts were telling me that he was simply trolling for information.

"Good, Al. So, what's up?"

"Oh, I was just wondering if you pitched Josephson to Bob yet, that's all." He inquired.

"Um, well..., I did mention the idea to Bob the other day, now whether he agrees with my recommendation or not we'll just have to see. Bob did say that he would mull it over, so I guess that's a step in the right direction anyway." I said, diplomatically.

"Yeah, that sounds very encouraging. So Jack, I heard that Bob went down to the State Capital yesterday. Was he in rare spirits this morning?"

I quickly thought to myself, "If Farnsworth thinks that I'm going to cough up any inside information about Bob, then he's completely off his rocker."

Frankly, I really don't know how Bob made out at the State Capital yesterday because he hasn't shared that information with me yet. I'm assuming that everything went "WELL," seeing how Bob sprang for the danish this morning.

Let's face it..., treating the staff to danish is not exactly typical behavior for Bob Watson!

But as long as I'm playing twenty questions with Farnsworth, I'd like to ask him, "Who in the hell is feeding you all of this inside information?"

Farnsworth definitely has a mole at WEALTH, or should I say a "rat," but whom?

Well, at that point it took every fiber in my being not to give Farnsworth a piece of my mind. I then demonstrated some restraint by simply saying, in a cheerful and professional tone of voice, "Um, well Al..., Bob seemed to be in good spirits today, but no more than usual."

So after hearing my vanilla response, Farnsworth simply said, "I see."

He then continued by saying, "So the special caucus is meeting next week on the WELL initiative, but you probably knew that already, right?"

"Um..., actually no, I'm not aware of that." I said, as I lied through my teeth, but for once in my life not feeling guilty about it.

There was a brief pause, and as I waited on the line, I was growing more impatient by the second. I then seized the moment and abruptly asked, "Is there anything else, Al?"

Farnsworth hesitated a bit, and then flippantly said, "Well…, actually there is."

"Well, what is it?" I asked, in a bit of a huff.

"Do you have a pencil handy, because I'd like you to write down a name?" He replied.

"Okay…, and what is this in regards to?" I asked, in a rather snippy tone.

"Just write down this name, James Brindamore. He's a close personal friend of mine, and I told him to be expecting a phone call from you." Farnsworth said, rather haughtily.

"Is this James Brindamore a new referral?" I asked directly.

Farnsworth laughed out loud, and boldly said, "Hell no! He's your ticket to State employment. He's the contact I've been promising to give you."

"Oh, okay…," I shockingly replied.

So after giving me James Brindamore's phone number, Farnsworth casually said, "Jim works at the State Office Building, and he's the Deputy Director of Personnel over there."

Which prompted me to say, "Wow…, he sounds pretty high on the food chain!"

Farnsworth laughed out loud again, and then replied in a rather smug tone, "Jack, what have I been telling you all along…, you scratch my back and I'll scratch yours."

As I continued listening to Farnsworth ramble on about nothing, I glanced up and saw Lenore walk into my office. Lenore then daintily sat down in the chair adjacent to my desk.

Lenore was wearing a very pretty blue dress and it was quite becoming on her. She was brandishing a radiant smile, and I must admit that I couldn't stop take my eyes off of her.

Farnsworth was still on the other end of the line, babbling on about something, but I was so consumed by Lenore's beauty that I had no idea what Farnsworth was even saying to me.

I then cut Farnsworth right off in the middle of his sentence, and hastily said, "Hey Al, I gotta go. Thanks again for the Brindamore tip, and I'll keep plugging away for Henry…, bye."

Lenore patiently waited for me to hang up the phone, and then innocently asked, "Hi Jack, how do I look for my interview?"

Uh…, as if she needed to ask me such a ridiculous question!

I enthusiastically replied, "Lenore, you look absolutely beautiful," and her radiant smile grew even bigger.

"Thanks, Jack. Do you think this dress is okay?" She quietly asked, as she delicately smoothed out the bottom pleats of her dress.

"Yes, it's perfect. Bob will be so captivated by your beauty that he won't hear a single word that you're saying in the interview." I said, admiringly.

"Oh stop…," she playfully replied, as she blushed and then bashfully bowed her head.

"So where's your bicycle? Is it out in the hallway? Would you like me to wheel it in for you?" I asked, in a teasing manner.

"Very funny, Jack. My Mom drove me in today. Speaking of which, I was wondering if you could give me a ride home later. Well…, that's if it's no trouble."

"No trouble at all, Lenore." I said, smiling.

While I finished up a report that was pending, Lenore quietly looked over the question and answer sheet that I drew up for her yesterday. She indicated to me that she studied the review sheet all night, and felt adequately prepared to answer any question that Bob posed to her.

As Lenore sat there, I noticed that she looked a little jittery. Just as I was about to ask her if she was all right, she nervously said, "Gee, I wish my stomach would stop doing cartwheels."

At that point, I suggested to Lenore that it might be a good idea for her to eat something, and that perhaps a little food may help settle her stomach. I then went down to the break room to see if there was anymore leftover danish from this morning, and as luck would have it I was able to nab the last one. I then brought the danish and a cup of coffee back to my office for Lenore.

As I handed Lenore the danish, I amusingly said, "Try not to spill anything on that pretty dress of yours Lenore. Coffee and raspberry stains may clash with that particular shade of blue you're wearing."

Suddenly, Lenore snapped at me by saying, "Jack, what are you trying to do…, jinx me?"

Lenore then put her coffee down in a huff, and moved as far away from the danish as she possibly could.

At that point, I tried to make amends by saying, "I'm sorry, Lenore. I was only trying to be funny. Listen, let me go and grab a couple of hand towels out of the break room for ya, okay."

Lenore seemed amenable to my suggestion, so I quickly ran down to the break room and snatched a couple of hand towels out of the linen cabinet for Lenore to drape over her dress.

Upon returning with the hand towels, Lenore immediately apologized for her abrupt behavior. She then proceeded to break the raspberry danish in half, and attempted to hand me the bigger of the two halves, to which I replied, "No thanks…, I already had two this morning."

As Lenore took a nibble of her danish, she perked right up and said, "Mmm…, this danish is delicious. Did you get this danish from Migliori's bakery?"

"Uh-huh…," I replied, with a satisfying smile.

Lenore continued by saying, "I thought so, especially the way Mr. Migliori swirls the raspberry filling. He's the best baker in town, well…, except for my Mom of course."

As I leaned back in my chair, I patted my paunchy belly and playfully said, "Well…, I've certainly had my fair share of danish from Migliori's bakery over the years. Can't ya tell?"

Lenore then popped the last morsel of danish into her mouth, and with a satisfying smile she said, "Boy, that really hit the spot, and my stomach feels a lot better now! Thanks, Jack!"

So after finishing her coffee and danish, Lenore and I spent a few minutes role-playing some of the questions and answers that I had prepared for her on the study sheet. I was quite impressed with how adept Lenore was in answering all of the questions that I posed to her.

Lenore was able to illustrate situations in an organized and succinct way, and I actually found many of her answers to be better than the ones that I had recommended she use.

Since Lenore wasn't assigned to go on the cleaning crew today, I suggested that this might be an opportune time for her to work on her internship report that was due on Friday. This was a rather lengthy assignment and part of her overall course requirement for her internship.

Around eleven-thirty there was a knock at my office door and it was Bob. Bob indicated to Lenore that he had a hole in his schedule this morning, and he was wondering if he could conduct the job interview with her now instead of this afternoon.

Lenore hesitantly replied, "Um…, sure, Mr. Watson. I'm just working on a writing assignment, but it can keep till later."

Bob quickly countered, "Are you sure Lenore, as a rule…, I generally don't like to interrupt people when their creative juices are flowing? Isn't that right, Jack?"

"That's right, Bob." I replied, echoing his sentiments.

Bob then turned to Lenore, and cordially asked, "So Lenore, shall we head down to my office?"

It was heading toward lunchtime now and my stomach was beginning to growl. I thought I might stroll down the block for a little fresh air, and perhaps buy a hot dog or two from Barney, who is the hot dog vendor down on the corner.

I also thought that getting out of the building for a little while may help kill some time, instead of just hanging around my office waiting for Lenore to finish up her interview with Bob.

As I approached the hot dog vendor, I affably said, "Hi Barney, give me two hot dogs with the works, but hold the pickle relish."

Barney handed me the dogs, and then cheerfully asked, "Would you like something to drink with that Jack?" (Obviously you can tell that I frequent the hot dog stand quite regularly, because Barney and I are on a first name basis.)

"Sure Barney, gimme a diet soda." I replied, as I rummaged into my pocket to pay him.

As I bit into my sumptuous hot dog, I had an interesting thought pop into my head. Why is it that most people don't mind splurging on the calories for their favorite food, yet when it comes to deciding on a drink they usually go with the diet soda?

Hmm..., perhaps the mindset being that the diet soda will somehow mysteriously offset the high calorie food that they're eating.

Well, as convoluted as that logic may be, it certainly works for me anyway!

When I finished devouring my two hot dogs, I glanced at my watch and saw that it was twelve-thirty. Lenore has been in her job interview with Bob for about an hour now, and by my calculations she'll probably still be in there for at least another thirty minutes.

Anyway, I discarded my trash, said "good-bye" to Barney, and then leisurely strolled up the block toward WEALTH.

As I opened up my office door, I was surprised to see Lenore. She was sipping on a diet soda, and quietly working on her written assignment at the corner table.

"Hi Lenore..., so how did you make out in your job interview?" I asked, alarmingly.

Lenore smiled at me, and then excitedly said, "Well, I guess you and I are colleagues now. He offered me the job and I said..., yes!"

"Fantastic! So how long was your interview?" I asked, reeling with excitement.

"I don't know…, probably about forty-five minutes." She said, very matter-of-factly.

"Wow! Well, I guess it didn't take Bob long to realize what a valuable asset you'd be for the agency. My interview lasted twice as long as yours did, probably because Bob needed all that time to figure out if he should take a chance on hiring me or not."

Lenore burst out into laughter, but then quickly rushed to my defense by saying, "Jack, I think you're indispensable. Bob realizes your value."

"Bob is it! So are you on a first name basis with the boss already?" I asked, with a slight grin.

"Jack, please…, don't tease me. Now that I'm employed here, Mr. Watson insisted that I call him by his first name." Lenore said, sheepishly.

"Really now…," I amusingly commented.

"That's what he said." Lenore stated, with a mischievous grin.

"Well, I'll have you know that I worked here for almost nine months before I was on a first name basis with Bob, and even then I only called him Bob behind closed doors."

Lenore quietly giggled, but then took a moment to be serious as she said, "Jack, thank you so much for all of your help. I couldn't have done it without you."

"So when do you start?" I asked, with great anticipation.

"June 1st," she replied, excitedly.

"Great! So not to pry, but are you happy with what Bob offered you? You know…, in terms of salary and benefits?"

"Yes…, I'm very satisfied with the offer, and I owe it all to you Jack!"

"Well, I may have helped, but you sealed the deal Lenore."

"Thanks, Jack. As a matter of fact, Bob commented on how well prepared I was in the interview, and not just in terms of my clinical skills…, if you know what I mean." She said, rather precociously.

I then replied, "Yeah, I think I know what you mean. My psychic vibes are telling me that Bob will be ushering me into his office sometime today, and not necessarily to compliment me on my exemplary supervisory skills. Bob is not overly fond of zealots, unless of course those zealots are drumming up business for the agency."

"Jack, what are you talking about? You've totally lost me." Lenore said, as she quietly giggled, and then displayed a look of puzzlement on her face.

"Oh nothing, I'm just rambling on…, babbling is what most people call it. Of course, if you wanna get clinical about it, I guess you could refer to it as engaging in some type of auditory hallucination, with deep-seated delusional thought. Harmless really, and I wouldn't be too concerned about it." I stated, as Lenore shook her head and quietly chuckled.

Lenore just held an admiring stare at me, and then quietly said, "Jack, you're funny. I wish my boyfriend could have your sense of humor."

"Boyfriend, huh…, now the plot thickens. I haven't heard you refer to a man in your life before. Is it serious?"

"Yeah, I guess so. He's working on his doctorate in clinical psychology. I think you two would probably get along quite well, because he has a tendency to over-analyze situations too, but not in the humorous fashion that you do." Lenore said, amusingly.

"Huh…, psych majors," I mumbled, as I quietly snickered to myself.

I then interjected, "I have my undergraduate degree in psychology. Sometimes I think the only reason I went into the field of psychology was to find myself."

"And did you?" Lenore asked, curiously.

"What…, find myself? No, I'm still looking, but I'm getting there." I said, chuckling.

"Glad to hear it," Lenore replied, gently.

Around two-thirty, Lenore finished up her written assignment and then handed it to me, so that I could look it over and submit it to Dr. Stevens for his review.

So since there was really nothing else for Lenore to do, I suggested that she take the rest of the day off, so that she could go home and tell her mother the good news about being hired.

Lenore was quite agreeable to my suggestion, but then suddenly realized that her leaving early might be an imposition on me because I had promised to drive her home.

I quickly reassured Lenore that it wasn't any trouble to drop her off because I had an errand to run, and that my errand was taking me right by her house.

Obviously, I didn't want to tell Lenore that the errand I was running was to swing by Migliori's bakery, so that I could order her a sheet cake for landing her first professional job.

We took the short ride over to Lenore's house, and surprisingly Lenore was as quiet as a church mouse the whole ride over. To be honest, I think she was still in shock about being hired.

Anyway, when we arrived at Lenore's house, I turned to her and enthusiastically said, "Well, here we are Lenore. You're probably gonna celebrate tonight, right?"

"Yeah, probably…, but I'm not exactly sure how yet."

"Well, you'll figure it out. Once again, congratulations and I'll see ya in the morning."

"Thanks, Jack. You've been so good to me these last six weeks." Lenore quietly said, and then she leaned toward me and gave me a tender kiss on the cheek.

"Well Lenore, thanks for making my first supervisory experience a positive one. Enjoy your celebration tonight, and I'll see ya tomorrow morning."

"Okay…, bye, Jack."

I drove away from Lenore's house feeling pretty good about myself. I know the Bible says that good works won't get you into heaven, but it must still count for something. After all, God is always watching, and as far as I'm concerned…, good works isn't exactly "chop liver."

At that point, I turned up the radio in my car, which is usually par for the course when I'm in an exceptionally good mood. I then pulled up in front of Migliori's bakery, and as I strolled into his shop, I was cheerfully humming the last song that was playing on the radio.

When I entered the bakery, Mr. Migliori was already waiting on a customer. He turned in my direction when he heard the cowbells clanging on the bakery front door, and when he saw it was me, he smiled and gave me a slight wave of his hand.

Mr. Migliori finished up with the customer that he was waiting on, and then he turned in my direction and pleasantly said, "Bon giorno, Jackie boy!"

"Hi, Mr. Migs. I was in the neighborhood, so I thought I would stop by."

"Bravo! It's-a-so-good-to-see-you,-Jackie boy. So-did-a-you-decide-whatta-da-cake-should-a-say?" Mr. Migs asked, gregariously.

"Yeah, I think I'd like the cake to say, "Welcome Aboard, Lenore." So what do you think Mr. Migs? Is it too corny?"

Mr. Migliori replied, "Hey, that-a-sounds-a-good-to-me. So-Jackie, who-is-a-Lenore? Is-a-she-any-body-that-I-a-know-a?"

"Well, yeah, maybe. Lenore said that her mother is a regular customer of yours. In fact, it's funny you ask because today Lenore bit into a raspberry danish that we bought from you this morning, and not only did she say that it was…, how do you say delicious in Italian…, oh yeah, delizioso, but the minute she tasted it she knew right away that it came from your shop."

"She-a-did, bravo!" Mr. Migs exclaimed.

"Yeah, I thought that was pretty amazing." I said, smiling.

"Bravo! Bravo! So-what-is-a-Lenore's-last-a-name?" He asked, with great interest.

"Richards, Lenore Richards," I replied.

"I know-a-Mrs.-a-Richards. She-comes-in-a-here every Sunday after Mass. She's-a-very-nice-a-lady. Her husband,-he-a-died, about three years ago. He had-a-da-cancer, and I know his-a-death was-a-very, come si dice…, how-a-you-say-a, oh yeah…, devastating for her." Mr. Migs said, sadly.

"Ah, I see. Well, Lenore was just hired today where I work." I stated, proudly.

"Bravo! So…, would-a-you-like-to-wait, or-a-come-a-back-domani, Jackie boy?" Mr. Migs asked, kindly.

As I scanned the display case, I saw that most of the baked goods were already picked over, so at that point I simply said, "I'll pick it up domani, Mr. Migs. I'll probably buy some other stuff to go with the cake. Is that okay with you?"

"Of-a-course, no-a-problem, Jackie boy. I'll-a-see-you-domani, and please say-a-hello-to-your-Mama-and-Papa-for-me…,-yes. All right, Pisano. Arrivederci!" He exclaimed.

"Arrivederci Mr. Migs, and grazie," I said, as Mr. Migs smiled and waved good-bye.

The next day I walked through the front door of Migliori's bakery, and the cowbells clanged, alerting Mr. Migs that he had a customer. Those same brass cowbells have been clanging on that bakery front door as far back as I can remember.

Anyway, Mr. Migs then walked out of the back room and immediately smiled upon seeing me. He then warmly said, "Jackie boy, bon giorno! It's-a-like-you-just-a-here, Pisano. Did-you-say-a-hello-to-a-your-Mama and Papa-like-I-asked-you-a-to-do-a?"

I replied, "Yes, of course Mr. Migs…, and they send their warmest regards, thank you!"

"Bravo! So-letta-me-go-and-getta-you-cake-a, Jackie boy. Help-a-you-self-to-some-fresh-a-coffee-on-a-da-counter, capisce."

"Thanks, Mr. Migs." I said, as he went into the back room to get the sheet cake.

Mr. Migs promptly returned from the back room and then placed the sheet cake down on the counter. Before boxing up the cake, he permitted me to peek inside and view his impeccable craftsmanship. It looked magnificent, and I particularly enjoyed seeing Lenore's name sprawled out in big fancy letters across the top of the cake.

As I stared down at the cake, I had a great sense of pride rushing through my entire body because I knew that I was instrumental in helping Lenore land her first professional job.

"So-do-you-like-a-da-cake, Jackie boy?" Mr. Migs asked, with a proud smile.

"Yes, it is bellisimo! Grazie, Mr. Migs…, you have certainly outdone yourself!"

Suddenly, Mr. Migs' smile grew even larger, and I could tell that he really appreciated my thoughtful and sincere words.

Mr. Migs then closed the top of the cake box and secured all four sides with a splotch of masking tape, so that the lid of the box would stay nice and snug.

He then warmly said, "So Jackie, can-I-getta-you-something-else-a?"

I pleasantly replied, "Yes, I'll take two dozen hard rolls, two dozen soft rolls, three dozen assorted danish, and a large tray of assorted cookies. I think that should do the trick Mr. Migs."

"Bravo, coming-a-up-a, Jackie boy." Mr. Migs said, cheerfully.

Mr. Migs threw my order together in no time at all. Once again, I loved watching Mr. Migs work, as if he was a great maestro…, conducting a symphony. He boxed and tied the parcels, and then lined them all up in a row on the top of the counter.

When Mr. Migs was done boxing up all of the baked goods our eyes locked onto each other, like two gunslingers. I then nervously said, "Hey Mr. Migs, you're not gonna hassle me about not paying you, are you?"

"Well Jackie boy, I'm-a-still-not-a-happy with-how-you-a-fool-la-me-da-last-a-time-when-you-a-paid-a-me-twenty dollars-a-too-mucha, capisce." He replied, with a sly grin.

"Yeah, I capisce…, but you never take any money from me Mr. Migs, so what do you expect me to do? You leave me no other choice, but to resort to trickery."

Mr. Migs laughed heartily, and then kindly stated, "Butta-Jackie boy,-I-hate-a-taking-you-money."

I smiled warmly at Mr. Migs, as I beseechingly said, "But Mr. Migs, you're in business to make a living, so please…, how much do I owe you?"

Mr. Migs then told me what I owed him, which still sounded too low but I paid him what he said anyway. As I was leaving the bakery, Mr. Migs came from behind the counter and helped me carry all of the baked goods out of his shop, and then place them into the backseat of my car.

As I was driving over to WEALTH, I was feeling rather merry, much like Ebenezer Scrooge felt when he realized that he didn't miss Christmas day after all.

When I pulled into the WEALTH parking lot, I saw C.D. getting out of his car. I then called out to him, "Hey C.D., c'mon over here and give me a hand!"

C.D. then ambled over to the side of my car, and when he peered into the backseat he saw me struggling with all of the various baked goods that I had just bought from Migliori's.

He then blurted out, "Geez.., what the hell did you do kid, buy out the whole bakery from that old Italian guy over on Andreano Avenue? I hope you bought some raspberry danish!"

I replied, "Don't worry, I took care of ya. Now would you please grab a few of these bakery boxes and help me bring 'em inside."

"Sure, kid. Where's the danish…, I'll bring that in!"

We managed to get all of the baked goods into the break room in one piece. C.D. then proceeded to get the coffee going, and he continued to clamor on about how good a raspberry danish was going to taste with his morning coffee.

I then heard some noise from up the hallway, so I knew that Bob had just arrived and was settling into his office. I then decided to walk down to Bob's office and say "good morning," and to let him know that I brought in some goodies and a sheet cake for Lenore.

As I was about to leave the break room, I saw C.D. fidgeting at the table. He was anxiously waiting to get the "green light" so that he could break into the danish. C.D. kinda reminded me of a little kid on Christmas morning, who couldn't wait to tear into the presents.

I then turned toward C.D., and amusingly said, "Hey C.D., you can dig in any time now."

C.D. jumped right out of his chair, and then made a mad dash for the pastry while saying, "Thanks, sonny boy! Don't mind if I do!"

I knocked on Bob's door, and I heard him quietly say, "Come in."

"Morning Bob, how's it going?"

"Good Jack, but I wish it was Friday, because it's been a long week."

"Yeah, you're right. Oh, by the way…, congratulations on hiring Lenore. She seems quite pleased, and I know she'll be an excellent addition to your staff."

At that point, I was bracing myself for what Bob was about to say to me next.

Bob then sarcastically said, "Yeah, thanks, but I pretty much had to break the bank to get her. It was quite obvious that she was well coached, as if someone had spoon fed her some inside information. She was able to counter my every move, yeah…, a real "wheeler dealer" that girl."

I replied, "What? "Wheel and deal," "broke the bank," who are you trying to kid, Bob? Lenore is not capable of such a thing."

"Well, that's exactly what I thought too. Then again…, maybe she was advised by someone who is very familiar with the inner workings of the agency. I will say this…, she is without question one of the best prospects that I've interviewed in a very long time." Bob stated, with a big smirk on his face.

"Yeah, not since that O'Leary guy anyway." I said, holding back the laughter and then waiting for Bob's brutal comeback.

Bob countered my witty remark by saying, "Uh…, excuse me Jack, but as I recall, I was pretty desperate in hiring someone when you applied for the position here. Lucky for me that you turned out as well as you did," prompting Bob to burst out into laughter.

I just glared at Bob, and then sarcastically said, "Ah…, thanks for the backhanded compliment, Bob. I really appreciate you putting things into perspective for me."

"My pleasure, Jack." Bob replied, as he continued laughing.

"Hey Bob, I hope I'm not stealing your thunder, but I took the liberty of buying a sheet cake this morning along with some rolls and baked goods. I thought we could have a little celebration today in honor of Lenore joining our staff. Is that okay with you?"

"Are you kidding! That's exactly the kind of initiative that I'm looking for in all of my subordinates!" Bob emphatically said.

"Good, I wouldn't want to usurp your authority." I replied.

"Nonsense Jack, as a matter of fact, since you already bought the rolls and all of the baked goods, then why don't I order up a large meat and cheese platter from Shaughnessy's Delicatessen? We can make it a full blown luncheon!"

"Hey, now you're talking Bob. It sounds like we're gonna have a pretty good day. Listen, we better get down to the break room before C.D. winds up eating all of the danish that I brought in. I'm just gonna go grab my coffee mug off of my desk, and then I'll see you down there."

"Okay, see ya in a few minutes, Irish." Bob affably replied.

Bob and I met up in the hallway, and then joined C.D. in the break room. From what I could tell, C.D. had already devoured two raspberry danish and he was eyeing a third.

C.D. was not only eating raspberry danish like it were going out of style, but he had consumed almost a whole pot of coffee as well.

Bob and I just looked at each other in utter disbelief, and then Bob amusingly said, "Hey C.D., you might want to pace yourself because we have a full day planned today."

C.D.'s curiosity got the best of him, as he asked, "What are you talking about Bob?"

I then beat Bob to the punch, as I smartly said, "We're having a luncheon today C.D., to celebrate Lenore's appointment to the counseling staff."

Bob smiled, and as he turned to pour himself a cup of coffee, I quickly handed C.D. a napkin so that he could wipe the raspberry jelly that was smeared on both corners of his mouth.

As C.D. wiped his mouth, he excitedly said, "A luncheon, well…, this day is getting better and better by the minute!"

It was almost eight-thirty, and Lenore should be arriving any minute now. As I was waiting for Lenore to come waltzing through the door, I was leaning toward her not going on the janitorial crew this morning because I wanted her to thoroughly enjoy her last day. For all intents and purposes her internship was over, so why not let her coast and simply enjoy the day.

It was now eight forty-five and still no sign of Lenore…, that's odd. Lenore is always on time and quite punctual, and although I'm somewhat concerned I'm not ready to call out the "National Guard" just yet. It then got to be nine o'clock, and still no word from Lenore.

Okay…, now I'm getting a little more concerned, especially since it's not like her to be late and not notify me.

As I picked up the phone to dial Lenore's number, she suddenly appeared in my doorway. As I fumbled to hang up the phone, I just stared at her in complete astonishment.

Lenore then dejectedly said, "Good morning, Jack. I'm sorry to be late, but as you can see I had a little problem coming in today."

"Well, yeah…, I can see that. Are you okay? I was beginning to worry about you. I'm glad you're safe, and I think in one piece. You've got bicycle grease all over you."

"Yeah, I know, my bicycle chain kept falling off the track on my ride in this morning. Oh brother, this is not the way I wanted to finish up the last day of my internship."

I then attempted to use a little levity in hopes of picking up her spirits, as I humorously said, "Gee Lenore, I think you have more grease on your slacks than you have on your chain."

Lenore sighed.

"Hey, tell ya what we'll do. Let's throw your bicycle in the trunk of my car and I'll drive you home, so that you can get cleaned up and put on some fresh clothes. How does that sound?"

Lenore replied, "Well, under the circumstances, maybe that's the best thing to do. We should probably tell Mr. Watson first before we go."

"Uh…, you mean Bob, don't ya?" I said, in hopes of making her laugh.

"Um, yessss, I mean…, Bob," she bashfully replied, prompting her to smile, and then sparking a pinkish glow to rise up into her cheeks.

Lenore went to use the restroom so that she could clean some of the bicycle grease off of her face, while I went to find Bob and apprise him of the situation.

When I found Bob, he was shooting the breeze with Ralph down on the contract floor. I conveyed to Bob what had happened and that I was going to run Lenore home, so that she could get cleaned up and change into some fresh clothes and I should be back in less than an hour.

Lenore was all set and ready to go when I met back with her at my office. I stowed her bicycle into the trunk of my car, and then we proceeded to take the short ride over to her house.

As we pulled up in front of Lenore's house, she turned to me and asked, "Jack, would you like to come inside and meet my mother?"

"Sure, why not." I casually replied.

We walked into the house and Lenore called out for her mother, but there was no reply.

Lenore then turned to me and said, "Gee, my Mom probably went grocery shopping. Oh well, why don't you make yourself comfortable on the couch, and I'll just be a few minutes."

"Okay Lenore…, take your time."

So while Lenore went into the bathroom to clean up, I sat quietly on the living room couch, soaking in the décor of the room, and admiring some of the various knick-knacks and family photos that were on display.

As I sat there, I was thinking to myself that despite having bicycle grease spattered on her from head to toe, Lenore still managed to possess a radiant beauty about her.

I then turned my head in the direction of the bathroom, where I heard the pitter-patter of water splashing in the shower, and the sweet sound of Lenore's voice humming a pretty melody.

For a split second there, I felt as though I was part of Lenore's family, well..., in a humorous sort of way anyway.

I then thought of a funny line that a good friend of mine would often say to all of his attractive female friends back in college, which was, "I love you like a sister..., somebody else's sister," and the mere thought of it prompted me to laugh out loud.

As I continued to sit on the couch, amusing myself with what I perceived to be extremely creative and funny thoughts, I noticed that the front door began to swing open.

At first, I thought my eyes were deceiving me, and what I was witnessing was nothing more than an optical illusion. However, as I continued to stare at the front door, I saw a petite older woman entering the home and she was juggling two large bags of groceries in her arms.

Obviously, this woman entering the residence was Lenore's mother.

As the older woman attempted to close the front door with her foot, she happen to catch a glimpse of me out of the corner of her eye. She then dropped the two large bags of groceries that she was holding, and let out an incredible shrieking yell.

The yell was loud enough to wake the dead!

Well..., what ensued next was simply beyond explanation, and mere words cannot describe the true gravity of the situation.

Lenore's mother kept screaming at the top of her lungs, as she scanned the premises for something to defend herself with, such as a bat, or some type of blunt instrument.

In an effort to show Lenore's mother that I meant her no harm, I then raised my arms up over my head and pleaded, "Wait Mrs. Richards..., I'm a friend of Lenore's!"

Despite standing under a cascade of running water, Lenore must've heard all of the noise and commotion that was coming from the living room. Lenore then grabbed a towel and rushed out of the bathroom and came charging into the living room to see what all the fuss was about.

As Lenore stood there in the middle of living room, she had nothing on but a scant linen towel, and she was desperately trying to figure out what all the yelling and screaming was about.

Well, as crazy as it may sound, but my attentions suddenly shifted from this screaming woman who was holding a weapon in her hands and ready to inflict serious bodily harm upon me, to just gawking at Lenore, who was draped in nothing more than a skimpy linen bath towel.

Lenore then shouted, "Mom, it's okay…, this is Jack O'Leary! I work with him down at WEALTH Industries!"

Upon hearing Lenore's pleas, her mother stopped yelling and then let out a tremendous sigh of relief. Mrs. Richards then bent down and started gathering up all of her groceries, which were strewn all over the floor, and I proceeded to help her pick up the groceries as well.

Once all of the groceries were safely picked up and placed on the table, Mrs. Richards then plopped herself down in one of the kitchen chairs, as if she were an oversized rag doll.

Meanwhile, Lenore continued to stand in the middle of the living room dripping wet, and wearing nothing more than a scant linen towel, which was quite revealing to say the least.

Although I felt extremely awkward standing there, my eyes kept drifting over to Lenore and the skimpy linen towel that was draped around her shapely physique. I felt compelled to say something, but I really didn't know what to say.

By now, Lenore's mother had gained her composure. Lenore stood next to her mother stroking her silvery hair, while saying, "Mom, are you okay? Would you like a glass of water?"

Mrs. Richards quietly replied, "No dear…, I just need to sit for another minute or two and collect myself. You on the other hand should probably excuse yourself and get some clothes on before that bath towel your wearing hits the floor."

Lenore then suddenly realized that she was standing in the middle of the kitchen with nothing on but a scant linen towel, and at the top of her lungs she shrieked, "Oh…, my God!"

At that point, Lenore immediately whisked herself out of the kitchen and made a mad dash toward her bedroom, which prompted Mrs. Richards and I to both quietly chuckle.

I then extended my hand to Mrs. Richards, and properly introduced myself by saying, "Hello, Mrs. Richards. My name is Jack O'Leary, and I'm sorry for startling you like that."

Mrs. Richards replied, "No…, no…, it's not your fault, I simply over-reacted.

It's very nice to meet you Mr. O'Leary. My name is Eileen Richards."

As we shook hands, Mrs. Richards then said, "Lenore has spoken so highly of you Mr. O'Leary. It's a pleasure to finally meet you, although I would have preferred a much calmer encounter than this."

"Yes, I agree." I replied, chuckling.

Mrs. Richards continued by saying, "I really want to thank you for all the help you've given Lenore. You're such a dear. How can we ever repay you?"

"Well, there's really no need Mrs. Richards. Lenore is a wonderful girl, and we're very lucky that she has decided to sign on with us at WEALTH."

Just then Lenore dashed out of her bedroom and rushed into the kitchen where Mrs. Richards and I were chatting. Lenore quietly smiled at me, and then walked directly over to her mother, as she soothingly said, "So how ya doin', Mom. Are you feeling better now?"

"Yes dear, I'm fine. Mr. O'Leary and I were just getting better acquainted." Mrs. Richards replied, in a more relaxed tone of voice.

"Please..., call me Jack, Mrs. Richards."

"So dear, why were you in the shower?" Mrs. Richards inquisitively asked.

"Well Mom, riding over to WEALTH this morning my bicycle chain kept falling off the track. In my haste to fix it, I wound up getting bicycle grease all over me."

"Oh dear...," Mrs. Richards remarked.

Lenore continued, "Jack was then nice enough to bring me home, so that I could get cleaned up and put on some fresh clothes. I then invited Jack into the house to meet you, but apparently you were out doing groceries, and, well..., I think you can figure out the rest."

"I see. Well..., I guess we've all had an exciting morning, but no worse for the wear." Eileen Richards remarked, as Lenore lovingly draped her arms around her mother.

"That's the spirit, Mrs. Richards!" I said, enthusiastically.

"Jack, please call me Eileen."

"Okay Eileen," I replied, softly.

"Jack, Lenore and I would like you to join us for dinner some evening. It would be a small token of our appreciation for all that you've done for Lenore."

"Yes Jack, you really must come to dinner sometime. Mom is an amazing cook, and she'll be happy to make your favorite dish. Right, Mom?"

"Um, yeah, okay, I accept. I'm free almost any evening." I said, pleasantly.

"Good…, it's settled then. Just let us know what's a good night for you, and I'll be happy to make anything that your heart desires." Eileen Richards stated, with a radiant smile.

"Thank you, Eileen. That's very thoughtful of you." I replied.

Lenore glanced at her watch, and then quietly said, "Jack, we should probably get going."

"Yeah, you're right. Say Eileen, we're having a small luncheon at WEALTH today to celebrate Lenore being hired, and you're certainly welcome to join us."

"What…!" Lenore exclaimed, in a surprised tone.

I quietly chuckled, and then explained, "Lenore is actually hearing about this for the first time, because I didn't get a chance to tell her this morning. Anyway, you're welcome to come by. In fact…, I insist that you join us. It would be a nice opportunity for you to see WEALTH, and to meet some of the people that Lenore will be working with."

"Sure, I'd like that. Thank you, Jack!"

"Great, Mom! It'll be fun to have you there!" Lenore replied, as she hugged her mother.

As we drove off, I tooted the horn to Eileen Richards, and then turned toward Lenore and said, "Well…, it's been quite a morning, and it should prove to be an even better afternoon!"

When we arrived back at WEALTH, I heard Dolly page me over the intercom. As I reached for the phone, Lenore whispered, "Jack, I'm gonna grab some coffee out of the break room. Would you like me to bring you back a cup?"

I quickly replied, "Yeah, thanks, and hey…, bring back some danish too, will ya."

"Okay, Jack. I'll scout it out for us." She said, with a smile.

"Good morning, Jack O'Leary."

"Jack, my boy…, how's it going?" It was the familiar voice of Dr. Stevens.

"Hi, Dr. Stevens. Hey, it's going quite well. Actually, I'm glad you called because I wanted to invite you to a little get together that we're having for Lenore today, who, by the way, is our newest member on the WEALTH counseling staff." I stated, proudly.

"Is that right? That's marvelous news, my boy! I wish I'd known sooner, I might have been able to rearrange my schedule. Unfortunately, I have a prior engagement so please accept my sincere apologies. I was just calling to see how you were progressing with all of the required documentation to satisfy Lenore's internship." Dr. Stevens said, smartly.

"Well, everything is completed, and to tell you the truth we're actually playing a little hooky today. Lenore just stepped out to get coffee. Oh, wait a minute, Dr. Stevens…, here she is now. I'm sure she wants to tell you the good news herself." I stated, cheerfully.

Lenore carefully placed the tray of coffee and danish down on the desk. I then handed her the phone, and she exuberantly said, "Hi, Dr. Stevens. So did Jack tell you the good news?"

"Yes…, yes…, my dear, its wonderful news! We're all so very proud of you! It won't be long until I'm sending you some eager young minds to supervise!"

Lenore then bashfully replied, "Well, before you do that I'll need to learn the ropes first. I wouldn't want you to place some poor impressionable young soul in my care quite yet."

"Ah…, a poor impressionable young soul, I rather like your candid characterization. Why it wasn't that long ago that you may have been depicted in those terms, my dear. The clumsy caterpillar has now transformed itself into a graceful butterfly." Dr. Stevens eloquently said.

"Oh, Dr. Stevens. I just love your flare for the dramatic." Lenore replied.

"So, my dear…, I understand that they're having a small get together in your honor at WEALTH today. Jack invited me, but regrettably I have a prior engagement that I really can't break. I miss our little chats, and I would love to see you soon. As a matter of fact, Jack has some reports that need to be dropped off to my office. Perhaps you could hand deliver them to me next week, so that we could have tea and visit." Dr. Stevens suggested.

"Hey, that sounds great Dr. Stevens. I'll call you next week to confirm a time, bye."

"Bye dear, enjoy your luncheon…, you'll be in my thoughts." Dr. Stevens replied.

Lenore and I killed the rest of the morning by going over some agency policies and procedures. Around twelve o'clock, I could hear Bob out in the hallway summoning people into the conference room for the luncheon.

Bob then ducked his head into my office, and enthusiastically said, "Soup's on…, down in the conference room."

"Okay Bob," we said, in unison.

When Lenore and I walked into the conference room it was wall to wall people. The room looked like a free for all, as everyone was helping themselves to the huge platter of cold cuts and salads that Bob had ordered up from Shaughnessy's Delicatessen.

As we all know by now, Bob rarely foots the bill when it comes to a free meal, so the WEALTH staff was taking full advantage of the situation and loading up their plates with food.

Eileen Richards was in attendance, as promised. As Lenore hobnobbed around the room, she had her mother by her side, as she proudly introduced her to all of her new coworkers.

When Lenore introduced her mother to Bob, Bob poignantly said to her, "It's a pleasure to meet you, Mrs. Richards. I now see where Lenore gets her stunning beauty from."

The luncheon wrapped up about one-thirty. Lenore and her mother began clearing the tables, but I insisted that they refrain from what they were doing and that I would attend to the task of straightening up the room. I then suggested to Lenore that she call it a day, so that she and her mother could enjoy a leisurely afternoon with each other.

Lenore certainly didn't need much convincing with regards to my suggestion, and then excitedly said, in one fell swoop, "Okay Jack, if you say so!"

As Lenore was helping her mother on with her sweater, I humorously interjected, "Listen Lenore, you better get that bicycle fixed. We certainly don't want a repeat performance of today. Isn't that right, Eileen?"

Lenore then spiritedly replied, "I'll get right on it, Mr. O'Leary!"

Mrs. Richards then gave me an unexpected hug and a tender kiss on the cheek, as she warmly said, "Jack, thanks again for everything. And don't forget to call us for that dinner."

As mother and daughter walked arm-in-arm out the front door, Lenore casually glanced back at me with an appreciative smile, and then gave me a slight wave "good-bye" of her hand.

I paused a moment, as I reflected on the time that I spent with Lenore. I then realized what a great sense of joy and accomplishment I had gained from the whole experience, and an experience that will undoubtedly stay with me for the rest of my life.

It took me about an hour to tidy up the conference room. As I was tying up the last trash bag, I was debating whether or not I should follow-up on the ominous yet intriguing State job lead that Farnsworth had given me the other day.

Essentially, I was operating on blind faith with regards to this job lead, and the sheer thought of it scared the hell out of me.

I mean how do I know if this James Brindamore even exists? For all I know this job lead may be nothing more than a hoax, or some sick practical joke that Farnsworth is playing on me.

Well, I guess I'll just have to take a chance and find out for myself, because the suspense was absolutely killing me.

By now, it was four o'clock and everyone was gone for the day, including Bob. By my calculations, I had just enough time to make that phone call over to the State Capital.

As I sat at my desk, I was trying to find the courage to dial the number that Farnsworth had given me. So after dialing the number, the call rang through and then suddenly a voice on the other end of the line said, "Good afternoon, State Capital. How may I direct your call?"

"Huh, so far, so good…," I thought to myself.

I hesitated a moment, and then cautiously said, "James Brindamore, please."

The operator replied, "One minute, please…, I'll connect you."

I thought to myself, "Wow, this guy actually exists! Now let's just hope that James Brindamore isn't the head janitor over at the State Capital!"

As I waited on the line, I was becoming more and more anxious by the second. The palms of my hands were getting sweaty, and I could feel the palpitations as my heart raced.

So after a few more seconds, a woman's voice came on the line and said, "Good afternoon, Mr. Brindamore's office. How may I help you?"

Still reeling with nervous apprehension, I replied, "Mr. Brindamore, please."

The receptionist then promptly asked, "And whom shall I say is calling?"

A surge of adrenaline went gushing through my entire body, as I uttered, "Um…, Jack O'Leary."

"One minute, Mr. O'Leary. I'll see if he's available." The receptionist pleasantly replied.

As I anxiously waited on the line, my heart was pounding like a drum. Moments later, I heard a rather deep and burly voice come over the line and say, "Good afternoon, Mr. O'Leary. This is Jim Brindamore. How may I help you?"

I hesitated a moment as I searched for the right words to say…, especially since first impressions are everything!

So after throwing caution to the wind, I then decisively said, "Hi Mr.

Brindamore, I was instructed by a mutual acquaintance of ours to give you a call regarding State employment."

Brindamore replied, "I see…, and whom may I ask is this mutual acquaintance of ours?"

Sure, at that point, I had great reluctance in uttering Farnsworth's name, but what other choice did I have. I then decided to cross my fingers and hope for the best, as I squeamishly blurted out, "Allan Farnsworth."

"Oh yes…, I do recall having a conversation with Allan a week or two ago with regards to someone giving me a call. I guess you're that someone, eh Mr. O'Leary."

"Please…, call me Jack, Mr. Brindamore."

"Okay, Jack. And why don't you call me, Jim. Now, if memory serves me correctly, you are a vocational rehabilitation counselor. Is that right, Jack?" Brindamore asked directly.

"Um, yes Jim…, that's correct."

"Well, we're always looking for qualified candidates to fill counselor vacancies throughout the State. Please don't hold me to this, but I think we're currently canvassing a list, and if memory serves me correctly, I remember seeing several of those job titles on statewide vacancy announcements." Brindamore said, in a very matter-of-fact way.

"Well that's very encouraging to hear, Jim." I replied.

"Of course, we could hire anyone we want on a provisional basis, but then he or she would ultimately have to take a test in order to become permanent for that particular job title. The person would then need to obtain a high enough score on the exam, so that they could be reachable on the civil service recruitment list." Brindamore explained.

"I see. So in order to secure a permanent position with the State there is an actual exam that needs to be taken?" I asked.

I then quickly wondered, "Geez! How in the hell did Farnsworth pass the test."

Brindamore replied, "That's correct, although there are other ways around taking the exam."

"I see. And what would that entail, Jim?"

"Well…, for instance, if an applicant has a physical or mental disability then the exam could possibly be waved. The State would then base their score solely on education, training, and experience."

"I see," I quietly answered.

Brindamore continued by saying, "Just keep in mind however that applicants need to furnish the State with medical documentation from a licensed medical specialist, who would then confirm to us that a disability exists, and also provide us with a clinical diagnosis as well."

"Really, well…, I have a visual disability, congenital cataracts, and I'm seen by my ophthalmologist on a yearly basis. Would that suffice in meeting the criteria of having the examination waved?"

Brindamore said, "Possibly…, and if that's the case then you would advance up the list and warrant high priority. We have a very strong affirmative action program that we're quite proud of."

"I see," I replied, attentively.

"Of course, this is simply a general overview of the system, and please don't hold me to this. I wouldn't want you to get your hopes up and be disappointed." Brindamore explained.

"Well, I'm really not trying to pin you down Jim. To tell you the truth, I didn't expect to cover this much ground in our first conversation. My sole intent for today was to just introduce myself, and express an interest in State employment."

"Hey, I understand. Listen Jack, I can mail out the appropriate medical forms to you, and then you can have your physician fill them out. Once the forms are completed, your physician can then mail them back to us here at the State Capital."

"Okay…, sounds good, Jim!" I replied, appreciatively.

Brindamore continued by saying, "So once the medical review board examines all of the information, then a determination will be made with regards to your disability status. If you meet their criteria, then you're on the fast track to getting hired and being placed on permanent status."

"Wow…, that's amazing! You've given me quite an overview today. Thank you, Jim."

"Well, I'm happy to be of service Jack. If you like I can slip these forms in the mail for you, unless of course you're planning on being in the vicinity of the State Capital next week."

Which then prompted me to think, "I may be out there next week with Bob for the WELL vote."

I then took the opportunity to say, "Well Jim, there's an outside chance that I might be in the vicinity of the State Office Building next week, Wednesday…, I believe. Perhaps I could pick up the medical forms from your secretary then. That is, if it's not too much trouble."

Brindamore countered my suggestion by saying, "Better yet…, call me next week when you have an approximate time that you'll be in the State Office Building, and then we can get together and chat. That way we can get better acquainted, and I can hand you the medical forms personally. Just remember…, any friend of Allan's is a friend of mine!"

I quietly thought to myself, "Allan Farnsworth is not exactly my friend. He's more of a nuisance, and at times…, a liability. But for now we'll consider him a friend."

So after taking stock of my rather contemptuous thoughts about Farnsworth, I then pleasantly said, "Sounds great, Jim. Thank you very much!"

Brindamore replied, "Don't mention it, Jack. I'll talk to you next week, bye."

As I hung up the phone, I simply couldn't believe my good fortune. I then quietly leaned back in my chair, and as I looked up to the heavens, I shouted at the top of my lungs, "Yesssss!"

CHAPTER THIRTEEN

Monday morning, you know the drill…, coffee with C.D., staff meeting with Bob, and then hitting the bricks with my skimpy bunch of job bank leads.

Since Joe died, it's been tough replenishing the job bank with any juicy new leads. It's as if some once and ancient fertile land has now suddenly and mysteriously vanished into thin air.

As I drove to my first appointment this morning, I had a passing thought of Lenore. I was thinking how much I missed her smile and her energy, and then wondering if she missed me too.

At some point this week, I'll need to find the courage to tell Bob that I'm looking into State employment, and more specifically…, my telephone conversation with Jim Brindamore last week.

To tell you the truth, I had intended to discuss the matter with Bob right after the Monday morning meeting staff, but I let that golden opportunity slip right through my fingers.

I don't know, call it what you want…, the Irish Catholic guilt or maybe even shame. I just feel like some sort of traitor, maneuvering behind Bob's back as I clandestinely plot my future.

Hey, Bob must realize that I can't work here for slave wages the rest of my life. Surely he expects me to look elsewhere, testing the waters…, and seeing what's available somewhere else.

Then again…, maybe Bob is hoping to groom me in taking over the reins of WEALTH when he retires someday.

Another reason I wanted to talk to Bob this morning was to ask him if he still wanted me to accompany him out to the State Capital on Wednesday for the vote on the WELL initiative.

I'm praying that the vote goes Bob's way, because it might take some of the sting out of me telling him that I'm contemplating leaving WEALTH and looking into State employment.

Of course, going out to the State Capital would not only be a great opportunity for me to experience our State Legislature in action, but it would also give me the window of opportunity I need to meet with Jim Brindamore. Both the special caucus vote and Jim Brindamore's office is located in the State Office Building, and essentially I'd be killing two birds with one stone.

Tuesday morning, and as I reached for the coffeepot to pour myself a cup of coffee, I could see that C.D. had already put a pretty good size dent in the first pot.

As always, C.D. was taking up shop at the break room table, as he leisurely perused the morning newspaper with a hot cup of coffee nestled by his side.

Anyway, I poured the remaining coffee that was in the urn, which was barely enough to eke out two mugs, and then decided to head down the hallway to say "good morning" to Bob.

As I was leaving the break room, C.D. began quietly snickering to himself, and then snidely remarked, "Hey kid, when did you start doing Dolly's job? Are you Bob's personal secretary, or just his errand boy?"

I paused a moment, and then light-heartedly replied, "Actually C.D., I'm more like Bob's personal envoy."

"His what! What's an envoy?" C.D. asked, with an extremely baffled look on his face.

I quietly chuckled to myself, and then simply said, "Why don't you look it up C.D., there's a dictionary on my desk. That is…, if you know how to spell it. See ya, later."

As I turned to exit the break room I started to lightly chuckle to myself, and as I headed up the hallway I chuckled even louder, when I heard C.D. mutter, "Wiseass, college boy."

Bob was working at his desk when I approached his office. I tapped on his door with my foot and vigorously said, "Good morning, boss." I then set the mug of coffee down on his desk.

"Morning, Jack. How's it going?" Bob replied, as he glanced in my direction.

"Doing well, Bob! So how was your afternoon off yesterday?"

"Oh, pretty good. I helped Sarah around the house, and then we had a couple of errands to run. Did everything go okay in my absence?" Bob asked, as he took a sip of his coffee.

"Uneventful, I made the rounds and I think we have some promising prospects. Oh, by the way, did I tell you that we might be having some subcontracting work coming our way from Donnelly Manufacturing, along with placing a small enclave of workers to clean their factory."

"Yes…, I heard. Quite impressive, Jack. Joe taught you well."

"Yeah, thanks, Bob. I think Joe would've been very proud of my networking skills. Oh, speaking of networking skills that reminds me, Mr. Migliori called me last night at home…,"

Bob interrupted me in midsentence, and humorously said, "Uh Jack…, I hope you're not expecting me to compensate you for taking work related phone calls after hours."

I quietly snickered at Bob's witty remark, and then said, "Do you remember me telling you the other day that Mr. Migliori is in the market to hire a bakery helper. Well, guess what…, he wants to know if we can place someone at his shop full-time. Do you believe it?"

"Hmm…, very interesting. Gee, maybe all those donuts that you've eaten over the past year from Migliori's bakery are finally paying dividends O'Leary." Bob sarcastically replied.

Bob continued by saying, "Well, if we do place someone at Migliori's, I want you to tell him that we will be waving all start-up fees and expenses, including salary for six months, or as long as necessary. Tell Mr. Migliori the reason we're extending this courtesy to him is because it's our way of saying "thank you" for the generosity he displayed to the Atkins family."

"Gee Bob…, it sounds like you're getting soft in your old age." I quipped.

Bob quietly scoffed at my amusing comment, yet I could tell by the expression on his face that he found a great deal of joy and contentment in extending this courtesy to Mr. Migliori.

As Bob leisurely sipped his coffee, he then perked up and commented, "Boy, that's good coffee. Well, at least C.D. can do one thing right anyway."

I then replied, "Ya know, Bob…, I'm surprised that C.D. never opened up a little coffee shop, or a "Mom and Pop" diner of some sort."

Suddenly Bob became quite animated, as he blurted out, "Are you kidding me? First of all, he's lazy, and secondly…, he'd drink up all the profits," prompting both of us to laugh.

"Yeah, I see your point Bob." I said, still chuckling.

"So are you still planning on going out to the State Capital with me tomorrow?"

"Yeah, if the invitation is still open."

"Definitely! I could use the company, seeing how it's almost a two hour ride." Bob said, as he took another savory sip of coffee.

"Great! Thanks, Bob." I replied, as I tried to contain my enthusiasm.

I then quietly thought to myself, "Jim Brindamore, here I come!"

"So what's on your agenda for today O'Leary?" Bob asked, as he turned his attentions back toward the work that was piled high on his desk.

"Well, I was flipping through the job bank yesterday, and I stumbled upon a lead that Joe had developed about six months ago, but there was no further follow-up indicated on the progress card. I thought I might check it out today." I said, as I took my last gulp of coffee.

"Good…," Bob nonchalantly replied, with his head deeply buried in his work.

As Bob continued to work at his desk, he piped up and said, "You've had a pretty good batting average lately O'Leary. Not only are you placing people into jobs, but you're procuring work for the contract floor as well. Ya know…, I took a big chance on hiring you O'Leary, but maybe now you're starting to finally earn that big paycheck I dole out to you each week."

At that point, Bob began to quietly snicker to himself, and when he glanced up from his work and saw the grimaced expression that I had on my face, he then let out a rip-roaring laugh.

I then stood up and sarcastically said, "I'll see ya later, Bob…, much later!"

As I was driving over to my first appointment, it suddenly dawned on me that I had forgotten to call the business that I was visiting this morning. I always make it a point to call ahead, not only as a common courtesy, but for another reason that I will explain shortly.

The name of the business that I was visiting this morning was called Spencer Trucking, and although I had their address, I wasn't quite sure of their exact location in town.

Usually when I call to confirm my appointment, I ask the person that I'm speaking with on the phone for directions, and whenever possible…, I ask them to provide me with as many landmarks as they can along the way.

The "landmark theory," remember?

As I have previously mentioned before, I need landmarks the size of billboards to get from one place to the other, so that I can concentrate on the road rather than slowing down to rubberneck. I'd just as soon not place myself or anyone else on the road in harm's way.

So given the fact that I didn't have the necessary landmarks needed to find Spencer Trucking, I guess you could say that it put me in somewhat of a predicament.

Dr. Stevens would often refer to this type of situation as an "impromptu improvisation," and as I recall he used that term quite frequently in class.

Essentially, the lesson that he was trying to convey to his flock of fledgling young counseling students was, "Okay stupid, you messed up..., now how ya gonna fix it!"

Well, I fixed it..., maybe not in the most conventional of ways, but the outcome was still the same.

Sure, I made a few wrong turns, and yes..., I got out of my car a couple of times so that I could run down to the corner of the block to get a closer look at a street sign or two.

I mean, yeah, I'll admit it..., what I was doing was certainly a little peculiar, and if someone was actually videotaping me then it might even wind up winning them some money on America's Funniest Home Videos.

I just kept driving around and driving around making the same wrong turns, as I scoured the same quadrant of city blocks looking for Spencer Trucking.

Then..., in the midst of all this confusion, I kept wishing that I was in a Star Trek episode right now, so that all I'd have to do is punch in the correct coordinates of Spencer Trucking into some fancy space-age gizmo, and I would be instantly transported to my exact location.

Now a device like that could prove to be one of man's greatest inventions..., and maybe even comparable to fire or the wheel!

Well..., don't ask me how, but I eventually found my way to Spencer Trucking.

I shut off my car, took a couple of slow deep breaths, and then tried to put the harrowing ordeal of the past forty-five minutes behind me.

Spencer Trucking was located in a very rundown part of town. The brick on the building was old and weathered, and there were no fancy signs or glitzy décor to catch one's eye.

Joe's job bank notes were pretty sketchy, but he indicated on the progress card that the company was a mid-sized trucking outfit, and that over the past two years the company has demonstrated substantial growth.

As I walked into the building, I encountered a receptionist sitting behind a small desk. I cordially introduced myself, and then proceeded to ask her if I could speak with the proprietor or whomever was in charge.

The woman then promptly said, "Oh..., well that would be Mr. Spencer. I'll see if he is available to speak with you."

Upon hearing her reply, I thanked the receptionist and then found a seat in the small waiting room.

So after waiting several more minutes, a rather stocky middle-aged man came barreling out of an adjacent office and then walked straight over to where I was sitting and bluntly said, "My name is John Spencer, I own this company. Whatta ya want?"

Mr. Spencer caught me completely off guard with his extremely abrasive demeanor. I really wasn't expecting him to be so abrupt. He didn't even have the common courtesy to shake my hand, and for a fleeting moment there I felt as if I was on the brink of fisticuffs with the guy.

So in an effort to right the ship, I introduced myself to Mr. Spencer and then proceeded to tell him a little bit about me and the agency that I represented.

As I began my spiel, I could see by the blank expression on his face that he wasn't the least bit interested in what I had to say. In fact, his face was becoming redder and redder by the minute, and he looked like a "hot water pipe" that was getting ready to explode.

Even before I could dip into my bag of tricks, and explain the incentive package that our agency offers area businesses who sign on with us, Spencer cut me right off at the knees and indignantly shouted, "What do you think this is pal, amateur hour?"

As I attempted to address Mr. Spencer, he rudely interrupted me again and bellowed, "Hey, I'm running a business here buddy, this is my livelihood. I don't have time to play nursemaid to a bunch of handicapped people with diminished capacity. I frown on damaged goods…, whether it's freight I'm hauling or the people who are under my employ. I'm not interested in anything that you're peddling, or being a part of your two-bit telethon. Do you get what I'm saying, pal?"

Well, I simply couldn't believe what Spencer just said, as I blurted out, "Excuse me?"

Spencer shouted, "You heard me…, I'm not interested in hiring any "geeks," "gimps," or "psycho's." I told that old guy with the big pot belly who was here once before not to pester me anymore! Don't you people communicate with each other down there?"

Although I wanted to give Mr. Spencer a piece of my mind, I thought I'd let cooler heads prevail, so I calmly said, "Well, first of all…, the older gentleman that you're referring to has just recently passed away, and I am now assuming his job responsibilities."

"Yeah, well…, that's not my problem," Spencer uttered, in a very flustered way.

I then got right up into Spencer's face, and firmly said, "Furthermore, I don't appreciate your tone of voice, or your vicious characterizations regarding the people that work at our agency. For your information we have some disabled veterans working at our agency, and as a matter of fact "pal," they were injured fighting for your freedom. Frankly, I'm appalled by your narrow-minded thinking, and you should be ashamed of yourself."

Spencer was at a total loss for words. I think he was completely shocked by my spirited candor, and all he could say at that point was "good day," as he stormed back into his office.

In a fit of sheer frustration, I gathered up all of my presentation materials and then shoved everything back into my attaché case, and then proceeded to make my way toward the door.

As I walked out of the building, Spencer's receptionist looked absolutely mortified, as she hung her head low and then softly said, "Good-day, sir."

On the ride back to WEALTH, I was thinking that this morning was nothing but a complete waste of time. Not only did I scour half the city looking for Spencer Trucking, but when I finally found the place I was subjected to an ignorant Neanderthal like John Spencer.

When I arrived back at WEALTH, I went directly to my office, closed the door, and then sat quietly at my desk licking my wounds and feeling quite sorry for myself. I kept ruminating over Spencer's cruel words, which seemed to keep gnawing at me like a giant toothache.

Why couldn't Mr. Spencer simply say that he wasn't interested in our program and just leave it at that? His contentious words spewed nothing but venom and hatred toward disabled people, and I found that to be very disturbing.

Honestly, I don't have a problem with people just saying, "no." It's their prerogative not to get involved with our agency if that's what they choose to do. But let's not go out of our way to maliciously slander, belittle, or minimize others because of homophobic fears or prejudices.

Around three o'clock, I decided to head over to Bob's office so that I could blow off a little steam from this morning's harrowing ordeal at Spencer Trucking, but when I went by Bob's office he was already gone for the day.

I then swung by the reception area to check my mail, and I saw a note in the slot from Bob that read, "Jack, something came up and I had to leave for the day. Let's plan on leaving tomorrow morning at seven o'clock sharp for the State Capital. The special caucus is convening at ten o'clock, that way we should have plenty of time to get there. See ya, tomorrow…, Bob."

When I went back to my office, I quietly sat at my desk and continued to reflect on the events of the day. Apparently those inflammatory remarks by Spencer really seemed to do a number of me, and not only caused me to be quite sad, but I was emotionally spent as well.

As I continued to sulk at my desk, I decided that it probably wasn't a good idea for me to share what happened at Spencer Trucking with Mom and Dad tonight for a couple of reasons.

First and foremost, it would be a breach of confidentiality. As much as I hate to admit it, but even a vindictive individual like John Spencer is entitled to his own opinions and his privacy.

Secondly…, Dad works as a truck driver and Spencer Trucking is a trucking outfit. That to me was a recipe for disaster, and mentioning it had too many potential negative repercussions.

The next day, before meeting up with Bob, I decided to swing by Migliori's bakery and pick up some fresh coffee and danish for our trip out to the State Capital.

Mr. Migs was beaming when he saw me walk through the front door of his shop wearing a jacket and tie. Although he was waiting on another customer, he interrupted his conversation with them and admiringly said, "Bon giorno, Jackie boy! You look-a-so-nice-a today!"

"Thanks, Mr. Migs." I quietly replied, as I waited in line.

When it was my turn to order, I asked for some coffee and danish to go, which then prompted Mr. Migs to swiftly say, "Coffee-anna-danish-is-onna-da-house today, Jackie boy!"

"Oh, today, huh…," I humorously grunted.

I then decided to outfox Mr. Migs, as I slyly said, "Mr. Migs, as a token of my appreciation for such prompt and excellent service, here is a ten-dollar tip!"

Upon seeing the ten-dollar bill on the counter, Mr. Migs excitedly replied, "Jackie boy, whatta-you-do, give me da-agita? That's-a-too-mucha!"

I calmly said, "Mr. Migs, if you have the right to treat me, then I have the right to treat you, capisce."

Mr. Migs thought about it for a minute, and then a smile swept across his face, as he enthusiastically replied, "Bravo!"

I smiled at Mr. Migs, and then warmly said, "Arrivederci, and grazie…, Pisano!"

As I was leaving the bakery, Mr. Migs began wagging his finger at me, as he amusingly uttered, "Next-a-time, I'll-a-be-a-ready-for-you, Jackie boy. Arrivederci…, and bon appetite!"

When I pulled into the WEALTH parking lot, I saw Bob nervously pacing back and forth next to his car. As soon as Bob spotted me, he began tapping the crystal of his wristwatch, as he exclaimed, "C'mon O'Leary…, let's get crackin'! We have a two-hour trip ahead of us. I think we'll take my car, I don't trust the road-worthiness of your vehicle, no offense."

I quickly replied, "Hey…, none taken. Unfortunately, with the meager salary that you're paying me, I can barely afford this "rat trap," Bob."

"Uh…, quite the clever comeback Jack. I'll let it slide this time because you at least had the good sense to stop off and pick up some coffee and danish for our trip." Bob commented, as we piled into his plush and elegant looking vehicle.

As Bob turned the ignition to his car, he glanced over at me and sarcastically said, "So, what's with the jacket and tie? Are you trying to impress somebody out at the State Capital?"

Suddenly, an icy chill went right down my spine by Bob's unexpected comment, and I immediately thought to myself, "Yeah, Jim Brindamore." But instead I smartly said, "Well…, I just wanna represent the agency in a professional manner Bob, that's all."

Bob just smiled, and quietly nodded his head.

As we drove toward the State Capital, Bob and I chatted the whole way out and we were never at a loss for conversation. Bob and I spoke of work, family, and we even touched on a few of our hobbies and outside interests.

There were times during our conversation when Bob asked me what my future career plans were. I really didn't know how to answer him, and found myself sidestepping the question each time he brought it up.

At one point during the trip I was so consumed in thought, - specifically in wondering how I was going to slip away from Bob today so that I could meet up with Jim Brindamore, - that Bob had to reach over and shake me, so that he could dislodge me out of my hypnotic state.

Quite honestly, I just couldn't find the courage to tell Bob the real reason why I was accompanying him to the State Capital today, and that my motives were less than honorable.

We reached the State Capital in two hours, just as Bob said we would. We parked the car in an all-day lot, and then we walked up the hill that led to the State Office Building.

Although I've been to the State Capital many times, I've never actually been to the State Office Building before. I was in absolutely awe of its brilliant and magnificent architecture.

Bob has been to the State Office Building many times over the years, and he knew his way around the complex like the back of his hand.

As we were walking through the front lobby, Bob saw a group of people milling about that he knew. We stopped and chatted with them for a few minutes, and then Bob casually introduced me to the group.

The people that we stopped to chat with were all Executive Directors of various agencies from all over the state, and like us they were all here today for the vote on the WELL initiative.

So after chatting several more minutes, we then excused ourselves and proceeded down the main concourse toward the hearing rooms where the special vote would be conducted today.

While en route, Bob saw a little coffee shop and then nonchalantly said, "Jack, we still have a few minutes before the proceedings get under way, so let me buy you a cup of coffee."

So while Bob paid for the coffee, I scouted out a corner table for us to sit down at.

As we leisurely sipped our coffee, we were captivated by all of the hustle and bustle of activity that paraded up and down the main concourse. There were men and women outfitted in their fancy power suits, as they smartly walked along clutching their briefcases. The view from the coffee shop thoroughly fascinated me, and I kept wondering where these powerful looking people were going, but more intriguingly…, what they were going to do when they got there.

So after finishing our coffee, we then merged with the pedestrian traffic on the main concourse, as we briskly headed toward the caucus rooms. We then hopped onto an escalator, which transported us up to the mezzanine level where all the caucus rooms were located.

As we filed into the main caucus room, there was a definite buzz in the air. I couldn't get over how stately the décor of the room was. There was elegant oak woodwork throughout the entire room, as well as exquisite looking chandeliers and marble everywhere.

We then ascended the long flight of stairs that led to the gallery seating. Bob informed me that there was a State law on the books that permitted all citizens the right to attend any of the proceedings that were being conducted in this room. At times, there were closed door sessions, which in that case prohibited the general public from attending the proceedings, however today's proceedings was an open forum, and from the looks of it a packed house.

So after finding our seats, I just sat back and soaked in all of the grandeur that surrounded me, and simply marveled at the amount of people that kept streaming into the room.

Bob would nudge me from time to time, so that he could point out some of the prominent and distinguished people that were sitting in the crowd. As the spectators continued to clamor, you could feel the electricity that was arcing throughout the entire room.

In a way, it kinda reminded me of opening day at the ballpark, and the only thing missing from today's spectacle was the smell of hot dogs and the refreshing taste of an ice cold beer.

As I panned the crowd, I spotted various news affiliates and production crews that were setting up their television equipment for live feeds and broadcasts. I also saw some familiar local and national reporters that were in attendance as well.

It's funny, but this "behind the scenes" experience made these celebrity icons seem more lifelike, almost ordinary, and nothing at all how the camera portrays them to be on the television.

There were production assistants running around making sure that their celebrity bosses looked perfect for the camera. I chuckled as I watched the way they fussed over their hair and make-up, and then double-checking their pearly whites for any leftover breakfast debris.

On the floor of the caucus room I saw some very prominent State politicians, who were surrounded by an entourage of personal aides. These aides were busy doting over these fat cats, as they brought them up to speed with some last minute briefings on the WELL initiative.

Suddenly a voice came over the microphone, which deadened the clamor of the crowd, as it stated, "Order! Order! May I have your attention, please! We're sorry for the inconvenience, but the special vote in today's caucus room will be delayed for one hour, at which time we will then be reconvening. Thank you for your cooperation and understanding!"

Bob then turned to me and snarled, "Rats! I was really beginning to get my hopes up that these proceedings would go off on schedule. I should've known better…, damn politicians!"

I on the other hand had a much different viewpoint than Bob, as I quickly thought to myself, "Saints b'praised! Now I can slip away from these proceedings and meet up with Jim Brindamore, while these "keystone" politicians get their act together."

At that point, I turned to Bob and asked, "Hey Bob, do you mind if I go exploring a bit?"

Bob replied, "Sure, Jack. I see some people across the way that I need to talk to anyway."

"Okay, Bob. I'll see you in about an hour."

I briskly walked down the long flight of stairs, and then exited the caucus room. Once in the hallway, I spotted a directory of names and offices.

As I scanned the directory, I spotted Jim Brindamore's name and office number, and then asked a security guard if he would point me in the right direction.

Suddenly my heart was racing with nervous anticipation, as I traversed hallway after hallway searching for Jim Brindamore's office.

I eventually found his office, well…, not without making a few wrong turns mind you. But that shouldn't come as any big surprise to hear, especially with the set of peepers that I have.

As I stood outside Jim Brindamore's office door, I was feeling extremely anxious. I then decided to take a couple of slow deep breaths, and as I walked through the outer door that led into his office, I prayed that I wouldn't succumb to a panic attack.

The print on the inner glass door read, "James Brindamore, State Deputy Director of Personnel."

Quite honestly, but not until this exact moment had I fully realized what a prestigious job title that Jim Brindamore held. And the very last thought I had before entering Jim Brindamore's office was, "How in God's name does Farnsworth know an important guy like this?"

As I entered the office, I came upon an older woman that was seating behind a desk. She smiled the minute she saw me, and then cordially said, "Good morning, sir. Can I help you?"

I nervously replied, "Uh, yes…, good morning. Um…, my name is Jack O'Leary. Is Mr. Brindamore available?"

The receptionist glanced down at her appointment book, and had a somewhat puzzled look on her face. She then asked, in a bit of a quandary, "Is he expecting you, sir?"

I hesitantly said, "Um, yes…, yes he is."

"Huh…, one minute please, I'll see if he's available." She courteously replied.

The woman then buzzed Mr. Brindamore's office and announced my name. After hearing his response, she glanced back at me and politely said, "Go right in, Mr. O'Leary."

"Thank you, ma'am." I replied.

As I opened the door, I saw that Jim Brindamore was on the telephone, and he seemed to be engaged in a very lively and spirited conversation with someone on the other end of the line.

At first glance, Jim Brindamore appeared to be in his late fifties, and he was a rather stocky and robust man. The desk that he was sitting behind was very old and worn, and if you ask me it probably should've been sitting out in the middle of some scrapyard somewhere.

Upon seeing me, Mr. Brindamore motioned for me to come into his office, and then pointed to a chair for me to sit down in.

While Brindamore continued to be engrossed in his telephone conversation, I nervously sat there waiting for him to finish up his call.

As I panned his office, I found it to be rather stark. On the wall behind his desk he had some diplomas and certificates, and every one of them was hanging either crooked or cockeyed.

In the corner of the room there was an old dusty bookcase, which had several family photos sitting in some chintzy looking frames, and then tucked behind the family pictures were a couple of plastic trophies that appeared to be bowling related.

Not to sound cruel, but Jim Brindamore's office looked more like an old storage closet than an office, and compared to Watson's office at WEALTH, well…, it was like night and day.

Brindamore then finished his phone conversation, and as he hung up the phone, he turned toward me and boisterously said, "So you must be Jack O'Leary? It's nice to meet ya, Jack."

He then reached across his desk and gave me a hearty handshake.

I replied, "Good morning, Jim. It's a pleasure to make your acquaintance too."

Jim smiled, and then gregariously said, "So what brings you to the State Capital today, Jack? I know it wasn't just to see me, right?"

I chuckled at his rather humorous comment, and then light-heartedly replied, "Actually Jim, I'm here with my boss. We're attending the special caucus vote today."

"Yeah, right. Isn't that the WELL initiative that I've heard so much about in the news?"

"Why yes…, I wasn't aware that you knew of it." I answered.

Brindamore quietly chuckled, and then was quick to say, "Jack, this is the State Capital…, nothing's a secret around here."

"Um, yeah…, I should've realized that." I replied, and feeling a bit naïve.

"Yeah, that's big news around the State. As a matter of fact, a good friend of mine drafted the proposal. His name is Bob Watson. Maybe you've heard of him?" Brindamore stated.

"Well…, actually Jim, Bob is my boss, and that's who I'm here with today." I said, as I suddenly felt the psychic energy that was swirling throughout the room.

"Uh, well…, isn't that a coincidence. Allan Farnsworth never mentioned that to me. Bob and I went to college together, and we were actually teammates on the college baseball team."

"Really…?" I replied.

"Yeah, that's right. Bob was an exceptional baseball player in college, and he wound up breaking all of the school records. As a matter of fact, Bob was actually drafted by the New York Yankees, and considered to be one of their top prospects." Jim said, with a reminiscent smile.

"Gee, Bob never mentioned that to me. I know he has a lot of sports memorabilia in his office, but drafted by the New York Yankees…, wow! I didn't know that."

"Yeah, well…, that doesn't surprise me because Bob is a very modest guy. Bob was a real hard throwing pitcher in his day, a southpaw, and I was his catcher…, can't ya tell." Brindamore amusingly said, as he leaned back in his squeaky office chair and then patted his portly belly.

I chuckled at Jim Brindamore's colorful remark, and then continued listening to him talk about Bob's illustrious baseball career.

"Yeah, Bob threw a couple of no hitters in college, and he had a string of shutouts too. All the baseball scouts said, "He's the next Whitey Ford," but unfortunately Bob blew out his arm. I heard he even struck out Mickey Mantle a couple of times down in Spring Training."

"Wow, that's amazing!" I said, and stunned to hear of Bob's great baseball prowess.

"So anyway…, here are the medical forms for your doctor to fill out with regards to your disability. Why don't you have your doctor complete the forms and then mail them directly back to me, and I'll handle the matter for you personally." Brindamore stated, reassuringly.

"Really…? Okay, I can do that. Thanks, Jim."

"Just remember, you're dealing with a bureaucracy…, and the process usually takes about six to eight weeks for the review board to make their final determination regarding your medical condition. Frankly, I don't really have any say in their decision, or else I would see what I could do to help you out. In the meantime, you can still apply for State positions and be hired provisionally." Jim nonchalantly said, as he leaned back in his squeaky office chair.

"I see," I replied, and trying to absorb everything that Jim was telling me.

"Do you know what the term provisional means Jack?" Jim asked, candidly.

"Um…, like temporary, right?"

Jim chuckled at my innocent response, and then quietly said, "Well, yeah…, but what it really means is that you can work for the State until an exam is offered."

"I see," as I nodded my head.

Brindamore continued by saying, "Now depending on the medical review board's decision, you will have one of two options. First, you will either be deemed disabled, thus waving the exam and automatically being made permanent in the position. Or, if not deemed disabled, you'll need to take the exam, pass it, and then be placed on an eligibility list. Once you're on the list you need to have a high enough score, so that you can be reached on the civil service list and be made permanent in the position."

"I see," as I continued to listen intently.

"Hey, I know this is a lot for you to absorb right now, but I wanted to familiarize you with the whole process." Jim said, assertively.

"Thanks, Jim. I appreciate you taking the time to explain it to me in such great detail."

"No problem, Jack. I'm glad to be of help. As a matter of fact, I did some checking this past week, and we're currently canvassing for a rehabilitation counselor position at a residential facility about three hours north of here. I don't know if that's anything you'd be interested in, but I could have my secretary mail you the job posting outlining all of the particulars."

"Yes…, I'm very interested. Thanks, Jim."

"Of course, feel free to use my name as a reference. They know me quite well at that particular facility." Jim said, casually.

"Gee, I don't know what to say Jim, you're treating me like family." I stated.

Jim laughed heartily, as he quickly interjected, "Oh yeah, well…, my kids might disagree with you. They sometimes think I'm a little too hard on them, but it's for their own good."

I quietly chuckled at Jim's comical remark, but then took a moment to be serious by saying, "Jim, I just want you to know that I'm not looking for a handout. I just want the chance to get my foot in the door, and earn things on my own merits."

Jim replied, "Well, that's exactly what I was hoping you'd say Jack. Listen, if you have any questions about anything that we've discussed today, or any new questions that you might think of in the coming days, then just give me a call, okay."

"Okay, Jim. I will…, and thanks again."

We shook hands, and as I was leaving his office he asked, "Hey Jack, do me a favor, will ya. Tell Bob Watson that I was asking for him, and please give him my warmest regards, okay."

Although I was quick to say "yes," I then wondered how I was going to pull that one off. The great wave of Irish Catholic guilt was once again seeping into the far recesses of my mind. I've painted myself into a corner, and now I've got to find a way to get out of this mess.

Jim then asked his secretary if she would take down my mailing address, so that she could mail me a copy of the job posting that we discussed. I once again thanked Jim for his time and all of his efforts, and then I was quickly out the door.

As I beat it back to the main caucus room, I kept racking my brains as to how I was going to break the news to Bob about my meeting with Jim Brindamore, and then wondering what Bob was going to say to me once he hears what I've said.

When I reached the main caucus room, I pushed through the massive oak door and then bounded up the gallery stairs where Bob was already seated. I no sooner sat down, when all of a sudden I heard the gavel sound, and a stately voice come over the public address system and say, "Ladies and gentlemen…, this meeting will now come to order!"

I immediately thought to myself, "Boy, talk about timing!"

As I sat down next to Bob, we exchanged smiles, and then we both turned our full-attentions toward the chairperson who was conducting the proceedings.

The opening remarks began and the framework was laid. What started out as a friendly sparring match, quickly transformed into haymakers being thrown, as the various committee members from both sides of the aisle voiced their opinions and then presented their arguments.

As I listened to the debates rage back and forth, it was becoming more and more clear to me that this wasn't a political issue, but more of a human rights issue. And for the first time since hearing about the WELL initiative, I was beginning to see things from Bob's perspective.

When Henry Josephson's name was mentioned it prompted me to chuckle. Bob and I exchanged glances, and although we desperately wanted to comment to each other, we simply held our tongues, because we didn't want to miss a single word being uttered.

Back and forth, back and forth, the arguments raged for almost two hours, but when everything was said and done, the WELL initiative passed by a comfortable margin.

When the chairperson announced the outcome of the vote, a resounding cheer echoed through the gallery.

It was as if the home team had just won the game on the very last play!

When Bob heard the committee's decision, it was like he just won the lottery!

Everyone in the gallery then made a mad dash toward Bob, so that they could pat him on the back and congratulate him on the outstanding job he did on the WELL initiative.

As I watched Bob shake one hand after the other, I felt as if I was in the presence of a celebrity.

In my eyes, I viewed Bob Watson as a human services icon, and I was proud that he actually considered me to be his young protégé.

So after being congratulated by what seemed like the entire gallery, Bob turned to me and hastily said, "Jack, I'm starving. Let's get the hell out of here, and go grab something to eat."

We descended the long flight of gallery stairs, and then slowly funneled our way out of the caucus room. We then ducked into a little delicatessen, which was situated right off of the main concourse, and we ordered up a couple of triple-decker sandwiches and something to drink.

While I scouted out a corner table for us to sit at, Bob splurged for lunch.

Bob was on a roll in doling out the cabbage today!

As I was about to take a hearty bite of my triple-decker sandwich, I amusingly said, "Boy, an ice cold beer would sure taste good with this sandwich. So Bob, when is the State Capital getting its liquor license?"

Bob laughed at my humorous quip, and then light-heartedly replied, "Ya know…, that's an excellent idea Jack. And that just might be the focus of the next grant proposal I write."

Yeah, Bob was certainly on top of the world right now, and there was nothing that could break his mood. Well, except for me telling him that I met with Jim Brindamore today.

So after we ate our tasty lunch, we exited the building and then made our way down the hill to where the car was parked. I was still pretty charged up from the events of the day, so I thought I would say something witty to encapsulate the day.

As I was opening up the passenger-side door of Bob's car, I enthusiastically said, "All's well that ends "WELL!" Right, Bob!"

Bob smiled, and he seemed to appreciate my amusing play on words.

As Bob turned the ignition to his car, he replied, "Well said, Jack! In fact, I just might use that clever little pun of yours as the title of the article I was asked to write for next month's Rehabilitation Journal. That is…, if you don't mind me pirating your quote."

I quickly interjected, "Hey, it's all yours Bob. You can compensate me for it in my next paycheck."

Bob then glanced at me, and gave me a sarcastic grin.

"So you're actually going to write an article on the WELL initiative, Bob?" I asked, as I fastened my seatbelt.

"Yeah, isn't that exciting? The chief editor of the journal contacted me the other day, due to all of the notoriety that the proposal received nationally, and they're even going to pay me a modest stipend for my efforts. Not a bad day's work Jack, if I do say so myself." Bob said, as he was preparing to enter the tollbooth, so that he could access the interstate.

We were roughly halfway home, when I found the courage to say, "So Bob, you didn't ask me how I spent my time during the morning recess."

Bob then momentarily pulled his eyes away from the road and glanced in my direction, as he quietly remarked, "Oh…, I guess it never occurred to me. So what did you do with yourself?"

"Well…, actually Bob, I met with someone who knows you, and he wanted me to convey his warmest regards to you." I said, pensively.

"Oh yeah…, and whom might that be?" Bob inquired.

"Jim Brindamore," I replied, anxiously.

"Really…? So how do you know Jim?" Bob asked, as he turned on his directional signal so that he could change lanes to pass a slow moving truck, which ironically was a Spencer Trucking tractor-trailer.

Seeing the name Spencer written in large bold lettering on the side of that tractor-trailer, seemed to catapult my mind into an immediate flashback to my unspeakable verbal altercation with John Spencer the other day. It made me so angry that I blurted out the word…, "asshole!"

"What did you say Jack?" Bob asked, in a quandary.

"Oh…, nothing Bob. I just had a passing thought, that's all." I replied, sheepishly.

"Okay, so what were you saying? Oh yeah…, something about Jim Brindamore." Bob questioned.

"Well, yeah…, I met with Jim Brindamore today. I got his name from Allan Farnsworth. Um…, I guess there's no easy way to tell you this Bob, but I'm seriously entertaining the idea of leaving WEALTH, and perhaps jumping over to State employment."

"You're kidding me, right?" Bob said, in a surprised tone of voice.

"No…, I'm not kidding Bob. I'm dead serious."

"So when did this come about?" Bob asked.

"Well Bob, to tell you the truth, I've been scrounging around for information on State employment for a while now."

"I see," Bob said, as he signaled back into the passenger lane after passing the Spencer Trucking tractor-trailer. Bob then resumed his cruise control, and kept his eyes fixed on the road.

"It's nothing personal, Bob. It's just that the salary and the benefits are much better with the State than what I'm presently receiving at WEALTH. Plus, I'll be getting married soon, and I need to plan for the future." I said, with conviction.

Just then Bob began to laugh out loud, almost uncontrollably.

As I looked at Bob in utter disbelief, I anxiously stated, "What's so funny, Bob? I thought we were having a serious conversation here."

Bob could barely control himself, but he did manage to say, "We are having a serious conversation. But there's something that you don't know and I do, and I think it's hysterical."

"Well Bob…, I wish you'd let me in on the gag because I'm almost on the verge of checking myself into the psych center, and being one bunk over from Henry Josephson. I've been dreading this conversation with you for months." I frantically replied.

"All right…, all right…, I'll tell you what's so funny." Bob said, still snickering.

Bob took a moment to compose himself, and then stated, "So Jack, correct me if I'm wrong, but you're telling me that Allan Farnsworth put you in touch with Jim. Is that right?"

"Yeah, that's right." I replied, candidly.

"So do you think Allan Farnsworth did that of his own volition?"

"Well, yeah!" I said, without hesitation.

"Okay, well…, how do you think Allan Farnsworth knows Jim Brindamore? After all, Jim is a very influential man in the State system. Do you really think that Allan Farnsworth associates with people in those types of circles?" Bob asked, with a big smirk on his face.

"I don't know. Farnsworth said that he would put me in touch with someone regarding State employment, and in exchange for the favor, he wanted me to convince you to reinstate Henry Josephson back at WEALTH." I said, with brutal honesty.

"I see…, and you believe him, huh?" Bob replied.

"Well, yeah…, and apparently he came through for me by giving me Jim Brindamore's name and number." I said, somewhat flippantly.

"Uh-huh, well…, you have a lot of faith in your fellow man Jack. I guess that's one of your more endearing qualities." Bob softly stated, while keeping his eyes fixed on the road ahead of him.

"So what are you getting at Bob?" I asked, with utter confusion.

"Jack, the truth is…, I instructed Farnsworth to give you Jim's name and number. He didn't do it on his own accord, although I'm sure he led you to believe that he did."

"What…!" I blurted out.

Bob continued by saying, "Jim and I go way back, we were college roommates together, and he was actually my teammate on the college baseball team as well. How do you think Farnsworth got his State job?"

"What! You mean to tell me that you hooked Farnsworth up with Jim Brindamore too?" I asked, in total disbelief.

"That's right…, and frankly Farnsworth is worth more to me now at the State level than he ever was at WEALTH." Bob said, decisively.

"Gee, I can't believe that you've known about this little charade of mine the whole time Bob. I feel so ashamed." I replied.

Bob then glanced at me with a consoling smile.

I then piped up and said, "I'm still very confused Bob. Why did you tell Farnsworth to give me Jim Brindamore's name in the first place?"

"Well…, I couldn't give you Jim's number, now could I?"

"I guess not," I mumbled.

Bob continued, "Jack, when I look at you I see someone who can be a real difference maker. I know that private agencies like WEALTH don't pay very well, and I thought a State position would afford you greater opportunities than what you presently have now."

"But using Farnsworth of all people…, why Bob?"

"Actually, Allan Farnsworth was the perfect man for the job, and you wound up falling for it hook, line, and sinker." Watson replied, with a big smirk on his face.

"Boy, I should've realized that I couldn't put anything over on you Bob." I said, with a little more cheer in my voice.

Bob chuckled, and then simply replied, "Well, that's why I'm the boss Jack. The game was rigged and you never stood a chance."

"So you decided to use Henry Josephson as a ploy?"

"Exactly! Because I know how much Josephson means to you, even at the risk of deceiving me." Bob replied, softly.

"So what plans do you have for me at the State level, Bob?"

"No plans, now Farnsworth…, that's another story. He's nothing but a complete idiot, and he couldn't find his way out of a paper bag even if you showed him. I was glad the day I was able to ship him off to the State." Bob said, with a big smile on his face.

"Hey Bob, you know that I've been happy at WEALTH, right? Well…, maybe not in the beginning."

Bob quietly chuckled, but then became a bit more serious by saying, "I know you've been happy here Irish. Listen, if things don't work out for you with the State then you can always come back. You'll always have a job with me here at WEALTH."

"Thanks Bob, but maybe you're jumping the gun in thinking that the State is gonna hire me."

Bob confidently said, "Jack, it's only a matter of time until the State comes knocking. Make no mistake, I don't want to lose you, but I also don't want to hold you back either."

"Thanks, Bob." I replied.

Bob continued by saying, "Jack, I'm well aware of the fact that you have had a lot of adversity in your life, which has prevented you from doing some of the things that you really want to do, such as not going into broadcasting for example. Frankly, I don't want you to add me to your long list of disappointments. I think you already have enough people on that laundry list of yours, especially someday…, when you're lying down on some psychiatrist's couch, and you start telling him all of your sob stories."

At that point, Bob glanced in my direction and we both laughed heartily.

Well, for the rest of the ride home Bob and I said very little to one another. I guess we said all that we wanted to say. I'm glad that Bob and I were able to clear the air, and that the cat was finally out of the bag regarding State employment. This was a tremendous hurdle for me to overcome, and now that everything was out in the open I seem to have a greater sense of relief.

When I arrived to work the next day I had a lot of catching up to do. As I rifled through my phone messages, I came across a message that read, "Please give John Spencer a call at your earliest convenience, thank you."

At first, I didn't know what to make of it. My initial thought was that Mr. Spencer wasn't done reaming me out from the other day, and that maybe he's had time to think of a few more choice comments to make regarding me and the people that I work with.

So seeing how my curiosity was piqued, I picked up the phone and dialed the number that was jotted down on the note pad, and after several rings Mr. Spencer's receptionist answered.

Upon hearing her voice, I seem to hesitate for a moment. I then found the courage to say, "Good morning, this is Jack O'Leary. May I please speak with Mr. Spencer?"

Spencer's receptionist then courteously said, "Yes…, right away, Mr. O'Leary. Can you please hold a moment?"

As I waited on the line, I quietly thought to myself, "This is very odd, and something is definitely amiss here."

A few moments later, I heard a rather subdued and contrite voice come over the line and say, "Good morning, Mr. O'Leary…, this is John Spencer. I appreciate you calling me back so quickly. I just wanted to apologize for my extremely rude behavior from the other day, and I hope you can find it in your heart to forgive me."

Although I was completely taken aback by his apparent remorse and heartfelt sentiments, I quietly said, "Apology accepted, Mr. Spencer. I understand your position of not wanting to get involved with our agency, and I respect that."

Spencer replied, "Actually Mr. O'Leary, I was hoping that you could swing by my office next week and explain your program to me in more detail. I'm also interested in knowing more about the disabled veterans that you have employed at your agency. Perhaps we could even use one or two of them here at our company."

"Why sure, Mr. Spencer. I would be more than happy to meet with you next week and discuss what our agency is all about." I said, in a rather surprised, yet high spirited tone.

"Good, okay, well, just set it up with my receptionist, and I'll look forward to seeing you next week. Thanks again for getting back to me so quickly, and for graciously accepting my apology Mr. O'Leary."

"Thank you, Mr. Spencer. I look forward to meeting with you next week as well."

As I hung up the phone, I thought to myself, "What the hell just happened?"

Quite honestly, I didn't think that I'd ever cross paths with John Spencer again.

Well..., at least not in this lifetime anyway!

In finishing out the week, Bob decided to splurge and throw the staff a little luncheon in honor of his victory for the WELL initiative. Other than me, I don't think that anyone else in the agency was particularly impressed with Bob's extraordinary accomplishment.

Be that as it may, it certainly didn't seem to prevent anyone from devouring the various platters of cold cuts and salads that Bob ordered up from Shaughnessy's Delicatessen, or the luscious sheet cake that everyone polished off from Migliori's bakery.

C.D. was certainly in his glory, and he had his plate piled high, as he kept shoveling the food into his mouth like coal into a scuttle.

The only time C.D. ever took a breath was when he incessantly said, "WELL done, Bob..., WELL done!"

C.D.'s comments were funny the first couple of times that I heard him say it, but as the afternoon wore on his persistent remarks teetered on obnoxiousness.

Bob just laughed when listening to C.D.'s annoying antics, and he simply didn't pay him any mind, because Bob was not going to let anyone or anything stand in the way of spoiling his landmark moment.

CHAPTER FOURTEEN

It's Monday morning, June 1st, and Lenore will be starting her first official day on the WEALTH counseling staff today. Bob was lucky to hire her, and I'm sure he'll grow to depend on her as much as he has grown to depend upon me.

Although I'm very excited to see Lenore today, I'm also feeling a little bit nervous too. I'm not looking forward to telling her that I'm contemplating the idea of leaving WEALTH.

Lenore was really hoping to work under my tutelage, and I'm sure that when I break the news to her it will come as a complete and utter shock. But then sooner or later she was going to find out about it anyway, and I'd rather she hear the news from me instead of from someone else.

As I pondered the situation, I saw Lenore come bouncing through the door. She looked totally refreshed and revitalized, and quite eager to start her new career. Lenore was donning a great big smile, and from the looks of it she had a brand new backpack and a shiny new bicycle.

Lenore then effervescently said, "Hello Jack, it's great to see ya!" She then propped her bicycle up against the wall, and scooted around to my side of the desk and gave me a big hug.

So after squeezing the life out of me, I replied with a big smile, "Lenore, it's great to see you too. You were definitely missed. I hope you enjoyed your time off."

"Ah, it was wonderful…, but I must confess that I really did miss you Jack."

"Likewise, Lenore. So I see that you've upgraded your mode of transportation."

"Yeah, Mr. Duffy over at the bike shop said that my old bicycle was beyond repair, so he wound up selling me a brand new one at a terrific price!"

"Great! So in case you were wondering, you have the office right next to mine. I think it might've been a broom closet at one point."

Lenore laughed out loud.

"Also, I made sure that you were all stocked up with office supplies, but if you should find that you need anything else then just let Dolly know."

Lenore smiled, and then enthusiastically said, "Thanks, Jack. I don't know what I'd do without ya!"

Suddenly, an icy chill went right down my spine by her innocent comment.

Lenore then hoisted her backpack over her shoulder, and eagerly said, "Well, I guess I'll get situated in my new office."

"Yeah, okay. Hey Lenore…, I'm heading down to the break room to grab some coffee. Would you like me to snag you a cup?"

"Oh yeah…, that would be great! I'll just be in my office getting organized."

As I walked into the break room, I immediately came upon its resident main stay C.D., who was plopped in a chair drinking coffee with his head deeply buried in the newspaper.

Now ordinarily I would pull up a chair next to C.D. and start shooting the breeze with him, especially with it being a Monday morning. But not today…, because today I was more intent on getting back to see Lenore than I was on scouring the sports page.

Once again…, the old Irish Catholic guilt was rearing its ugly head at me, because I knew that I just couldn't slip in and out of the break room without at least saying something to C.D., so I blurted out, "Morning C.D., how's it going?"

At that point, I really didn't care what C.D.'s response was so long as I made the effort to say something to him.

"Hey sonny boy, things are swell. C'mon, pull up a chair…, I wanna talk to you about last night's game. What a barn burner that was, eh!" C.D. exclaimed, as he sipped his coffee.

Again, I was solely intent on pouring two cups of coffee for me and Lenore, and then getting the hell out of there, but I did manage to say, "You're right…, it was a heck of a game!"

Still scanning the sports page and never once looking in my direction, C.D. nonchalantly asked, "So kid, how many home runs does Hughes have this season?" C.D. then leisurely waited for me to respond to his question, as he continued to peruse the sports page.

Obviously, C.D. was expecting me to pull up a chair next to him and hash out last night's game over a hot cup of coffee. But what he didn't know was that I had other plans.

So after pouring myself two cups of coffee, I turned to make my getaway. I then noticed that there was a box of apple turnovers on the counter, so I carefully lifted the lid and nabbed the last two apple turnovers that were in the box. With my stash of goodies in hand, I prayed that C.D. wouldn't turn around at that exact moment and catch me.

Once again, C.D. had no idea of the movements happening behind him, because his nose was so buried in the newspaper that you could barely see the top of his shiny bald head.

C.D. then asked me a second time, but this time he asked a little more forcefully, "Kid…, how many homers does Hughes have?"

By this time, I had managed to safely tiptoe my way out of the break room with my stash of goodies in hand, and I was essentially home free from being detained. I must say that I was rather proud of my deceptive ploy, and I got a real kick out of the fact that I was able to put one over on my old pal C.D., who still had no idea of what was happening behind him.

Despite it all, I did manage to turn toward C.D., and without missing a beat, I shouted an answer to his question by saying, "Hughes has fourteen homers!"

Upon hearing my rousing response, C.D. flinched. He then turned his body completely around in his chair to ask me another question, but then saw that I was nowhere to be found.

At that point, C.D. had a rather dumbfounded look on his face. He scratched his head, shrugged his shoulders, and then sauntered over to the coffeepot to pour himself another cup of coffee. C.D. then nonchalantly lifted the lid to the box of apple turnovers, but then discovered that the box was empty. C.D. then cried out, in his classic whiny voice, "Why kid…, why?"

C.D. then took his cup of coffee back to the table, where he had been perched all morning, and resumed reading his newspaper.

As I gingerly tiptoed my way into Lenore's office, she looked up and witnessed my juggling act. She immediately jumped out of her chair and grabbed the two mugs of coffee from my hands, as she amusingly said, "Geez Jack, you look like a circus act!"

I replied, "Maybe so…, but mission accomplished Lenore."

In a playful whimper, Lenore whined, "Jack, you're gonna get me fat bringing me this apple turnover. Don't you know that I can't say no to an apple turnover?"

I then precociously said, "Oh, really! So what else can't you say no to Lenore?"

Lenore just stared at me with those deadly lavender blue eyes of hers.

I then humorously interjected, "Uh…, correct me if I'm wrong, but didn't the doctor say that he wants you to gain fifteen pounds? Well, I'm just following doctor's orders Lenore."

As we sipped our coffee and nibbled on our danish, we attempted to catch up on each other's lives for the past two weeks. Lenore mentioned to me that she saw Bob's interview on the evening news regarding the WELL initiative, and she was ecstatic that the vote went in his favor.

I then told Lenore that I had accompanied Bob to the State Capital for the WELL vote, and then proceeded to fill her in on all of the details of the day, except of course..., the one little detail about my meeting with Jim Brindamore.

Quite honestly, I just couldn't bring myself to say anything to her about my meeting with Jim Brindamore because I was afraid that it might put a damper on things and spoil the moment.

It was getting close to eight-thirty now, and out in the hallway I could hear Bob's voice say, "Let's go, people! It's time to put down your coffee and danish and head down to the conference room, ASAP."

Upon hearing Bob's stirring announcement, Lenore jumped right out of her chair and then reach for her pad of paper and pen for the staff meeting. Seeing her reaction prompted me to quietly chuckle because Bob rarely summons people into the meeting like that.

Then again..., maybe Bob was trying to act tough today because it was Lenore's first day, and he wanted to make it clear right from the start who was running the show around here.

Actually, I've come to realize that Bob is not the ogre that people make him out to be. I've seen a dramatic change in Bob over the past year, and I'd like to believe that maybe in some small way I've contributed to softening his mood.

As we entered the conference room, Bob apologized to Lenore for not stopping by her office to officially, "welcome her aboard." Bob indicated that he had some pressing business to attend to this morning, but he did make it a point to ask her if there was anything she needed.

Lenore was quick to say, "No sir..., Jack has been getting me up to speed."

Bob replied, "Excellent! Thank you for taking care of matters for me Jack."

Lenore and I sat down at the table, and as we waited for the meeting to begin my eyes seemed to be glued on Bob.

As usual, Bob took his place at the head of the table, and although he was trying to be patient, I noticed that he kept glancing at his watch and tapping his fingers on the table at a feverish pace. Bob seemed a bit pressed for time, and in a real hurry to get the meeting started.

So when the meeting finally commenced, Bob's first order of business was to introduce Lenore to the group, and they responded by giving her a quiet round of applause.

Lenore then stood up and meekly replied, "Thank you, everybody."

Although she was blushing, I could tell that she was very appreciative of the recognition. It then prompted me to reflect back on my first staff meeting experience, and it made me smile.

So after dispensing with the formality of introducing Lenore to the group, Bob was now ready to get right down to business.

Lenore had her paper and pen at the ready, while I just sat back with my hands folded totally engrossed in watching her. Throughout the meeting Lenore was taking copious notes, as she studiously wrote down every word that was streaming out of Bob Watson's mouth.

Watching Lenore was very entertaining, especially since we all know by now that Dolly always attends the meeting and records the minutes, and then distributes the minutes to each of the counselor's so there's really no need for any of us to take notes.

In hindsight, I guess I should've gently nudged Lenore and given her the heads up, but watching her unbridled enthusiasm unfold as she wrote down everything that was being said, well…, it was just too precious to pass up. Anyway, I'll make it a point of telling her later.

The staff meeting lasted its usual length. As the counselors paraded out of the room, I was hoping that maybe one of them would've taken the time to wish Lenore "good luck," but such was not the case.

As Bob was exiting the room, he turned back towards Lenore and wished her "good luck," and then followed up his rather gratuitous comment by saying, "Lenore, if you have any questions at all then just ask Jack. I think he knows the ropes by now. Right, Jack?"

I replied, "Um…, yeah, that's right, Bob. Although, C.D. does have more seniority than me," which prompted Bob to lightly chuckle, as he headed back toward his office.

"Well, I guess I better get crackin' on those case files. I'll see ya later, Jack."

"Yeah, okay. See ya, Lenore. And don't forget…, if you have any questions then just ask."

I grabbed a cup of coffee out of the break room, and then went straight back to my office so that I could finish up a few reports.

As I quietly sat at my desk, I had this crazy premonition that Dr. Stevens would be calling me sometime today to inquire about Lenore.

Then again…, I guess it doesn't take a rocket scientist to have a hunch like that.

After all, it's not unusual for a university professor to acknowledge one of his prize student's on their first professional day.

Well, as the Irish often say…, "May God strike me dead!"

But the thought of Dr. Stevens no sooner left my mind, when all of a sudden Dolly buzzed me on the intercom and said, "Jack, you have a call on line one, it's Dr. Stevens."

I quickly thought to myself, "Aha..., my psychic powers seem to be getting stronger, because I almost had Dr. Stevens' phone call timed to the second."

"Hello, Dr. Stevens. I know this sounds crazy, but I was just thinking of you. I had a hunch that you'd be calling me today." I enthusiastically said.

"Is that right? You know me quite well, my boy. This solidifies what I've been telling you all along Jack..., that you have very strong instincts." Dr. Stevens replied, with panache.

I laughed at his amusing comment, and simply said, "Well..., I just wish that these strong instincts that you keep referring to could help me conjure up six winning lottery numbers."

Dr. Stevens chuckled at my rather astute wisecrack by saying, "Dear boy..., now what would you do with all that money? You'd wind up losing your purpose in life."

"Uh..., somehow Dr. Stevens, I think I could learn to adapt," which prompted both of us to laugh quite heartily.

"Yes, well..., in any event, I was just calling to see how our young protégé is faring. I trust she is settling in nicely?" Stevens inquisitively asked.

"So far, so good..., and she's cracking the case files as we speak Dr. Stevens."

"Wonderful, you're such a grounding influence, my boy. Bob Watson is lucky to have you there Jack."

"Thanks, Dr. Stevens. Hey, while I have you on the line I was hoping to tell you something, and I would appreciate it if you kept it confidential for now."

"Sounds rather serious, Jack. What is it?"

"Well, if the opportunity presents itself, I'm considering changing jobs and pursuing State employment."

"Really, well..., the State salary and benefits are certainly more substantial than what you're currently earning at WEALTH. And I'm sure it will be quite a blow to Bob Watson when he learns of the news." Dr. Stevens said, boldly.

"Actually Dr. Stevens, Bob already knows. I really can't get into right now, but Bob was quite instrumental in putting me in touch with a very influential contact at the State Capital."

"My, my, that certainly sounds quite intriguing, and a story that I would love to hear about sometime, perhaps over tea." Dr. Stevens remarked, with his usual flare for the dramatic.

"Yeah, sure, it might even qualify as one of those believe it or not stories. You know what they say…, truth is stranger than fiction. Right, Doctor?" Prompting both of us to laugh.

"So have you broken the news to Lenore yet, Jack?"

"No, not yet…, and that's why I wanted you to keep it under your hat for now. I'm looking for the right moment to tell her."

"Yes, I thoroughly agree, and I'm quite confident that you'll find the right moment to tell her, my boy. Well, if there's nothing else…, would you please be so kind as to transfer me over to Lenore's office phone. I'd like to properly welcome her aboard in her new assignment."

"Sure, I'll transfer you Dr. Stevens."

"Thanks, my boy. Call me…, if you need a reflective ear."

The week at WEALTH was relatively uneventful, however on a more personal note, I did manage to mail out the medical forms that I received from Jim Brindamore a few weeks ago.

Dr. Pierce, who is the ophthalmologist that has been treating me since I was a young boy, was able to complete the forms and provide me with a clinical diagnosis.

Despite the heavy backlog of patients that were sitting in his waiting room, Dr. Pierce was gracious enough to fill out the forms while I waited. In his professional opinion, Dr. Pierce feels that my visual disability should qualify me in satisfying the State medical review board's criteria. However, if I should have any difficulties with regards to their decision, then Dr. Pierce said that he would be happy to make a phone call or write a letter on my behalf.

Upon leaving Dr. Pierce's office, I thanked him profusely for taking the time to document my medical condition. And on the drive home, I found myself laughing uncontrollably, because I realized that I was thanking Dr. Pierce for attesting to the fact that I couldn't see worth beans.

Once again, Jack O'Leary's life continues to be a total enigma, and a life that not only presents some major challenges at every turn, but also a life that defies logic or reason as well.

Thus far, Lenore has done remarkably well at transitioning into her new position. Her work ethic and organizational skills are beyond reproach. She familiarized herself with the case files in record time, and she is now setting up appointments and fully engaged in counseling sessions. She seeks me out from time to time for clarification on agency policy and procedure, but other than that she is on her own and doing a splendid job.

Lenore manages to spend a large portion of her day on the contract floor, and without question, she has demonstrated a lot more bravery than I had exhibited during my early days.

Of course, in my own defense, Lenore did intern here and she has me to lean on, but more importantly…, she doesn't have anyone on her caseload that even closely resembles Michael Wallace or the notorious Sampson's.

That being said, it still doesn't negate the fact that she is doing a superb job, and that she is truly an exceptional person.

One morning, Lenore scurried into my office and quickly shut the door behind her, and then whispered in a troubled tone, "Jack, every time I go into the break room I see C.D. in there drinking coffee and reading the newspaper, and what's more…, he always calls me rookie. I don't think he even knows my name."

Upon hearing Lenore's concerns, it took every fiber in my being not to laugh out loud. I certainly didn't want to minimize Lenore's feelings by laughing in front of her, but I did indicate to her that Bob is fully aware of the situation and that he will handle the matter in his own way.

And as far as the rookie comment goes, I explained to Lenore that C.D. possesses some very limited social skills, and what she may construe as being condescending, he views as a way of befriending her.

Although I tried to explain the situation to Lenore in terms that she could understand, I could tell by the troubled look on her face that she was not buying my explanation whatsoever.

When Lenore finally left my office, I could hear her quietly mumbling under her breath, "Getting paid to drink coffee, huh…, it just doesn't make any sense to me at all."

Well, it's been about three weeks now since I mailed out the medical review forms to Jim Brindamore. The other day Jim was nice enough to send me a confirmation letter stating that he was in receipt of the medical forms that I sent him, and that he would keep me posted if he heard of any new developments regarding my case.

Once again, Jim reiterated to me in the letter that it takes roughly six to eight weeks until a decision is made in my case, so he strongly advised me to exercise some patience in allowing the process to play out.

In the meantime, Jim suggested that I send out a resume and an application to the facility that he had made mention of on the day we met at the State Capital, and to feel free to use his name as a reference on the application.

This morning I'm scheduled to meet with Mr. John Spencer over at Spencer Trucking. Apparently, Mr. Spencer has been out of town for the past ten days, and his receptionist has had to call me several times to reschedule our appointment.

Oh, speaking of phone calls..., yesterday I received a very interesting phone call from Mr. Sampson. Mr. Sampson actually called me from Arizona, and then went on to say that the reason he has not been in contact with me of late is because he and his wife have been on vacation.

Anyway, I thought I was going to literally fall off my chair in laughter when he told me the story of his being on vacation with his wife Charmayne, and his older brother Amos.

Amos, who I have never met before, but apparently works as a city bus driver, decided to take Mr. and Mrs. Sampson on a transcontinental vacation. The purpose of the trip, in Mr. Sampson's own words were, "To see America..., before we all die!"

Apparently, Amos loaded up Mr. and Mrs. Sampson into an RV rental, and then embarked on a six-week vacation out west.

Uh, all I can say is..., that must've been a pretty big RV!

To tell you the truth, I was absolutely shocked that Amos would even consider an undertaking like that. Even if my life depended on it, I don't think I would've had the courage or the intestinal fortitude to be cooped up with the Sampson's for that amount of time.

I laughed out loud when I heard Mr. Sampson emphatically say..., "Boy, that Grand Canyon sure is a pretty big hole!"

As I listened to Mr. Sampson describe his cross-country adventure, our conversation was certainly a far cry from the first time we chatted. I can still vividly recall my stomach churning every time the telephone rang for fear that it was the Sampson's on the other end of the line.

So after finishing up my conversation with Mr. Sampson, I thought I would do a little investigative work, so I called the restaurant that the Sampson's work at and the manager of the restaurant corroborated Mr. Sampson's story.

When I asked the manager why he failed to inform me of the Sampson's absence, he nervously said, "Well..., I was afraid that you might send me a replacement."

Upon hearing his reply, I burst out into laughter. I then told the restaurant manager that I would've only sent him a replacement if he had requested one.

In wrapping up my conversation with the restaurant manager, I made it a point to say, "In the future please let us know the Sampson's whereabouts, and don't be afraid to call me if you're having any additional problems or concerns."

To which he replied, "A year ago, I was ready to fire the Sampson's, but now they are two of my best workers. I've seen a dramatic improvement in both of them over the past year, and if you have anymore clients at your agency like them, then please send 'em my way!"

When I hung up the phone, I was filled with a great sense of satisfaction. It was very heartwarming to know that someone other than myself has come to appreciate the tremendous progress that the Sampson's have made over the past year. It made me realize that all of the hard work and sleepless nights that I have endured with the Sampson's was finally paying off.

As I was heading out the door for my appointment at Spencer Trucking, I heard Bob call out to me, "Hey O'Leary, are you getting ready to make the rounds?"

I alertly replied, "Yeah, but first I have an appointment at Spencer Trucking, Bob."

Bob then amusingly said, "Oh yeah, well…, just to play it safe, you better take a baseball bat with ya."

We both laughed, and then I quickly interjected, "Well Bob…, that won't be necessary because Mr. Spencer and I patched things up the last time we spoke."

"Really? All right, well…, good luck Irish. Check in with me later, I wanna make sure that you come back in one piece." Bob quipped, as he slid a few coins into the vending machine for a mid-morning snack.

As I walked through the front door of Spencer Trucking, Spencer's receptionist warmly greeted me by saying, "Good morning, Mr. O'Leary. I'll tell Mr. Spencer that you're here."

Moments later, Mr. Spencer came sprinting out of his office to greet me. As we shook hands, he affably said, "Sorry for all the cancellations, Mr. O'Leary. The last couple of weeks around here have been pretty hectic, but I'm glad we're finally getting the chance to meet."

To which I replied, "That's quite all right, Mr. Spencer. I completely understand."

Spencer then cordially said, "Please…, follow me."

We walked into a small adjacent room. Upon entering the room, I was quite surprised to see a carafe of coffee and a large platter of assorted pastry sitting on the table.

As I sized up the pastry, I cunningly said, "I'll bet you bought those baked goods from Migliori's bakery."

Mr. Spencer was quite taken aback by my rather astute observation, and with a slight chuckle in his voice, he replied, "As a matter of fact, I did. Are you familiar with that bakery?"

"Huh…, do I know Migliori's?" I amusingly commented.

I then light-heartedly said, "My family has been buying baked goods from Mr. Migliori ever since I can remember. It's the best bakery in town, but you didn't need me to tell you that. You really shouldn't have gone to this much trouble though, Mr. Spencer."

Spencer quietly stated, "Well Mr. O'Leary, it's my way of saying I'm sorry for the way I conducted myself at our last meeting. In fact, my receptionist…, even at the risk of being fired, reprimanded me on how despicable my behavior was."

"Well…, perhaps I caught you on a bad day." I said, diplomatically.

Spencer staunchly replied, "Hey, let's not sugarcoat it Mr. O'Leary, I was a real jerk that day. After you left, all I thought about for the rest of the day were the disabled veterans that work at your agency, and it got me thinking about my Dad who served in WWII. My Dad has since passed away, but I know what a proud patriot he was in fighting for this country."

I then gently said, "Well, as I recall, I said a few choice words myself Mr. Spencer. That wasn't very professional of me, and I apologize for my rude behavior as well."

"To tell you the truth, Mr. O'Leary…, I gained a lot of respect for you that day, especially in the way you stood up to me. You weren't the least bit intimidated by me and I like that."

"Well…," I sheepishly uttered, and for one of the few times in my life, I was at a complete loss for words.

"Listen Mr. O'Leary, now that we've dispensed with all the apologies, I thought we could sit down and enjoy some coffee and pastry, and you could tell me a little bit more about your agency."

"Sure, but before we get started Mr. Spencer, I just wanted you to know that my Dad also fought in WWII, and I too have a great respect for veterans as well. And what's more…, I think you and I have a lot more in common than we think." I said, as I helped myself to a danish, while Spencer poured the coffee.

"As a matter of fact, Mr. O'Leary…," I then interrupted Mr. Spencer in midsentence and said, "Please…, call me, Jack."

Spencer replied, "Okay, Jack. And please call me, John."

"Thank you, John. Now what were you saying?"

Spencer continued "Well Jack, you're right…, we do have a lot in common. In fact, I asked around about you, and as it turns out I know your Dad. He's a trucker…, right?"

I lightly chuckled, and then replied, "Yeah, he's a trucker…, and he's been sitting behind the wheel for over thirty years."

"Well Jack, when I found out that I vilified the son of a trucker, I felt absolutely terrible."

"Hey John, forget it…, I'm not one to dwell in the past. What's done is done. Let's just go from here and see where it takes us, okay." I said, optimistically.

Spencer replied, "All right, but I was wondering…," Spencer hesitated a moment, but then continued by saying, "did you tell your Dad that we had words, you know…, that you and I were bumping heads the last time we met?"

I quietly answered, "No John…, everything we do here is strictly confidential."

"That's good, because I'd hate for him to find out what a complete jackass I was to his son." Spencer replied, which prompted both of us to laugh heartily.

"So John…, let me tell you a little bit about our agency. I think you'll be pleasantly surprised." I said, as I opened up my briefcase and then plunged right into my spiel.

I spent about an hour talking to John Spencer about WEALTH, and the types of services that we offered. When I finished the presentation, John Spencer seemed quite impressed with what he heard and thought that it was very educational.

So after hearing what I had to say, John decided to hire two people from our agency to work at his company, and his exact words were, "Let's get 'em started, ASAP."

As soon as I heard the magical ASAP reference, I immediately thought of Bob Watson, and at that moment I felt as though fate was giving me a gentle nudge.

One of the positions that John Spencer wanted to fill at his company was on the loading dock, and he needed someone who was strong and could work without any physical limitations.

The second position called for someone who might be able to work reliably as a bookkeeper in the business office.

Obviously, Michael Wallace fit the bill for the loading dock position, and the other position was targeted for a man named Bob Hodge, who had some prerequisite business skills.

John Spencer seemed to take an immediate shine to Bob Hodge, who was severely wounded in the Vietnam War, and as a result of his injuries Mr. Hodge is now a paraplegic and confined to a wheelchair.

Although Mr. Hodge receives a disability check from the military every month, he desperately wants to work in the business sector and live a more normal and productive life.

So after hearing Bob Hodge's courageous story, John Spencer was literally brought to tears, and he was quite insistent that Bob Hodge start working at his company immediately.

When we were all done, John and I shook hands and he thanked me for my time. I then conveyed to him that it must've been destiny that brought us back into each other's lives again, which then prompted him to ask me why I should make such a bold and grandiose comment.

I then proceeded to tell him that on a recent trip back from the State Capital, I saw several Spencer Trucking tractor-trailers on the interstate. For me seeing those trucks was a sign, and perhaps even an omen that he and I would somehow be reunited again.

So after listening to my insightful illustration, John seemed to gain a great deal of solace and contentment, and I dare say…, maybe even altered his perspective on the way he views life.

Upon returning back to WEALTH, I went straight over to Bob's office. I knocked on his door and then enthusiastically said, "Hi Bob, I'm back. And not only am I in one piece, but I also have some terrific news too!"

Bob looked up from his work, and then inquisitively asked, "Oh yeah…, and what might that be O'Leary?"

"Well, I just placed two clients over at Spencer Trucking!"

"Really? Well congratulations…, that's great news!" Bob exclaimed.

I then excitedly said, "John Spencer wants one person to work on the loading dock, and the other person to work in the business office! Can you believe it?"

Bob smiled, and then warmly interjected, "Of course, I believe it. Why wouldn't I? After all, you were trained by Joe Atkins, weren't you?"

I quietly nodded my head and smiled contently.

Bob continued by saying, "Based on your last encounter with Mr. Spencer, I wouldn't have thought it possible. So, what changed?"

"Well, I really don't know Bob. He told me that he knew my Dad, so maybe it's a truck driver thing. You know…, teamsters are all fraternal brothers. Then again, perhaps guilt got the best of him, and now he's trying to atone for his reprehensible behavior."

"Yeah, maybe even a little bit of both." Bob remarked, as he listened intently.

"Then again…, I did mention to him that we provide services to disabled veterans, which prompted him to think about his Dad, who was a veteran of

WWII. But, uh…, I'd rather not say anymore than that Bob."

"Oh, really? Are you sure there isn't anything else that you'd like to tell me Jack?"

"Um, no…, we'll just leave it at that Bob. The bottom line is that we now have two new placements at his company. It wasn't the most conventional placement that I've ever had, but I couldn't be happier." I stated, proudly.

"Well Jack, not to dampen your spirits, but I need you to take a little trip out to the psych center for me and check up on our old buddy Henry Josephson."

"Ah, c'mon Bob…, I've already done my time at the psych center and now it's time for someone else to go out there? I think we need to "Share the "WEALTH" a little around here, don't you agree." I said, and whining like a spoiled child.

"Huh, "Share the WEALTH," you know…, I've always enjoyed that little catch phrase, and it's probably my most favorite expression." Bob said, as he leaned back in his sleek leather chair and smiled appreciatively.

I then countered his whimsical remark by saying, "Don't try to butter me up, Bob. Anyway, I thought ASAP was your most favorite catch phrase."

"Touché, Jack. But c'mon…, we've already been down this road before. Besides, you have such an excellent rapport with Mr. Josephson." Bob said, fighting back the laughter.

"A rapport…, is that what you call it? Don't you think you're stretching things a bit Bob?" I groaned, as I flopped down into the big cushiony leather chair across from Bob's desk.

"C'mon Jack, it won't be so bad. I've already spoken with Ms. Brown, and she said that she can free up some time out of her extremely busy schedule, so that you can spend a few minutes with your old pal Josephson. You'll be in and out of there in no time at all. Plus, it'll give you a chance to get reacquainted with Henry again, you know…, to catch up." Bob said, as he was on the verge of laughing hysterically.

"Reacquainted, sure Bob…, the only thing I'll be reacquainted with is hearing Henry tell me, "Do you know God loves you, brother?" Not exactly what I'd call getting reacquainted."

Upon hearing my sarcastic rendition of Henry Josephson, Bob roared with laughter, as he barely managed to say, "I told Ms. Brown that you could be out there by two o'clock today."

Bob was laughing so hard that his eyes began to water, and it prompted me to say, "I'm glad you find this so amusing Bob. I'm supposed to be doing job placement remember."

As Bob continued to laugh heartily, he then blurted out, "Hey Jack, I owe ya.

But technically…, Josephson is still on your caseload."

I then waved the white flag and replied, "Ah…, forget it Bob. Actually, it's me who owes you. After all, you put me in touch with Jim Brindamore. So now we're even-steven, right."

"Jack the ledger is clear." Bob said, smiling.

"I'll admit, I am slightly curious as to how Henry is doing." I commented, as I rose from Bob's big cushiony leather chair.

As I turned for the door, I quietly said, "See ya later, Bob. Oh…, and I'll tell "God" that you were asking for him brother."

Later that afternoon, I drove over to the psych center. When I got there I swung by the security office and picked up my visitor's pass, and then carefully negotiated my way through the many long, dark, and cavernous hallways that led to the infamous Ward 19.

I rang the doorbell to Ward 19, and then waited for someone to unlock the door. When the door finally opened, I flashed my visitor's pass to the attendant and then entered the unit.

As soon as I stepped onto Ward 19, I was overpowered by the incredible stench of cigarette drenched air that permeated every crevice and square inch of the living unit.

This tsunami of pungent air put an immediate strangle hold on my respiratory system, and made it almost impossible to breathe. As I made my way over to the front desk, I then did my best ventriloquist act, as I mumbled, "Is Stella the ward charge available?"

The attendant at the front desk then informed me that Stella was indisposed at the moment, and could he be of any assistance to me.

Before responding to his question, I took another quick gasp for air, and then told the attendant my name and my reason for being here today.

The attendant then instructed me to wait in the visitor's lounge, which by no means was a safe haven in escaping the land of second-hand smokedom, but it certainly beat the alternative.

En route to the visitor's lounge, I took out my handkerchief and placed it over my nose and mouth, and then hunkered down in the extreme rear of the room.

It then occurred to me that if Bob forces me to come back out to the psych center again, then he may need to requisition me a gas mask from the local army-navy store.

As I struggled to breathe whatever little oxygen was in the air, I found myself alternating between holding my breath and taking short shallow breaths. I was attempting to do everything in my power to minimize the amount of vile second-hand smoke that I was forced to breathe.

Of course, using this technique can only last for so long, and I quickly realized that I was beginning to hyperventilate.

Suddenly, I had all sorts of crazy thoughts and ideas swirling through my head, as I sat there waiting for Henry and Ms. Brown to show up. I'm sure that all of these bizarre thoughts that I was having were largely attributed to the onset of anoxia. I kept focusing on my breathing, much like a woman would do in child birth.

As I happen to glance up, I saw Ms. Brown barrel into the visitor's lounge. She caused me such a start that I took too deep of a breath, and then went straight into a coughing jag. As I glanced back up at Ms. Brown, she appeared as though she had lost some weight.

Perhaps she burned a few fat cells when she and the "posse" were out searching for Henry a couple of weeks ago.

Anyway, I stashed my handkerchief into my pocket and then stood up and extended my hand to greet her.

Ms. Brown then looked me straight in the eye, and with her sickening syrupy smile said, "Hello Mr. O'Leary…, it's so nice to see you again!"

I thought to myself, "What a crock of shit that is! You're no happier to see me than I am to see you. You didn't even have the common decency to pick up the telephone and give me one lousy phone call when Henry was missing for almost two months."

So putting my rather contemptuous thoughts aside, I simply said, "Good afternoon, Ms. Brown. Thank you for meeting with me on such short notice."

She then nervously replied, "Yes, well…, would you like to take a seat?"

I then asked, "Will Henry be joining us?"

She curtly replied, "Oh yes…, however, I thought we could chat first."

"Okay, well…, would you like to start, or should I?" I asked, cordially.

She then said, "Well, perhaps you can start by informing me as to what Henry's status is now that the WELL initiative has been passed."

"Oh, well…, I was under the impression that Mr. Watson had already addressed those logistics with you. No matter, anyway…, in a "nutshell," oh…, pardon my choice of words, Ms. Brown." I said, and then I lightly chuckled to myself.

Ms. Brown wasn't the least bit amused by my Freudian slip, as she just glared at me with her steel blue eyes. She then yanked her notepad out of her briefcase, and then said in a bit of a huff, "Please…, continue."

"Well Ms. Brown, we're certainly willing to entertain the notion of having Henry resume his work evaluation at WEALTH. That is…, as long as he's not displaying any ill effects from his recent ordeal with his brother Simon."

"Yes, well…, Mr. Watson alluded to that also." She curtly replied.

As I listened to her ill-conceived comment, I quietly thought to myself, "Why do I always have to show her my cards, yet she always seems to play her cards close to the vest?"

I then nonchalantly asked, "So how's Henry doing?"

"Fine," she said, and being her usual vague self.

I thought to myself, "Fine, who are you trying to kid? Henry is far from fine."

So then I asked, "Well, let me ask you this Ms. Brown? In your opinion, do you think Henry should continue with his vocational evaluation at WEALTH?"

She candidly replied, "In my opinion, I think it's a little too premature."

I then thought to myself, "Wow, the milquetoast actually took a stand!"

So after a brief pause, I then asked, "Okay, but what if Henry came back to us part time, say…, two or three days a week?"

"Perhaps," she said, in a wishy-washy manner.

Suddenly, I was beginning to lose my patience, and no doubt…, the alveoli in my bronchial lobes as well, due to the cigarette drenched air that I was being forced to breathe in.

I then stated, in a rather cogent and precise way, "Well Ms. Brown, our agency is not only concerned with the vocational development of a person, but with their social development as well. I certainly think that Henry could use some polishing in his social development, and then maybe in time we can start focusing on the vocational aspects of his life."

"Perhaps," she said, once again.

I was thinking to myself, "Is that all she's going to say is "perhaps?" What is wrong with this woman?"

It suddenly occurred to me that the psych center was the perfect place for Ms. Brown to be working, especially since all of her comments could be characterized as being very non-descript, and quite similar to the idiopathic diagnoses that all of these "dime store" psychiatrists are slapping on all of their patients that reside here.

At that point, it was quite apparent to me that my conversation with Ms.

Brown was absolutely futile and destined to go nowhere, so I asked her if I could see Henry now.

Ms. Brown then simply replied, "Certainly, I think we've covered everything."

I thought to myself, "Well, not everything…, but let's not stay here any longer than we have to, or else there may be a "code blue," and I'll need the crash cart to resuscitate me."

A few minutes later, Ms. Brown returned to the visitor's lounge with Henry. Henry then extended his small nicotine laden hand to me, in much the same way he had in all of the other previous times that we'd met. We then shook hands, well…, that is to say if you wanna call it a handshake, because his grasp was as limp as overcooked spaghetti.

As I observed Henry, I noticed that he still had that faraway look in his eye, which indicated to me that he didn't recognize me at all.

Anyway, we all sat down and I commenced the meeting by asking Henry a few benign questions, in hopes that these simple inquiries might evoke some type of spark out of him.

So after several unsuccessful attempts of trying to break the ice, it became quite clear to me that our conversation was going nowhere fast. At that point, I simply cut to the chase, and asked Henry if he would like to come back to WEALTH Industries and work with us again.

As I waited for Henry's reply, the look on his face gave me the distinct impression that not only did he not comprehend my question, but that he didn't even know what galaxy he was orbiting in.

Henry then replied, in a low and quivering tone of voice, "Do you know God loves you, brother?"

I immediately thought to myself, "I knew he was going to say that, and if Bob Watson was here right now he would be on the floor laughing hysterically."

Anyway, I wound up spending a total of fifteen minutes with Henry, and of those fifteen minutes, about fourteen minutes and thirty seconds of it was essentially a staring match.

As Henry gazed at me, he kept oscillating his head back and forth like a small kitchen fan, and never once blinking his eyes. The time I spent with Henry, though brief, was certainly ample enough time in appraising his state of mind, or should I say lack thereof.

Frankly, I didn't see anything different from the last time that Henry and I met, so I guess in that respect his little escapade with his brother Simon didn't make him any worse for the wear.

For all intents and purposes, Henry still resembled "Our Lord and Savior, Jesus Christ." And in his mind, and I use the word "mind" quite loosely, he's still doing "God's Work."

We concluded the meeting, but nothing of any real significance was accomplished today. Henry was essentially the same, and so was Ms. Brown for that matter.

As I said my "good-byes" to Henry and Ms. Brown, I then turned for the door. I was halfway out the door, when I heard Henry's faint quivering voice call out, "Messenger...," which prompted me to look back in Henry's direction.

In an eerie tone of voice, Henry quietly uttered, "I'll be praying for you brother. Go in peace..., for I am always with you."

Henry then made the "Sign of the Cross," and reverently bowed his head.

At that point, I really didn't know what to say. As I slipped out the door, I just smiled and gave Henry a slight wave of my hand in acknowledgement of his kind and gracious words.

When I arrived back at WEALTH, I went straight down to Bob's office so that I could apprise him on how my meeting turned out with Henry over at the psych center.

As I tapped on Bob's door, I sarcastically said, "Hi Bob, I'm back from purgatory."

Bob then amusingly quipped, "Purgatory..., huh! Well, I see that you've upgraded your description of the place from the last time you were there O'Leary."

"Well, so much for my in and out over at the psych center Bob. I wound up gnawing on some of the same old issues that you and Ms. Brown had already covered. She is still quite dense, and lacks any semblance of a sense of humor, just in case you were wondering."

"Jack, to be honest with you, I don't really care to hear about Ms. Brown or the sense of humor she lacks. I'm more interested in knowing how our little friend Mr. Josephson is doing."

"Well, he seems like the same old Henry to me Bob."

"Excellent! That's exactly what I was hoping you'd say to me Jack. You know I trust your judgment implicitly." Bob said, smiling.

"Yeah, I know you do Bob, especially when my judgment coincides with what you want to hear, right?" I replied, and we both laughed.

Well for the past two weeks, Bob and the psych center have been trying to hash out a start date for Henry Josephson. Apparently both sides can't seem to agree on the correct number of hours that Henry should attend WEALTH.

In order for WEALTH to qualify for federal funding, then Henry needs to attend the program for a specific number of hours each week, but the psych center is not willing to budge on the number of hours that Bob is requesting.

As a matter of fact, the other day I happened to overhear Bob on the telephone, as he shouted at the top of his lungs, "For crissakes, Ms. Brown! We're not running a charity here!"

Quite frankly, you would think that the psych center would love nothing more than to have Henry out of their hair for as many hours as they possibly could every day.

But when it comes to the psych center…, there's really no rhyme or reason to them whatsoever!

On a more personal note, I received a letter in the mail from the State facility that I had sent my resume and job application to a few weeks ago. This facility is a residential facility that houses mentally retarded individuals, and is commonly referred to as a developmental center.

Essentially, the letter thanked me for my interest in their facility, and upon review of my application, they may be calling me to schedule a time to meet and talk about the position.

Last night, I had dinner with Lenore and her mother. Eileen Richards made good on her promise of fixing me a delicious meal, as a way of saying "thank you" for helping out Lenore.

The highlight of our dinner conversation was rehashing the story that brought us all together for the first time, and we laughed so hard that our stomachs ached.

The following week, I received a phone call from a Ms. Rita Spinelli, who works as an Associate Personnel Director at the State facility that I had forwarded my resume to.

Ms. Spinelli indicated to me that she reviewed my resume, and wondered if I was interested in scheduling a time to discuss the position and to also take a tour of the facility.

So after chatting with Ms. Spinelli for a few more minutes, we agreed upon a day and a time for me to come and visit the developmental center, and discuss the position in greater detail.

As I hung up the phone, it then occurred to me that the time has finally come for me to bring Bob up to speed on my news about State employment.

Bob and I have not broached the subject of State employment since returning back from the State Capital, and when he hears the news I hope it doesn't come as a complete shock to him.

The next day, I waltzed into Bob's office with two piping hot cups of coffee and a big smile on my face, as I enthusiastically said, "Morning, boss! Here's a hot cup of "Joe," just the way you like it!"

As Bob snatched the cup of coffee from my hand, he suspiciously remarked, "A hot cup of "Joe" just the way I like it, huh. So..., what do you need Jack?"

I quietly chuckled at Bob's rather animated reaction, and then replied, "Is it that obvious, Bob? Well, actually..., I need tomorrow off because it's kinda important."

"Oh yeah, why..., do you have a hot date with your fiancé?" Bob asked, as he leaned back in his sleek leather chair, while taking a few savory sips of his coffee.

"Actually Bob, I have a job interview at a State facility tomorrow."

"I see. Well, if you ask me..., I think that was rather presumptuous of you to be making arrangements like that without clearing it through me first. Wouldn't you agree, Jack?" Bob stated, as he attempted to sound tough, while grinning behind his coffee cup.

"You're right, Bob. I'm not following proper protocol, but I was somewhat nervous on the phone when they called." I said, backpedalling.

"Nonsense, I'm only kidding with ya..., you did the right thing. Hey, you're the one that needs to demonstrate flexibility, not them. So where are you interviewing at tomorrow?" Bob asked, as he nonchalantly sipped his coffee.

"Well, it's a state developmental center that's about two hours north of here. Are you familiar with it?"

"Why yes..., I'm very familiar with it. In fact, I know the Director of that facility quite well, and he's a very good man." Bob replied, emphatically.

"Geez Bob..., is there anyone in this field that you don't know?" I humorously remarked, as I shook my head, and smiled in amazement.

"Hey Jack, when you've been working in this field for as long as I have, then you eventually get to know everybody." Bob answered, and we both laughed in unison.

"I'll remember that for future, Bob." I replied, still chuckling.

"So is this the job posting that Jim Brindamore gave you?" Bob asked, as he leisurely sipped his coffee.

"Yeah, I thought I would give it a look-see." I said, casually.

"Sure, of course..., although not that I'm trying to sway you one way or the other, but that's heavy snow-belt country up that way. When you drive up there tomorrow you'll be enjoying a beautiful June day, but just keep in mind what January and February will be like up there. Weather wise, it's a whole different ballgame than what we're used to dealing with down here."

"Yeah, you're right, Bob. And I appreciate the advice, but I need to see the place for myself and then make an informed decision."

"Okay, well…, if you need any last minute words of advice then you know where to find me, but if not then good luck tomorrow Irish." Bob said, in a very sincere tone.

"Thanks, Bob." I replied, as I rose from his big cushiony leather chair, so that I could get ready to start making the rounds.

Later that afternoon, I happen to pass by Lenore's office and saw her working at her desk. I quietly tapped on her door, and then casually said, "Hi, Lenore."

Lenore smiled, and then pleasantly replied, "Hi Jack, c'mon in."

"Okay…, but continue what you're doing, I can wait." I casually said.

As I sat there waiting for Lenore to finish up the progress report that she was working on, I couldn't stop admiring her stunning beauty. But what intrigued me even more was the intensity she displayed in writing her reports.

Lenore then put down her pen and looked me straight in the eye, and affably said, "So, what's up Jack?"

"Well…, I just thought I'd come by and say, "hi." I haven't talked to you in a couple of days, and I just wanted to see how things were going?" I cordially replied.

"Things couldn't be better! So what's going on with you Jack?" Lenore asked, with her usual vim and vigor.

"Well…, I have some news." I quietly replied.

"Oh yeah, what is it?" Lenore inquired, as her face lit up with anticipation.

"Well, I'm taking tomorrow off because I have a job interview at a State facility, which is about two hours north of here." I said, and sounding almost blasé about it.

Suddenly, Lenore's effervescent smile disappeared, and her radiant glow was then transformed into a look of complete and utter shock, as she incredulously replied, "Really…?"

I could tell that Lenore was shaken by the news, so I tried to downplay any enthusiasm I had about the impending job interview by saying, "Well, at the very least, I'll get educated as to what types of vocational programs they provide their clients up there."

Quite honestly, I'm not really sure if Lenore heard a single word I said. She continued to be in a state of shock, and I felt as if I had just totally obliterated her "couldn't be better" day.

Lenore then inquisitively asked, "So do you know much about the position?"

"Actually no," I replied.

"Wow! Well, you must be pretty excited, right?" She asked, in a deflated tone of voice.

"Yeah…, but I'm also a little bit nervous too." I replied, and still downplaying my enthusiasm.

"So are you going to take the job if they offer it to you?" Lenore asked, as she braced herself for my reply.

"I don't know, yeah…, probably. The State pays six thousand dollars a year more than what I'm currently making now, and they have an excellent health care package and a really good pension plan." I replied.

"So does Bob know yet?" She asked, timidly.

"Oh yeah…, he knows!" I replied, in a very demonstrative voice.

Lenore seemed a bit startled by my animated tone, and then asked, "So he must've been quite surprised when you told him, right?"

"Well, it's a long story, and I really can't get into it right now, but suffice to say he wasn't too shocked to hear the news." I replied, as I quietly rehashed the whole Farnsworth-Josephson scenario in the deep dark recesses of my mind.

"Gee, that sounds like quite a story Jack." Lenore said, mystified.

"Oh, it is, trust me…, and comparable to that of a Hollywood script." I replied, and we both quietly laughed.

"Well, good luck tomorrow Jack. Not that you'll need it, because you're just the kind of person that every agency is looking for in a great counselor." Lenore said, kindly.

"Thanks…, Lenore." I softly replied.

As I left Lenore's office, words can't express how incredibly sad I felt, - and dare I say…, but maybe even sadder than the day Joe died.

Chapter Fifteen

It's Friday morning, and in a little while I'll be leaving for my job interview at the developmental center. Dad is downstairs making breakfast and Mom is doing some last minute ironing, as she tries to smooth out a few of the wrinkles on my suit.

I haven't worn my suit since Joe's funeral, and when I tried on my trousers this morning, I discovered that I had a pretty tough time squeezing into them.

It took me almost fifteen minutes to fasten the damn button!

So before heading downstairs, I took one last look at myself in the mirror, and I realized that the waistband on my trousers felt so tight that it looked like it was ready to explode. I then prayed to God that the button wouldn't pop off sometime today.

Well…, at least not until my job interview was over anyway!

I've always fought the battle of the bulge, but wrestling with that button this morning was a real wake up call for me, and perhaps serve as the motivation I need to start thinking about losing a few pounds, especially since my wedding day is right around the corner.

As I sat down to a hearty breakfast, Mom was admiring how nice I looked in my clothes, and Dad was putting the finishing touches on writing out the directions for my trip.

So after devouring my breakfast, Dad pulled up a chair next to me and went over the directions step by step, and assured me that his way was the fastest and easiest way to get there.

Dad being the trusty truck driver that he was not only wrote out the directions turn by turn, but he even went to the trouble of drawing me a little map as well, and highlighted specific landmarks that I would be passing along the way.

The "landmark theory…," remember.

So after examining the directions that Dad handed me, I humorously quipped, "Gee Dad, these directions look more like a treasure map than a road map."

Dad replied, "Very funny, Jackie boy…, you'll be thanking me later."

Mom then piped up and frantically said, "Jackie, your father is just trying to help you out, your eyesight…, remember! We wouldn't want you to get lost and be late for your job interview, or God forbid getting into a car accident and winding up in the hospital."

I paused a moment and reflected on what Mom said, and then appreciatively replied, "You're right, Mom. Thanks…, Dad."

As I reached for the car keys, Mom and Dad wished me "good luck," and then I was quickly out the door.

Once safely on the interstate, I glanced at the directions that Dad wrote out, and I lightly chuckled to myself when I saw what he wrote down for my final destination, which read, "X marks the spot, matey!"

The trip went according to plan, and it was precisely two hours long just as Dad had predicted. Dad's directions actually came in quite handy, and I have to say that a couple of times along the way his artwork prevented me from making a few wrong turns.

Dad always says, "If you wanna know how to get somewhere and get there fast…, then just ask a truck driver!"

Quite honestly, I really didn't know much about the facility that I was visiting today. I opted not to ask Bob anything about the place, even though he strongly encouraged me to do so.

To tell you the truth that was a very tough decision for me to make, especially since Bob knows the Director personally, and it would've afforded me a golden opportunity to access some inside information.

The bottom line was that I wanted to be offered the job on my own merits, and not be accused of resorting to some sort of preferential treatment or back room nepotism.

So after exiting the interstate, I turned onto to a very quaint and scenic country road. A few miles down, I spotted the landmark that Dad had diagramed for me on the "treasure map."

As I continued to drive along I saw a sign that read, "Developmental Center Straight Ahead," and then about a quarter of a mile down the road I veered onto a paved driveway that was densely wooded on both sides.

Continuing up this wooded driveway I came upon a clearing, and then witnessed the unfolding of many stately looking buildings coming into view. These majestic fortresses looked like medieval castles - made of brick and stone, and they were all sprawled out on an incredible piece of property. If I didn't know any better, I would've thought I was standing on a major college campus, instead of a facility that houses developmentally disabled individuals.

For me the one question that still remains was, "What's lurking inside these imposing and exquisite structures, and more importantly…, can I rise up to the challenge?"

As I scanned the quadrant of surrounding buildings, I saw a sign that read, "Human Resources Office This Way." Upon entering the building, I approached the receptionist that was sitting in the front lobby, and cordially asked her if I could speak with Ms. Rita Spinelli.

Moments later, Ms. Spinelli walked into the front lobby and greeted me. She then invited me into her office, where coffee and danish were waiting for our general consumption, and I immediately interpreted this as a very good omen.

We sat down and made ourselves comfortable. As we engaged in a few light pleasantries, I then reached for a raspberry danish off of the tray. As I sunk my teeth into that mouthwatering treasure, I seemed to forget all about my little tug of war match this morning with my trousers.

So after finishing my tasty danish, I then reached for the trashcan to discard my napkin. As I extended my arm to toss the napkin from my hand, I thought I heard a faint popping noise.

At first, I wasn't quite sure what to make of it. But as I slowly leaned back in my chair, I realized that the waistband on my trousers suddenly felt a helluva lot more comfortable, and then I distinctly heard the sound of plastic hitting the floor underneath my chair. This confirmed my suspicions that the button to my trousers had come loose.

I quickly thought to myself, "Shit…, of all the times for this to happen, it would have to be right in the middle of my State job interview."

Although I attempted to act like nothing happened, I could feel my heart racing a mile a minute. Obviously, I couldn't bring this little faux pas of mine to the attention of Ms. Spinelli, or else she might think that she's in the company of a total incompetent.

Up until now, I thought I was doing a pretty good job at impressing Ms. Spinelli, but all of my efforts could go right down the drain if she discovers that she's sitting across the table from some bungling idiot whose button just popped off in the middle of a job interview.

Every so often, I found myself discretely searching the floor around my chair in hopes of spotting the lost button. But then realizing that even if I did find the button, how in God's name would I manage to nab it without Ms. Spinelli noticing.

Once again…, the proverbial albatross was wrapped firmly around my neck!

Not only has this ill-fated bird already prevented me from attaining my lifelong dream of a career in broadcasting, but it may very well preclude me from getting a lousy State job as well.

So before embarking on our tour, I decided to take one last stab at locating my button, so I knelt down on one knee and pretended to tie my shoe while giving the floor one last look.

Unfortunately, my roll of the dice came up snake eyes, because after scanning the floor one last time the button was simply nowhere to be found.

So at that point, I quietly recited a quick Hail Mary, and then prayed to God that my pants wouldn't fall down sometime today.

Well…, at least not until my job interview was over anyway!

Ms. Spinelli was a very young and attractive woman, but also someone who possessed a wonderful personality as well. I found her to be an extremely kind and easy-going person, and she seemed like the perfect choice for recruiting impressionable young men like me.

En route to our first stop on the itinerary, she insisted that I call her Rita, and I reciprocated by asking her to call me Jack.

As we walked along, Rita provided me with a brief history of the facility, in terms of when it was first founded and some of the names that it's been referred to over the years, such as, the "House for Idiots," "Asylum for the Deranged," and "State School for the Handicapped."

Although I found these names to be rather repugnant, Rita explained to me that the field of mental health has grown leaps and bounds since its inception, and that over the years society has learned to take a much kinder and humane approach towards individuals with disabilities.

Rita then concluded the history lesson by saying that the facility was the oldest institution in the State, and that it has been proudly serving the community for over one hundred years.

As we continued to stroll along and look at the various points of interest, I found myself having a very enjoyable time. Interestingly enough, but the thought of having a missing button on my trousers never once entered my mind.

Throughout the tour Rita gave me the latitude of asking her all sorts of questions, and the questions that she couldn't answer she said that she would check on for me. I felt quite at ease on the tour, and I could definitely see myself working here if the opportunity ever presented itself.

Around twelve o'clock, Rita and I walked over to the cafeteria to get a bite to eat.

As I reached for a lunch tray, Rita told me to order anything I wanted to off of the menu because lunch was her treat.

I then replied, "Boy, you're really giving me the red carpet treatment today Rita."

Rita laughed, and then quietly said, "Well, it's all part of the recruitment process Jack."

After lunch, Rita and I visited some of the residential buildings. Although the living units were crowded, they were bright and cheery and actually seemed quite homey for an institution.

In talking with the staff, I found them to be quite dedicated, and from what I could gather they demonstrated a good working knowledge for the clients that they cared for.

As I visited one living unit after the next, it suddenly dawned on me that what I was experiencing today was a dramatic contrast from the smoke-filled environment and stodgy rigid staff that Henry Josephson's living unit portrayed at the State psychiatric center, and it made me realize that not all State facilities were necessarily the same.

So after taking a tour of the residential units, we then visited some of the vocational programs that were in operation. I found these programs to be very rudimentary, yet functional, and I was actually thinking of ways in which I could make these vocational programs better.

Rita then introduced me to an older woman named Alice Albright. Ms. Albright was in charge of all of the vocational programs here at the developmental center, and if I were offered the job she would be my immediate supervisor.

Ms. Albright and I spent the better part of an hour discussing ideas, and having a lively exchange of questions and answers. I found her to have a keen sense of humor, and she struck me as someone who was a real visionary and very committed to her work.

During our conversation, Ms. Albright mentioned to me that she knew Bob Watson, and that she was quite aware of his role as being the driving force behind the WELL initiative.

So after finishing up with Ms. Albright, Rita met back with us and then proceeded to thank Ms. Albright for her time. Before continuing on with the balance of our tour, Rita then momentarily pulled Ms. Albright aside and spoke with her in private.

As I waited for Rita and Ms. Albright to conclude their conversation, I was wondering if they were exchanging notes regarding hiring me, or merely discussing dinner plans for later.

By now, it was four o'clock and the tour was over. Rita and I went back to her office and made ourselves comfortable. She then asked me if I had any questions or concerns, to which I attentively replied, "No…, not really."

At that point, Rita looked me straight in the eye and calculatingly said, "Jack, I'm prepared to offer you the vocational counselor position, that is…, if you're still interested?"

Needless to say, but I was completely taken off guard by her unexpected yet very enticing offer, and at that point I really wasn't expecting a decision to be made so quickly.

So not really knowing what to say, I simply replied, "Rita, can I think about it over the weekend, and then get back to you next week?"

Rita pleasantly said, "Absolutely! Here's my business card, with my direct office phone number listed on it. I would appreciate you calling me back with a decision, ASAP."

"ASAP," I amusingly thought to myself, as I slid her business card into my pocket. Of all the catch phrases that she could have possibly said, she chose "ASAP," Bob's patented phrase.

Suddenly, I felt as if I was receiving psychic messaging from Bob, and that fate was giving me a gentle nudge in reassuring me that everything would eventually turn out just fine.

As I was leaving Rita's office, she turned to open the door for me. As I stepped toward her, I happen to glance down at the floor directly in front of me, and there it was…, - hidden in plain sight, - the button to my trousers.

So without even blinking an eye, I quickly reached down and snatched up the button and then tucked it into my pocket before Rita even realized what had happened. We then shook hands and cordially said "good-bye," and I told Rita that I would be in touch.

Well…, the two hour ride home felt like a five minute joyride!

As I cruised down the highway, I had the wind blowing through my hair, as I listened to some of my all-time favorite rockn'roll songs that the classic rock radio station was cranking out.

When I arrived home Mom and Dad met me at the front door, much like they had a year ago when I interviewed at WEALTH. Mom had supper waiting for me and Dad was pouring me an ice cold drink, as he peppered me with all sorts of questions.

Every so often, Dad would ask me, "So Jackie boy…, how good were those directions that I gave you, huh?"

Mom kept telling Dad, "Jack Sr., will you let the boy tell his story, and for goodness gracious would you please let him eat."

That evening my fiancée come over to the house and we hashed out all of the pros and cons of taking the developmental center job, and at the end of the day we all came away with the same conclusion, - that I should take the State job at the developmental center.

Although I really didn't need much convincing, it was very reassuring to know that Mom, Dad, and my fiancée were all behind me one hundred percent!

So I guess the only thing now is breaking the news to Bob Watson. It probably won't come as any big surprise to Bob when I tell him. I know that Bob doesn't want to lose me, but at the same time he doesn't want to stand in my way either.

Bob realizes that he can't compete with the State in terms of their salary or benefits, and that his job market pool consists of recruiting inexperienced counselors who are in dire need of gaining field work experience.

In addition to that, Bob is resigned to the fact that when he hires a greenhorn right out of graduate school, like he did me, that the clock is ticking…, and that he needs to get as much mileage out of them as he possibly can before they start entertaining other offers.

So it would seem that my days at WEALTH Industries are numbered. A year ago, I would've never thought that I'd find this much contentment at WEALTH. But now I'm on the verge of leaving, and I pray to God that I'm not making the biggest mistake of my life.

It's Monday morning, and as I pulled into the WEALTH parking lot, I noticed that I didn't see Bob's Lincoln Town Car nestled in its usual spot.

As soon as I walked through the front door, I could immediately smell the intoxicating aroma of fresh brewed coffee. I stowed my backpack in the office and then headed straight down to the break room so that I could grab a cup of C.D.'s high test.

When I lumbered into the break room, I saw C.D. assuming the position. He was sitting quietly at the table, leisurely perusing the sports page and seemingly unaware of my presence.

As always, C.D. had a piping hot cup of coffee faithfully by his side, and he looked like he didn't have a care in the world. I lightly chuckled to myself as I watched him for a second or two, and then greeted him by saying, "Good morning, C.D., so how's it going?"

C.D. glanced up from his newspaper, and then said in a rather carefree tone, "Morning, sonny boy. Things are swell. So how did ya make out with your job interview on Friday?"

As I poured myself a cup of coffee, I was somewhat stunned by his bold inquiry, as I hesitantly muttered, "Oh…, you know all about that, huh?"

"Why sure, kid. You know that nothing's sacred around here!" C.D. said, in jest.

As I stirred my coffee, I wasn't finding the humor in what C.D. was saying. If the truth be told, I was feeling a little miffed, and almost violated. I didn't like the fact that everyone in the place knew where I was on Friday. Other than Bob and Lenore, no one else knew why I took Friday off, and I'm quite certain that neither one of them would've said anything to anyone.

At that point, I really didn't know how to respond to C.D., as I just kept staring down into my coffee, stirring it in a mesmerized fashion.

C.D. then asked me a second time, but this time a bit more forcefully, "So kid, what gives…, did you get the job or not?"

Again, I felt really uncomfortable talking to C.D. about this, especially since I hadn't even had a chance to talk to Bob about it yet. So at that point, I tried being very nonchalant about it by saying, "Well, I'm under consideration, I guess."

In an effort to change the subject, I decided to pull up a chair next to C.D. and casually ask, "So what's new in the world of sports?"

C.D. then turned his attentions back to the newspaper and replied, in his usual animated way, "Well, let's see…, the home team lost again last night, but you probably knew that already."

"Yeah, they stink lately." I said, as I was perusing the box scores.

C.D. put the newspaper down rather abruptly, and then flippantly said, "You know…, you really should stay right here at WEALTH, kid. This job is a piece of cake, plus where are you ever gonna find a better cup of coffee in your life than the one that I make."

All of a sudden, C.D. began to howl with laughter, and was apparently quite amused by his simple-minded sense of humor.

"Well C.D., we'll see what happens. Hey, is Bob coming in today?" I asked, and making another valiant attempt at changing the subject.

As C.D. poured himself another cup of coffee, he casually replied, "Yeah, he called earlier and said that he's running late. Hey Jack, have you ever known Bob to miss a Monday morning staff meeting. I mean it's the one time all week that he can gather us all together, and then yell at us for not doing our job!"

C.D. and I continued to dissect the sports page, and every so often he would bring up my job interview on Friday. I was careful not to say too much because C.D. is a gossipmonger.

Hey, I really like C.D., but I also know what he is capable of too. Essentially, C.D. and the word confidentiality don't usually appear in the same sentence.

Actually, I've come to the conclusion that C.D. is a narcissist, and that he's so wrapped up in his own little world that he's not really worried about anyone other than himself. I wouldn't necessarily call him selfish, but he seems to lack the capacity in knowing how to be a true friend.

So I guess the question that I keep asking myself is, "Why does C.D. mean so much to me?" And the only plausible explanation that I can come up with is, - I really enjoy his company.

Looking back C.D. was the only person here at WEALTH who actually went out of his way to get to know me, and as time went by we managed to cultivate a pretty good friendship.

Quite honestly, C.D. was my only source of comic relief when I was trying to keep my head above water with the likes of Michael Wallace and the notorious Sampson's.

So I guess that's why I overlook a large portion of his flawed personality, and almost view him as some sort of "funny" uncle, who keeps visiting me unannounced, but can't quite take the hint that I'm not interested in nurturing any type of long term relationship with.

As I went to pour myself a second cup of coffee, I saw Bob walk into the break room, who then amusingly said, "Hey O'Leary..., save some coffee for the people that haven't had their first cup yet."

I then pretended to pour the remaining coffee into my mug, but then stopped short, as I playfully said, "Get in here, Bob. There's still enough coffee for one full cup."

C.D. put down the newspaper, and then said in his usual dramatic style, "Well..., I guess it's time for me to do my magic again."

So while C.D. proceeded to make another pot of coffee, Bob and I exchanged some light pleasantries. Bob took a sip of coffee, and then gestured for me to follow him down to his office so that we could talk in private.

Once again, I certainly didn't want to discuss anything in front of C.D., because saying anything while he's in the room is comparable to taking out a full-page ad in the newspaper.

As Bob and I were leaving the break room, I called out to C.D., "Hey C.D., I'll see ya at the 8:30 staff meeting!"

C.D., who was still throwing the coffee together, simply said, "Okay, kid...," as he whistled a happy tune, and then flipped the switch on the coffee maker to brew up a fresh pot.

Bob and I walked down to his office and made ourselves comfortable. He then casually asked me, "So how did you make out on Friday with your job interview?"

I replied, "Well, they offered me the job Bob."

"Yeah, well…, I'm not surprised to hear that. So you said yes…, right?" Bob asked, as he took a leisurely sip of his coffee.

"Actually, I said that I'd get back to them this week. But after discussing the matter at length with my fiancée, I think I'm going to take the job Bob."

"Congratulations!" Bob said, as he displayed a half-hearted smile.

"Yeah, thanks, Bob. I'd like to call them today and give them my decision."

"Sure, Jack." Bob quietly replied.

Just then there was a knock at the door. I couldn't see who it was because the door was obstructing my line of sight, but once I heard the voice I could tell that it was Lenore who said, "Hi Bob, could I talk to you for a minute?"

Lenore stepped into Bob's office, but when she turned to sit down, she saw me seating in one of Bob's big cushiony leather chair, and in a flustered tone of voice she said, "Oh…, I'm sorry, I didn't know you were in conference with Jack. I'll come back later."

"Wait Lenore…, Bob and I are finished talking." I quickly replied.

"No…, no…, that's okay, Jack. It'll keep till later." She said, in an apologetic tone.

"Are you sure?" I answered.

"Yeah, I'm sure. So how did your interview go on Friday?" She asked, pensively.

"Um…, it went well. They actually offered me the job and I think I'm going to take it, but I'd appreciate it if you didn't say anything to anyone just yet." I replied, with a faint smile.

Bob could sense the tension in the air, so in an effort to lighten the mood, he humorously interjected, "So, uh…, you'd rather I not say anything at the staff meeting this morning Jack?"

"Heck no…, they'll find out soon enough Bob!" I emphatically said.

Bob flinched by my spirited response, and Lenore quietly snickered.

Lenore then raised her right hand, as if taking an oath, and categorically stated, "Jack, you have my solemn vow that no one will hear anything from me," prompting Bob and I to both chuckle at Lenore's unsolicited, yet high-spirited gesture.

"Well Lenore, it's not you that I'm worried about, it's C.D. that really concerns me. He's commonly referred to around here as the local town crier." I said, facetiously.

Bob piped up and amusingly quipped, "Really..., I thought he was the village idiot!"

At that moment, we all roared with laughter. In the midst of all of our laughter, who should come waltzing into Bob's office but none other than C.D., as he curiously asked, "What's all the commotion about? What did I miss? Oh yeah..., coffee's on!"

"Thanks C.D., we'll be right down." Bob said, as he took out his handkerchief and wiped his watery eyes, due to his uncontrollable laughing jag.

We all grabbed some coffee, and then headed down to the conference room for the Monday morning staff meeting.

Now this might sound a bit paranoid for me to say, but as I walked into the conference room, I thought I detected a fair amount of whispering and side-glances being cast in my direction from the other counselors around the table. I had the distinct impression that all of the counselors were kibitzing amongst themselves about my job interview on Friday, and wondering whether or not the "fair haired boy" was in line for a new job.

In my opinion, the counseling staff are nothing more than a bunch of busy buddies, who seem to be totally preoccupied with the affairs of others. I wish I could say that at least one of them had a single redeeming quality, but then that would be stretching things a bit.

Well..., with the exception of C.D. of course, but I guess technically he doesn't count.

In commencing with the meeting, Bob looked as though he had a full agenda to cover this morning. As always, Dolly was recording the minutes of the meeting, and she was writing fast and furious to keep up with everything that was flying out of Bob's mouth.

Bob knew that the minutes of the meeting was the only leverage he had in insuring staff accountability, and thus not allowing the counseling staff to shirk their duties or responsibilities.

In fact, Bob is so fanatical about recording the minutes of the meeting that he has a separate filing cabinet in his office, which contains all of the minutes of every staff meeting ever conducted for the past thirty years.

And to take it one step further, the files are all catalogued and cross-referenced for easy access and accessibility.

So the last order of business in this morning's staff meeting was to inform the group that Henry Josephson would be resuming his work evaluation at WEALTH next week.

Bob proceeded to give a brief overview of what lengths it took to get Henry reinstated back into the program, but as I glanced around the room, I could tell by the expression on the counselor's faces that they weren't the least bit interested in knowing any of the gory details.

As Bob continued to address the group, I could hear some quiet mutterings and a few moans and groans and "oh brother's" from around the table, and it caused me to quietly chuckle.

Once again, despite my indifference for the other counselors, I must confess that I found their snide remarks and animated comments this morning to be utterly hysterical.

So after informing the group about Henry, Bob wrapped up the meeting by proudly saying, "Kudos to Jack O'Leary for placing Michael Wallace and Bob Hodge at Spencer Trucking this week. Great job, Jack!"

Although Bob meant well by his comment, I was embarrassed beyond belief. At that point, I simply smiled and gave Bob a slight nod of my head in recognition of his kind words.

Dollars to donuts…, but I'm sure Bob's flowery remarks nauseated the other counselors to no end, especially since the counselors all knew that singling me out like that was Bob's subtle way of giving them a little zinger for not doing their job.

Lenore on the other hand was beaming. And after listening to Bob sing my praises, she smiled and reverently bowed her head, as she gave me a quiet round of applause.

So after the meeting concluded, I said "good-bye" to Lenore and then went directly back to my office so that I could give Rita Spinelli a call and inform her of my decision in accepting the position at the developmental center.

Before dialing the number, I took a moment to construct a few ideas in my head as to what I was going to say to Rita. I then dialed the number, and Rita quickly picked up the phone on the first ring.

"Hello, Rita. This is Jack O'Leary." I said, nervously.

"Hi, Jack. So have you made up your mind regarding the position?" She asked, directly.

"Yes…, I would like to accept the position Rita." I replied, without hesitation.

At that point, I quietly chuckled to myself because everything that I had rehearsed in my mind before placing the call to Rita went straight out the window.

Rita then effervescently said, "That's wonderful! Well…, that's what I call starting the week off right. I really think that you'll be happy here Jack."

"Yeah, thank you, Rita. I feel really good about my decision too. I was very impressed with what I saw the other day, and I think that the developmental center will be a really good fit for me." I replied, confidently.

"I agree. Well…, you come very highly recommended, and not only by your supervisor Mr. Watson, but also by Mr. Jim Brindamore, who as you know is our State Deputy Director of Personnel. Quite honestly, we don't get too many candidates with recommendations out of his office. You must be very special Jack." Rita said, cheerfully.

"Gee Rita, I had no idea that Mr. Brindamore even provided you with any input." I humbly replied.

"Well, there's a lot of behind the scenes activity that goes on in the hiring process Jack."

"So it would appear. Well Rita…, when would you like me to start?"

"ASAP," she promptly said.

Once again, the ASAP reference caused me to lightly chuckle and then think of Bob. Somehow it's only fitting that Rita should continue to use that little catch phrase with me.

I then said, "Well, how about a week from today. That is, if I can clear it with my boss?"

Rita replied, "That would be great! Perhaps you can get back to me after you speak with Mr. Watson."

"Yeah, okay, that sounds like a plan Rita."

"Great, Jack! Oh, by the way, I did check on housing and we do have some availability for you to utilize until you can secure your own accommodations. In addition to housing, we have laundry facilities and storage for your belongings as well." Rita said, thoroughly.

"Wow, that's terrific! Thanks, Rita. That's a huge load off of my mind." I replied.

"No problem, Jack. I'm happy to be of service. Okay, well…, let me just say welcome aboard, and call me back when you have a definite start date. Congratulations, Jack!"

So after hanging up the phone with Rita, I decided to swing by Bob's office and update him on the situation. As I walked up the hall, I saw Lenore exiting Bob's office and she appeared to be rather upset. When I caught up to her, I asked with concern, "Lenore, are you okay?"

Lenore glanced at me momentarily, but then looking away she hurriedly said, "Um…, yeah, I'm okay Jack. I can't really talk right now because I've got some people waiting for me down on the contract floor, so I'll see ya later, okay."

As I watched Lenore make haste toward the two double doors that led to contract floor, she pulled a tissue out of her hip pocket and then wiped her eyes. This confirmed my suspicions that she had been crying.

I quickly headed up the hallway toward Bob's office. When I tapped on his door, he was fully reclined in his sleek leather chair aimlessly gazing out the window. Bob was in such a deep train of thought that he didn't even bother to turn around to see who was knocking on his door.

I then hastily asked, "Excuse me, Bob…, but I just saw Lenore leaving your office and she appeared to be crying. Is everything all right with her?"

Bob quietly replied, "Don't worry, she'll be okay Jack. She's just upset about you leaving that's all." I could detect some sadness in Bob's voice as well.

"Yeah, well…, this is very difficult for me too Bob. I hope you realize that."

Bob swiveled his chair around so that he could face me, and in a heartfelt way he said, "I know it is Irish. I'm gonna miss you too. So did you make that phone call to Ms. Spinelli?"

"Yeah, Bob. They'd like me to start next Monday. Well…, if that's okay with you."

"Well, can you tie up all of the loose ends by Friday?"

"Yeah, I can Bob." I said, confidently.

"Well, if that's the case then its official, Friday will be your last day. I think you should start informing the staff immediately, or if you prefer I could make a general announcement over the intercom." Bob humorously suggested, in an effort to lighten the mood.

"No! No intercoms, Bob. I'll handle telling the staff myself. It shouldn't be too hard, all I need to do is tell C.D., and the rest of it will take care of itself. We all know how good C.D. is at keeping a secret." I said, sarcastically.

Bob smirked, and then quietly replied, "You're absolutely right."

So after pausing a moment, Bob then continued by saying, "Well, since Friday is your last day, it will give me a few days to plan a little "good-bye" party for ya."

"Thanks, Bob. Well…, I guess I better get crackin' on tying up all those loose ends."

As I beat it down to my office, I was thinking that I had a lot to do in a very short amount of time, but I was quite confident that I could get it all done by Friday. There were letters to be sent out, phone calls to be made, and people to meet with.

By now, everyone in the agency has heard the news that I'm leaving. I must say that it's been very heartwarming for me to see so many people go out of their way to thank me for all that I've done over the past year, and that the place won't be the same without me.

I especially welcomed some of the comments made by several of the line supervisors, in particular, Ralph and Smitty.

Initially, Ralph and Smitty thought that I was nothing more than a "snot-nosed" kid with a fancy college degree, but as time went by they grew to appreciate my efforts, and I'm proud to say that I managed to earn their respect along the way as well.

The next day, while enjoying a hot cup of coffee with C.D. in the break room, he surprised me by saying, "Boy, you must be pretty well-liked around here kid. Yesterday I overheard some of the line supervisors singing your praises, and take it from me, they usually don't have anything good to say about any of the counselors."

So after listening to C.D.'s off the cuff comment, I was almost tempted to say, "Gee C.D., don't base their actions on how they treat you."

But seeing how I'm a product of parochial school education, I decided to take the high road and not say a word, so I merely accepted C.D.'s backhanded compliment in stride.

Well, as the week wore on it was my definite impression that Ralph was genuinely going to miss me. Every time he saw me, whether in the hallway or on the contract floor, he would pull me aside and find something to talk about, even the most insignificant of things.

As I've said before, Ralph didn't particularly care for any of the other counselors on staff, and I guess it would be fair to say that none of them were particularly fond of him either.

Yet, when it came to me, Ralph made an exception. Due to the fact that I had such a solid relationship with Joe Atkins, then that essentially entitled me to a "free pass" with Ralph, and a pass that none of the other counselors were issued.

Ralph basically looked out for me, especially after Joe died. Ralph made sure that all of my clients on the contract floor were being well-cared for, and I'm sure that this preferential treatment on the part of Ralph was just one more reason why most of the counselors on staff didn't genuinely like me.

Funny though, I noticed that none of the other counselors went out of their way or did even the slightest thing to better their situation with Ralph.

Let's face it, this wasn't exactly "rocket science" that we were dealing with here!

The only thing needed in greasing the wheel with Ralph was an ounce of human kindness and a little bit of common sense, which really wasn't asking too much at all.

Lately, Lenore has been maintaining a very low profile with me. She's certainly cordial when she sees me, but she's definitely keeping her distance. I've noticed that she always seems to be in a real hurry to go somewhere else, instead of just stopping to chat with me. This is a side of her that I haven't seen before, and it's taken me completely off guard.

Yesterday, I received a very touching phone call from John Spencer. John conveyed to me that the two men we placed at his company were doing exceptionally well.

I smiled when I heard John emphatically say, "Michael Wallace and Bob Hodge are exceeding my expectations!"

Furthermore, John stated to me that he has taken a real liking to Bob Hodge, especially since John is a Vietnam veteran himself, and that over the past several weeks, John and Bob have both shared some mutual experiences with each other from their stint in the War.

John was so impressed with Michael and Bob that he wanted to know if we had anyone else at WEALTH who might be a good fit for his company, which prompted me to amusingly think, "Spencer Trucking may become the "mother lode" of all job placements for our agency!"

At that point, I reassured John that I would certainly pass along his sentiments to the next job placement specialist coming on board.

In closing, John took a moment to be serious, and poignantly remarked that he would always be forever in my debt for having his conscience raised regarding the disabled.

As I hung up the phone, I reflected on what John said, and at that point I experienced an indescribable sensation of joy wash over me, as if the Holy Spirit had just touched my very soul.

CHAPTER SIXTEEN

Well, here it is, Friday…, and it's my last official day at WEALTH. I arrived earlier than usual this morning because I wanted to soak up every last moment of today that I possibly could.

A year ago, I would've left WEALTH in a heartbeat, especially if some other job offer had come along that sounded even remotely appealing. But today, well…, I find myself eagerly coming into work before the crack of dawn.

Who'd a thunk it?

As we all know by now, Bob is usually the first person into work every morning, but it's still a "horse race" between C.D. and me as to who arrives into work next.

I've actually pondered the many reasons as to why C.D. gets into work so early every morning, and the only plausible explanation that I can come up with is that perhaps the allure of doing nothing all day long motivates him.

That, or else his wife kicks him out of the house as early as she possibly can, so that she can enjoy a little peace and quiet for the rest of the day.

Then again…, maybe C.D. simply wants to have some "alone time" with the coffeepot, well…, for a little while anyway, before he's forced to share with the rest of the WEALTH staff.

So after stowing my belongings in the office, I then went down to the break room so that I could get the coffee going. While I waited for the coffee to finish brewing, I sat down at the break room table and started reading the sports page.

Moments later, C.D. came strolling through the break room door with his coffee mug in hand, as he boisterously said, "Hey, what are ya doin', kid? Don't ya know that today is your big day! You should've let me make the coffee!"

"Uh…, that's okay C.D., I don't mind." I casually replied.

C.D. took a sip of the freshly brewed coffee, and then said with a satisfying smile, "Boy, that coffee tastes pretty good. I taught you well, grasshopper!"

So after chatting several more minutes with C.D., I detected some noise up the hallway, which meant that Bob was most likely settling into his office. I then decided to pour two cups of coffee and head down to Bob's office, so that I could shoot the breeze with him for a little while.

I then excused myself from C.D., who by now had turned his full-attentions toward the sports page, and was too engrossed in the box scores for idle chitchat anyway.

As I approached Bob's office, I saw that he was fully reclined in his sleek leather chair, and he was aimlessly gazing out the window.

Just as I was about to knock on Bob's door, I saw him breakdown into tears. I was so stunned by Bob's outward show of emotion that I almost dropped the two mugs of coffee that I was holding. I've never seen Bob cry before, not even at Joe's funeral.

I then realized that I couldn't let Bob know that I happened upon him like this, so I quietly made an about face and tiptoed my way back down the hallway towards the break room.

When I finally crept my way back toward the break room, I could see C.D. at the break room table, leisurely sipping his coffee and still quite engrossed in the morning newspaper.

At that point, I decided to shout at the top of my lungs, and loud enough so that Bob would clearly hear me down in his office, "See ya later, C.D.! I'm going down to Bob's office!"

Upon hearing the unexpected shrill of my voice, C.D. flinched…, and almost jumped completely out of his chair. He then turned his entire body around in my direction and scowled.

As I slowly proceeded up the hallway towards Bob's office, I began to quietly snicker to myself, when I heard C.D. mumble, "What the hell is wrong with that kid?"

C.D.'s reaction, and what's more…, the perplexed look he had on his face was simply hilarious.

But then after a second or two, C.D. shrugged his shoulders and then shifted his full-attentions back to scanning the sports page again, as if nothing had happened.

When I reached Bob's office, I tapped on his door with my foot, as I cheerfully said, "Good morning, Bob. I've got a hot cup of "Joe" for ya."

Bob then swiveled his sleek leather chair around in my direction, as he quietly replied, "Great! That's just what the doctor ordered. Thanks, Jack."

I placed the mug of coffee down on Bob's desk, and then proceeded to sit down in the plush cushiony leather chair adjacent to his desk. This is a chair that I have grown quite fond of sitting in over the past year, and I've relished every minute in it.

As Bob reached for his coffee, I could tell that he had been crying. His eyes were all puffy, and I could detect the glistening remnants of watery tears that had just been wiped away.

Although it saddened me greatly to see Bob so distraught, I opted not to charter those waters, or attempt to make any inquiries with him regarding his apparent melancholy state.

Bob then took a sip of his coffee, and satisfyingly said, "Boy, C.D. certainly outdid himself this morning. That's one of his better cups of coffee."

I paused a moment, and then proudly said, "Well, actually Bob..., I'm the one that made the coffee this morning."

Suddenly Bob became quite animated, as he staunchly remarked, "What...! You mean to tell me that all this time you could make coffee this good! C.D.'s coffee skills are the only thing keeping him in a job. Thanks a lot, Jack! I could've fired him a long time ago, if I knew that you could make coffee this good. Just imagine all of the money that I could've saved the agency."

"Very funny..., Bob." I sarcastically replied.

Bob's smile then expanded.

I then continued by saying, "So anyway..., I finished everything that had to be done Bob. Whoever takes over my caseload shouldn't have any surprises or messes to clean up."

"Good..., thanks for taking care of that Jack." Bob replied.

I then interjected, "Oh, by the way..., I had a very nice conversation with Mr. Migliori yesterday when I stopped by the bakery."

"Oh really...," Bob replied, as he leisurely sipped his coffee.

"Yeah, Mr. Migliori told me that he couldn't be happier with Kevin Riley as his new full-time bakery helper." I answered.

Bob nodded his head and replied, "Excellent, well done..., Jack!"

I continued by saying, "In fact, Mr. Migliori said, and I quote, "Jackie boy, thatta-Kevin-is-a-pretty-smart-a-kid,-and-he's-a-really-catchin-on-ta-da-job. Thanks-a-so-mucha-for-a-bringin'-him-to-a-me,-Pisano!"

At that point, Bob began laughing harder than I've ever seen him laugh before. I could tell that Bob got a real kick out of listening to the animation in my voice, especially in how I was able to annunciate Mr. Migliori's broken English. It gave me a great sense of joy to see Bob laughing, especially when only a few short minutes ago he was sobbing inconsolably.

Bob then said, "Jack, your colorful rendition of Mr. Migliori was so lifelike that

I felt as if I was standing right there in the bakery with you…, nibbling away on an apple danish."

Although I was glad that I could snap Bob out of his doldrums, it suddenly dawned on me that after today I wouldn't be around to cheer Bob up anymore, which made me incredibly sad.

Bob continued, "Hey, that's great news about Kevin Riley. I know he'll be sorely missed down on the contract floor, but placing him at Migliori's will be a great opportunity for him."

I then replied, in a wee bit of an Irish brogue, "T'at it will…, t'at it will!"

Bob then asked, "So let me ask you something? Did Kevin Riley get the job at Migliori's because he was the most qualified person we had at WEALTH, or because of his Irish heritage?"

As I pondered the question, Bob then leaned back in his sleek leather chair and cracked a wry smile, as he waited for me to respond.

I then looked Bob dead in the eye, and said with a straight face, "Well…, I'll need to consult my files first, but I'll be sure to get back to you on that by the end of the day Bob."

Bob chuckled at my humorous comeback, and simply uttered, "Uh-huh…, thanks, Jack. Bob then continued by saying, "So have you heard the latest rumor?"

"Um, no…, what rumor are you referring to Bob?"

"Well, now that you're leaving, C.D. has decided that he may want to take over the reins of job placement after all, especially now that Migliori's bakery is one of our client companies."

I quietly chuckled, and then replied, "Well, that sounds like vintage C.D., if you ask me."

Bob continued by saying, "And to take it one step further, C.D. is apparently taking all the credit for placing Kevin Riley at Migliori's. He told everybody down in the break room that the only reason he stops by the bakery every day to buy a raspberry danish is because he's laying the groundwork to place more clients at Migliori's. Can you believe the nerve of that guy?"

"Well Bob…, you keep telling me that C.D. has a warped perception. Something to do with his not being breast fed as a baby, right?" I amusingly stated.

Bob continued, "Listen, if I do decide to reassign C.D. to job placement then he better get his head in the game, because if he thinks for one minute that he'll be twiddling his thumbs all day while he's cramming raspberry danish into his mouth, then he's got another thing coming!"

"Shhhh…, now just simmer down Bob. It's not worth getting upset about. C.D. has been working for you for over twenty-five years, so isn't it time that you just accept him for who he really is before you wind up giving yourself an ulcer."

Bob nodded his head, and then calmly replied, "Yeah…, I guess you're right O'Leary."

There was a brief pause, and then Bob light-heartedly said, "So, I thought we'd have your "good-bye" party around noontime. I've got everything ordered from "Super Burger," because I know you fancy their gourmet cuisine."

"Super Burger, huh…," I replied, as I smiled in appreciation of Bob's sarcastic wit.

Bob quietly laughed, and then held an affectionate stare at me.

"I feel a little uneasy today Bob." I said, as I stared aimlessly out the window.

"Yeah, well, good-bye parties are not easy. I've been doing this job for over thirty years, so I guess my good-bye skills are a little rusty. Sorry to say…, but I'm a little short on advice for ya, Jack." Bob stated, as he took another savory sip of his coffee.

"Well, yeah…, for you personally, but you're certainly no stranger to good-bye parties, especially since you've thrown quite a few over the years, right." I then began to laugh out loud.

Bob suddenly realized the point that I was making, and then replied, "Oh, I get it now…, you're referring to my staff turnover issue, aren't you? Ah, very funny Jack, and you're right, I have orchestrated a few good-bye parties over the years. But why would a good little Irish Catholic "guilt-ridden" altar boy like you broach such a sore subject like that with me. It's not a very Christian thing for you to do, especially when you know that staff turnover is a chronic problem in human services, and a major source of worry for Executive Directors like me."

I stopped laughing for a moment, so that I could sarcastically say, "Yeah, I know it is Bob, especially when Executive Directors like you pay their counselors such measly salaries."

With a coy smile, Bob then matched my witty comeback with a witty comeback of his own by saying, "Well, that may be…, but sometimes out of sheer desperation, Executive Directors are forced to hire people that they might not ordinarily hire."

"Uh…, you wouldn't be referring to the day that you hired me now, would ya Bob?"

"Well, I'll just let you gnaw on that one for a little while O'Leary." Bob said, as he smiled and then joined in on the laughter.

It was good to see Bob laughing again. Bob has certainly had a lot on his plate these last few months, and my leaving WEALTH is only further complicating matters for him. After all, Bob will not only be down a counselor, but he'll also be down a friend as well.

Bob then reached across his desk and handed me an envelope and said. "Here Jack, I've got something for you."

I took the envelope from Bob's hand and opened it up. Inside the envelope was a check in the amount of fifteen hundred dollars, which prompted me to hastily ask, "So what's this for?"

Bob replied, "Well, it's for all the unused vacation and sick time that you've accrued over the past year. It should come in handy buying furniture and such for your new apartment."

"Really…, I had no idea. Are you sure the agency doesn't need the money Bob?"

"Huh…, that's just like you O'Leary, worrying about the needs of others instead of yourself. Hey, you earned it, and it's yours."

"Okay, well…, if you say so. Thanks, Bob."

As Bob opened up his accounts ledger book, he nonchalantly said, "Oh, by the way, your presence is requested down on the contract floor. Ralph and Smitty brought in some pastry for ya from Migliori's bakery, so why don't ya head down there and I'll see ya in a few minutes, okay."

"Yeah…, okay. Hey, thanks again for the check Bob." I said, as I slipped the envelope into my pocket, and then headed out the door toward the contract floor.

As I pushed through the two double doors that led onto the contract floor, I suddenly stopped dead in my tracks, as I saw the entire WEALTH staff gathered in full brigade.

Even the "notorious" counseling staff was all present and accounted for!

As soon as the crowd laid eyes of me, they gave me a rousing round of applause. Which not only took me by complete surprise, but it left me utterly speechless as well.

At first, I really didn't know what to make of it.

Was their spirited ovation due to my leaving, or because they could now dig into the mouthwatering array of pastry that was sitting so picturesquely in front of them.

Well, whatever the reason…, I was deeply touched.

And then of course there was C.D., who was standing front and center and chomping at the bit, so that he could have first dibs at the vast assortment of delectable goodies that were staring him smack in the face.

C.D. then impatiently whined, "C'mon kid, pick one…, so that we can all dig in," which of course prompted everyone in the room to laugh heartily.

While everyone continued to laugh, I reached for the nearest danish on the tray, which then prompted C.D. to quietly grumble, "Ah gees…, that's the one I wanted."

So as everyone helped themselves to coffee and danish, I pulled up a chair and then sat down at one of the tables that was arranged for the gathering.

As I sat there I felt like some sort of famous dignitary, as people approached me one by one, shaking my hand, and congratulating me on landing my highly coveted State position.

In the midst of all the excitement, I then felt a light tap on my shoulder. When I turned to see who it was, I was delighted to see that it was Lenore.

Lenore smiled, and then sweetly asked, "Hi Jack, do you mind if I join you?"

"Please do…," I replied, as I scooched over to make room for her to sit down.

People continued to congratulate me, and although I appreciated their kind and thoughtful words, I seemed to be more intent on sneaking a peek at Lenore every chance I could.

As Lenore nibbled away on her danish, she listened intently to each passerby wish me good luck and sing my praises. This was actually the first time in over a week that Lenore and I have spent any amount of time together, or said more than two words to each other. I missed her company, and I was overjoyed to be sharing this spotlight moment with her this morning.

About twenty minutes later, Bob stopped by and joined in on the festivities. Bob mingled freely with the staff, but every time I glanced his way he seemed to have me dead in his sights.

I felt like the Pope, as people stood waiting in line so that they could have their private audience with me. Even people who I thought didn't particularly like me were making the effort, so that they could spend a quiet moment with me and say a few parting words.

By now, it was approaching 8:30 and the party was beginning to wind down. The clients were now starting to arrive and settling into their respective work stations on the contract floor. As people scattered, Bob quickly reminded everyone that the luncheon for me was at noon.

C.D. was so excited by Bob's stirring announcement that he began rubbing his hands together like a little kid, and then saying the word "goody" over and over again.

Many of the clients knew that it was my last day, but some didn't. The clients that were hearing it for the first time were extremely animated, in terms of their comments, body language, and facial expressions.

In my view, the old adage of, "Out of the mouths of babes," should be rewritten to say, "Out of the mouths of babes…, and the developmentally disabled."

As I listened to the outpouring of affection that these clients were demonstrating toward me, I was deeply moved, as they repeatedly said, "Don't leave us, Jack. Please.., don't leave us!"

So after spending several more minutes with the clients on the contract floor, I decided to head over Bob Watson's office. As I tapped on Bob's door, I saw him working at his desk.

I then casually asked, "Hey Bob, do you need me for anything this morning?"

Bob replied, "Um, no…, not really Jack. You're all caught up with your work, right?"

"Yeah, I'm all caught up Bob."

"Okay, then get lost…, if you need to." Bob said, chuckling.

"Thanks, Bob. I'd like to swing by Spencer Trucking and say "good-bye" to John Spencer. While I'm over there I'll take a peek on Michael Wallace and Bob Hodge, and see how they're doing as well." I said, with great anticipation.

"Sure…, go ahead. We've got everything under control here." Bob stated, confidently.

"Great! Thanks, Bob. I'll be back in a couple of hours."

"Okay, see ya later, Irish." Bob said, as he resumed crunching the numbers of the overhead accounts ledger.

When I arrived at Spencer Trucking, John Spencer's receptionist greeted me by saying, "Hi Jack, how's it going? So what brings you by today?"

"Hi Mary, well…, I was hoping to see John and speak with him for a few minutes."

"I see, well…, I think that can be arranged. He's just finishing up on a conference call. So would you like a cup of coffee while you wait?"

"No thanks, Mary. I'm all set."

"Okay, well…, you can keep me company while you wait for Mr. Spencer." Mary said, as the telephone rang and she turned to answer it.

A few moments later John Spencer walked out of his office, and when he saw me sitting in the reception area, he was quite surprised to say the least.

As John approached me, he extended his mighty hand and affably said, "Hi, Jack. So did you come by to tell me that you've decided to stay on in your present position?"

I let out a hearty laugh and replied, "No John, I'm still taking the new job. I just thought I'd come by to see how Michael and Bob are doing, and to just say that I'll miss our friendship."

"Likewise, Jack." Spencer said, sincerely.

I then commented, "It's funny…, but even though you and I have only known each other for a few short weeks, I feel as though we've known each other for years."

"Yeah, I feel the same way Jack. It's probably because we have a lot in common, in terms of our blue collar upbringing and our Irish tempers, no doubt." Prompting both of us to laugh.

John then invited me out back to the loading dock, where he proudly pointed out Michael Wallace hard at work. Michael was busy loading boxes onto tractor-trailers, and the sheer look of joy and contentment on his face indicated to me that he had an affinity for this type of work and that he really found his niche.

As I watched Michael work I had a reflective moment, and I recounted the day that he stormed into my office and attacked me for no apparent reason. Based on that incident alone, who would've ever imagined that he'd be holding down a real job someday? Certainly not me!

At that point, I was very proud of Michael, and of myself. Although, if memory serves me correctly, Bob was the driving force behind us not throwing in the towel on Michael.

Was it foresight on Bob's part to keep Michael in the program, or was his decision purely based on the almighty dollar?

Who knows, and if you were to ask Michael that question he'd probably say, who cares!

We then swung by the business office and met up with Bob Hodge. Bob was hard at work crunching the numbers, balancing the books, and performing the same types of duties that Bob Watson does with the overhead accounts ledger at WEALTH.

When speaking with Bob Hodge, he certainly looked to be in his element. We all chatted for a few minutes, and then I shook Bob Hodge's hand and wished him well in his new career.

As John Spencer walked me out to my car, he reiterated once again that he would certainly entertain having more referrals placed at his company.

For a fleeting moment, I wondered if perhaps the Sampson's could somehow "fit into the equation" here at Spencer Trucking.

Hahaha! Only kidding..., the Sampson's are doing just fine right where they are!

Once again, I thanked John Spencer for signing on with the agency, and as we shook hands, I good-naturedly said, "Hey John, the next time that I'm back in town I'll stop by and visit with ya, but this time the pastry from Migliori's bakery is on me!"

John Spencer burst out into laughter, and then gregariously replied, "Jack, it's a deal!"

When I arrived back at WEALTH, I walked past the conference room and observed Bob and Lenore setting up for the luncheon. From what I could see they had everything under control and spared no expense. The room was all decked out with colorful balloons, party streamers, and a very pretty blue and white gingham tablecloth that adorned the conference room table.

I decided not to disturb Bob and Lenore as they primped the room because I didn't want to spoil the moment. As I snuck away, I chuckled to myself and thought, "Bob has this good-bye party thing down to a real science. Lord knows, he's certainly had a lot of practice at it!"

It was approaching noontime now, and I was getting ready to make my way down to the conference room for the luncheon. Before leaving my office, I decided to scribble down a few words on a piece of paper, just in case I needed to say something gratuitous at the luncheon.

As I pondered the right words to say, there was a light knock at my office door. When I looked up I saw Dr. Stevens standing in the doorway, and he was smiling from ear to ear.

I then jumped right out of my chair, and enthusiastically said, "Dr. Stevens, what a pleasant surprise! I wasn't expecting to see you here today! Thank you so much for coming!"

Dr. Stevens then replied, in his own inimitable way, "Jack, my boy..., I couldn't pass up an opportunity to see you off and wish you well in your new assignment."

We shook hands and gave each other a hearty embrace. I then decided to have a little fun with Dr. Stevens by saying, "It's so wonderful to see you again, Doctor. Have you lost weight?"

Dr. Stevens amusingly replied, "Dear boy, is your eye condition worsening! As a matter of fact, I should abstain from eating at this luncheon altogether. I can barely buckle my trousers."

I quickly interjected, "Speaking of which…, I think they're ready for us down in the conference room, shall we?"

"Yes, by all means my boy, I'm completely famished!" Dr. Stevens amusingly quipped.

Dr. Stevens and I walked into the conference room and it was a sight to behold. There were mounds of hors d'oeuvres, large platters of cold cuts and salads, and best of all…, the desserts were all from Migliori's bakery.

Need I say more?

Mr. Migs also provided us with a full sheet cake, which of course was free of charge, and on top of the cake there was an inscription that read, "Best of Luck, Jackie Boy!"

As I gazed at the inscription on the cake, I felt as if I was celebrating my tenth birthday all over again. But that's okay…, because it's a feeling that I've come to know and cherish.

When Lenore spotted Dr. Stevens and I enter the room, she walked over to where we were standing and gave each of us a big fat hug. Dr. Stevens was so overcome with emotion that it prompted him to say, "It's so wonderful to be here with my two young protégé's!"

Lenore then enthusiastically said, "Listen boys…, plates and silverware are over on the left so please help yourself!"

As Dr. Stevens and I made our way over the buffet table, I noticed that Bob Watson was nowhere to be found, however C.D. was eating enough food for an entire army. His plate was overflowing, and he was shoveling the food into his mouth like there was no tomorrow.

Just as I was about to dig into the mouthwatering array of delectable delicacies, C.D. glanced in my direction, and then gave me one of his patented smiles and a big thumbs up.

As I smiled and nodded my head at him, he then proceeded to shovel an ungodly amount of food into his mouth. He then attempted to say something to me, but his words were so garbled that I couldn't make out a single word that he was trying to say.

And if that still wasn't embarrassing enough, C.D. then began to laugh out loud, and the food that was crammed in every nook and cranny of his mouth began spewing in every direction.

What might seem like an awkward moment for most people…, really didn't seem to faze C.D. in the least.

As I stood there watching C.D. in utter disbelief, Dr. Stevens leaned into me slightly, and then devilishly whispered, "Is that chap a close personal friend of yours, Jack?"

Dr. Stevens then began to lightly chuckle to himself, and as we both paraded down the buffet line, I quietly chuckled as well.

By now, there was a steady flow of traffic streaming in and out the conference room. Everyone was busy helping themselves to the sumptuous array of food that was on display. Some stayed and kibitzed, and others made a hearty plate and then brought it back to the contract floor, so that they could provide adequate staff coverage in keeping the operation out back afloat.

Apparently Bob was single-handedly covering the contract floor, and deploying the staff in shifts, so that they could enjoy some food and have one last chance to say "good-bye" to me.

People kept coming up to me left and right and stating that I would be sorely missed. Dr. Stevens was smiling like a proud father when hearing people sing my praises. I was humbled by their heartfelt sentiments, and even found myself on the verge of tears a couple of times as well.

Just then I saw Bob enter the conference room. He went straight over to the buffet table and fixed himself a quick plate, and then smartly sat down at the table to join us.

As Bob unfurled his napkin, he made his apologies for being late by saying, "Sorry I couldn't get in here any sooner Jack, but we had a deadline to meet down on the contract floor."

"Duty calls, Bob." I said, smiling.

"Yeah, well…, I had to "crack the whip" in order to get the work done this morning. You can appreciate that, right Dr. Stevens?"

We all laughed at Bob's humorous comment, as Dr. Stevens robustly said, "Indeed I can, Bob. I'm quite aware of the trials and tribulations of running a top notch program like yours. It's so good to see you again!"

"Likewise, Doctor. It's always a pleasure to see you too."

Bob continued by saying, "So Dr. Stevens…, now that Jack is abandoning us, I'm in the market for filling a counselor position. Do you have any eager young minds graduating from the university that are in the same league as Jack and Lenore?"

Dr. Stevens then spiritedly replied, "Well…, that's a pretty tall order to fill Bob. However, I may have one or two students that I would characterize as having potential."

Lenore and I quietly snickered at Dr. Stevens' witty remark.

Bob then said, "Good…, then tell them to come see me, ASAP. I might have an interesting proposition for them."

I then chimed in and said, "In other words, Dr. Stevens…, they'll be overworked and underpaid!" Which prompted all of us to laugh out loud, including Bob.

Dr. Stevens then rushed to Bob's defense, as he emphatically stated, "Well, that might be Jack, but you and Lenore will never find a better training ground than WEALTH Industries to hone your skills. Bob and the WEALTH staff do a marvelous job here!"

"Thank you, Doctor. I couldn't have stated it any better myself." Bob replied, as we all laughed heartily.

"The food is good…, wouldn't you agree, Jack?" Bob casually said, as he took a generous mouthful.

"Delicious, Bob. Thank you!" I replied, appreciatively.

"You're welcome! So…, did you get a chance to see your old buddy Henry Josephson this morning Jack?"

"No…, you mean he's here today?" I replied, with utter surprise.

"Yep, the psych center dropped him off about an hour ago. He's going to be hanging around here for a couple of hours today so that he can get re-oriented to the place." Bob said, as he finished his meal and then wiped his mouth with his napkin.

"Re-oriented, huh…?" I quipped, which prompted Bob to slightly chuckle.

"How is the poor chap doing Bob?" Dr. Stevens innocently asked.

"Well, he's breathing…," Bob amusingly stated.

"So when is Henry's official start date Bob?" I asked, with interest.

"He's slated to come back to us full-time starting Monday. Part-time would've been more prudent, but in order to qualify for federal funding then Josephson needs to attend the program full-time. I guess I shouldn't complain because Mr. Josephson will be generating a lot of revenue for WEALTH, and certainly help pay a few bills around here. Especially this rather expensive meal I just laid out for you Jack," prompting all of us to laugh heartily.

Dr. Stevens glanced at his watch, and then softly said, "Well, my boy…, it's time for me to bid you a fond adieu. I have another pressing engagement that I need to attend. I'd like to wish you all the very best in your new assignment, and just remember…, if I can ever be of any assistance to you my boy, then please don't hesitate to call on me."

"Thanks, Dr. Stevens. It's comforting to know that you're only a phone call away. Thank you so much for coming today, it really meant a lot to me." I said, sincerely.

Dr. Stevens replied, "The pleasure was all mine Jack. Actually, I owe Lenore a debt of gratitude for informing me of this very auspicious occasion."

"Oh, and Doctor…, don't forget to mention to your graduates that we have an immediate opening here at WEALTH, and that they can contact me if they have any questions." Bob stated, in a very professional tone.

"That's right, Dr. Stevens. But if they'd like to hear the unedited version of working here, then they can contact either me or Lenore." I said, and we all laughed heartily, including Bob.

Bob stopped laughing for a moment, and then replied, "Well, I'm not too worried about Jack because he'll be gone, but I may need to start screening all of Lenore's incoming phone calls. Remind me to make a note about that to Dolly," prompting everyone to laugh once again.

"Ta-ta, everyone!" Dr. Stevens flamboyantly said, as he shook my hand and gave Lenore a peck on the cheek.

Bob then turned to me and casually stated, "Well, it looks like the party is beginning to wind down. There's still a lot of food and baked goods left over, and I want you and Lenore to have first crack at bringing some of it home. I'll be making a general announcement later for the rest of staff. Well, I've got a few things to attend to out back, so I'll catch up with ya later."

It was almost three o'clock, and the clients will be punching their time cards very shortly. If I was going to see Henry Josephson then I better get down to the contract floor quick.

As I headed out back, Lenore emphatically called out to me, "Jack, make sure you say good-bye to me before you leave," and I assured her that I would.

When I reached the contract floor, I panned the room to see where my old buddy Henry Josephson was, but he was nowhere to be found.

In the midst of looking for Henry, people were approaching me left and right, shaking my hand, patting me on the back, and wishing me all sorts of luck in my new job.

Obviously, I was pleased to receive their adulation, but for some unexplained reason I was more intent on finding Henry and having a few parting words with him. Despite circling the contract floor twice, I was still unable to locate Henry, which threw me into a bit of a tailspin.

I then approached Ralph and asked, "Hey Ralph, where's Henry Josephson?"

Ralph quickly replied, "Oh, he just left..., not even two minutes ago Jack. If you hurry then you might be able to catch him out in the parking lot."

"Thanks Ralph," I said, as I high-tailed it toward the back door.

Sure enough, as I ran out into the parking lot I spotted the psych center van pulling away with Henry. Although I tried my best to get the attention of the driver, he apparently didn't see me in his rearview mirror.

To my surprise, Henry must've heard all of the yelling and commotion happening behind him, and he actually turned his head in my direction and saw me waving my arms in the air.

Henry quietly bowed his head, and then reverently made the "Sign of the Cross" with his right hand. In acknowledgement of his kind and thoughtful gesture, I smiled and waved "good-bye," and then watched the psych center van turn the corner and disappear into a cloud of dust.

As I stood there in the middle of the parking lot, I had a reflective moment, and prayed that some way, somehow..., Henry's elevator would someday manage to make it up to the top floor.

When I walked back into the building, Ralph called out to me, "Hey Jack, were you able to catch him?"

I replied, "Nah..., they peeled out of the parking lot before I could get their attention. Hey Ralph, how did Henry seem to you this afternoon?"

"Well..., he seemed like his same old self to me." Ralph said, straightforwardly.

"Okay, thanks, Ralph."

Ralph and I shook hands, and then we said one last "good-bye" to each other.

As I turned to walk away, I felt Ralph grab my arm. He then gave me an unexpected hug and warmly said, "I just want you to know that the place won't be the same without ya. Take good care of yourself, kid."

"Thanks, Ralph. Hey, do me a favor, will ya. Can you keep an eye out for Lenore? Will you take care of her like you took care of me?"

Ralph smiled, and then replied with utter assuredness, "You can count on it, kid."

I left the contract floor and then walked directly over to the time clocks, so that I could say some final "good-byes" to the clients as they all lined up and punched out for the day.

As I stood there saying one heartfelt "good-bye" after the next, I had an overwhelmingly amount joy in my heart. There were smiles, tears, and yes..., even a few puzzled looks. But then in an instant, - the clients were all gone and the place resembled a tomb.

Suddenly the eerie quiet of the building was strangely reminiscent of my first day at WEALTH, when I arrived early that morning so that I could make a good impression on Bob.

Isn't it strange how the chain of events in our lives always seem to come full circle?

So, here it is…, 3:45 on a Friday afternoon, and everyone has gone home for the day with the exception of Bob, Lenore, and myself. Bob permitted the staff to leave fifteen minutes early today so that they could get a jump on the weekend.

Could it be possible that Bob Watson is getting soft in his old age?

Anyway…, as I sat at my desk I suddenly experienced an anticlimactic moment.

I guess it finally hit me that this was it, and that in roughly fifteen minutes from now I will be "closing the book" on my career here at WEALTH Industries.

Mom thought it might be a nice idea for me to write out a few note cards to some of the people that have meant so much to me during the course of my time here. So I decided to use the remaining minutes I had to write out note cards for Bob, Lenore, C.D., Dolly, and Ralph.

As I was writing out the note cards, there was a quiet knock on my door. I looked up and saw that it was Bob, which then prompted me to say, "Hey Bob…, what's up?"

Bob then hastily replied, "Hi, Jack. Listen, I just remembered that I promised Sarah that I would accompany her to a four o'clock appointment today. I really wanted to stay and walk you out, but as you can see I'm running late. Can you do me a big favor and make sure that all of the lights are turned off out back, and that all the doors and windows are secured?"

I quietly answered, "Sure, Bob. Just like old times, right? Even though it's my last day, you still wanna squeeze every drop out of me that you possibly can."

Bob lightly chuckled, and then once again he relied on his incredible wit to say, "Well Jack, technically…, you're still on the clock. Besides, I think you need to feel some sense of obligation towards me in helping pay off that rather expensive meal I just had for you earlier."

I then countered Bob's witty remark by saying, "Hey, you're not playing the guilt card, are ya Bob? You of all people should know that I'm saturated in guilt as it is."

Bob smiled, and then genuinely said, "I'm really gonna miss ya, Irish. Make sure you stay in touch, okay."

As I gazed up at Bob, I could tell that he was barely holding it together, as I staunchly replied, "Absolutely, Bob!"

Bob smiled, and then extended his hand and quietly said, "Okay, well…, I gotta go. I'll talk to ya soon, bye."

As we held a firm handshake, we stared warmly into each other's eyes with deep mutual admiration, and then Bob exited the room.

Moments later, there was another knock at my door, and this time it was Lenore. I looked up and pleasantly said, "Oh, hi Lenore…, c'mon in."

Lenore replied, with a quiet smile, "Hi Jack, I just saw Bob leave. You two really got to be very close. I hope that I can develop the same relationship with him as you had."

"Oh, you will…, because you're the heir apparent." I said, confidently.

"What do you mean by that?" She asked, with an innocent chuckle in her voice.

"Well…, just that Bob will come to rely on you as he has relied on me. And he'll make you a better counselor, and an even better person than you ever imagined." I said, sincerely.

"Like he did with C.D.?" She quipped.

I roared with laughter, but then was quick to say, "Well…, let's not forget that Bob is human. Sure, he's had a few counselors fall through the cracks over the years, but I don't think he has anything to worry about with you. Besides, I did all the heavy lifting for ya!"

Lenore laughed, and then she stared at me with those piercing lavender blue eyes of hers. She then quietly said, "Well…, I'm heading out."

"Yes, I can see that." I replied, as Lenore stood there holding her bicycle in the doorway.

There was a brief pause, and then Lenore said, "Jack, I just wanna thank you for everything that you've done for me."

Lenore then propped her bicycle up against the wall and gave me a tender embrace.

We held each other for a moment, and then I gazed into her dazzling and hypnotic lavender blue eyes and said, "Actually Lenore, it's me who should be thanking you. You filled a void in me when Joe Atkins died. When Joe died, I felt very hollow inside…, but then you came along and I was able to convert the sadness of his death into a sort of cathartic energy by training you in your internship. And we even managed to have a few good laughs along the way too."

Lenore paused a moment, and then said with a coy smile, "Well, like you always say Jack, there are no coincidences, and that things definitely happen for a reason.

Huh, you know…, I think I'm beginning to buy into this predestination theory of yours Mr. O'Leary."

"You've learned much grasshopper, so now it's time for you to leave the nest and flourish." I quipped, prompting Lenore to quietly giggle and then smile.

"Gee, thanks for sharing that Joe Atkins story with me Jack." Lenore said, in a very comforting way.

"Well, just keep paying it forward Lenore, and "Share the WEALTH" with the next person who comes on board." I stated, profoundly.

"I will, Jack. Well…, I guess I better get going. Promise me that you'll stay in touch!" She said, adamantly.

"I promise…, I promise…," I replied, with a big smile.

Lenore then gave me one more hug, but this time it was so big that it almost squeezed the life out of me. She then reached for her bicycle, and as she turned to leave, she looked back at me one more time and I could see that her eyes were welling up with tears.

I walked out into the hallway, so that I could catch one last glimpse of Lenore.

As she wheeled her bicycle out of the building, she turned toward me again and said, half crying, "See ya around, Jack."

"See ya, Lenore." I softly replied.

I then walked over to the window and watched Lenore hoist her dainty little frame onto her bicycle, and as she slowly peddled away, I could see her wiping the tears from her eyes.

Although it broke my heart to see her cry, I took great comfort in knowing that we shared some very memorable moments together, and memories that will stay with me for a lifetime.

So after saying "good-bye" to Lenore, I went out back to make sure that all of the lights were shut off and that all of the doors and windows were secured as Bob had asked me to do.

When I came back to my office, I gathered up the note cards that I had written out and then placed each designated card squarely on the desk of Bob, Lenore, Dolly, C.D., and Ralph.

As I walked back to my office, I quietly thought to myself, "Well…, my work here is done."

I grabbed my backpack and slung it over my shoulder, and then tucked the small cardboard box that I had packed all of my personal effects into under my arm.

Before shutting off the lights, I glanced around my tiny little office one more time to make sure that I wasn't forgetting anything.

As I shut off the lights and closed the door behind me, I thought of the "WEALTH" of knowledge that I had acquired, and the "WEALTH" of experience that was within me now.

At that moment, it finally occurred to me that "WEALTH" meant so much more to me than money, and I prayed that I was making the right decision in taking the State job.

As I turned the ignition in my car, I paused a moment, and then quietly chuckled to myself, as I finally realized, "WEALTH has truly made me a very "rich" man."

END

Post Script

I hope you enjoyed the story, and please feel free to send me any thoughts or comments you might have about the book, or perhaps even mention who your favorite characters were in the story to my email address, stemmer947@gmail.com

Also, be watching for my next book entitled, "The State School," which is the sequel to "Sharing the WEALTH," and see what interesting adventures are in store for Mr. Jack O'Leary.

About the Author

Jack Dempsey was born in New York City in 1954 and lived his formative years on Long Island, New York. In 1976 he graduated from SUNY Brockport with a BA in Psychology. He earned his Master's degree in Rehabilitation Counseling in 1979 from Hofstra University on Long Island. After graduate school he worked thirty years as a Vocational Rehabilitation Counselor for NYS OMRDD and retired from that position in 2010.

Dempsey's main intent for writing this book was to provide the reader with a light-hearted fictional story of a profession that he has enjoyed being associated with for all of his adult professional life. Mr. Dempsey is married to his wife Kristin for over thirty-eight years and has four children and currently resides in Upstate NY.